THE H

AN ESPIONAGE THRILLER SERIES
BOOK 1

SAUL HERZOG

AUTHORCONTACT

1

The question isn't *who*, or *what*, or even *why*, though they will matter soon enough.

No. At the outset, there is only one question.

How?

How did she get here?

How did it happen?

How did everything go so horribly awry?

Had there been a stranger in the bed all along, as Roman would have put it? A rat in the house? A traitor in her midst?

Or was it just a plain, old-fashioned cock-up?

She wants it to be the former. Betrayal. Treachery. A mole. Otherwise, the truth—that the Ruskies simply got the better of her—is too painful to contemplate.

She sits motionless, erect as a lamppost on a steel-framed chair. Her wrists are zip-tied behind her back, and her ankles are cinched to the chair's front legs.

Her hair hangs disheveled, matted with sweat and blood. Mascara streaks down her cheeks like soot. And though she can't see it, she feels the blood seeping into the fabric of her coat.

She doesn't remember the screaming.

She doesn't remember falling to the ground.

What she does remember is the dogs. The heat of muscle and jaw, the sickly wetness of tongue and saliva, and, of course, the teeth—bone-white in the stark light of the guardpost.

She doesn't remember the pain—that has already been siloed, locked away behind a mental firewall. But she does remember the closeness. The intimacy of the animals. Vicious, but in control. Never frenzied. They could have torn her throat out, ripped her apart like greyhounds on a screaming hare. But they didn't. They knew exactly how far to take her.

The guards never moved a muscle. Never flinched.

They'd stood and watched like statues carved from ice. Like they were being offered a demonstration of what the dog could do.

She remembers forcing herself not to struggle. To lie still. Play dead.

And she doesn't struggle now. There would be no point.

At best, she could hope to tip over the chair, slamming her body against the raw concrete floor. She's been trained not to make futile gestures like that, not to expend emotion when it will do no good. She's been trained against spitting in the eye of an enemy that's already got her beat.

Things don't have to be fair, she's been taught. They don't have to be just.

The only law they must obey is the law of logic. The only god they serve is what happens next. Everything else is dogma. Heresy.

She closes her eyes. And sees his face.

Roman Adler.

Of course it's him. Who else would it be?

She has hours left to live—maybe. No family. No legacy. She's known lovers—maybe even love—but it's his face that comes to her now. And it's his voice she hears in the silence.

"We do not charge machine gun nests with bayonets."

He has a thousand lines like that. Clean. Cynical. Lethal.

Each a shard of glass in the soft tissue of Washington's illusions. He is, perhaps, the last true realist. The last man unbought by theories of what *should* be, what *ought* to be, rather than what simply *is*.

"You know the two most dangerous words in the English language?" he once asked.

She didn't.

"It," he said, raising a thumb. "Depends," he finished, raising a finger.

"It depends?"

"It depends," he said again, "is the biggest threat facing the West since three hundred Spartans held off the combined might of the Persian Empire. Since the Visigoths sacked Rome. Since the fall of Troy."

This is his gospel—chiseled into the hard stone of his mind by one thing and one thing only. Experience.

And now, sitting in this frigid, concrete tomb on some forgotten edge of the sprawling Russian expanse, she realizes she is going to die for it.

She is going to die for his gospel.

America, the West, the great *Pax Americana*, is struggling for its existence. It is fighting not to be thrown on the ash heap of history. If it fails, it will burn.

And burn. And burn.

History allows no other outcome.

Roman once showed her a satellite feed, live-streamed from orbit, and put his finger on Russia. On China. He waved it over Iran and North Korea and called them the new axis. The rising counterweight to everything history thought it knew. Everything it thought it had learned.

"History doesn't care about right or wrong," he told her. "It doesn't care about the hard-won lessons of our forefathers. It is a plow in a November field. And we are mice in a burrow."

She's spent more time with him than perhaps any other living person, but she doesn't know how much she believes his words.

She was born into a different world. A different America. His gospel isn't the only one available to her. There are others.

She remembers the old speeches.

Fear itself.

A house divided.

Morning in America.

They sound like myths now—slogans for a country that no longer exists. They were the certainty Roman was born into, the certainty of the GIs who came home from Europe knowing they'd defeated the greatest evil the world had ever known. The certainty of Harry S Truman when he dropped not one, but two atom bombs on his foe.

He'd had eighty-five percent support for that decision. Eighty-five.

She doubts a president today could get that much support on whether the earth is round.

Who was it that said—*Some stories are true that never happened*?

They might as well have said—*Some stories that did happen are no longer true.*

Or, more starkly—*There is no truth. No past. Nothing that happened... happened.*

The world Roman knew is gone. That's the only certainty now.

She starts to shiver and tries absently to calculate how much time has passed. It is impossible. She was unconscious when they brought her in. All she knows—from a small, high window too narrow to escape through—is that it is night, and it is snowing.

And, from some distant part of her mind, she remembers that it is Christmas. How fitting, she thinks, that it be the day she dies.

Footsteps approach, and she holds her breath.

A bolt slams—the sound of metal on metal, like so much of human history—and the door groans open, heavy on its hinges.

Icy air knifes through the room as a lone man enters.

Her interrogator.

That was the delay. They'd been waiting for him.

In some buried part of her, she knows this will be the last face she sees.

All the paths of her life—every fork, every joy, every betrayal—led to this.

This cold, dark room. This stubbled man in a crisp, tailored uniform.

He is older than her. Fifties, maybe sixties. He was probably a soldier already when she was born.

He takes his time lighting a cigarette, exhaling a cloud of smoke, then says in Russian, "Let's start with your name."

She doesn't answer.

She's been in rooms like this before. She knows what's coming. And she knows that for all her grit, for all her fortitude and resolve, in the end, she will crack. Everyone does.

After the cigarettes have been stubbed out on her skin, after the razor blades have been slid beneath her fingernails and her face has been battered to a soft, bloody pulp, she will crack.

And let's not forget she's a woman.

There are tortures that happen in the dark—between a man and a woman—that even the CIA's own documents don't describe. Not the pain. Not the humiliation. Not the wet animal stink of it. Things unwritten in the reports. Unspoken in the air-conditioned debriefing rooms back in Langley.

True stories that never happened.

So why resist?

We do not charge machine gun nests with bayonets.

We do not spit in the eye of the enemy.

Except when we do.

Because she knows something her interrogator doesn't.

She knows who trained her. She knows who she still believes in. She knows who stands watch against the creeping, sprawling darkness.

Roman Adler.

The ghost in the machine. The shadow in the dark place.

The policeman.

So she looks up slowly. Her lip split. Her voice raw.

"Here's spit in your eye."

2

Forty-eight hours earlier…

Toko Sakhalinsky raised two fingers at the waitress and held up his empty mug. She was scribbling an order at the next table over and acknowledged him with a curt nod. A moment later, she was refilling his cup with the thin, brown liquid that passed for coffee in the place.

It was faintly bitter—like the taste on your fingers after peeling off a latex glove—but Toko didn't say anything. He'd expected more from New York City—he'd tasted better coffee at truck stops on the Kolyma Highway—but he wasn't one to complain.

"Everything all right?" the waitress said, twitching to get to her other tables. "Ready to order?"

"I could use more cream," he said in his stiff, stilted English.

"And something to eat?"

"I already told you, I'm waiting for someone."

"All right, no need to get snippy."

He leaned out of the booth and watched her leave. Not young, probably his age, old enough to remember Soviet times if she'd been born in Russia. Under her brown uniform she was all flesh and thigh and jiggle—just how he liked it.

He picked at the foil lid of a creamer and emptied four into his cup, added three sugars—in defiance of doctor's orders—and stirred the bitter mess into something tolerable.

Outside, sleet fell in glassy sheets. It hadn't let up since his plane landed, and the traffic struggled against it. He watched a city bus take a too-fast turn, spraying slush and almost causing an accident. Horns blared. Cars skidded. Drivers swore.

Not so different from Yuzhno, he thought. If anything, here was worse. More cars. More pedestrians. More drivers who didn't seem to give a damn who or what they hit.

He checked his watch. His contact was late.

The diner sat just around the corner from the Russian Mission to the UN—a thirteen-story building on 67th Street that also housed the Belarusian mission and, unofficially, a little-known outfit under the intentionally vague name of *The Nevsky Permanent Subcommittee of International Liaison and Protocol Affairs*.

Those who knew of its existence tended to call it the Nevsky Committee. Or simply, the Committee. Though it wasn't a committee at all, and had absolutely nothing to do with liaisons, protocols, or any other aspect of Russian diplomacy. It was, in fact, an SVR *active measures* unit, not tasked with intelligence gathering—for which there was a plethora of other agencies—but actual boots-on-the-ground work. Dirty hands work.

Wet work, as they'd called it in the KGB.

That meant surveillance of persons of interest. Intimidation of dissidents. Pressure on uncooperatives. And yes, assassination. Everything the pansies at the diplomatic corps were too delicate to touch.

Similar units operated out of the embassy in Washington, and the consulate in Houston. The closure of consulates in San Francisco and Seattle had made the West Coast trickier, but not by much.

Moscow had always reveled in the laxness of American domestic surveillance. At GRU headquarters—the enormous, concrete structure known affectionately as the *Fish Tank,* or alternatively the *Aquarium*—they said cynically, and ungrammatically, that America was *The Land of the too much Free.* At the *Forest*—as SVR's base in Yasenevo was known—they called it simply *Zombieland.*

Operations that would have been unthinkable in Moscow—or anywhere under the Russian domestic surveillance regime—were routine on US soil.

Which was why the Committee could bring in men like Toko—men willing to get their hands *very* dirty, for the right price—with almost laughable ease.

The whole thing was headed by a particularly charmless SVR functionary named Vasily Morozov. Toko had heard him called *Moron-ov* more than once, and had worked with him at some of his previous postings—Germany, Britain, Poland, Hungary. He was the archetypal Moscow yes-man—soft-palmed, addicted to bribes, lily-livered in the face of superiors, and forgettable to the point that even his enemies never thought of him. Which was probably why he'd survived so long—part of that Moscow breed that thrived not in spite of its mediocrity but because of it.

The waitress was back, and Toko looked up at her like he'd never seen her before in his life.

"Ready to order?"

"How many times do I have to say this—"

"Look," she said, flashing a feistiness he wouldn't have minded seeing more of, "it's the middle of lunch hour—"

"I'm well aware of the hour."

"So, if you're not going to eat, I need the table for someone who is."

"I can't just sit and drink my coffee?"

"This isn't a waiting room. I've got a section to run."

"This is ridiculous. In my country, they wouldn't dream of treating a customer like this."

"In your country, they probably aren't working for tips."

"*Tips?*"

"Please God, tell me you know what a tip is?"

"Oh, I know what a tip is."

"My lucky day," she muttered.

"I just don't believe in them."

She clenched her jaw, exhaling slowly.

Toko studied her. He'd have liked to ask her back to his hotel for a lesson in customer relations. She clearly had some frustrations to work through.

"What'll it be?" she said impatiently. "Otherwise, I'm giving your table to that guy in the suit."

Toko looked toward the door, where a three-hundred-pound man was bursting out of a gray flannel suit. For a second, he thought it was Morozov. "He does look like he'll rack up a bill."

She didn't smile.

After a beat, Toko gave in. "Fine, you want me to eat, bring something."

"It's not that I want—"

"No, no," he said, brushing the air with his fingers. "Bring food. And a refill while you're at it."

"What would you like?" she said, reaching for the menu.

"You choose."

"I don't—"

"*You* choose," he said again, refusing to look at the menu.

She narrowed her eyes, then turned and vanished. She returned almost immediately with a sandwich on rye, fries, and an enormous pickle.

"What's this?" he said as she clanked the plate down in front of him.

"What does it look like?"

"How'd it come out so fast?"

"It was made by mistake."

"For someone else?"

"Do you get the impression we're making sandwiches for fun back there?"

"And this is normal? This is how you treat your customers?"

"You said bring food. If you don't want it—"

"No, no," he said, blocking her as she tried to take it back. "I'll eat it. I'm really not here to cause trouble."

"Right," she said flatly.

"I'll need mustard."

"Yeah," she said, already walking away.

"And ketchup," he added. "And more coffee."

From the way she stormed off, he doubted she'd return with any of it, and he took the top off the sandwich. Hot butter, melted cheese, grilled kraut, corned beef. Absolute perfection, he thought, like the sway of her thighs.

She came back with the condiments, throwing them on the table like she hoped to break something. "Everything good?"

He'd just taken a bite, and he nodded, then muttered through the mouthful, "I thought I asked for more coffee."

She left, and he picked up the ketchup bottle and shook it. It was stuck, and he pounded the base with the heel of his hand.

The bell chimed above the door, and a man entered, briefcase in one hand, umbrella in the other.

Morozov.

He wore a flimsy coat and leather shoes, as if he'd dressed for a stroll on the Black Sea in summertime. Toko took one look at him and, not for the first time, was struck by how deeply unattractive he was. Not that anyone would have mistaken Toko for an underwear model, but Morozov was in his own league—balding, tubby, bad skin with an unhealthy pallid sheen. The suit, expensive, looked decidedly cheap on him, and Toko doubted he'd have been able to close the top button of his collar without pinching flesh. If Moscow's bureaucratic class had physical form, this was it.

"Over here," he said, raising his hand for Morozov to see.

Morozov approached, shaking out the umbrella, spraying water.

"Watch it," someone snapped.

"You watch it," Morozov shot back, sliding into the booth. Then, in Russian, "You couldn't wait to eat?"

"I did wait."

"We said two, didn't we?"

"We said one," Toko said, a blob of ketchup finally exiting the bottle and landing on the table next to his plate.

Morozov eyed it as if it were an insult to him personally. "Charming."

Toko wiped it with his napkin. "You want to order something?"

"We should begin."

"Here?" Toko said, chewing with his mouth open.

Morozov looked around, gauging the room. "It's a good place," he said. "Usually."

"For talking?"

"Why not?"

"You're not serious?"

Morozov shrugged.

Toko waved at the waitress. "Hey, sweetheart, my friend could use some service."

"They don't talk like that," Morozov muttered.

"Oh, don't be such a pussy," Toko said, eyeing the waitress. She glared back from behind the counter. "She likes it."

If she did, she wasn't showing it.

Morozov let out a labored sigh, then lifted his briefcase to the table.

"Not here," Toko said.

"I know what I'm doing."

"You want to discuss ops in a diner? You're dumber than you look."

"It's just logistics. Car rentals. Pickups. Times and places."

"Anyone could be watching."

"This isn't Russia. No one's watching. You could shoot a man in the middle of Fifth Avenue—"

"Even still."

Morozov looked ready to argue and Toko gave him a long, dead stare. Then shrugged.

"What's that?" Morozov said.

"What?"

"*This*," Morozov said, mimicking the shrug.

Toko shook his head.

"You'd better get with the program," Morozov said. "You know what happens if this goes sideways."

"Sure."

"I'm not playing around."

"Neither am I."

"You're being difficult," Morozov said.

"Difficult?"

"*Pissy.*"

"I've been sitting here for an hour waiting for your fat ass—"

"Don't say that."

"Say what?"

"You know what."

"I'm *terribly* sorry if I injured your delicate sensibilities—"

"Hey!" a new voice, deep and angry.

They both looked up.

A massive man in a grease-stained chef's jacket towered over them. "You fellas need to leave."

"Who are you?" Toko said, though you didn't need a detective to figure it out.

"I'm the guy telling you you've got a problem."

"A problem?"

"There's no problem," Morozov said. "My friend here wants to say sorry—"

"I don't want to say anything."

"You're the one who gets fresh with servers?" the cook said to Toko.

"English isn't his first language," Morozov offered.

"I was just being friendly," Toko said, pulling a pen from his pocket. "Looks like she could use a friend." He scrawled the name of his hotel on a napkin. "If you want a tip," he said to her, "call and ask for 303."

"The only place she's calling is the police station," the cook said.

"Why? She's got so many offers she has to beat them off?"

"That's it," the cook said, stepping forward. "Out!"

"We're not going anywhere," Toko said.

"Yes, we are," Morozov said, grabbing the briefcase and slipping a hundred-dollar bill on the table.

"I'm not finished with my sandwich."

Morozov was already walking toward the door. "Why do you always have to be such a hard ass?" he said over his shoulder.

Toko looked down at the hundred, then swapped it for a fifty from his wallet.

He made a phone gesture to his ear. "Call," he said again to the waitress. "I'll have a real nice tip waiting. You'll see."

3

Toko was pelted by sleet as he hurried out.

"What are you so upset about?" he called after Morozov, who was a few yards ahead and struggling with his umbrella in the ungodly wind. "You know we couldn't talk in there. It was way too public."

"And this is so much better," Morozov said as a bus sped by, spraying his shoes in slush. "Perfect!"

"Call your driver," Toko said.

"Driver? My office is right up there."

"You didn't walk. Not in those eight-hundred-dollar calfskins."

Morozov gave him a hard stare before pulling out his cell and barking into it. Then he said to Toko, "For the record, I did walk."

It didn't matter. Two minutes later, a black town car with diplomatic plates pulled up and they got in.

"Where to?" the driver said over his shoulder.

"Circle the block," Morozov said. "Slowly."

As the car joined the slow-moving traffic, Morozov raised the privacy screen. "Better?" he said to Toko.

"You're the SVR officer," Toko said. "You tell me."

Morozov looked at him as if contemplating whether or not to kick him out of the car. Then he put on his seat belt and adjusted the vent by their feet, aiming the warm air at his sodden shoes.

"So what have you got for me?" Toko said.

Morozov pulled the briefcase onto his lap and flicked it open. A brown manila envelope sat on top of the other documents, and he handed it to Toko. From its weight, Toko guessed there was a phone inside, along with papers.

"That's all the details you'll need for now," Morozov said. "Maps. Schematics. Instructions. Targets. They're purposely obfuscated in case they fall into the wrong hands."

"This isn't my first rodeo."

Morozov nodded. "You'll get updates on the phone."

"So that's how the phone will work?"

"Very funny."

Toko looked at him for a moment, thinking.

"What is it?" Morozov said.

"It's just..." Toko began.

"Just what?"

"Where's this operation coming from?"

"You're asking that now?"

"Yes."

"I recommended you for this, don't forget. I hope you're not going to make us both look like idiots."

"You recommended me for a reason."

"Because I wanted a job done."

"Because you wanted the best of the best."

"There are five other guys I could call right now. Any one of them would take your place."

"Then go ahead. Call them."

Morozov said nothing.

Toko nodded. "You can't."

"Because you're so special," Morozov said sarcastically. "You and your *special skills*. Like Sean Connery."

"Sean Connery?"

"Whoever."

"Liam Neeson."

Morozov made to reply, but, for once, words failed him. He turned to the front—the sleet was coming down so hard the wipers were barely keeping up. They'd turned onto a side street and were now stuck behind a delivery van with its hazards on. The driver honked, but the van didn't budge.

"Look," Toko said, "I'm just asking where the order originated. It's a valid question."

"Bit above your pay grade, though, don't you think?"

"Not if it's from the *rezidentura*."

"Always looking to cover your ass."

"I need to make sure this isn't some harebrained scheme cooked up here in New York—"

"It's from Moscow," Morozov said, cutting him off.

"Be specific."

"Yasenevo. Top floor."

"You're sure of that?"

"I can show you the authorization code if you like."

"I *would* like."

Morozov regarded him with his beady eyes. They both knew that wasn't going to happen. The code would identify exactly who'd initiated the order—and if there was one thing the brass at the Forest knew, it was how to keep their hands clean.

"But you've seen it?" Toko said.

"I have," Morozov lied.

Toko weighed the information. "I suppose I'll just take your word for it, then?"

The Honeytrap

"The top floor isn't in the habit of explaining itself to the likes of you, Toko Gromovich."

"I know that. I just need to be sure."

"The order's good. It's from the top. I think the price made that much clear."

"I'm not complaining about the price, but it's only worth something if I'm around to spend it."

"That's up to you, Toko. Get the job done, get home in one piece, and you'll be able to cash in your chips for good. One last job and you're a made man. Don't think I don't know what you were up to this time yesterday."

"Yesterday?" Toko said.

"You spoke to that realtor in Barvikha. That building you've had your eye on. The one with the swimming pool and the electric parking spots. You want to live the high life. That's nothing to be ashamed of. You want Yanukovych and Bashar al-Assad as neighbors. I get that. Really, I do."

"All right," Toko said. "Point made."

And the point was made. As soon as Toko received the wire—twenty-five percent of the total, paid in advance—he'd called his realtor. There was a three-bedroom he'd been eyeing for a while. Room for himself, a nanny, and his three-year-old daughter. Less than a kilometer from his ex-wife's new place. It wasn't the oligarchs and émigrés that attracted him to the neighborhood. It was her.

And they both knew the New York *rezident* didn't pay like that. Nor would he have had access to Toko's phone calls in Moscow. This was coming from higher.

"The Committee's really not in the business," Morozov continued, now satisfied they were on the same page, "whatever else you may have heard about us, of starting wars."

"I've heard nothing at all of you," Toko said curtly.

Morozov smiled again. The man knew an insult when he

heard one. "Be that as it may," he said, eyeing Toko like he was seeing him for the first time, "I must say, I'm a little surprised at your reaction."

"No, you're not."

"I think this order is, shall we say, testing your..."

"My what?"

"*Fortitude*," Morozov said. "Your stomach for what needs to be done."

It was a fair statement, though Toko doubted there was an operator on the list who wouldn't have balked at a plan like this. For all he knew, some had already turned it down. Calling in a man from Moscow was not standard procedure. The New York *rezidentura* had plenty of its own assets.

"I'll say this," Toko said. "I've never seen a plan of this magnitude."

"What of it, Toko?"

"The casualties—"

"Let's not speak of casualties."

"I'm just saying, US mainland civilian casualties. We all saw how they reacted to 9/11."

"There you go again, speaking above your pay grade."

Morozov wasn't wrong. It didn't matter what he thought anymore. He'd taken the money. Seen the envelope. He was already in too deep. The top floor didn't believe in refunds.

"There's nothing wrong with my stomach," he said.

"Are you sure? I'm more than happy to tell the *rezident*—"

"All right," Toko said. "Enough."

"Really?"

"Stop being a prick. You know I didn't sign up for this. You know *you* didn't either. That's all I'm saying."

"Fine. You've said it. Feel better?"

"You're not going to tell me you didn't blink when you saw the order?"

"It's neither here nor there whether I *blinked*."

"But you did, didn't you?"

Morozov gave him a long look. "What is it you think we signed up for?"

"Forget it," Toko said.

"No, really, Toko. I want to know."

"You've been toeing the party line since the day you left the academy."

"I'm a *patriot*," Morozov said. "Nothing more."

"You think this is patriotism?" Toko said, holding up the envelope.

"What would you call it?"

Toko said nothing. Then, after a beat, "I like to call a spade a spade."

"And that helps you sleep at night, does it?"

"I don't sleep at all," Toko said.

Morozov looked at him. His face had gone flat. "No, Toko Gromovich. I don't suppose you do." They both knew what he was thinking.

"You know what this is?" Toko said.

"Tell me. What is it?"

Toko knew better than to say it, there were ears everywhere, but he did anyway. "*Terrorism*."

"So you're against killing now? An assassin with a conscience? Rich, coming from you."

"What's that supposed to mean?"

"You know what it means. You and your little *peccadilloes*. Your *proclivities*, I suppose the police might call them. I know what you do after you get your dick wet."

Toko saw red. He'd have liked to throttle Morozov right there and then, but he forced himself to remain calm.

"You know," Morozov continued, "I have to report back to Moscow after this meeting, right?"

"I have no doubt."

"Every word."

"Report all you want. I'll do the job. My record proves that much, if nothing else."

"Well, aren't we lucky? I suppose we should be giving you a clap on the back for doing your job."

"I'm going to put this thing in motion, Morozov. Think about that for a second. Actually think about it."

"A medal, then? The Order of Lenin?"

"You're a funny man," Toko said, though neither of them laughed. "The man who pulls the trigger has a right to call it what it is."

"And that's the word you choose? *Terrorism*? That's how you think of defending Russia?"

"Defending Russia?" Toko scoffed. "Now I think you really are mad."

"I choose to think of it that way."

"This isn't about what you choose, it's about facts, and a lot more people than me will be calling this terrorism when it's done. Believe me."

"Hmm," Morozov said, thinking.

The thing about Morozov, as Toko well knew, was that he was first and foremost a politician. He had to be. More than intelligence, more than operations, he was a creature of the Kremlin—steeped in doublethink and the instincts necessary for survival.

Sitting in that government car, they both knew there was a good chance everything they said was being recorded. *Crimethink* was a word coined by Orwell, but it might as well have come straight from the SVR training manual. And it was something Toko was coming dangerously close to.

Because in Vladimir Chichikov's Russia, even the trigger man didn't get to call a spade a spade.

Morozov, keenly aware of this, chose his words as carefully as ever. "First of all," he said, "let's get one thing clear. *Terrorism* is the occupier's term."

"Occupier?"

"Yes."

"What occupier?"

"Can I ask you something?" Morozov said, his tone so measured now that Toko was sure he was speaking for the benefit of microphones.

"You can ask whatever you like."

"Have you heard of the FLN?"

"No."

"Front de Libération Nationale?"

"Just make your point."

"I'm asking if you're familiar with their politics."

"The politics of the *Front de...*" Toko started, making a vague gesture. "Liberation? Something French? I don't know. Africa?"

"Exactly," Morozov said. "Algeria, to be precise."

"Algeria," Toko repeated.

"They were called terrorists, too. In their day."

"I get it," Toko said. "Everyone's a terrorist. Until they win and rewrite history."

"See," Morozov said, letting out a mirthless laugh. "You're not as obtuse as you let on."

"You can talk all you want, but it doesn't change the fact that innocent people—"

"Innocent?" Morozov scoffed, making a slow, circular motion with his finger, like a blackjack player asking for a hit. "Show me one innocent person in this country, and I'll call the whole thing off."

It was Toko's turn to laugh. "No you won't."

Morozov shrugged. "Before you start rolling your eyes at me, think about this. The 1950s. The Algerian War of Independence—"

Toko looked at his watch. "Look, Morozov, I came in person as a courtesy—"

"You came because you took the money. You sucked on the tit. Now you can shut up and listen."

Toko had already opened the envelope. He could see materials lists, pickup locations, the location of a target dam, and instructions for sabotaging diesel fuel. There was a lot to do.

What he pointedly did not need was a history lecture.

"You said terrorism," Morozov went on. "You chose that word."

Toko slapped the envelope against his palm. "You don't have to be a physicist to see what the end goal is here."

"The end goal? That's an interesting phrase."

"And why's that?"

"Because our end goal is the same as it was for the Algerians."

"Wasn't Algeria a French colony?"

"Algeria was the underdog," Morozov said. "They were the occupied people."

"And they became terrorists," Toko said.

"They became guerrillas."

"Guerrilla, terrorist, freedom fighter. Just a matter of perspective, right?"

"Stop interrupting," Morozov snapped. "That's not what I'm saying."

"ISIS, Al-Qaeda, the IRA—I get it. Those are the tactics you're advocating."

"Not the tactics," Morozov said, slapping the envelope in

Toko's hand. "You see any car bombs in there? Suicide vests? It's the calculus I'm advocating."

"You want to turn the world into Gaza? Into West Belfast?"

"I want them to lose the will to fight. I want them to retreat."

"Retreat? These maps are of Richmond, Virginia."

"I credited you with more imagination."

"What imagination are you talking about?"

Morozov leaned forward slightly, his voice low and urgent. "The whole world is an occupation, Toko. America is a cancer. We can't move. We can't breathe. One day, we'll wake up and their boots will be on our necks. They'll be on the streets of Moscow, the gates of the Kremlin, and it will be too late. They'll come for our wives, Toko. Our daughters. They'll come to Barvikha too, and who will they find there?"

"Enough," Toko growled.

"*Your* daughter, Toko. That's who."

"Don't you bring her into this."

"That's why terror is the answer," Morozov said. "Pain is the only language they understand."

The car started moving again. Outside, the sleet thickened—hard pellets of ice hammering the glass.

Toko looked down at the envelope, then out at the blur of taillights and city streets.

It had begun. The calculus of terror.

4

Oksana Tchaikovskaya was freezing. She ducked into the entryway behind her for shelter. The incessant sleet of the past few days had given way to a few hours of light snow, but the extreme weather was by no means behind them. Blizzard conditions were expected to continue right through the holidays.

Manhattan high-rises made deep chasms of the streets, and a flurry of snow whipped by her as if caught in a wind tunnel. She hugged herself through her cropped cashmere jacket, regretting her decision to wear something so impractical. *Style above substance*—always her downfall. And not just with clothing.

She looked good, though—the jacket was a perfect knockoff of a Valentino she'd seen on Fifth Avenue, minus the four-thousand-dollar price tag, and she'd paired it with Saint Laurent sunglasses and some high-heeled black leather boots that made her look and feel almost exactly like Charlize Theron's character in *Atomic Blonde*. The look suited her bleached hair and delicate Slavic features. The glasses would have hidden her face, too—if she hadn't taken them off when it got dark.

She looked at her watch. *Come on,* she thought, lighting another cigarette. She hated the things—wasn't even really smoking—but they gave her a reason to loiter. Getting it lit was no easy task, and she turned toward the wall and cupped both hands to shield it from the wind. When she looked up, the bus that had been blocking her view had moved on, revealing, across the street, the brightly lit showroom of the *Tsaritsa* Art Gallery, bedecked in twinkling Christmas lights.

This was not going to be an easy job, she thought, scanning the thirty-foot windows that spanned the first three floors of the forty-story tower. The glass in the windows was bulletproof—she knew because she'd seen the permit application filed with City Hall—and light spilled from them onto the sidewalk, casting the passing pedestrians in a pallid glow.

Really, she shouldn't have been considering the job at all. Art galleries weren't her thing. Midtown wasn't her thing. Never mind that this particular stretch of 57th was known colloquially as Billionaire's Row. Security in the neighborhood was intense.

But she couldn't let that stop her. She wouldn't. This was not an ordinary job. It was personal. She looked at the big black-and-white photo of the gallery's proprietor—the extravagant socialite and general man-about-town, Proctor Sifton—and felt her blood boil. It was the face of a man she'd imagined killing, not once but a thousand times. She'd even googled how to buy an illegal firearm, though, of course, she hadn't gone through with it. She wasn't a killer. Just a thief. Jesse James. Robin Hood.

She didn't steal from ordinary people.

Proctor Sifton wasn't a corporation, though. He wasn't another faceless Wall Street bank or Fortune 500 company. He was an individual. An art dealer. A Joe Schmo. He just happened to be a Joe Schmo who, a month earlier, had slipped ketamine into her drink and had his way with her while she was unconscious. How many others had he done the same to? Oksana had woken up after her one and only date with him to find herself lying on a green velvet sofa with blood between her legs and no idea whatsoever of where she was or how she got there.

The feeling—raw, bottomless—wouldn't fade. Wouldn't heal. She couldn't eat. Couldn't sleep. That wasn't going to change until she made him pay.

That was how it worked. *Make them pay. No matter the cost.*

She remembered lying on his sofa in the dark, afraid to move in case he was still there. She listened but heard nothing. No breathing. No presence. And only very gradually did she begin to piece together what had happened to her. She realized that she was in his gallery, on the upper level, where he kept his private desk and files. She'd been to the gallery enough times to recognize the place. She loved the art. That was how she'd met Proctor in the first place.

From the sofa, she'd looked down at some of the most beautiful—and valuable—Russian paintings that would ever be sold on the private market. She'd been taken in by it all. The glamor. The glitz. She could admit that. She'd allowed herself to be seduced.

But now, the artworks, suspended from a vaulted ceiling on invisible wires, each one bathed in a pocket of light as if held in place by some supernatural aura, would be forever tinged by an unspeakable agony, a deep revulsion that lingered in the pit of her stomach like a poison.

As the fog of the sedative wore off, the memories of the night before came rushing back to her in sudden, disjointed fragments. She remembered the bar where she'd met up with Proctor, a late-night place in Tribeca that he'd suggested. She'd been there before, which made her trust the place, and it hadn't seemed like *that* bad of a date, at least not by her admittedly lax standards. If she'd had one criticism, other than his looks—he was twenty years older than her and had definitely let his gym membership lapse—it would have been that he hogged the conversation. What he talked about was interesting—Russian art, catnip to Oksana—but he didn't share the air. He talked in a steady monologue that allowed no interruption.

He'd once sold a Kandinsky in a Mandarin Oriental elevator. "Some hedge fund guy," he'd boasted. "Recognized him as soon as he stepped in. Ninety seconds later, I'd closed a deal for thirty mil."

"Mil?" Oksana said innocently.

"Million," he said, smirking. "US dollars."

He'd told her he currently had a Malevich and a previously unknown Soutine. Malevich wasn't her thing, but Soutine, she adored. She might have gone back with him willingly just to see it. He'd suggested it.

"Come and I'll show you my *greatest masterpiece of all*," he'd said.

Oksana only smiled. She hadn't made up her mind. There was the art, the glamour, but also his pasty, pockmarked skin, bulging gut, and brash manner. And, though she hadn't gotten close enough to confirm it, she suspected his breath smelled.

"Excuse me a moment," she'd said to buy herself a second to think. "Ladies room."

That had been her mistake. She hadn't actually left a

drink on the table—she was clued in enough not to be that stupid—but they had just ordered a second round from the waiter. She was gone only a minute, not as long as their first round of Sazeracs had taken, but when she got back, the drinks were on the table, the amber liquor glimmering in hand-cut crystal glasses like liquid gold. Who'd have thought there was horse tranquilizer in one of them?

But there was, because things got woozy fast after that, so much so that when he offered to call her a ride, she didn't even have the strength to object. When it arrived, it wasn't a yellow cab but an unregistered black car, and she barely noticed him getting in behind her.

It was pretty much curtains after that.

Now, out in the cold, looking up at the gallery's elegant granite façade, its gold trim and intricate art deco detailing, taking in the millions of Christmas lights, the wreaths and ornaments, the piped-in music, it was hard to believe something so terrible had happened inside.

In the month since it had happened, she hadn't been able to shut her eyes without images of it—some real, some conjured by the darkest recesses of her imagination—flooding her senses like a nightmare she couldn't wake up from.

Keep your enemies close, she thought. *Keep them close, and make them pay for what they've done. No matter the cost.*

That was what she'd been told. And that was why she was back. Those words.

Maybe they weren't words to live by, but they were one of the most vivid memories she still had of her mother. It was strange, given that she couldn't have been more than four or five when she'd heard them—and, thinking back now, she couldn't even remember if they'd been said in English or Russian—but those words, her mother's admonishing face and the sudden vehemence in her voice, were as clear to Oksana as if they'd been said only yesterday.

Make them pay. Make them burn.

She'd been a little girl, and they'd been on their way home from school, Oksana and her mother. They walked past the Russian Consulate building on 91st Street, which just happened to be a few blocks from their home on 95th. Oksana remembered pointing out the Russian flag that hung over the building's entrance.

"Daddy's flag," she'd said.

Even at that age, she'd recognized it from one of the few photos they had of her father—standing in full uniform in front of a thirty-foot-high flagpole outside the central administrative office of the Lipetsk Combat Training Center. Her father was young in the picture. It had been taken before Oksana was born. He was facing the flag, saluting it.

It was then that her mother had said the words. "Make them pay, *Ksyusha*." That was what her mother called her—Ksyusha. "Keep them close and make them pay, no matter the cost."

If Oksana—a twenty-four-year-old from New York who remembered nothing of her homeland and knew precious little of her parents' tragic deaths—could be said to have anything constituting a *worldview,* a *philosophy* of life, it was contained in those words. That memory.

That truth.

There were enemies.

And they would pay.

Just like Proctor Sifton.

5

Roughly four thousand miles from where Oksana stood—across the Atlantic, over the frigid Labrador Sea and the Gulf of Finland, past the endless Russian taiga—another woman hugged herself through an impractical coat. She was a little older than Oksana and cut a striking figure with freshly bleached hair, white as snow, held in place by a pair of oversized Fendi sunglasses that looked more like ski goggles. Her name was Margot Katz.

She watched as an air hostess cranked a large mechanical handle, stumbling forward as the door jerked suddenly open. She nearly tumbled out into the wind, and Margot grabbed her.

"Oh my God," she cried in Russian, raising her voice over the raging storm outside. The wind caught her hat and sent it flying away into the night.

"A blizzard," Margot shouted.

The woman nodded adamantly. "Be very careful on these stairs."

Margot braced herself, then stepped out into the maelstrom, clutching the cold steel of the stair rail for support. Out on the runway, a ferocious polar vortex whipped across a desolate expanse of concrete with nothing but the plane and a waiting shuttle bus in its path. She made it to the bottom of the stairs, where a man in an orange parka waved her with a flashlight toward the bus. Just ten yards away—and still she hesitated.

"Go, go, go," the man yelled.

She was the first off the plane, the first to make it to the bus, and she tucked herself into a seat as far from the door as she could get, grateful more than ever for the thick, faux fur she was wearing. The coat, frankly, was ridiculous, chosen specifically to distract the FSB, but no one could say it wasn't warm. She clutched the collar, pulling it tightly around her neck, and remembered the look on Foxtrot's face when she first saw the receipt for it. Foxtrot—not her real name, but what she went by at the Bookshop—was Roman's number two, had been for decades, and was as diligent with expense accounts as she was with CIA kill orders.

"What on earth do you call this?" she'd gasped in her perfectly enunciated English accent, holding up the receipt.

"What does it say it is?"

They were in their office, a little hideout above a bookstore on DC's Dupont Circle—the last place on earth anyone would expect to find an elite spy unit, and Foxtrot had been scrambling to prepare documents for Margot's trip. "A forty-five-hundred-dollar coat, Margot?"

"It was on sale."

"You're going to get us audited."

Margot knew that wasn't true. Roman Adler, head of their unit, was one of the few in Washington who truly could spend without fear of an audit. His budget was comprised entirely of dark money, completely off the books, subject to precisely zero congressional oversight. Even the CIA Director didn't know what was in it.

Margot took the coat out of a Macy's shopping bag and held it aloft like some pelt she'd just brought back from a hunting expedition.

"That's the most ridiculous thing I've ever seen," Roman said.

"It's got a job to do."

"You're not going as a *Tverskaya* streetwalker," he said.

Margot put the coat on defiantly—a luxe, white fur that extended from her neck all the way to her ankles, and which looked like it had been harvested from a litter of baby seals. As Roman's eyes grew in horror, she also put on the designer ski goggles she'd bought to go with it, at a cost of another twelve hundred dollars.

"You're going to blow the entire operation," he said.

"Am I?" she said, turning to show him her back. If he'd thought it was bad before, he was truly aghast now. Spread across her back in enormous red letters, as if someone had purposefully ruined the coat with paint, was the word *Balenciaga*.

"You look like you've been attacked by PETA," Foxtrot said.

"It's faux," Margot said. "Relax."

Though in truth, even she felt uncomfortable in it. These days, even faux fur was too much, and she wouldn't have been caught dead in it on the streets of Washington.

But she wasn't going to be wearing it in Washington.

She looked out the window of the bus as the remaining passengers disembarked the rickety Ural Airlines vessel that had just brought them in from Istanbul. The flight had been touch-and-go, almost canceled a number of times due to the storm, and the passengers—barely thirty in all—hurried down the steps as if abandoning a sinking ship. The usher was still waving them with his flashlight, and Margot thought they wouldn't have looked any more desperate if they'd been holding one of those ropes mountain climbers used to stay together. Even the flight crew, the last to get on the bus, looked frazzled. More than one hostess had lost her hat.

The bus wheezed to life, ferrying them to a terminal that was as eerily empty as the plane had been. Margot looked at her watch—it was just after one AM, but even at nighttime, it was rare to see such a major hub so deserted. She hurried along with the rest of her group, passing a shuttered McDonald's, rebranded as *Tasty's*, the new logo still very much evoking the original, and a Starbucks that had been relaunched as *Stars Coffee*, its branding barely distinguishable from the Seattle original. Indeed, if she looked at the sign close enough, she could still read the 'bucks' lettering under a thin coat of white paint. This was it—this was what an economy severed from the global order looked like. It wouldn't be long before China went the same way.

She presented herself at passport control, the only passenger not in the line reserved for Russian citizens, and waited twenty minutes while seven uniformed officials, including an FSB warrant officer and two senior sergeants, pored over her false, hastily-issued documents. Foxtrot had worked a small miracle to get everything together in time for the flight, but Margot still worried as another two guards came over to examine them.

"Purpose of your trip, Miss...."

"*Pechvogel*," she said for the tenth time—an unlucky bird, a fitting alias. "I already told you. I'm here to provide language services at the embassy."

"*Russian* language services?"

"Correct," she said in Russian. Everything they'd said had been in Russian.

"At the *American* embassy?"

She didn't even give an answer to that. Her credentials were American—a false diplomatic passport, a visa, a diplomatic note, and a full assignment letter and travel itinerary. The itinerary said she'd be in Moscow seven days—and wouldn't be leaving the city. The assignment letter said she worked as an interpreter and would be conducting language performance reviews for secretarial staff. It was precisely the type of work the FSB was likely to believe of a female staffer—a fact Foxtrot was all too aware of, and had been taking advantage of since the KGB days. "They love to underestimate us, darling," she'd once told Margot. "Lean into it. Give them just enough rope to hang themselves."

Margot didn't know Foxtrot's real name. She didn't need to. Nor did she know the details of her life, though she imagined they included places like Wycombe Abbey and Cheltenham Ladies' College, Knightsbridge and Ascot Racecourse. She always managed to conjure an impression of impeccable English aristocratic breeding.

"And you'll be staying…" the FSB officer started.

"On-compound," Margot said cooly. "Is this going to take much longer?"

The officer stared at her for long enough that it made her feel awkward. "It will take what it takes."

She said nothing. The truth was, she wasn't surprised to be getting the third degree. She was traveling on diplomatic papers at a time when Moscow's relations with Washington were at their lowest ebb in decades.

"You've been to Ukraine," the officer said, flicking through the passport. Foxtrot purposely put that in to make the papers look less sanitized.

"I've been to a lot of places."

He nodded gravely, then told her to take a seat. She looked at the thin, plastic bench by the wall, before walking over and sitting down on it. She was fairly certain she was the last passenger in the building.

She crossed her legs, tried to look natural, and tried not to think about all the ways this could go sideways. It wouldn't take much. A misspelled name. A date in the wrong format. She'd done her share of hostile border crossings, but nothing ever prepared her for the cold, surgical scalpel of Russian suspicion.

More phone calls followed, more waiting, and she half-expected to be brought to a private interview room. After about an hour, she was finally called back up to the desk where the officer stamped her passport and, separately, her visa, pounding the documents with his stamp as if trying to break the thing.

"Go on," he grunted.

She went through to the baggage carousels where, surprise, surprise, her suitcase was nowhere to be found. Important embassy personnel sent their luggage ahead by diplomatic courier, but she was traveling as an interpreter, and had carried her own luggage. There was nothing in it she couldn't replace, and nothing that would give her away as a spy, but it did take her another half-hour to find someone from the airline to file the claim with.

Finally, she left the terminal. Outside, a cab waited. Behind it, brazen and unmistakable, was a black BMW with tinted windows.

6

Toko sat in a white Toyota SUV, registered to a shell company, and fought the urge to slam his head into the wheel. He'd been stuck in bumper-to-bumper traffic for over an hour. One more inane joke from the drive-time hacks and he'd shoot someone—or himself.

The song that had been playing—a Christmas song performed, apparently, by chipmunks—ended, and the hosts came back with gusto.

—All right, folks. If you're still with us, we're still with you. And if you're southbound on I-95 right now, ouch. Carmageddon, am I right?

—It really is that bad, Trevor. The latest from the weather desk is that this system off the Atlantic is just getting bigger and bigger. They're calling it a once-in-a-generation Nor'easter. One jackknifed tractor-trailer north of Baltimore and boom—twenty-five-mile backup. Traffic's being rerouted.

The Honeytrap

—And what about people already south of that Elkwood interchange, Nina?

—I hate to say it, but those folks are in it for the long haul. We're talking hours, Trevor. With freezing rain still falling, it's going to be a while before any of them get moving again.

They cut to more Christmas music.

A quick look at the map told Toko that he was indeed past the Elkwood interchange. No detour for him. He was well and truly stuck, and that was not good news. It didn't help that the heat from the vent was blasting into his face, drying his eyeballs. And the wipers shrieked across the glass like a trapped animal, shredding his patience.

He looked at the clock on the dashboard. He'd already been on the road longer than the entire journey was supposed to take, and he'd scarcely covered half the distance.

He sat clenching his teeth, weighing his options.

—And that was *Let it Snow* by the legendary Vaughn Monroe. One of my favorite moments in film history was when they played that song over the ending credits of *Die Hard*. Do you remember that scene, Nina? The camera pulling away from Nakatomi Plaza, everything in ruins, and then that song comes on?

—*Die Hard*? Now, there's a Christmas classic. Trevor, what, in your opinion, is the greatest Christmas movie of all time?

Toko switched them off, then reached behind the seat for the half-eaten packet of chips he'd thrown there a few hours earlier. Old Bay, they called it—a strange flavor he'd never had before. It reminded him of a stew seasoning he'd known as a child. That thought, combined with the incessant sleet pelting his windshield at an almost horizontal angle, gave him a sudden sense of nostalgia. It wasn't so different, he thought, from the weather of his childhood on Sakhalin Island, where cyclonic storms blew in off the Sea of Okhotsk so ferociously that even Stalin's *Gulag* had struggled in the face of them. He didn't think of that place often, though this trip seemed to have stirred something up. In his memory, his childhood was one unbroken ice storm. Not snow, never snow. Only frozen rain—cold, wet, sharp as shrapnel.

He pulled out his phone and pinched the map, zooming in on his location. The last exit he'd passed was five miles back. If he had to, he would get on the shoulder and drive the wrong way back to it, but he could see on his phone that even if he did that, the surface roads for miles around were a gnarl of gridlock. According to the traffic data, the only way out of his predicament was forward, past the accident, and onto the empty highway beyond. If he managed that, he'd have the road virtually to himself as far as Baltimore.

He tossed the chips onto the passenger seat and wiped his hands on his pants. Then he checked his mirrors and pulled into the median shoulder, ignoring the angry honks from the cars behind. He'd seen emergency vehicles speed by on the shoulder earlier, but the sleet had built up so quickly that their tracks were no longer visible. Putting a lot of faith in the Toyota's winter tires, he picked up speed and hurtled forward into the darkness. He pushed forty—too fast for the conditions—but if he went any slower, some wise-ass would pull out and block him.

It was ten minutes before he saw the flashing lights of the emergency vehicles. The accident was a multi-vehicle pileup involving a semi, jackknifed and blocking the rightmost lanes. From the number of ambulances—he counted six—as well as the other emergency vehicles, he guessed there'd been fatalities. There were two fire trucks, as well as a slew of police cruisers, but no tow trucks or other equipment for clearing the road.

A single cop, bundled up like an Arctic explorer, faced the backed-up traffic. He wasn't letting anyone through. As the radio had said, it didn't look like anyone would be getting past for some time.

Toko was approaching too fast, but he resisted the urge to slow down. To do so now would be to admit defeat. The cop would pull him over. At this speed, and with the road as icy as it was, stopping wasn't an option even if he wanted to. The cop would know that instinctively, which would stop him getting in the way.

Toko sped right by the cop, past the emergency responders and their vehicles, past the wreck itself, gambling the police would be too busy to worry about one rogue driver.

After the accident, the conditions grew immediately worse. With no traffic, the sleet had time to build up to a thick carpet of ice. He went on as fast as he dared, which was only about twenty miles per hour, keeping one eye on his rearview. He continued like that for a few miles, but as he approached the very first exit after the accident, saw the flashing blue and red lights of the police behind him.

He swore under his breath.

Just one car—a big black SUV. He could run, but that probably wasn't a good idea. It would mean, at best, ditching his vehicle and arranging a replacement. It could be done—but it would take time and wasn't without risk. Morozov wouldn't be pleased either.

He slowed down.

For a meeting with a cop, the location could have been worse. A dark stretch of road with a high divider blocking the view of the oncoming traffic. Tall pines lined both sides. He'd let the cop stop him, and if things didn't go his way, he'd kill the cop, take the exit, and ditch the Toyota. He'd done worse for less.

He came to a halt just before the exit and reached for the glovebox. Inside was a legally registered Glock 19, put there by the SVR, and he took it out and checked that it was loaded. The gun was nothing special, but it was reliable, easily concealable, and common enough that it wouldn't implicate the embassy if he used it. He placed it between his seat and the door, where he could reach it easily. Also in the glovebox was a fresh slate of false documents, all carefully prepared by the Committee and arranged neatly in a plastic document holder with the name and logo of the Geico insurance company on the cover.

In the trunk, he had a few gallons of bleach, ammonia, ammonium-nitrate fuel oil, two empty jerrycans, and five kilos of regular white sugar. He also had tools, a flashlight, and a hard case containing electronic cell-activated trigger devices and detonators. Most were legal, over-the-counter products, even the triggers and detonators. In combination, however, and in the back of a car driven by a man with a pronounced Russian accent, they would definitely set off alarm bells if discovered. They were concealed by nothing more than the SUV's built-in retractable cargo cover.

The police car pulled up behind him and stopped. Toko sat motionless, his two hands on the wheel. The cop took a minute, then got out of his car and approached, one hand holding a flashlight and the other at his waist, near his gun. He was doing everything by the book. Their side of the highway was dark, completely devoid of cars, isolated. It was just Toko and the cop now.

The cop rapped on the window with the flashlight. Toko peered out and saw a kid—early twenties, fresh-faced and inexperienced. He cracked the window six inches—a blast of sleet pelting him in the face as he did so.

"Know why I pulled you over?"

Toko cleared his throat. "I choose to remain silent."

The cop nodded at that and let out a brief sigh. Toko was keenly aware of where the cop's hands were and where his own gun was. He didn't doubt he could beat him to the draw.

"I'm going to need to see your license and registration."

Toko took his time getting the license out of the document holder—it was a New York license, and the name on it matched the vehicle registration. When he got it out, he didn't pass it through the crack in the window but held it up against the glass, forcing the cop to go back to his cruiser for his mobile terminal. When he returned, he crouched toward the window, reading the text with his flashlight and checking the photo. He removed the glove on his right hand to enter the details. "Registration," he said when he was done.

Toko repeated the process, holding the registration to the glass and forcing the cop to do everything again in the cold.

"You sped past an accident back there," the cop said after confirming the documents.

Toko said nothing.

The cop sighed again. "Have you got anything in the back of the vehicle?"

"I do not consent to a search," Toko said in his heavy accent.

The cop seemed to be at a loss for what to do. He still hadn't put his glove back on, and the sleet was coming down hard. The cold would reduce his dexterity.

"I'm going to have to ask you to step out of the vehicle," the cop said.

Toko considered reaching for the gun, it would have been the easiest thing in the world, but the look on the cop's face told him it might not be necessary. Instead, he said to the cop, "This interaction is being recorded."

The cop looked the car over, searching for the camera. "What are you?" he said. "Some kind of lawyer?"

Toko said nothing.

The cop said nothing either, then repeated his previous command. "Step out of the vehicle, sir."

Toko said, "Am I required by law to step out of the vehicle?"

The cop hesitated, and Toko added, "Am I being detained, or am I free to go?"

"You're being pulled over for a lawful stop."

"For what?"

The cop looked at him for another moment and their eyes locked. Almost imperceptibly, Toko gave him a shake of the head, as if warning him of something. Neither said a word. Seconds passed in silence. Toko turned his gaze forward, looking at the vortex of sleet in the arcs of his headlights. He was acutely aware of the cop's stance, his position, his lack of movement. It was a moment of stasis—a coin spinning in the air. It couldn't spin forever. The superposition had to collapse. Heads or tails. Life or death.

Which way would it go?

Then the cop said, "All right, you're free to go. Next time you see an accident like that, stop like everyone else."

Toko said nothing. Shut the window. Shifted into gear.

Then he drove into the storm, eyes fixed on the mirror.

The cop didn't follow.

Heads. This time.

7

Oksana didn't remember arriving at the gallery. Didn't remember being taken out of the car. What fragments she could summon felt like things that had happened to another person—like she'd been floating above her own body, watching it being broken from a great distance.

What she did remember—vividly—was waking up afterward. She remembered lying there, cold, thinking about the texture of the velvet against her bare skin. She remembered touching the mess between her legs, a sickly mixture of blood and bodily fluids that made her retch when she realized what it was.

She didn't panic, though. She remained strangely calm. She tried to get up from the sofa but lost her balance. And then, Proctor himself—rising from the darkness like some prehistoric sea creature—caught her. He'd been watching the whole time, and even as she leaned on him for support, as he helped her with her dress and shoes and brought her wordlessly to the door, the only thing stopping her from clawing his eyes out was the shock still numbing her senses.

She didn't give in to the rage. Not then. Not yet. She swallowed the bile and made herself a promise—revenge, when it came, would be total.

When they got to the door, Proctor opened it, and the light from the corridor spilled in, assaulting her senses anew. There'd been a comfort, if it could be called that, in the darkness. A sense that what had happened wasn't quite real. That it could be concealed. The glaring fluorescence of the corridor was like suddenly being exposed to kryptonite. Her head spun, and she lost her balance again, only this time it was the wall that stopped her from falling.

"Elevator's down there," Proctor said, pointing down the corridor, and she remembered very clearly the mechanical clicking of a pin tumbler lock as he shut the door behind her. It was an old-style lock, original to the building's construction, and something that an art dealer of Proctor's caliber might have had the wherewithal to upgrade. Oksana made note of it—even in that addled state, her thief's brain worked. She noted the door's construction and its place in the corridor, unmarked but for a small 'Staff Only' sign. She noted how far she was from the elevator bay and the number three stenciled on the brick wall directly opposite. It was a service corridor, utilitarian and undecorated, reserved for staff and deliveries, and she logged every detail.

She would need them when she came back.

The building was a 1940s landmark, once the beating heart of the New York art world. Most galleries had moved on, replaced by luxury retail—but not this one. The *Tsaritsa*. Proctor had owned it for fifteen years, but for six decades before that, it had been *the* place in the city to find the most valuable Russian art. Collectors from all over the world, even from Moscow, came to place bids at its biannual auctions.

Oksana was still in the doorway of the building across the street, still shivering, still pretending to smoke cigarettes. An armored vehicle rounded the corner onto 57th, and she found herself adjusting her hair as a means of concealing her face. She noted the two uniformed guards inside the vehicle and the distinctive logo on its side—Muldowney Consultants. Her jaw clenched. Not good. Muldowney was the most notorious private security firm in the city, and the most formidable. It recruited exclusively from ex-military, men and women who were not gun-shy, and its guards were more heavily armed than any others in the city. They were also more likely to kill an intruder. Oksana knew this because they displayed the statistic prominently in their marketing materials. She'd come across them in the past, and, every time, had promptly dropped the job. Once she saw their skull and bones logo, she pulled the plug. Without exception.

She couldn't go up against contractors who advertised their kill count. She worked alone. Unarmed. Her wits were her only weapon. No job was worth dying for, and no job was worth killing for.

She knew that Muldowney operated out of a dispatch center across the East River in Queens, sending heavily armed guards in quasi-military vehicles over the Queensboro Bridge with unrivaled response times. To where she was now, it would take five minutes tops for them to respond to a nighttime alarm.

During the day, when traffic was heavier, their response would be slower. That made it essential that she carry out the job as soon as possible after the gallery closed for the night. She looked at her watch. According to its website, the gallery shut at seven. Details were everything in a job like this. How many staff stayed until closing, how long it took them to lock up, and whether anyone remained behind afterward, were all critical pieces of information. From what she could see now, there was just one person still inside, a woman in a prim polka dot dress who looked about Oksana's age. Oksana wondered if Proctor had ever brought her to Tribeca for a drink.

At a few minutes before seven, the woman started turning off the lights. Oksana watched her go through the nightly routine. The only question she had was whether anyone was left upstairs. From where she was standing, she couldn't see, but she knew that Proctor kept his desk up there, as well as his files and a walk-in Diebold Nixdorf safe. If he was up there—if he made a habit of being there past closing time—she needed to know.

The woman in the polka dots finished up, leaving on just the overnight lights. These included spotlights on some prominent paintings, as well as dim recessed lighting over the stairs and on the upper level. Oksana watched her climb the staircase, then watched her emerge from the building's main revolving doors a minute later.

They were the same doors Oksana had come out of the night Proctor drugged her. She watched the woman descend to the sidewalk and hurry off in the direction of Madison Avenue, buffeted by the wind. She checked the time. Five after seven. If that was how it went every night, it was perfect. Traffic was still heavy enough on the Queensboro that there'd be time for her to get in and out. Earlier also meant more people in the building and more traffic on the street, making her presence less conspicuous.

She remained where she was for another ten minutes, watching for movement on the upper level. There was the nightlight but nothing else. Nothing to suggest Proctor was up there. She looked at her watch again and was about to call it a night when a man in a pinstripe brushed past. He happened to be speaking Russian into his cell, and when he scanned a key card to access the building, she flicked away her cigarette and caught the door behind him.

"*Spasiba*," she said when he looked back.

He was surprised, but she met his eyes coolly, following him into the lobby as if she belonged there. He was still on the phone while they waited for the elevator, still speaking Russian, and she glanced at her own phone to appear natural. When the elevator arrived, he stepped aside for her to enter first. She avoided the control panel, noting it required a key card.

"Floor?" he said when the doors shut, now in English.

"Three," she said, voice steady.

He scanned his card, looking her over, head to toe. Mid-forties. Wedding band. She knew what he was thinking.

He ended his phone call and was about to strike up a conversation when the doors opened.

"Are you Russian?" he said as she stepped out, speaking again in their native tongue.

She looked back, but the doors were already shutting, and she gave only a shrug in answer. The truth was, she wouldn't have known what to say to him. Her birth certificate said she was Russian—issued twenty-four years ago by the Central Clinical Hospital in Moscow. Her parents had certainly been Russian, not that she'd ever really known her father. Her mother, she did remember, and from the few photos she had of her, knew she bore a striking resemblance to her. She'd been a dancer. She'd even made it all the way to the Bolshoi. Oksana, like all orphans, clung to every glimmer of a memory of her as if her life depended on it.

The Honeytrap

The years they'd spent together in the attic on 95th Street were the happiest of her life. They were all the childhood she'd had.

Her father was dead and buried before they ever left Moscow, and while her mother spoke of him fondly, she did not speak of him often. Something had gone badly there, though Oksana never found out what it was.

In any case, it all ended with the sudden death of her mother when Oksana was just six. The next ten years were spent going in and out of foster homes, group homes, and whatever other facilities the esteemed New York City Administration for Children's Services had at its disposal.

Oksana still went back to the old address on 95th Street. The place was different now—no longer broken up into cheap apartments—and she would stand outside and look up at the attic dormers, trying to figure out which one had been theirs. She could clearly remember her mother sitting in the sunlight, her golden hair glowing like fire, telling stories in her clipped Russian. Oksana spoke the language fluently and always felt a pang of emotion when people told her she carried that same Saint Petersburg lilt.

Survival. That was the first thing her mother taught her. But it wasn't the only thing.

The corridor was flanked on both sides by offices for various businesses, and at the end was a large window overlooking the entrance she'd come in by. She walked to it and stared out. Directly across the street, she had a perfect view into the *Tsaritsa's* upper level.

And there was no mistaking the man she saw sitting there.

He was at his enormous desk, typing on a laptop, his hairy chest visible even at this distance through the few open buttons of a garish orange and purple shirt. Oksana choked back the rising bile in her throat and wondered how she'd ever thought she should date such a monster. Was it protection she'd been chasing? Power? Or something uglier —something rotten she still didn't want to admit?

She marked the time on her watch and realized her hand was shaking.

"Hey," someone said from behind her. She turned to see a group of three women who'd just come out of one of the offices. "Can we help you?"

The woman who spoke was wearing a pair of cat eyeglasses with heavy black rims that made her look like a librarian. The other two were holding coats and briefcases, clearly headed home for the night.

"Oh," Oksana said, trying to look relaxed. "I'm waiting for someone. He works for…" she scanned the directory, "Global Equity Partners."

"GEP?" the woman said skeptically.

"Yes," Oksana said, maintaining her gaze.

"Their office is that way," another woman said.

"Right," Oksana said, holding her ground. "Well, he said wait here."

They stared at her, and the one in the glasses said, "It's just, we don't usually get visitors up here."

Oksana said nothing. If she wanted to force the issue, she would let her.

It turned out she didn't, and the three of them entered the elevator, the one in glasses looking back at Oksana like she was on to her. Oksana turned back to the gallery.

Proctor had risen to his feet and was switching off his computer. He walked over to the door, where Oksana remembered there was a control panel for the alarm system, and pushed a button on it before turning out more lights, leaving the upper level in darkness. A minute later, he emerged from the revolving doors.

Oksana watched him through squinted eyes.

He was going to pay. That was their way. Her mother's way.

Make them pay, Ksyusha.

8

Margot sat in the back of the cab, eyeing her driver. She wondered if he was on the FSB payroll, too. It wouldn't have surprised her. By now, nothing would.

Behind, the three-series was tailing so closely it would be a miracle if it didn't rear-end them. Did he want to be seen? Was intimidating embassy interpreters the new norm?

"He's close," she said to the driver.

He nodded. "I just don't know..." he said quietly before letting his words trail off.

"Don't know?" she said.

He cleared his throat. "I'm saying, I don't know who teaches them how to drive. The road's as slippery as a...." His words trailed off again.

"Slippery as a what?" she asked, amused.

He caught her eye in the rearview. "Oh, you're bad."

"You're the one who said it."

He shook his head, allowing himself a smile. "I thought you people were all prim and proper."

"*Us* people?"

"*Amerikántsy*," he said.

"Is my accent that bad?" she said. She hadn't given him the address of the embassy but a hotel near it, and one of the criteria for operating in Moscow was that she could pass as a local. A slip-up in that regard could be the difference between life and death.

The driver shrugged. "It's okay. Just a little...."

"Prim?"

"Maybe," he said, making a face like he was trying to pick out the flavor of a wine. "Too proper. Like a newscaster or something."

"I see. I'll have to work on that."

"Don't worry about it," he said. "Really, it's the hotel that gave it away. No one stays at the *Romanov*."

"My boss does."

He nodded, and again, she wondered if he was FSB. Outside, the streets were so deserted she wondered if there'd been some incident she hadn't heard about. The weather was bad, and it was the middle of the night, but for a city of twenty million—the biggest in all of Europe, by some measures—something felt off. It was as if the whole place had been abandoned, like in one of those Zombie Apocalypse films.

Visibility was so poor the driver had to sit up over the steering wheel, peering out through his wipers as they squeaked back and forth across the windshield.

They passed an intersection, and the lights weren't working. They weren't even flashing yellow. A car sped by, mere feet in front of them, and the driver jammed the brakes. They skidded to a halt, avoiding a collision by inches.

Behind them, the three-series blared its horn, skidding into the lane next to them.

Margot winced. "That was close."

Even the driver was startled. "Prick," he muttered, looking at the three-series. It slipped back in behind them when they started to move. "You don't think—"

"Think what?" she said.

"That he's...."

"Following us? It wouldn't surprise me."

"Who are you?" he said, peering at her anew in his mirror.

"Nobody," she said. "A pencil-pusher. I work for the embassy."

"I better not get in any trouble for this."

"You won't," she said, pulling her cell from her purse. It was vibrating, and when she looked at the screen, she saw Bryce's name. For some reason, a wave of apprehension washed over her. It was usually *verboten* to take a call like that, but her comms protocol on this job was different. "Bryce?" she said. "Everything okay?"

"I've been trying to reach you."

"I just got in," she said. "My flight was delayed." He knew she was in Moscow, though he thought she worked for the State Department. He had no idea what she really did.

They'd been going out for almost two years, though they lived separately. That was Margot's call. He had a beautiful townhouse in Cleveland Park—a place with a yard, a large deck, and a spare room that would have made a perfect nursery—but Margot didn't want to move too fast. Concealing what she did was hard enough living separately.

"Relationships never end well in our line," Roman told her when she first mentioned it. "Get out before it gets messy."

It was advice Margot promptly ignored. In fact, she

wasn't sure it hadn't inflamed her feelings for Bryce—and her determination to make the relationship work.

More recently, he'd told her, "He's going to propose, just so you know."

"Excuse me?"

"I have access to his credit card history. Unless he's shopping at Tiffany for someone else."

Margot had been completely taken aback by the announcement. "You don't think that's something I might have liked to be surprised by?"

"Not if you value your current role."

"Oh, I see," she'd said. "Nip it in the bud—every glimmer of happiness I might have on the horizon."

"This isn't good. Trust me."

And a part of her knew he was right. If she ever truly wanted to move beyond dating, there would be serious implications. It wasn't just the practicalities of keeping the truth hidden—her contract imposed ironclad legal obligations, particularly the requirements of her *Top Secret* clearance, with its *Special Access* designation. The designation alone required manual re-issuance from Foxtrot every twenty-one days, along with disclosing every person she'd spent more than twenty-four hours with.

Roman Adler required undivided loyalty from his people. There was no room for sharing.

"I don't want to be alone forever," she'd said. "If Bryce proposes, I'm going to accept."

"It would mean changes."

"No kidding, it would mean changes. I'm thirty-one years old."

"You've got time."

"Not if I want a family."

"And do you?" he'd said, as if it were the most preposterous idea he'd ever heard.

She didn't answer. She hesitated. But if she hadn't been certain then, she was now. She didn't want to end up like Roman—alone, surrounded only by ghosts, vanquished enemies, hollow victories that meant nothing. She wanted a real life.

"Honey, what's the matter?" she said into the receiver, keeping an eye on the driver as she spoke. She knew that every word she said was potentially being recorded—by Roman as much as the FSB.

"There's something we need to talk about," Bryce said.

"Is everything all right?"

"Everything's... not all right."

"What's happened?" she said, trying to picture his face. She calculated what time of day it was in DC and said, "You're not still at work, are you?"

"I'm not at work."

"It sounds noisy."

"I'm at George Washington."

"George Washington?"

"The hospital."

"Oh my God—"

Don't freak out. I'm all right."

"What happened?"

"I'm fine. It was a small car accident."

"Oh God."

"Stop!"

"I'm sorry, I'm just—"

"Listen, there's something I need to tell you."

"Okay," she said, taking a deep breath.

"You'll find out anyway, so...."

"Find out?"

She could hear voices in the background—nurses, maybe. Ambulances. The drone of an intercom. He paused for a moment, then blurted it out. "I wasn't alone in the car."

She felt an instant pressure in her throat, as if someone had grabbed her by it. She tried to speak, but no sound came out. A knot clenched in her chest, tight enough to stop her breath. She knew what this was. She knew what he was going to say.

"Margot?" he said. "Are you there?"

"I'm here," she breathed, the words scarcely audible.

"I'm only calling because you were going to find out anyway."

"You keep saying that."

"I've been trying to come up with a way—"

"Who is it?"

"Calm down."

"Who is it?" she said again, voice rising. "Who was in the car?"

He said nothing for a moment, then, "Cynthia Snider. You met her at the—"

"Company gala," she snapped, suppressing an urge to throw up.

"Right," Bryce said. "Well, now you know—"

She tried to open the window but it was locked. "Stop the car," she said in Russian.

"Look," Bryce said, and she could hear the distance in his voice, the frosty dispassion of a man who was already gone. She'd been telling herself for months that it wasn't there, but there was no denying it now.

"Pull over!"

The car stopped and she opened the door, taking deep breaths of the cold air as she fumbled one-handed with her seat belt. "Why are you doing this?"

"Come on, Margot. You know why."

"No, I don't," she lied.

"Don't make this difficult."

"*Difficult?*"

"You always make everything so—"

"Don't do this," she gasped. "Please don't do this." She hated herself for saying it, for sounding so desperate, but once it started, she couldn't stop. "Please don't leave me, Bryce. I'll do better. I'll be better—"

A pause. Then, as if from miles away, a voice she no longer recognized. "Cynthia's pregnant."

The seat belt unbuckled, and she threw her head forward, retching violently onto the pavement.

She spat, wiped her mouth with the back of her hand, then held up the phone. "Hello? Bryce? Are you there?"

He was gone.

She looked back at the tail car. It had stopped too, and it sat by the curb idling, its driver watching her from behind the glass.

Motionless. Predatory.

Like a carrion bird circling something already half-dead.

9

Irina Volkova lay restless in her bed, staring at the sliver of light entering the room through the curtain. She'd been staring at it for an hour, telling herself it was moonlight, though she knew it was just the sodium glow of Kutuzovsky Prospekt eight floors below. She kicked off her blanket, a tangled mess, and sat up in the bed.

She shouldn't have broken contact, she thought. She should have kept broadcasting. If they were risking her life anyway, what was the difference?

In the room next to her, on a beautiful Cavour writing desk she'd overpaid for in Florence, sat a hundred-watt, 1960s-model, army shortwave radio transmitter. In the attic above, hidden behind the building's own insulation panels, was an enormous directional antenna pointed directly at Berlin, sixteen hundred kilometers away.

She got up and went to the window. An ungodly blizzard was tearing through the city, and she'd never seen the streets so desolate. The few cars that dared to be out were struggling against the wind. She watched them, wondering if *they* were out there now—FSB men in a van full of equipment—hunched over scanners, listening in on headphones like a Gestapo radio unit.

By rights, she should have gotten rid of the transmitter the moment the FSB started raiding offices. But she couldn't —it had been her father's. Instead, she'd disconnected the antenna and removed the battery. Still, she was running a terrible risk keeping it. Sooner or later, they'd close the noose. She looked down at the street for anything resembling a van with an antenna on the roof, or even a phalanx of police cars with their sirens blazing—at this point, it would almost be a relief to see them coming—but there was nothing.

Only snow, swarming like locusts in the headlights of the cars.

She replayed in her mind the conversation she'd had with Zubarev's secretary eight hours earlier. The Americans had called a meeting, and it didn't track. Either the ambassador had forgotten completely how things were done, or it was a ham-fisted attempt to put Irina and Margot in a room together. Her gut told her it was the latter, and it was shockingly dangerous.

Margot was smarter than that.

The bosses had stepped in.

The secretary's name was Zoya, and—for some reason Irina still hadn't gotten her head around—Zubarev seemed to be sweet on her. In the world of the Central Federal District, secretaries getting their asses pinched was as common as breathing oxygen—but Zoya's ass might have been expected to be an exception. Zubarev was no spring chicken—but Zoya was seventy if she was a day, with thinning hair and an ass so corpulent her chair had to be custom-made. On more than one occasion, Irina had witnessed her eat an entire family-sized supermarket lasagna for lunch.

"What's all this, then?" Irina said, sauntering over to her desk, trying to look nonchalant.

"What does it look like?" Zoya said, dipping a chocolate-filled *ponchik* into a mug, and promptly dripping coffee all over the printout.

"It says *Meeting with US Ambassador.*"

"So you *can* read!" Zoya said sarcastically.

Irina hadn't exactly expected her to be helpful, but she wasn't about to take her crap, either. "I read that article you left open on your screen, too," she said. "What *is* facesitting, anyway?"

Zoya turned beet red, but she still wasn't ready to play ball. "Ask your stallion next time he's got you on your back, *slut.*"

"You can do better than that," Irina said coolly. She'd been called *slut, whore,* and a whole lot worse by the fine ladies of the secretary pool a thousand times. She no longer felt a thing.

They'd made their point. She'd crossed the line. She'd slept with the top dog. Not the boss—they'd all dropped to their knees for him long ago—but the boss's boss. The emperor himself. Vladimir Chichikov.

In fact, Zoya should have been a whole lot more careful because Irina was *still* sleeping with him.

Perhaps not as frequently as had once been the case—five years had passed since she'd first charmed him by spilling coffee all over his shirt in a Center 16 corridor—but he still found his way to her bed when the mood struck.

Not coming to her bed literally—the President of the Russian Federation didn't make house calls. Not anymore.

But, he'd send a bodyguard—a knock on the door, a tap on the shoulder—and she'd be whisked off to a waiting car to answer the presidential summons. They might bring her to the Kremlin. Or the residence outside the city. Or to a private jet and on to Sochi, or the Valdai Residence in Novgorod, or even overseas. Once, she'd even been brought to the Kremlin Situation Room. She'd never forget the glass of the conference table against her spine, or the hundred screens above her showing live troop movements in the Donbas. She'd literally watched men die in real-time while the *Savior of the Motherland* buried his face between her thighs.

It wasn't the life she'd dreamed of.

Whore. Traitor.

She hadn't been born for it. Nothing about her life predicted it. You didn't spend your whole childhood training for the military just to betray your country.

And Irina's training had begun when she was thirteen. That was when she told her father she wanted to follow in his footsteps. The announcement came in the form of an application fee—for Lyceum 239, the elite technical school where he'd started his own journey as a radio specialist thirty years earlier.

He'd gone on to serve with distinction during the Soviet war in Afghanistan, and Irina had every intention of following his example. It wasn't just his radio that was in the next room—she had his portrait, too, and his letter of commendation signed by Yuri Andropov. In a silver frame, protected by glass and backed by crimson velvet, were his seven medals of valor. On the bookshelf sat his first edition of *Dead Souls,* a gift from his own father on the eve of his deployment.

It all looked more like a shrine than an active espionage operation.

But that was what it was.

On the desk next to the radio were some less sentimental items—a notebook and pencil, an ashtray, some Prima cigarettes, and a box of matches.

After decoding a message from Margot, Irina would open the window, light a Prima, then burn the message in the ashtray. Often, while smoking the cigarette, she'd look at the black and white photo of her father, dressed in uniform before his first tour of duty, and wonder what he'd make of it. Of his daughter passing secrets to the enemy. Two words came to mind, echoing the opening of a book title he'd loved.

Whore. Traitor.

Her father, above all else, had been a patriot. He took the ideal of *Motherland* seriously. He believed in the flags and banners, the parades and uniforms, the tombs and monuments.

What would he think, if he saw what she had?

The corruption.

The cynicism.

The callous waste of life—by men who would sacrifice an entire generation on the altar of their own glory.

Would he understand?

Would he agree?

Or would he call her what Zoya had? *Whore*?

Or worse? *Traitor*?

Perhaps she'd get to find out.

But for now, there was Zoya and her *ponchiki*.

"Zoya Mikhailovna," Irina had said, taking one of the little doughnuts and popping it in her mouth. "Who called this meeting?"

They'd locked eyes, but it was Zoya who gave first. "The Americans."

"And they requested Zubarev by name?"

"It's still his department, isn't it?"

"But why?" Irina said. "They've never done that before."

Zoya tapped her mug with a ballpoint pen.

"Come on. Don't pretend I can't make this ugly."

"Oh, and what would you do?" Zoya said, defiant. "Write me up? Zubarev would lose a lot of sleep over that."

"If you don't smother him first."

A beat.

"What did you say?"

"I said, why did they call the meeting?"

"Embassy security," Zoya said curtly.

"Embassy security?" Irina repeated, flat.

"You got a problem with that, *pillow princess*?"

"It's a bit vague, isn't it?"

"Look," Zoya said, snapping the box of *ponchiki* shut and dropping it into her enormous purse, "if you think I'm staying late with the likes of you—"

"Just tell me what you know."

"What I know?" she sneered, stuffing the rest of her things into the purse. "As I'm sure you're aware, no one shares their reasoning with us lowly secretaries."

She shut down her computer and began a rocking motion, building momentum to heave herself out of the chair.

"How's your grandson?" Irina said.

That stopped her.

She looked up, and there was fire in her eyes—hot and instant. Irina hated herself for using it. She knew the grandson was the only thing this woman cared about in the world.

But she twisted the knife anyway.

"I hear he dodged another draft call."

"Don't you bring him into your sordid little—"

"I'm just saying," Irina said, her voice syrupy and cruel even to her own ear. "He's awfully lucky."

Zoya exhaled slowly through her nose. "Something about embassy airspace," she muttered.

"What's that?"

"Embassy airspace," she said again, enunciating exaggeratedly.

"Do embassies have airspace?"

"Police helicopters," Zoya said. "Regular Moscow police helicopters."

"They've been flying over the embassy?"

"Yes, they have. And, according to the ambassador, they've been far too low."

"And that's what the meeting's about?"

Zoya shrugged. "Now, if you don't mind," she said, grabbing hold of the desk with both hands and building up the momentum again, "why don't you fuck off?"

With all her might, she pulled herself to her feet. It was a sight to behold, and Irina watched her walk across the office like a ship under sail, her legs lost in her billowing skirts. When she was gone, Irina stared after her toward the elevator, her mind racing through the possibilities.

One thing was certain. A meeting in Zubarev's office was suicide. She had to stop it.

She pulled on her housecoat and slippers, nearly tripping over her cat on the way to the kitchen.

"Careful, Pushka," she chided, making her way to the refrigerator. The cat rubbed against her legs, and she bent down to pick her up. "What do you want?" she said, muzzling her nose into Pushka's lustrous fur.

She took milk from the refrigerator and poured some for Pushka. Then, on a whim, she poured a cup for herself too.

Irina didn't ordinarily drink milk, she only kept it for the cat. But she poured some now into a white mug and placed it in the microwave. Then, she watched it rotate in the little light.

The microwave was a Miele—best of the best. She still remembered the feeling in her gut the first time she saw it.

Chichikov hadn't been at the viewing, of course. It had just been her and the bimbo realtor, nipples showing through her silk dress, and four of Chichikov's ubiquitous bodyguards. At the end of the viewing, she was told that the four-thousand-square-foot apartment, with its fourteen-foot ceilings, parquet floors, and wrought-iron railings on the balconies, was already hers.

"I don't want to be a kept woman," she'd told Chichikov.

They were lying next to each other in his enormous bed at Novo-Ogaryovo.

He'd said back, "I want you to know what you're worth."

He'd meant it as a compliment, a gesture of affection, but the transactional undertone stung. She knew what she was in that place—she knew her role. She'd heard how the guards spoke behind her back. *Blyad*, they called her. Or *deshyovka* if they were feeling generous.

"I was FSB when you found me," she said, running her finger around his pink nipple. "Don't turn me into one of those women at the Mercedes Bar."

He'd looked at her curiously then. "You're not like the others."

Others, she'd thought bitterly. Chichikov had wives, ex-wives, multiple mistresses with whom he'd had children. Irina never forgot that. She wasn't an equal. She was a possession. Part of a harem.

And there was no such thing as choice in that world.

You took what they gave.

You became what they said.

And as well as becoming a mistress, she became pregnant.

The microwave dinged, and she reached in for the cup. It was hotter than expected, and she almost dropped it. She picked it up using her sleeve as a sheath and brought it to the counter. When she sat, Pushka was immediately on her.

"Shh," she whispered.

She blew on the milk and sipped. It tasted like childhood—radios and laughter on her father's lap.

Then she opened her briefcase and pulled out Zoya's coffee-stained distribution list. She read over the names and noticed that there'd been a last-minute correction on this copy. It was different from the one distributed via email. The ambassador's interpreter, Carla Stellenbosch, had been crossed out. In Zoya's angular scrawl, another name had been added.

Peggy Pechvogel.

Irina opened her laptop, typed in the name, and hit enter.

Whore, Traitor, Soldier, Spy.

The screen blinked once, then began to populate.

10

The rest of the drive went smoothly for Toko despite no letup in the weather. He pulled off the highway at a place called Yellow Tavern, and filled his tank, as well as the two five-gallon jerrycans in the trunk, then went inside.

"Anything else for you?" the clerk said.

"Coffee."

"It's self-serve."

"I see," Toko said. "Just take what I want?"

"Cream, sugar, it's all there."

Toko filled an oversized cup with coffee, topping it off with six packets of real sugar and something called French Vanilla flavor enhancer. He also picked up a depressing-looking shrink-wrapped sandwich and—in a snap decision—two candy bars sitting by the checkout.

He paid, climbed back into the car, fired up the engine for heat, and ate the sandwich where he sat. He chewed mechanically, watching the people scurrying in the downpour. Flood warnings had crackled all day on the radio and everyone was in a hurry.

One man came out of the store with two large cases of bottled water and promptly slipped on the ice. He fell flat on his ass, water bottles bursting everywhere. Toko watched him limp to his vehicle.

Soft, Toko thought. Weak. These people were citizens of a decaying empire. They were withering on the vine. They deserved what was coming.

He had to tell himself such things. Any sane man would. Not that Toko qualified.

Morozov saw America as a dark power, an ever-expanding cancer. Toko didn't see it that way. He wasn't fighting an empire. He was going to hurt these people where they lived. He was going to hurt their children in their beds while Christmas trees twinkled in the living room.

Another woman slipped on the ice, flailing with an umbrella and a phone.

He finished the sandwich and took a long sip of coffee. It tasted like a warm milkshake. Only here, he thought, would they sell coffee in twenty-ounce containers—and invent something as ridiculous as a coffee flavor enhancer. It did taste good, though, and when he bit into the Reese's NutRageous candy bar, the rush of sugar was as pleasurable as any drug.

This place, he thought, squinting at the Exxon lot through sleet-streaked glass, was as far from the world of his birth as it was possible to imagine. Watching these people, it was easy to see them as another species, their thoughts and worries as alien to his own as if from another planet. They'd grown up with refrigerators and microwaves, color TVs and credit cards. They'd grown up in the sunshine.

And yet, thinking of his daughter, there was another uncomfortable truth he couldn't square. Katya—already insisting on Kasia, after a Polish TikTok Star—had more in common with these people than she ever would with him. She lived in Moscow and had never been within four thousand miles of the island of his birth, though she'd been to the United States. Twice. Even to Disney World. With her mother—the money-grubbing whore—and her new husband—the family-stealing cuckoo. It was a strange thought, but the distance from Moscow to Yuzhno was almost as far as the distance from Moscow to this very gas station.

And Katya, his only love, was one of them. She was on their side. And the world she would inherit, for all his efforts, would be defined not by the apartment in Barvikha, not the bedroom he planned or the private school he'd already paid the exorbitant fees for, but by this act of terrorism he was about to commit.

This blackened offering.

It would be ash in her mouth.

He slapped himself hard. Too much thinking wasn't good. Then he bit back into the NutRageous. It wasn't bullets that would kill him. It was the sugar. Probably already had.

He let out a long sigh, then bit off another mouthful. It was a slippery slope, he knew, all this thinking. A man like him was better off not thinking. Keeping his mind blank. That was how he'd been trained. If he was wrong in what he was doing now, then all the experiences of his life, everything in the long path that had led him to this point, were wrong also. And if a life could be wrong, it could just as easily be meaningless. It didn't matter. *This* didn't matter. What he was going to do didn't matter. *Nothing did*.

The comforts of nihilism. That was what Chichikov's regime offered the world. There was no such thing as right and wrong, good and evil. All justifications were meaningless. Unnecessary. Chimeras of our own devising. Fairy stories for children.

"Cavemen told stories before killing mammoths," he'd been taught. "Stories when crops failed, when death hovered near. But the stories didn't matter, Toko. Only that they killed. Only that they survived."

In Chichikov's Russia, even schoolchildren were taught that survival was the only morality. That failure was the only sin.

His first handler had put it plainly. "There are Russian girls shipped in containers, Toko. Seven—eight years old. Huddled like cattle."

Toko didn't need to check that fact. He'd heard the crying himself behind the steel doors of the containers at Yuzhno's port. Sometimes, he still heard it.

"The world is many things, Toko. Coca-Cola, Britney Spears, Michael Jackson. But the girls in containers are just as real. Chernobyl is just as real. And anything that's real can be brought to their shores."

And so, here he was.

Mokroye delo, they called this work in Russian. *Wet work.* In KGB times, vast departments, like *Spets Byuro 13*, worked on little else. In those days, entire bureaucracies, thousands of men and women who got up in the morning and looked at themselves in the mirrors of their Moscow apartments, had dedicated their entire working lives to tracking down and killing the enemies of the Russian State.

And who could say they were wrong to do it?

Fifty million Russians lost their lives in the first half of the twentieth century fighting defensive wars. Wars started by Western powers. Wars in which the explicit goal was the annihilation of the Russian nation and the permanent enslavement of its people.

So, Toko tried not to lose too much sleep over the things he did for his country. Against fifty million, what was one? Or two? What was a thousand?

Reality was subjective. How could it not be?

Toko had been born in a *Yaranga*—a hand-built, semi-underground hut made of driftwood and animal skins, and dug into the thin, stony soil of a land so hostile that even Stalin's Gulag struggled to survive it. He came from the extreme east of the extreme east of Russia. It was a place that had only ever been used as a penal colony, first by the Tsar, then the Imperial Japanese—who called it *Toyohara*—and finally by the USSR. It was a place of punishment and exile, of forced labor and death. Crossing the Strait of Tartary—or the frigid Sea of Okhotsk—was like crossing the Styx. One-way, and only in chains.

Toko's father was a border guard at the port. He sat around getting drunk on *Zhigulevskoye* beer and smoking cheap, filterless cigarettes.

His mother was a native of Sakhalin—a mix of Nivkh and Ainu blood—and looked more Asian than Russian to Russian eyes. His parents weren't married, and—from what fragments Toko had been able to piece together—the relations they'd had were not entirely consensual on his mother's part. Not that he'd ever been able to ask—she'd died giving birth to him. Apart from his genetics—his high cheekbones, lustrous black hair, and robust, stocky build—the only thing he'd really gotten from her was his name.

After her death, her people wrapped him, still screaming and covered in blood, in a grain sack. They'd left the sack with the porter of the Oblast Children's Hospital No. 1 in Yuzhno, along with a note, written in the hand of the porter, explaining what they knew of his origins. He might have died then, but with the aid of the note, he found his

The Honeytrap

way to his biological father, where he had a second chance to die.

Luckily or not, depending on one's perspective, the father didn't kill the unasked-for infant but rather passed him into the cold, unloving hands of his own mother. She was originally from Western Russia and had been exiled as a child, along with her family, to Sakhalin during the Stalin years.

It was she who raised Toko, and, being a good Russian, quickly set to scrubbing the pigment from his skin with a wire brush. It almost killed him.

He grew up in Yuzhno as a Russian, attended Russian school, and had no further contact with his mother's people. He never learned their language. When he tried to track them down in adulthood, their settlements no longer existed. Their language was what was termed a *linguistic isolate*. Something had happened in the past to cut them off from the great tides of human history. They'd remained apart. Other. Toko felt that in his bones.

By age fifteen, he was working at the same port as his father, though in a different capacity. Rather than border guard—drunk twelve hours a day and dressed in the drab uniform of the Federal Border Service—Toko became a smuggler. He worked the other side. By that time, his grandmother was dead, and he'd long since been kicked out of his father's government flat in *Kholodilka*. It didn't matter. He earned more in a month than the government paid his father in a year. The Soviet economy was collapsing, and Toko was cashing in on the ocean of contraband pouring in from Japan and Korea and a dozen other markets.

His ability to blend in among Asians and Russians alike was an asset. So, too, were his natural aptitudes for logistics, local languages, and doing what needed to be done. A man of his abilities was destined to attract the eye of the security apparatus, and pretty soon, he wasn't just smuggling, he was making sure the party bosses got their share.

From there, it was just a small step to becoming a full-fledged SVR hitman—a *wet worker*, or *likvidátor,* as they called them then—on the same government payroll as his father, though on a better scale.

Toko wasn't a patriot.

But as long as they paid what they promised—never a fact to be taken for granted—he kept his mouth shut and followed orders. He was the reliable dog.

He dialed Morozov and pulled the map onto his lap.

"You're in Richmond," Morozov said when he picked up.

"You're tracking me?"

"Of course we're tracking you. And you're lucky the weather held. You took your sweet time getting there."

"Has Moscow finalized the target?" Toko said.

There were a number of potentials—all parts of the Surry County Flood Prevention Plan, published publicly by the Virginia Department of Conservation. That such sensitive information was out in the open—the flood controls along the entirety of the James River were completely public—was another example of America's failure to make difficult choices. There was such a thing as too much freedom. Too much openness.

"Toko, that waitress?" Morozov said.

"What waitress?"

"The one from the diner. You gave her your number?"

"Ah?" Toko said, an agonized expression crossing his face.

For all his justification—all the talk of terrorism and innocent lives—Toko Sakhalinsky was a troubled soul, a fractured man. A man at war with himself and his own urges.

"Did she ever call?"

Toko ignored the question. "Give me the target," he said.

Morozov hesitated, still thinking about flabby thighs and brown skirts, no doubt. Eventually, he said, "Target C."

The map on Toko's lap was a detailed Army Corps floodplain study—also public domain—and the target was marked as plainly as any other point of interest. "Bosher's dam," he said, opening the wrapper on the second candy bar. "It says here it's a low-head concrete weir."

On the same map, just downstream, was a residential cluster called Glenwood—rows of low-income prefabs packed along a bend in the floodplain like tin cans. There was an elementary school there. He committed its name to memory without meaning to.

"That's the one," Morozov said.

"You don't want me further downriver, then?" The briefing note was unclear on that point.

"No," Morozov said. "Those are harder targets. There's been enough rain that C will do. Failing which, the secondary is scarcely a mile away."

"Got it," Toko said.

He stared at the map. Chocolate melted in his hand. Then he started the engine.

11

Harry Cassidy drove his brand new F-150 at a dead crawl. He wasn't even pushing twenty but had already had a near miss. The frozen rain hadn't just turned his shift into a twelve-hour-long endurance test, it had also covered the road in an almost sheer sheet of ice. One wrong move, and he'd be in the ditch. Having just signed a five-year financing deal on the truck, he had precisely zero intention of letting that happen.

It was late, he was tired, and to top it off, he had six missed calls and fourteen increasingly irate messages from his wife, Sheryl. She'd been expecting him hours ago, and the single message he'd sent telling her he'd be late clearly hadn't cut it. He was very tempted to step on the gas.

But he resisted the urge. He wasn't a hurrier. He wasn't impulsive. Slow and steady, that was his motto—and as Lead Safety Engineer for one of the largest nuclear plants on the Eastern Seaboard, it was a good one. He prided himself on having his head screwed on straight. It was part of his self-image, along with the hard hat, the steel-toe boots, and the obsolete company-branded pocket protectors clipped to his shirt. As far as he knew, he was the last person at the plant still using them, and he was fairly certain he was running down a supply that hadn't been re-stocked in over a decade.

When people called him a geek—which they did often—he took it as a compliment.

On the wall of his office, next to a posed family portrait Sheryl had insisted on paying good money for, were nine framed certificates—his degrees from Virginia Tech and Michigan, his INPO certs, and his NRC license.

He'd earned each the hard way, and took pride in it.

So no—he wasn't about to hurry.

And he sure as hell wasn't going to end up in a ditch, calling out the plant's tow truck for rescue. He would drive like a grown-up and take his time. He was so late he was in the dog house anyway.

He glanced at the clock on his dash, and in the split second it took, almost lost control.

"Good grief," he said aloud, righting the vehicle and reducing his speed still further.

He was on a concrete road—known as Hog Island Road—that wound through a few miles of forest and a state nature reserve before terminating at a security check. Some local farmers and hikers, and two logging companies used the road in summer, but in winter it was exclusively plant traffic.

The plant itself was located on a crook in the James River near where it emptied into the Chesapeake. Though mostly hidden by forest, it wasn't as remote as it felt, sitting just a few miles from settlements on the opposite bank.

Keeping both eyes on the road, he called Sheryl and braced for what was coming. Instantly, her voice filled the cabin. "Where the hell are you?"

"Honey, I know. I'm sorry."

"You're supposed to be helping with Christmas. I was worried sick."

"I messaged—"

"Oh, I *got* your message. Your *one* message. Three freaking hours ago."

"It's been an absolute zoo. The river's higher than I've ever seen it. I couldn't get away."

"And you couldn't call?"

"This is the first chance I've had. I *just* left."

"Well, you'll be lucky to get home at all. Cathy Davenport said they're closing the bridge."

The bridge she was talking about was a four-mile causeway over the James Estuary that connected the south side of the river, where Harry now was, with Newport News, where he and Sheryl lived. If it was closed, it meant a lengthy detour.

"The beltway's open?"

"What am I, Google Maps?"

"I'm just asking—"

"Cathy also said the Hanscombs have been flooded out."

The Hanscombs lived four houses down. If they were flooding, it didn't bode well. "How?"

"Their basement started filling with water. I don't know how."

"What a nightmare!"

"So, *that's* what I've been dealing with. They're calling it the storm of the century. A once-in-a-hundred-year thing."

"That's what a century is."

"Yeah, well, smarty pants, do you think you might want to be with your family when it strikes?"

"You know I'm on my way."

"Well hurry up. I've been seriously considering packing up the kids and taking them to my parents."

Harry took a deep breath. She knew that would get to him. Sheryl's father was a truck mechanic and avid doomsday prepper. One of his favorite pastimes, when he wasn't too busy buying crossbows, was questioning Harry's ability to protect his daughter and grandchildren when the shit hit the fan. And yes, that was how he referred to them—*his* daughter and *his* grandchildren—especially in front of Harry.

Taking a turn just a tad too fast, Harry felt the slide of his tires as they lost traction. "Oh, no!" he gasped.

"What is it?"

He regained control and righted the truck, then slowed down even more. "It's the road. Slick as an ice rink."

"Well, if you're planning on getting stuck in a ditch, let me know now so I can pack the things—"

"Sheryl, that's enough. I'll be home in an hour."

"An hour? In this?"

"A little longer."

"A lot longer, and that's *if* the bridge is open."

Harry rubbed his temples. He just wanted to get home in one piece—and without a fight. "I'm sorry," he said. "I know I'm late. I should have tried harder to call."

"That's all I'm trying to say."

Twenty years of marriage had taught him well. "You're absolutely right, hon."

"I just want the kids to see their father before FEMA shows up at the door."

"I'll be there as soon as I can."

"Well get home in one piece. Oh, and while you're at it, could you pick up some bottled water?"

"Bottled water?"

"And batteries. Double-A."

"What kind of storm do you think we're in for?"

"They're for the flashlight. I just want to be prepared."

"All right, I'll pick up batteries and water."

"The kids will be in bed."

"I know," he said with a sigh, then heard the beep of another call. "See you soon." He hung up and answered the second call. It was the control desk—the plant manager, in fact.

Harry's voice immediately changed. This was the real Harry—the one who spoke in acronyms and contingency plans. "Pete? Tell me."

"Did you leave?"

"You know I did."

"Yeah, well, I'm going to need you to turn around."

"I'm at my twelve-hour cap."

"Priesenhammer just crashed. He's not going to make it."

"Is he all right?"

"He's fine. Skidded on ice and rear-ended a minivan. He's sitting in the back of an ambulance right now. They say he needs an X-ray or some shit."

"Well, I'd love to help out, but twelve hours is twelve hours."

"This is an emergency, Harry."

"You're telling me. I just spent the last twelve hours dealing with your emergency."

"No. They're saying the water level sensors are out."

Harry took a beat. There'd been nothing wrong with them when he left his station ten minutes ago. "Which ones, Pete?"

"Extractor pumps."

That was what he was afraid of. "You're sure?"

"I think I know what a bad—"

"Get a team out to clean off the ice. Pronto."
"Already done. Completely defrosted."
"And the readings?"
"Nothing. We're blind."
"Those pumps can't flood."
"That's why I'm calling, Har."

The plant's Westinghouse reactors used a simple *once-through* cooling system—river water in, river water out. As long as the James kept flowing, gravity did the rest. Except in exceptionally bad weather, such as the present, when the river rose above the loop's outflow level. When that happened, only pumps could keep the flow going.

But the pumps needed to be at exactly the right level. Too high, and all they pumped was air. Too low, and they flooded. And they did not like getting flooded. No sir. Flood those, and you didn't get a do-over.

Harry eased off the gas. With the river as high as it was, the pumps were mission-critical. Which meant his union cap was out the window.

"So you're on your way back?" Pete said apprehensively.

Harry sighed. "I'm on my way back, but get those pumps out of the water now."

"What about the heat?"

"Get them out, Pete."

"Harry, tell me you're not going to *SCRAM* my plant two days before Christmas."

"We're a ways from that yet, but we can't risk flooding those pumps. A sensor problem, we can handle. It's a software issue. A glitch. But those pumps are specialized pieces of—"

"You're lead safety. We pull them when you get here."

"Pull them now. Hadfield can handle it."

"You're five minutes away."

"And if that control circuitry gets wet, the nearest repair crew is in Quebec, Canada."

"Harry, I don't mean to be the guy who cried wolf here—"

"Pete, relax. We can handle this."

"Without pumps in the loop, we're not getting any flow."

"Like you said, I'll be there in five—"

"And without flow, the water gets hotter and hotter. Then it boils. Then it superheats. Then we're operating the world's biggest pressure bomb."

"None of that's going to happen. Did you pull the pumps?"

"Order sent down to Hadfield. I'm going to get a real nice call from the governor over this."

"Yeah," Harry said. "It's better than the alternative."

He hung up and looked in his rearview. There were headlights approaching. He switched on his hazards and waited for it to pass. The last thing he needed was someone ramming him while he was doing a U-turn.

The lights drew closer, then red and blue flashers came on. He hadn't realized it was security. He rolled down his window and waited for it to pull up.

The guard did the same, then said, "You Harry Cassidy?"

"Guilty as charged. Pete send you?"

"In case you didn't pick up the phone."

Harry nodded. "I picked up."

"So you'll follow me back? They said it's life and death."

"I'll follow," Harry said, "but I'm going to need you to do something for me."

"What's that?"

"Call my wife. Tell her something real big's come up."

12

Freedom, for Irina, came soaked in blood.

Not right away—certainly not when armed guards dragged her to Chichikov's clinic in Kuntsevo. There, she was subjected to every manner of medical brutality. *Mifepristone*, they told her, when she demanded to know what they were testing for. *Misoprostol*, too—every compound, natural and synthetic, that might induce abortion.

"Abortion?" she'd cried, tied to the bed like a criminal. "You think I did this to myself?"

And they did think it. For weeks, they thought it. And one of their procedures, something called *Dilation and Curettage*, ended up puncturing her uterine wall, ensuring she'd never get pregnant again.

"Act of God" was the final conclusion, delivered to Chichikov nine weeks to the day after the miscarriage— after she'd been dragged, kicking and screaming, from her bedroom.

It was the first time she'd set eyes on him since it

happened, and through the glass of the observation room, she heard him say to the doctors, "You wasted her."

"Sir," the doctors protested, "the complications—"

"She's ruined," he added. "Useless."

Chichikov left then, and a few moments later, guards dragged out the doctors. Irina learned later they'd been executed—strangled with coat hangers, one of the tools they'd accused her of using.

The ordeal wasn't the first she'd seen of Chichikov's dark side.

But it was the beginning of her resistance.

At first, her only hope was for escape. She'd wanted to get as far from Chichikov as humanly possible—out of Russia, if she could. That became difficult when, despite all that had happened, he kept finding his way back to her bed. He came so often that suicide started to feel like the only way out. And that was when her path crossed with Margot's.

At first, she'd known only that Margot was American, and pegged her as just another of the endless stream of Western girls looking to make it big in Moscow. She asked her for paper towels in the restroom of a flashy nightclub. An inauspicious beginning if ever there'd been one.

But soon, Margot had pieced together not only who Irina was sleeping with, but also her Center 16 background. And that was when a plan began to come into focus.

"You don't want to escape," Margot said to her, hastily refreshing her lipstick in that same restroom some weeks after their first meeting. "You want to get even. You want to nail his dick to the wall."

Irina didn't hesitate. "I want to cut it off and feed it to him."

By that time, Irina was no longer completely captive. She'd persuaded Chichikov to transfer her from a secret wing at Novo-Ogaryovo, where he'd been keeping her, to the apartment at Kutuzovsky Prospekt.

"I'll let you go," he'd said, "because it was my doctors who spoiled you. Made you half a woman."

Those words had been a slap in the face, but she'd swallowed her emotion whole. "And because you promised," she added.

"You're still mine, though. I'll have you whenever I want, however I want. Don't ever forget that."

"Of course," she'd said, giving him a faint smile. What else could she say?

Weeks would sometimes pass without a word. Then, without warning, his guys would show up twice in one week, whisking her away in a black car. Occasionally, in those very early days, he even came to the apartment in person, accompanied by an entire SWAT team that secured the building from top to bottom. He seemed to like coming. He'd walk around in a silk dressing robe and make his own coffee in the mornings, or sit at her kitchen counter reading the morning papers with a cigarette in his hand—a taste of normalcy he couldn't get elsewhere.

She'd become his refuge.

And it was one of life's eternal ironies that it had been he who tracked down the R-130 base station.

"A housewarming gift," he said, presenting it.

"Is this really his?" she whispered, though she already knew it was. She'd have known her father's shortwave anywhere.

"Look at the bottom."

On a sticker bearing its frequency range, 1.5 to 12 MHz, were the initials VV.

"Vasily Volkov," Chichikov said. "I assure you it's his. He was the only operator in the unit, and this was their only base station. There's no one else it could have belonged to."

"They still had it?"

He shrugged. "About the job. You know you can't go back to Center 16. Too many people there know where you've been."

"But you promised me—"

He raised a hand, stopping her short, then reached into his jacket and pulled out an envelope.

"This is the best I can do," he said. "Take it or leave it."

When he left, the envelope was still on the counter, unopened. Inside was Irina's fate—and for a long moment, she didn't dare touch it. Center 16 had been her one goal in life—everything she'd ever worked for—and he'd already said she couldn't go back.

All those years, all that work, and for what? Turned out he'd been right. *Wasted.*

Hers had been a very particular upbringing, a very particular education. Graduated from the Lyceum at seventeen, gone on to MathMech in St Petersburg, then a covert cryptography program at Moscow State. From there, Center 16 was the only path. She'd trained in SIGINT, fieldwork, counterintelligence. Mastered six languages. Passed the screenings for *Sovershenno Sekretno*, Russia's top security clearance.

Before Chichikov ever laid eyes on her, she'd worked on the nuclear codes, top-level military doctrines, the entire inner wiring of the Russian war machine.

Now, all that was to be replaced by whatever was written inside this creased envelope. Somewhere, her father's voice echoed, "First, the noise, Irinka. Then the signal."

She peeled it open slowly. The paper inside bore the seal of the Central Federal District—not a promising start.

The role was intelligence analyst, something adjacent to her work at Center 16 but nowhere near as technical. It wouldn't engage the skill set she'd spent years perfecting. And it wouldn't put her anywhere near the top decision-makers.

But then she saw who she'd be reporting to—Leonid Zubarev.

Was it a trap? That was her immediate response. She and Margot had met four times already, always in the same restroom at the Mercedes, but this blew everything they'd been plotting out of the water.

It was like Chichikov had just handed her a razor and asked her to shave his throat.

Zubarev was far more important than his flamboyant title—*Plenipotentiary Envoy*—suggested. That role was just a cover. His true position was Chairman of the *Sovbez*, the Russian Security Council, and his office within the Central Federal District acted as its *de facto* secretariat. Reporting to him meant a front-row seat at the beating heart of Chichikov's security apparatus.

That was how she knew what was coming. Through snatched data packets, fragments of overheard conversation, stolen files.

Something worse.
Something on US soil.
Something that would bring America to its knees.

She didn't know the specifics. The files—laden with schematics, computer code, and 256-bit encryption—couldn't be hacked by a lone operative. They required the combined efforts of an intelligence complex.

So she'd passed them to Margot the best way she could think of—shipped by a courier specialized in trafficking illegal art. With the Russian elite liquidating assets at an unprecedented rate, it was the one method that wouldn't raise eyebrows.

Naked corruption.

The object she'd shipped was no *Mona Lisa*, it was a drab old oil painting her father had picked up somewhere, and an auction listing in New York wouldn't draw eyes beyond the narrow world of niche Russian art collectors. But she didn't need a crowd—just a ping.

On a CIA tracer.

And how to make sure that tracer was running?

The easiest way would have been to fire up the R-130. That was the method she and Margot had relied on in the past.

But it was out of the question now. Center 16 was sweeping the airwaves, and the FSB was raiding offices—ripping computers from desks, arresting Irina's peers left, right, and center. A broadcast would be suicide.

So she'd done something far simpler. She'd bought an ordinary tourist postcard from a kiosk in Red Square, wrote the painting's name on the back, then sent it via regular Russian Post—paying extra for express stamps—to Margot Katz, care of the US Embassy in Moscow.

A basic plan, slipshod, hit-or-miss—but if there was a way to trace the sender of a postcard—short of watching them drop it in the mailbox—Irina didn't know what it was.

Hit-or-miss was the right descriptor, though. Especially *miss*.

Because if the plan had worked, getting the files would have been as easy as walking into the gallery in New York and taking the painting off the wall.

Instead, Margot was in Moscow, and the US ambassador was pestering Zubarev's office for a meeting about police helicopters.

That would never do.

Irina climbed down the rickety ladder carefully, a small portable hard drive clutched in her hand. If all this skulking and plotting ever led to her death, it would be because of this little drive.

She reached the bottom and waited for Pushka, who'd followed her up to the attic, then slid the ladder back up to the ceiling on its retracting springs.

In the kitchen, her laptop was still on the counter, next to her empty mug of hot milk. On the screen was the result of her database query. A single hit. A woman who'd passed through passport control at Sheremetyevo not three hours prior.

Peggy Pechvogel. Thirty-one. American. The photo left no doubt.

The hair was different, a bottle blonde rather than her natural brown, and she was looking decidedly conspicuous in her white fur coat, but there was no denying who it was.

Margot Katz.

This was who Zoya had scribbled in on the distribution list in place of the ambassador's usual translator.

They'd decided they couldn't wait. They'd come for her.

There was a moment—half a breath, maybe less—when Irina seriously considered bailing on the whole thing. Deleting the files. Throwing away the drive. Walking away and letting the secrets rot. But that was the voice of fear, and fear was a luxury she no longer permitted herself.

She exhaled, already mourning the cost of what she was about to do, then got up, went to the bedroom, and got dressed. Once, she might have chosen something beautiful. Not anymore. Everything was practical—black pants, flat-heeled boots, a warm coat with a high collar. In the office were the Prima cigarettes, bought for just this purpose, and she put them in her coat pocket. Then she went back to the kitchen and put out extra food for Pushka. She also wrote a quick note for the superintendent—*Away on business. If not back in two days, come get Pushka.*

She glanced one last time toward the office. She remembered her father at the radio. She couldn't have been more than eight or nine, and could still smell the solder and dust of the old rig, hear the faint hiss of the speaker between bursts of static.

"First, the noise, Irinka," he said, guiding her small hand across a scrambled frequency map. "Then, the signal. The enemy will blur the line—that's their job. But you won't blink. You won't falter. You'll never abandon your post."

Now, his little Irinka was cracking open the secrets of the motherland and laying them bare for that same enemy to see. Maybe it would cost her life.

But she'd heard enough noise.

Now came the signal.

Now came the truth.

13

Toko checked his watch. It was still dark outside, but time was definitely against him. Any further delay, and the sun would be up before the job was done. He crawled along a divided highway west of Richmond, the conditions worse than ever, though there was so little traffic it hardly mattered. He was searching for a concealed turnoff—a rutted track hidden in the trees. It was used by locals to get to a gravel road below, and he knew it was there from satellite images.

The gravel road was closed to the public and gated with a *No Trespassing* sign. It paralleled the east branch of the Tuckahoe Creek Railway Line and ended at a dirt lot overlooking Bosher's dam.

He looked again at the satellite view on his phone. The imagery was two years old and taken in summertime. Finding the turnoff wasn't so easy when the ground was covered in ice.

He arrived at the position marked on the map and pulled over. Peering into the bare branches of a thick cluster of hickory and maple, he searched for what he knew was there—a small electrical substation. He drove forward at walking pace, hugging the shoulder with his hazards on, and was about to throw the car into reverse and double back when he saw electrical poles poking out above the trees. He followed the wires, and sure enough, there was the substation.

He eased off the road and cut the engine. Then he took the gun from the glove box and put it in the waist of his pants. The sleet was still pelting down, and he braced himself before stepping out. He went first to the trunk for his parka, gloves, and padded winter boots. He put them on while leaning against the car, then grabbed his flashlight and set off into the brush.

He walked down the slope toward the substation, and found the gravel road. There were multiple sets of fresh tire tracks in the slush and his pulse picked up. There hadn't been any at the gate.

He trudged on as far as the parking lot and immediately saw that he had a problem. Beneath the single electric light illuminating the lot were four parked vehicles. All had their lights on and engines running.

There was a late model Toyota Corolla, a black Honda Civic with tinted windows, a Ford Focus with aftermarket rims, and a Hyundai Elantra, its windows steamed up like the inside of a greenhouse. Kids, he thought, wondering how they'd managed to get there. There must have been another route through the surrounding farmland.

He shut off his flashlight and watched them. The dam was there as expected, and the sluice gate was right by the river bank, easily accessible. It was only the cars that were the problem. Local kids, he guessed—out late, fooling around, jeopardizing his operation. He was fully authorized to kill for this job, and he had no qualms in doing so, but four cars, likely with two kids in each, eight in total—that would be pushing it. Eight bodies would be national news. Helicopters. Dogs. The works. They'd find the damaged sluice. It wouldn't be long before some detective grasped the implications—the dam, the storm, the nuclear plant fifty miles downriver.

No, killing these kids wasn't an option.

Better to try his luck with the secondary target. He walked back to the SUV, fired up the engine, and pulled open the Flood Prevention Plan. Spreading it across his lap, he found the next target on the list, another low-head weir, scarcely a mile away, at a spot just before the river forked around a small island.

He pulled back onto the highway, crossed the river, and exited almost immediately onto a small county road that skirted the river's south bank. The road was lined on both sides by tall, bare trees. To one side was the river, and on the other, the ground rose steeply toward the backs of secluded million-dollar homes, all set back at least a hundred yards and accessed by another road. There was no traffic.

He drove about half a mile before seeing the dam. It wasn't much to look at—another squat, concrete structure with a visible sluice to control water flow.

He stopped the car and got out. First job was to unload. As he got to the trunk, he saw the headlights of an approaching car. He waited for it to pass, then reached inside for two heavy sacks of ammonium nitrate.

Ammonium nitrate was a commercial fertilizer, but this had been powdered and mixed with fuel oil. He hoisted the sacks onto his shoulders and made his way down the slope of the river bank. Halfway down, he slipped, hit hard, and kept going.

The concrete column of the sluice abutted the river

bank, and he piled the two sacks against it, then went back to the Toyota for the bleach and jerrycans of gasoline. The rain never let up, soaking him to the skin. The explosives—cheap, anonymous, effective—had been chosen because they were foolproof. They left no signature, no source. Just blast and rubble. In all likelihood, it would read as vandalism, not sabotage.

Still, if the fertilizer got too wet, it wouldn't ignite. He threw plastic over it, then scrambled for the detonator.

He was taking it from the trunk when another set of headlights approached. He waited, then saw the familiar blue and red flashers of a police car on the roof. They came on silently as the car drew near. With a sigh, Toko pulled off his right glove with his teeth, threw it into the back of the SUV, and reached for the gun at his waist. He drew the gun but kept it concealed in the cuff of his parka. Then, he turned to face the cop.

There was no light but the cruiser's flashers and the Toyota's dashboard glow.

Toko waited as the cruiser came to a halt, trying to look unthreatening, his arms by his sides. After a few seconds, the door opened, and a cop stepped out. He was a young guy, fair-haired with a patchy scruff of beard on his chin.

"What's the problem, sir? This is a no-stop zone."

Toko didn't know if the cop's arrival was coincidence or if someone had called him, but he didn't intend to find out. Without saying a word, he pulled his gun. The look of surprise on the cop's face was tender. Heartbreaking, even.

Toko fired two shots into his chest and watched him stagger backward. The shots rang out as loud as thunderclaps, but Toko knew they wouldn't travel far in the rain. The cop was wearing a vest, but he fell to the ground nonetheless. Utterly in shock, he squirmed on the ground, struggling to get his gun from its holster. Toko walked over calmly, pressed the barrel against the man's forehead, and pulled the trigger.

Blood. Brain. Bone.

Scattered like gravel across the tarmac.

Toko scanned. The road was empty. The houses on the slope—dark, distant, shielded by trees. He leaned into the cruiser, switched off the lights, and checked the laptop on the dashboard. The screen showed only the logo of the local police department.

Moving quickly, he lifted the cop by the armpits and dragged him down the slope of the river bank. The water was flowing ferociously, and Toko knew that the next stretch of the river was relatively obstacle-free. There were some pronounced bends about a mile downriver, and a few miles after that, there were shallows around Belle Isle and Mayo Island. He shoved the body into the water, trusting it to take him that far.

The body immediately disappeared into the darkness.

Soaked and caked in mud, Toko went back to the police car. Its engine was still running, and he got into the driver's seat and drove it about half a mile downriver, where he found a small parking lot for a golf course. He parked in the corner of the lot, as far from sight as possible, killed the engine, and took the mobile police scanner from its holster on the dashboard. Then he locked the car and flung the keys as far as he could in the direction of the river.

On the walk back to his own vehicle, a single car passed. He doubted it would matter. It wasn't a stealth mission. The explosion would attract some attention, and it certainly wouldn't take long to find a missing police cruiser.

Maybe the cop had logged his location. Maybe someone had seen something. But there was nothing he could do about that now. He got back to the Toyota and all was as he'd left it.

Moving very quickly, he retrieved the detonator and hurried back down the slope to the weir. He shoved the jerrycans and bleach tight against the fertilizer, opened the lid on one of the jerrycans, and hung the detonator over the gasoline. Then he resealed it, swept his eyes over the setup one last time, and climbed back up the slope.

When he reached the SUV, he got the electronic trigger from the trunk and climbed back into the driver's seat. He started the engine. Ever since his first Lada, he'd never fully trusted a car to start when he needed it. This one started fine, and he pulled another fifty yards down the road.

Then he pressed the trigger.

An orange bloom rose and vanished over the river like a dying star.

14

Margot had a multi-room suite at the Romanov—king-sized bed, memory foam mattress, down-filled duvet. The sheets were Egyptian cotton, and the blackout blinds kept everything as dark and quiet as a tomb. None of it did a whit of good. Even Trazodone and Ativan, medications she'd been told not to mix because of their potency, hadn't helped.

She tossed and turned, fixating on Bryce and Cynthia, picturing them in all the varied scenarios an office affair conjured. The compulsory elevator quickie. Cynthia bent over his desk. She even pictured her riding him like one of those mechanical bulls. Pure fantasy—choreographed by a porn director—but imagination was a powerful thing.

She pictured the two of them lying next to each other after sex, slick with sweat, and wondered if they'd talked about her in those moments. Mostly, she wondered how long it had been going on. How long she'd fooled herself into thinking everything was all right. How long she'd let it happen.

Cynthia Snider was a junior associate at Bryce's law firm,

though she could have fallen back on a career as an underwear model if the law didn't work out. She wasn't younger, exactly—Margot was thirty-one, and Cynthia had to be close to that—but she was a different breed. A higher-octane model. Cynthia was one of those girls who was always giggling and flirting, forever bending over or sticking out her perky tits.

"Would it kill her to wear a bra?" Margot said to Bryce after she first met her. "She looks like she just stepped out of a walk-in freezer."

"She does not."

"Seriously," Margot continued. "What are those? Two grapes?"

Bryce had laughed it off, all light-hearted and jolly, but from the first, Margot pegged Cynthia for exactly what she was—a threat. Not consciously, perhaps. Margot wasn't the jealous type. But Cynthia stood out. *This was the girl*, Margot remembered thinking, that Bryce made small talk with at the water cooler. This was who he was with when he stayed past midnight to close those big deals.

When the clock next to the bed showed six AM, she decided she'd had enough. She got up and made coffee, then brought it over to the sofa, along with her cell, resisting the urge to call Bryce. There was no operational reason why she couldn't call him. Her personal comms protocol was wide open. In fact, she was encouraged to clutter the airwaves with as much personal noise as possible. It was part of her *controlled identity*, as they called it.

"Peggy Pechvogel?" she'd asked when she saw the name, holding up the passport like it might sting her.

They'd been in the back of Roman's government-issue Cadillac Escalade, a car he used only in cases of the most extreme urgency, and they were speeding along I-66 toward

Dulles. Like everything else in this mission, the briefing had been cobbled together last minute.

"It was all we could pull up from the roster," Roman said.

"It means bad luck," Margot said. "In German."

"I know what it means," Roman said. "There wasn't time to be picky."

"Good thing I'm not superstitious."

Roman looked at her and sighed. Just a few hours prior, they'd been reamed out by the entire National Security Council, and the words still rang in their ears.

She glanced over the protocol.

"Instagram? I don't even use it."

"Peggy Pechvogel does."

Margot logged into the account. Beaches she'd never walked. Dogs she'd never owned. Friends she'd never met. Even Foxtrot's AI found her real life too bleak to emulate.

"You all right?" Roman said.

Margot didn't reply. The truth was, she didn't like the setup. Relying on the ambassador, showing up on *Hummingbird's* home turf unannounced—it was risky. Worse, it was sloppy. It would be a miracle if it didn't land *Hummingbird* in hot water, even if they did manage to pass a message—and Margot still had no idea how they would pull that off. A brush pass would have been one thing, just about possible in a setting like that, but it would require *Hummingbird* to actually have a message she was willing to pass. Given that she'd failed all communication attempts for five days, that seemed doubtful.

But it was all they had, and if there was one thing everyone at the Council had agreed on, it was the need for drastic action. They didn't care why *Hummingbird* had stopped communicating. And, evidently, they didn't care about endangering her life. Or Margot's. They just wanted what they wanted.

What Margot also saw—and she shouldn't have been surprised by it, but she was—was just how willing Roman had also been to put her life on the line. Not that that wasn't part of the territory—Margot knew better than anyone that you didn't work at a place like the Bookshop because you valued your personal safety—but the way it had gone down at the meeting, the way the decision had been made, something about it had frankly shocked her.

Even as the plan was being pitched, she'd half-expected someone in the room to put a stop to it. God knew they weren't happy with what had been achieved so far. They'd liked what they were getting, but when they found out the source, all hell broke loose. They'd been positively apoplectic, especially the president.

And yet, no one pulled the plug. As they complained about its legality, they'd been only too willing to send Margot back into the fray for more.

"Margot?"

"I'm fine, Roman."

On the drive to the airport, there'd been a part of her that thought Roman might yet put his foot down, cancel the mission at that late hour, and come up with a better plan. But he hadn't. Instead, he'd pulled out his bottle of Pepto-Bismol and took a big swig.

Wiping his mouth, he said, "For what it's worth—"

"Don't," Margot snapped.

"I'm sorry, Margot."

"I said, don't."

"Their reaction was unwarranted."

Margot clenched her jaw. "Holman wanted me arrested."

"She blusters. It's what she does."

"You're sure?"

He didn't answer. He took more Pepto-Bismol, and she knew he was stalling for something.

"What is it?" Margot said. "You look like you're waiting to be called in for a root canal."

"The file," he said.

She nodded. The meeting hadn't resulted in handcuffs and charges of treason, but it had resulted in what was known as an exceptional executive order. The president had forced the Bookshop to turn over its case file. That included *Hummingbird's* identity. It was all to be turned over to Gabriella Wintour's office. As far as Margot knew, it was the first time in Bookshop history that such an order had been made, and it meant she was flying off to Moscow now with less cover than even their most mundane operations ordinarily had.

"I'm sorry I told them anything," she said.

Roman nodded. "It's okay. You had no choice."

"This is what we get for keeping secrets."

Roman was screwing the cap back on the Pepto-Bismol. "Keeping secrets is the entire reason we exist," he said.

Margot knew she should let the matter lie, but there was a part of her that refused to do so. There was a part of her that couldn't stop blaming Roman for the way it went down.

She'd recruited *Hummingbird*.

But Roman ran the show. He called the shots. And it was he who'd chosen not to loop in the president.

The only reason the Council knew anything was because he'd panicked. They'd lost contact with *Hummingbird*, and Roman had made the mistake of asking the Council for help. It had been a disaster. The whole fiasco, if it didn't land Margot in prison, might yet cost her her career. And this mission—her flying half-cocked to Moscow while the case file was being bandied about the Council like one of those old chain emails—might well cost her her life. And Irina's.

"Not from the president."

Roman hesitated—a flicker of guilt, maybe even regret—but she saw it. "What's that?" he said.

"Keeping secrets from the president. That's not why we exist."

He said nothing, and she decided to move on. She'd said it. He'd heard her.

"Quite the social life I have," she said, holding up her phone and showing him the Instagram feed.

"You should have seen Foxtrot's face," he said, "when the computer magically started filling everything out. She used to slave over that by hand."

Margot nodded. "And it says here she wants me to make innocuous personal calls?"

"We don't know how closely you'll be watched," Roman said, "but we have to cover all the bases. We're already at a disadvantage, so anything you can do to make your personal traffic look as normal as possible will help. You're there as an embassy hire. A civilian. That means logging in to civilian email, browsing socials, even shopping for underwear."

"*Underwear?*"

"Or whatever."

"You'd love that."

"I'd love anything that made you look like a normal person."

"You make it sound like I'm not one."

He raised an eyebrow. "How many women your age have zero digital footprint?"

She let it go. "You want me to call home, too?"

"Your *beau* knows you're going to Moscow, doesn't he? It would be weird not to call."

"If I want to get him killed."

"Don't you?"

She smiled thinly. "Ha ha."

"We'll scramble the metadata. They won't be able to trace it to him. Just make sure he doesn't reveal his name and address while he's on the line, and he'll be fine."

"This is messy," Margot said.

"It's hasty," Roman said. "Not necessarily the same thing."

"None of our usual protocols are being observed."

"You're the one who decided to fly out with zero notice."

"I know, but..."

"Margot, it's the best we can do."

"And the file," she said. "Wide open."

"It's not *wide* open."

"The whole Council was on that circulation list."

"I know," Roman said, and she could see the tension on his face. A distribution list that long, even if the names were at the very top of the national security apparatus, with the very highest levels of clearance, was his absolute worst nightmare. A mission like this, a source as valuable as *Hummingbird*, out there on laptops and email inboxes and who knew how many secretary's desks.

It was not how the Bookshop operated, and for good reason. Roman Adler had burned his whole house down more than once because of a suspected leak. Under normal conditions, even he and Foxtrot didn't have details they didn't absolutely need. He hated being exposed.

"We'll have to trust...." He started, then stopped himself.

They held each other's gaze then, a fraction of a second

too long, and she almost thought he was going to say something personal.

Thankfully, he thought better of it.

The driver brought down the privacy screen. "Approaching the departure terminal, sir."

Roman nodded and put the screen back up, keeping his gaze on Margot. "Things have changed over there. It's not the Russia we—"

"I know," she said.

"The slightest slip-up now could cost you."

She knew Moscow wasn't what it had been. For twenty-five years, everyone had played nice. That was over now. The handshakes, the hydrocarbon deals, the glossy G8 summits—all done. The Cold War hadn't ended. It had mutated.

George Clooney eating blinis and Gisele Bündchen partying it up in nightclubs wasn't coming back.

"I mean it, Margot. The party's well and truly over."

"I wasn't planning on going to any discos if that's what you're afraid of."

"What about fashion shows?" he said, eyeing the coat.

"Very funny."

He smiled, but it was a thin, hollow smile. He was worried. "I think I know why she went dark," he said.

"What?"

"Foxtrot only just got word, but there was a big raid at Zubarev's office. Dozens of arrests. Computer equipment was torn off people's desks and confiscated. Phones were searched. Hard drives scanned."

"What were they looking for?"

Roman shrugged. "Could have been anything or nothing."

Moscow was in a state of intense paranoia. The FSB, the

GRU, Center 16, they'd all been stinging themselves like scorpions, purging their ranks of the slightest trace of treason, real or imagined. "Was *Hummingbird* among—"

"No, no. Not as far as I could tell. But the timing can't be a coincidence."

"You think the raid was for her?"

"Judging from the names of those arrested, there seems to have been a *Sovbez* connection."

"So she's out on a limb?"

"A long one."

"Do you think she took something? Something they know is missing?"

Roman let out a long sigh. "I don't know," he said. "But you need to act like you're being watched from the moment you step off the plane. Even with your cover intact, you're not safe. The way things are going, even a translator is at risk of being picked up. Trust no one. Everyone's hostile. "

"It's always been that way," she said, raising an eyebrow.

"Well, now, more so," Roman said, smiling that thin smile again. "Act like you've got nothing to hide—but hide everything."

"I know," she said.

"No visible precautions. That means personal comms in the clear. Regular taxi cabs and hotel rooms. Reservations for dinner beforehand. As if you want to be followed."

"This is 101, Roman. I know how to lay a pattern."

The car pulled up outside the terminal. He still looked like he wanted to say more.

"You regret any of this?" she said.

"No."

"Not telling the president? Not looping in the Council?"

"That would have handed Kyiv to Chichikov."

Margot wasn't so sure, but she didn't argue. She got out of the car, pulling her bag with her, avoiding eye contact.

"Margot," he called.

But she shut the door without answering.

Now, in the hotel room in Moscow, she took a sip of coffee and wondered if she should have. She could have said something to him. He was an old man, after all. They got sentimental.

They weren't the only ones.

She looked at her phone screen.

An emotional, teary-eyed call to Bryce would serve her cover well. That sort of personal drama was exactly the noise that would distract the FSB. It would give her legend color. It would make her believable.

Like the Balenciaga.

The training manual called it *playing it straight,* sinking into one's cover, living the role.

But she didn't make the call.

It wasn't pride. It was the fact that Cynthia was pregnant.

That was the absolute. That was the fact that no amount of screaming and crying would change. It was the one thing stopping her from calling him right then and there and literally begging him not to leave her.

Because if there was one thing Margot Katz couldn't bear, it was the idea of being alone. That was how she'd fooled herself—putting up with a loveless, hollowed-out cusp of a relationship when she already knew it was over.

Because the altnerative was so horrible.

She opened the Instagram app and started scrolling.

She knew what she was looking for. There'd been pictures before on Bryce's socials that had clawed at her, and the account Foxtrot made had full access. She scrolled now past Bryce's mountain biking trips and snaps of his Jack Russell Terrier.

There.

A group shot from an office party she hadn't been invited to. It showed a fresh-faced Cynthia, dressed to kill in a sequined dress, looking directly at Bryce. It wasn't definitive by any means, Bryce wasn't even looking back, but Margot remembered how the picture made her feel when she first saw it. Even then, she'd known something was up. She zoomed in on Cynthia's face, asking herself why she hadn't confronted him when she had the chance. He'd have called her crazy—it was nothing more than a glance, a moment caught on camera of a woman looking across a room—but they'd both have known better.

She'd felt it in her gut, and ignored it anyway.

She scrolled on. Jack Russells. Moody shots of whiskey glasses, cigars, rare Japanese vinyl.

Then another.

This one was from the Bar Association conference in Honolulu last summer. Bryce had said he was going with two other partners, both men, and Margot had taken him at his word. She'd told herself there was no reason to doubt him. But there'd been a photo from that trip, posted by one of the other partners, that had gotten to her. It showed Bryce in a goofy Hawaiian shirt holding a Mai Tai. He'd never wear that shirt, never order that drink. Someone had handed him both—and he'd said yes.

But again, she'd brushed it off.

Told herself she was crazy. There was no smoking gun. No lipstick on the collar. No panties in the sofa cushions. No whiff of Chanel in his Mercedes.

But she'd known. Something wasn't right, and she'd refused to admit it. The nights they spent together—always at his place, always with an overnight bag because she didn't keep clothes or even a toothbrush there—grew fewer and farther between. Their dates grew stilted, forced. The emoji-filled texts became so infrequent that whole days passed without the familiar ding on her phone.

And she'd put up with it. Worse, she'd welcomed it. She had secrets of her own to protect, a false life with Roman and Foxtrot that needed to be upheld at all costs, and if that meant crippling her relationship with Bryce, it was a price she'd been willing to pay.

What was it they said? The worst lies are the ones we tell ourselves?

The truth was, the relationship had ended a long time ago, its death unmarked and unmourned. There'd been no fight. No tears. And Margot had shut her eyes because it allowed her to go on telling herself she wasn't alone in the world.

It allowed her to ignore the fact that any time she let someone get close, they left.

She shut the app and looked up from the phone. The sun had begun to cast its first oblique rays over the Russian metropolis, and she got up and went to the window. Another day in Moscow.

Clear. Still. Frigidly cold.

Like the life she'd created.

15

Toko ditched the Toyota at a Walmart off I-64, as ordered. Morozov's people would tell him in the morning if he was to go back for it or find another vehicle. He put the scanner, detonators, gun, and maps in the carryall and left everything else where it was.

In the store he bought a change of clothes—the ones he had were soaking wet—and changed in the store restroom.

Then, he called a cab.

"Awful weather," the driver said as he climbed into the back seat. She was an Indian woman, possibly Pakistani, with a thick accent. Toko said nothing in reply, shifting uncomfortably in his new clothes.

"Can you turn the heat up?" he said, opening a booking app and searching for hotels in central Richmond. He wanted someplace small and independent, not tied into a global reservations system.

"And where are we going?"

He finalized a booking and said, "An inn called The Patrick Henry. You know it?"

"Patrick Henry," she repeated. "Give me liberty, or give me death."

"What's that?"

"That's Patrick Henry," she said. "Changed history, supposedly."

"Good for him," Toko muttered, adjusting the collar of his cheap shirt.

They drove, Toko with his head against the glass, watching the dreary streets go by. Sleet lashed the windows.

He glanced at the driver. Pretty—for a cab driver. He wondered if that was a liability behind the wheel. She probably had a wrench under her seat.

"So that was the Civil War?" he said, making conversation. "The Patrick Henry thing,"

"No," she said. "War of Independence. Seventeen-seventies."

"Same era as the constitution."

"A few years before."

They hit a pothole, and Toko's head knocked against the window. They'd entered the older part of Richmond, a distinctly historical area, and he looked out at the period buildings, the old-style street lamps, the quaint side streets. It all reminded him of one of those cozy Christmas movies. His daughter would have liked it.

He glanced again at the driver, and she gave him the faintest smile.

"You know your history," he said.

"It's in the air around here."

He looked at his phone—they were four minutes out from the hotel—and he wondered if he could get her to come up to the room with him. It wasn't a lot of time to work with, but often, less was better. And he'd never had an Indian before. Or Pakistani. Whichever she was. He wondered if she'd break easy. "There was a rebellion in my own country at the same time," he said. "Seventeen-seventies."

"Oh?" she said, looking again in the mirror. "And what country would that—"

"Russia."

"Right," she said, trying not to look surprised.

"I look Chinese. I know."

She shrugged.

"I'm from the far east. The Pacific Ocean."

"I see."

"And at exactly the time America was having its revolution, we were having one of our own."

"I didn't know that," she said.

"Because it failed," Toko said. "History has no place for failure."

She thought for a moment. "I don't know if that's true."

"Name one man in the history books who failed."

"Adolf Hitler failed. Mussolini failed. Josef Stalin failed."

Toko smiled. "Did they?"

She glanced at him again.

He said, "You should be teaching this stuff."

She smiled again. "So what happened? Your revolution?"

"The leader was named Pugachev. He rebelled against Catherine the Great, but he never claimed to fight for liberty. His great quote was, *I am your Tsar*," Toko said dryly.

"I see."

"He was cut to pieces in Bolotnaya Square."

She gave him a sidelong glance.

They rounded a corner and saw a police car, flashers on, parked by the curb.

He reached inside his coat. His thumb brushed the safety.

"Don't stop," he said.

The car slowed. A cop stepped out. Toko's heart ticked once.

Then the cop waved them on.

Toko exhaled, peering out as they passed.

"Nothing to be afraid of," the driver said.

"Sorry," Toko said. "Where I come from, it's not just the criminals who worry about police."

"Maybe it's not as different as you think here."

Toko shrugged. "You say that, but in my opinion, America and Russia are as different as two countries could be. Two separate arcs through history. Two separate planets."

They drove past a grand white building with classical porticos and columns. Toko looked up at it.

"State Capital," the driver said. "Used to be the capital of the Confederacy."

"This close to Washington?"

She nodded. "Closer than you'd think, isn't it?"

They rounded another corner, and she brought the car to a halt. "This is it."

He looked out at the inn. "Coming up?"

She blinked.

"Leave the meter running."

"Mister—"

"When's the last time you did something crazy?"

"This crazy? Never."

He shrugged. "Suit yourself. I'm gone tomorrow."

He handed her a twenty, and something in his smile made her hesitate.

"One night. One hour. You won't regret it."

She shook her head, then said, "What are you after, exactly?"

"More history lessons," he said, then turned and walked away.

As he was checking into his room, she appeared in the lobby. He smiled, more to himself than her, and they didn't speak in the elevator.

The room was the same colonial style as everything else they'd seen. Comfortable though—and picturesque, with antique furniture, a gas fireplace that was already burning, and real oil paintings on the walls of American pastorals.

As soon as the door shut, he pounced on her. He couldn't help himself.

Later, when she was gone, he lay on the bed in post-coital bliss, listening to the police scanner. The fire was still burning, and his gaze fixed on the oil painting above it.

What if it had been America that dismembered its revolutionaries, he wondered. The room he was in was three centuries old. When his people still lived under sealskins, men in this city had brick fireplaces and oil paintings.

There was some chatter on the police radio, and he listened. The storm was causing mayhem—downed power lines, burst water mains, car accidents, road closures. Whole neighborhoods were without power, and it was the same story up and down the coast. In the havoc, the police still hadn't realized they were a man down.

No mention of the explosion, either. Just flooding. Everywhere.

Toko picked up the hotel phone and called the concierge. "Room service," he said.

The concierge went over the menu with him, and he ordered a steak, fries, Coca-Cola, and two pieces of lemon meringue pie. One thing he would never bring himself to do was criticize American food. He would criticize the politics, the social ills—there were a million Kremlin-approved talking points on such matters, and he'd parrot any of them—but he wouldn't criticize the food.

When the room service arrived, he took the tray from the waiter at the door.

"I can bring it in for you."

"Not necessary," Toko said, shutting the door without giving a tip or word of thanks. Immediately, he reopened it. "Ketchup?" he said.

"Oh, right away, sir."

"I asked for it earlier," he lied, without knowing why. "Bring ice, too," he said. "Lots of it. In a bucket."

The waiter hurried off, and Toko shut the door again. He placed the tray on the small table by the fire, then went to the window and looked out at the street below. All was as eerily quiet as when he'd arrived. The only car out there was the cab, parked legally where the driver had left it. He glanced at the bathroom, and his mind leaped to that dark place it so liked to go.

The cab driver. The waitress in New York. So many others.

Then, as if possessed, he crossed the room and tore into both pieces of pie with his hands, gorging like a starving man, shoveling the food into his mouth.

He was just licking his fingers when the knock came. He wiped his mouth and went quickly into the bathroom. He caught a whiff of perfume while washing his hands but avoided looking at the tub. Then he toweled, shut the bathroom door, and went to the door.

"Your ketchup and ice, sir," the waiter said, handing him a miniature bottle of Heinz ketchup and a metal ice bucket. Toko took them wordlessly, staring at the ketchup.

"Everything all right?" the waiter said.

Toko shut the door, locked it, then went to the table and

sat down. He poured the entire bottle of ketchup on the steak and began eating. He ate mechanically, without tasting the food, only pausing when something came through on the scanner.

They were talking about the missing cop now. His last check-in had been from Cherokee Road, where he'd been responding to a domestic. Toko looked at his map. The location of the dispute wasn't so far from where he'd killed him. It was less than two miles from where he'd dumped the patrol car. Far enough, he thought, to buy him the time he needed. He'd be gone soon enough.

He finished the steak, picked up the tray, and placed it in the hallway outside his door. Then he brought the ice into the bathroom and dumped it in the tub without looking down.

Afraid of what might be looking back.

16

Margot dozed on the sofa, only woken by the sudden clang of the hotel phone. She looked at her watch, then stared at the blinking red light on the receiver.

"This is the front desk," a voice said.

"Yes?"

"Apologies, ma'am—you asked to be notified."

"The luggage?"

"It just arrived from the airport."

"Did they say anything?"

"Say anything?"

"About the reason for the delay?"

"It arrived by cab, ma'am."

"Of course," she said.

"I can have someone contact the airline if you like."

"Please do," she said, knowing it was pointless, but also something a conscientious interpretor might do. "And send the bag right up. All my toiletries are in it."

"Of course."

She hung up.

It was possible the bag had been genuinely delayed—Margot herself had nearly missed the connection in Istanbul—but more likely, it had been scooped up by the FSB. Sitting alone on the carousel while she was stuck at passport control, it would have been too easy a target to ignore. Not that it meant her cover was blown. It was just the FSB being the FSB. They were nothing if not thorough, and a bug inside the compound was a bug inside the compound, even if only in the luggage of a language tutor.

There was a knock at the door, and she let in the bellhop, watching closely as he wheeled in the bag on a brass luggage cart. "Over there's fine," she said, indicating the closet. She had to wonder about him too, now—about everyone—and scanned for anything that might be off. An ill-fitting uniform, a stray price tag. She saw nothing.

When he was gone, she turned to the suitcase, eyeing it like a bomb, primed and ticking. She had to assume it was bugged—riddled with location trackers, mics, signal interceptors—whatever the Aquarium could think of.

Up to this point, she'd been fairly confident the room itself was clean. She'd arrived unannounced, without a reservation, which meant no prior warning for a surveillance crew. She'd said at passport control that she was going to the embassy, but by the time she got downtown, it was so late that a check-in at the hotel wouldn't have raised any undue suspicion.

It was just the bag she needed to be wary of.

There was a time when worrying this much over a suitcase might have felt paranoid. Not anymore. The terrain had shifted.

And it wasn't like she could simply scan it. If it contained any bugs, she would have to live with them.

Never show you're being vigilant. That was how the manual put it.

Roman had a more colorful way of putting it. "Always pee with the door open," he said.

That was what he'd told her before her first visit to Moscow, back when she was still green on the workings of denied areas. The phrasing caught her off-guard.

"Excuse me?" she'd said.

"Always let them believe they've got the jump on you," he said. "Always let them think they're two steps ahead."

"Let them see me piss?"

"Act like you're not being watched, even when you know you are. *Especially* when you know you are. Act like you're not even aware of the possibility of being watched, like you've got nothing to hide. That way, when you *do* have something to hide—"

"The manual already says all this."

"Well, my job is to drill it into your head."

This was back when she still suspected him of wanting to get inside her pants.

Now, she *knew* that he did.

But she also trusted him. She'd taken the lesson to heart, that one and a dozen others, and they'd saved her life more times than she could count.

Roman's Rules, she called them, though they were basically just a rewording of standard operating procedures to be as politically incorrect as possible.

Never be the only one clothed at an orgy.
Never wear underwear if you plan on flashing your cooch.
The only way to hide your tail is to flash your tits.

He could have as easily said *blend in, be prepared, misdirect*.

"I don't see why you have to make everything so...."

"Crass?" he'd said, utterly unperturbed.

"Yes."

"Look, Margot, this stuff is life and death. Would you think someone who'd just peed with the door open knew they were being watched?"

"No, but—"

"And what of someone who *did* shut the door? Would you ask yourself, why is she shutting the door? There's no one else there. Does she know we're watching? Why hasn't she farted? She's onto us."

"Why hasn't she *farted*?"

"Everyone farts, Margot. When they're alone in a room, they fart. You spend hundreds of hours surveilling people, you know that stuff. The FSB knows that stuff. In their bones, they know it. People take their shoes off when they're alone, they loosen their belts, they scratch their ass and sniff the finger."

"They do *not* sniff their—"

"The point is, if you're ever playing for the camera, they'll know. So don't do it. And for God's sake, don't be delicate."

"*Delicate?*"

"Yes."

"Do you tell your male assets not to be *delicate*?"

"I don't send male assets where I'm sending you."

They'd locked eyes then, but he refused to back down. No apology. He meant what he said and was standing his ground.

Eventually, she shook her head. "Fine, but your way of saying things makes you sound like a lech."

"*Lech?*"

"Creep."

"Do you think I care what I sound like?"

"I'm telling you as a favor," she said. "I'd hate to see you caught up in some sort of *complication*."

"Complication?"

"Harassment complication," she said. "Sexual complaint. Don't pretend you don't know what I'm talking about. Times have changed since you came up the ranks. You're going to have your eye on the Kremlin, on Beijing, and some suit in the Government Accountability Office will lop your head off without you ever seeing it coming."

It had been his turn to say nothing, and for a moment, she thought she'd gotten through to him. The truth was, he was a dinosaur. A remnant from a time long past. HR was a bigger threat to him than a vial of novichok ever would be.

He looked at her for a long beat. Then, "I lose sleep over our mission, Margot. You will, too, when you see what we're up against."

"I wasn't saying—"

"There's no room for distraction. We need to be focused. Because if we fail, there won't be a Government Accountability Office. There won't be an office of any kind. We'll be back in the Stone Age. Or we'll be speaking Russian. Or Chinese. The niceties of democratic society? Gone. All of it blown away like ash in the wind."

"God, Roman, calm down. I was just—"

"We're going to make sacrifices, you and I, that would make the pencil pushers in Congress literally shit their pants. Unspeakable things."

"I get that, Roman."

"Things that would give ordinary, God-fearing folk nightmares. Taxpayers wouldn't stand for what we're going to do. Voters wouldn't stomach it. Heads would roll if they ever found out."

She'd wanted to argue, but his face stopped her cold.

"We're the viper in the nest, Margot. The scorpion in the bed. Coiled. Still. Ready to strike." His voice dropped low, but he was still animated, a fleck of spit clinging to his lip. "There are no good guys in this game."

"Okay!" she said, frustration rising. "I get it."

"Do you?"

"Yes!"

"Because when the shit hits the fan, I'm the only one who'll be there, Margot."

"I get it. I do."

He softened. "You're going to do things that will make your own skin crawl. I'm telling you because I know. I wear the scars."

She nodded slowly. "I know, Roman."

"You'll wake in the night, drenched in sweat. Your skin cold. Terrified. And you'll come to me. And when you do, I'll ask you to do it all again. And worse."

"I said I get it."

"That's what we're preparing for. Darkness you never imagined. And my job is to get you ready."

"I understand," she said. "I'm in. All the way."

He nodded. "So if I say *cooch* or *pussy* or *tits*—it's because those words cut to the bone. Like our job does. They grab you by the throat."

"I hear you," she said quietly.

She never forgot that conversation. He'd left the room afterward, leaving her to think, and she had thought. And she'd made a decision.

She'd decided to follow him. Not because she admired

him. Not because she liked him. But because she believed what he said. She knew it was the truth.

Wherever he led, wherever he went, however dark it got, she would follow.

And it had served her well.

She'd seen the mistakes other parts of the agency made —mistakes that would have been unthinkable under Roman's watch—and she'd seen the cost of them. Lives were lost. Objectives were lost. The nation lost ground. NATO lost ground. And those losses didn't go away. They had to be made up. Other men and women had to go out and risk their lives to make them up. The currency of their game was flesh and blood. It was bone and gristle. It was a game of inches, and those inches were paid for in lives on the battlefield.

And if they failed, everyone would pay the price.

Margot squinted at the suitcase. It was time to *pee with the door open*. She picked up the hotel phone and called down to the front desk. "Room service, please."

"Of course, madam."

She ordered a croissant, preserves, coffee, and orange juice. When the waiter arrived, she made sure to speak loudly and clearly, telling him in Russian where to put the tray and asking how far away the embassy was and whether she'd need a taxi to get there. She already knew the answers, but if the suitcase was bugged, she wanted anyone listening to know that it was up and running.

When the waiter left, she sat down and ate the food, taking her time to enjoy the pastry, the homemade jam, and the Vologda butter that, alone, almost made a visit to Russia worth it.

She purposely got butter on her fingers and sucked them clean—loudly.

She acted like no one was watching.

Then, she got up and went to the suitcase, unzipped a compartment on the front, and pulled out a small first aid kit. The kit contained an extremely compact foil blanket like the ones used by EMTs. This one had been modified with a fine metal mesh that allowed it to act as a Faraday shield. She unpacked it, draped it over the suitcase so that it was completely covered, then shoved the whole thing into the closet.

Time to stop flashing. Time to cover up.

In Roman's parlance, time to *don her panties*.

She looked at her watch, then powered off her phone, removed it from its case, and released the SIM with a small pin that she kept in the lining of her wallet. She replaced the SIM with another, specially modified, that was also hidden in the wallet, then powered the phone back up and went into the bathroom. She shut the bathroom door and turned on the water in the shower.

While personal comms were in the clear, almost begging to be intercepted, operational comms were another matter. The encrypted SIM relied on signal-masking software in the phone that connected to dedicated hardware located on the top floor of the embassy, just a few hundred yards away. Any call she made now would be routed through it, then relayed through an NSA satellite. Theoretically, it was as secure as a hardline inside the embassy.

She dialed a series of one-time access keys and waited. When Roman picked up, his voice was raspy, as if she'd woken him. She looked at her watch. It wasn't yet dawn in Washington.

"You weren't sleeping, were you?" she said.

"Resting my eyes."

"This call was scheduled down to the minute."

"I'm awake," he said, clearing his throat. He then fell into a fit of coughing.

"You all right?" she said. "You sound like you've got a dick in your mouth." Some of his vulgarity may have rubbed off on her over the years.

"That's my girl," he said through a phlegmy laugh. "Ever the lady."

"You don't pay me to be a lady."

17

"Classy," Roman said. "I'll have to remember that."

"It's all yours," Margot said.

"And the flight? Not too uncomfortable?"

"Tolerable."

"I saw a storm on the radar."

"We hit some turbulence."

"And the airport?"

"What about it?"

"Anything untoward, Margot?"

"*Untoward*?"

Roman glanced at his watch. It wasn't yet dawn, but already the president was late.

"Well, they weren't exactly rolling out the red carpet, if that's what you're asking."

"But they accepted your papers?"

"Of course they did. Why wouldn't they?"

"I'm just getting the lay of the land, Margot. No need to get testy."

"*Testy*? You're stalling. Something's happened, hasn't it?"

She was right, of course, something *had* happened, but

Roman was under strict orders not to get into it with her. Not until the others had arrived. That was what his operational autonomy had come to. "Margot, please."

She let out an exasperated sigh. "Everything went as expected. They questioned me, I gave them the legend, the paperwork checked out, and when I finally got through, my luggage wasn't there."

"Of course it wasn't."

"And my cab was followed."

"FSB?"

"Had to be."

"Just the one car?"

"As far as I could tell. Standard-issue three-series. The driver was cockier than ever. Didn't even bother to hide it."

"And your cab?" Roman said. "Anything off about that? About the driver?"

"If there was, he hid it well. Honestly, all things considered, it went pretty smoothly."

Roman nodded to himself. "We'll see about that," he said quietly. He was already thinking of the personal call she'd received in the cab—the one from the love interest. The Casanova of Cleveland Park, as Roman thought of him. He decided not to bring it up. It would only add to her distraction.

"Seriously," Margot said, her voice sharp. "What's going on? Why are we talking about luggage and cab rides?"

Roman glanced out the window. The South Lawn was as snow-strewn and desolate as any Siberian waste, the wind clawing at the White House.

There was a noise at the door and he looked up. It opened a crack, but it was just the usher peering in. It shut again before Roman could ask about the coffee he'd ordered.

He looked again at his watch. He was in the Eisenhower Executive Building—grand, overbuilt, and full of ghosts—but where he and the president always met. It was more discreet than meeting at the White House, and Roman was a stickler for not drawing attention.

"Well," Margot started, "if you're not going to tell me what's happened, I may as well hang up."

"Hold on, Margot. Hold your horses." He winced—immediate mistake. He knew it the instant the words slipped his lips.

"Hold my *horses*? Roman—I'm locked and loaded. I just flew halfway around the—"

"I know, I know," he said, acutely aware of how she'd react when she found out they were waiting for the others. She'd left for Moscow as a matter of extreme urgency, after one of the ugliest Council debates Roman had ever witnessed. There'd been calls for Margot's head. Calls she be arrested, even. Charged with treason.

She'd taken it personally.

She wasn't in Moscow now just to bring in *Hummingbird*. She was there to prove herself. *Holding her horses* wasn't part of the agenda.

"*Hummingbird's* made contact," she said. "That's what this is. She knows I'm here."

"Sit on that thought, Margot."

"How does she know? Airport security?"

"We're not the only ones being read in."

Silence. He could almost feel the tension pull taut. Margot breathed, then said, "Excuse me?"

"President insisted."

"Insisted on what? Being on an ops call? What's he going to say? To be careful?"

"He thinks he's helping."

"Helping? The president? That's the dumbest thing you've ever said to me."

Roman sighed. He didn't blame her. She was in the field, a live wire, in play, and the Council was making her wait for nothing. They were putting her in her place, putting them both in their place, showing them who was boss.

And it wasn't just mean. It was dangerous.

Hummingbird had re-established contact. She'd followed one of the agreed protocols. There was only one thing to do next, and it didn't take a committee to know it.

"It's not just him, either."

"Oh, fuck this."

"Margot!"

"No, Roman. The rest of them can all go—"

"Chain of command," he snapped. "As much as we hate to admit it, we do still answer to a higher power."

"Oh, that's rich. *You* telling *me* about the chain of command? Who are we even waiting for? Don't tell me it's Dumbledore."

Dumbledore was her less-than-genius nickname for Dominic Doerr—the president's newly-anointed *wunderkind,* the youngest ever director of national intelligence. Not yet out of his thirties—barely out of diapers, as far as Roman was concerned—he was a Silicon Valley billionaire. He was also a tech bro, complete with sculpted beard, flashy sneakers, and an ever-present Patagonia vest.

Roman found him insufferable. "God, I hope not," he muttered.

"Because if it is, we might as well just pull the plug right now."

"Let's wait and see how it plays out."

"Can you at least give me a heads-up? Are we still looking for a meeting at the *Sovbez*?"

"Margot, I can't say."

"Come on. If I'm about to get reamed all over again—"

"No one's getting reamed—"

He could hear the fire in her voice, the hunger in her belly. Doerr wasn't the only one who'd called for her head. Half the Council had piled on.

Brutal to watch.

And completely predictable.

She was Roman's creature, after all. His creation. Her fortunes rose and fell with his. And though it might not look it, Roman Adler was a man fighting for his life.

"This changes everything," she said. "If she's made contact, we don't need the meeting."

She was right. *Hummingbird* was back inside the comms pattern. That meant there were better ways to pass messages than forced meetings at the *Sovbez*. Safer ways.

And Margot's survival at the agency depended on them.

Because the last one *Hummingbird* had sent—right before she went completely dark—was that something worse than the invasion was coming.

Something catastrophic.

An attack on the homeland.

More was supposed to follow, but it never did.

And that silence was what kept Roman up at night. Why he was losing sleep. Why he'd sent Margot in blind, unprepared, half-cocked.

Because he knew in his bones—if *Hummingbird* said something was coming, it was.

And yet, how had he done it? How had he let her get on that plane.

They hadn't even waited for a government jet. She'd flown commercial. An overnight bag, a fur coat, and a legend slapped together by tech they barely understood. That was the prep. That was the groundwork.

Sending her in like that wasn't just a mistake. It was a sin.

And if anything went wrong, he'd never forgive himself.

He'd come up the ranks old-school, the hard way—East European back-alleys, stale cigarette smoke and cold coffee, pistols and Minox cameras. He knew how fast things could go wrong in conditions like these. He'd seen it happen a hundred times.

There was a knock on the door, snapping him back to the present. "One second, Margot, that's them." But it wasn't. It was the usher with his coffee. He set it down on the table, then looked up.

"Something the matter?" Roman said.

"You sure you're in the right place?"

"Am I sure?"

"It's just, you look...."

Roman was wearing the plain livery of the Secret Service's Uniformed Division—Thorogood shoes, sergeant's epaulets, the works. He knew he looked like a mall cop, but it wasn't the usher's job to point it out.

"What did your security read tell you?" he said.

"It checked out."

"Well, that should be good enough, shouldn't it?"

The usher nodded.

"Just forget I'm in here," Roman added. "Forget everything about me."

The man didn't look convinced, but he left the room, and Roman said into the phone, "Sorry, Margot, a *Stasi* agent here thinks—"

The line was dead.

She'd hung up on him.

The Honeytrap

He looked at the screen to confirm, then crossed the room and sank heavily onto a two-hundred-year-old *chaise longue*.

He couldn't call her back, either. Not as securely as if she initiated the call.

He poured coffee into a china cup, straightening his tie as he did. He stirred in milk, then leaned back and put his feet on an antique coffee table.

She'd call back. She had to. He hadn't told her which protocol *Hummingbird* had used.

He took a sip, dripping coffee onto his crisp white shirt.

"Perfect," he muttered, dabbing at it with a napkin.

He was very tired. He hadn't slept a wink. Every time he tried, he thought of Margot.

The usher peeped in again, then retreated before Roman could say anything. It wasn't the first time the disguise had caused confusion. The other members of the Council found it very amusing whenever he was inadvertently asked to hold a door or fetch a chair. He didn't care. Unlike the rest of them, he couldn't afford to be clocked as a person of interest. He was a creature of the shadows. No fanfare. No limousines. No name on the guest list.

If he got his way, no foreign adversary would ever know he existed.

One of his predecessors, the Director of Clandestine Services following the Kennedy assassination, had made it his habit to show up for all Oval Office meetings dressed as a White House cook. There was even a memo addressed to LBJ explaining why he always required so much notice for meetings. "Cooks don't arrive in town cars," he'd written. "They take the bus. And DC buses run late."

Roman loved that. The man had been the only cabinet-level official during the Cold War never ID'd by the KGB.

He'd been able to walk his dog along Sixteenth Street, right by the gates of the Soviet Embassy, and no one so much as looked his way.

That was tradecraft.

That was the standard Roman pursued.

And besides, the Thorogood Oxfords were the most comfortable shoes he owned.

18

Gabriella Wintour, the president's National Security Advisor, was not having a good morning. It had started with an emergency four AM phone call from her ex—always a nice way to start the day—and continued downhill from there.

"What do you mean, is she here?" she barked into the phone, jumping out of bed as if just realizing there was a rattlesnake in it. "You said you'd have her for the goddamn week—"

"Just check her room," her ex-husband, the high-powered lobbyist, Felix Westport, said.

They were talking about their fourteen-year-old daughter, Cassie, who was currently going through a rebellious phase that had very definitely crossed the line into problem territory. Overnight, Gabriella's sweet little girl had gone from Ariana Grande and Disney princesses to dark eyeliner and *deathcore* music loud enough to prompt two HOA complaints.

"Are you telling me you've lost her?" she said, breathless, as she rushed down the hall to Cassie's bedroom.

"I haven't lost her," Felix said, though she could hear the worry in his voice. "She must have snuck out. Her window's wide open."

"I thought that house had security up the wazoo. Your words."

"Is she there or not?" he said frantically.

"She's not," Gabriella said, scanning the perfectly unslept-in bed.

Fifteen minutes later, she was driving down the shrub-lined driveway of Felix's eight-bedroom mansion, gravel spraying behind her as she skidded to a halt. Felix, caught in her headlights like a startled deer, was standing waiting on the front porch.

"Where is she?" Gabriella gasped, jumping out of the car.

"Relax," Felix said. "She's all right."

Gabriella clocked the suitcase at the door. Ditching his own daughter this close to Christmas? Even for Felix, this was a new low. "Where did you find her?"

"Next door." Felix glanced across a manicured lawn toward the enormous Tudor-imitation house in the next lot. On the second floor, a single light was on.

"*Next door?*"

"She has a friend there," he added.

"Let me guess. This friend is a boy."

Felix sighed.

Gabriella gave him a withering look. "And does this boy have a name?"

Felix shrugged, and at that moment, she would have happily gone to prison for strangling him. "I don't know," he said. "The place was on the market. New people just moved in."

"Felix! It's four o'clock in the morning."

"She snuck out. What was I meant to do?"

"You were meant to *watch* her, to *parent* her. Remember what that is?"

"Don't start. You're hardly mother of the year."

Those words stung—Gabriella was all too aware of her shortcomings in that department—but she was not about to let him gaslight her over it. She looked at the suitcase. "Tapping out already? I thought you had big holiday plans."

"I assumed when you said you were coming...."

"I was coming to make sure she's all right."

"Yeah, well, you might as well take her. I was thinking of flying out to Aspen, but everything's been canceled because of the storm."

"You could keep her here. She's been looking forward to it."

"She doesn't want to be here."

Gabriella gave him another withering look. She couldn't believe she'd spent the best years of her life with this man.

"I need you to take her," he added weakly. "Something's come up. *We*—"

Gabriella raised a hand, cutting him short. "It doesn't matter," she said. "I don't want to hear." The *we* in question was him and his new child bride, Avalon. He'd picked her up—along with hair plugs and a vintage Testarossa—to replace the life he and Gabriella had spent the best part of twenty years building together.

"Where's my daughter?"

Felix opened the door and led her through a cavernous foyer. They found Cassie in the kitchen, sitting next to Avalon and looking decidedly unperturbed with a tub of Van Leeuwen dairy-free ice cream in front of her. It was Gabriella's first time inside the house, and she was taken aback by the opulence. The Christmas tree must have been twenty feet high, bedecked in lights, glass beads, and red Lindt chocolates that hung like berries from the branches. Through a set of grand Venetian doors, she could see the turquoise glow of a hot tub, warm even now, in the middle of the worst winter storm on record.

"Don't you look pleased with yourself," she said to Cassie, who just happened to be wearing the pink velour tracksuit Avalon had bought at the mall a few months earlier. It had the word *Juicy* printed across the ass, and Gabriella had told her more than once what she thought of it.

"Mom, don't make a big thing out of this."

"A big thing? Where the hell were you, Cassie? Who were you with?"

"Gabriella, please," Avalon started, but Gabriella gave the woman—who was all of nine years older than Cassie, closer to her in age than she was to Felix—such a look she instantly shut her mouth.

"I was with a friend," Cassie said.

"A friend? What friend?"

"His name is Cody. Cody *Richards*," she added wistfully, as if imagining taking the name for herself.

"And what age is this Cody Richards?" Gabriella said.

When Cassie didn't answer, Gabriella pulled out her phone and fired off a message to the security desk at her office. The reply came instantly—name, address, social security number, date of birth, criminal record, school transcript. The record was clean, thankfully, but as Gabriella did the math, she suddenly felt sick to her stomach. Cody Richards was seventeen.

"Gabby," Felix said, "are you all right?"

"You're white as a ghost," Avalon added.

She looked at the three of them—Felix in the Ralph

Lauren housecoat she still remembered picking out for him at Nordstrom, Avalon in a silk robe that made her look like a Japanese geisha, and Cassie, who'd just spent the night, for all intents and purposes, with a grown man—and suddenly felt like a stranger in the room.

"You," she said to Cassie, "*out!*"

"But mom—"

"*Get* in the car."

Cassie stormed off, and Gabriella followed, grabbing the suitcase from the porch on her way and flinging it into the back of her SUV without allowing Felix to help. She got into the car and almost hit him when she pulled away, driving like a bank robber down his driveway.

"Mom!"

"Don't '*Mom*' me, Cassie Westport."

"We were just—"

"I don't want to know."

"He's just a boy."

"He's seventeen."

"Avalon says—"

Gabriella drummed the wheel with her fingers. "Do *not* bring Avalon into this."

"She just thinks that you're—"

"I mean it, Cassie."

Avalon—as well as being a home-wrecker, in Gabriella's eyes—had put herself through college with the help of a little website called sugardaddy.com. Felix wasn't yet aware, but Gabriella wouldn't have minded being present when he found out. In any case, Avalon's thoughts on parenting were about as relevant at that moment as the weather on Jupiter.

"Today of all days," she muttered, thinking of what lay ahead of her at work. She instantly regretted it.

Cassie went quiet, then said, "Sorry if my acting out doesn't fit with your busy schedule."

"Honey!"

"And thanks for ruining my vacation plans."

"I didn't—"

"Dad told me you vetoed their plans to bring me along."

That was a lie. Gabriella didn't even know what the plans were, she'd never been asked anything about them, and she would have happily allowed Cassie to go anywhere with her father as long as it was safe.

As usual, however, Felix hadn't included Cassie. Gabriella had no idea how to break that to her. She couldn't tell her she'd been dumped by her own dad on Christmas, so instead she said nothing, allowing Cassie to believe it was all her fault.

They drove the rest of the way in silence, Gabriella chewing on the logistical kink this threw up. She hadn't booked time off for the holidays. She'd expected Cassie to be with her father. Now, with what was going on in Moscow, she wasn't sure how much time she'd be able to take off. There was a very real chance Cassie would be home for Christmas—with only Mrs Koeffer for company.

That guilt had gnawed at her when she left for work an hour later.

❄

"Gabriella?" President Calvin Westfahl's voice cut in. "*Gabriella!*"

"Yes, Mr President."

"You're a million miles away."

"Sorry, sir."

"The report?"

The Honeytrap

They were marching down one of the Eisenhower Building's interminably long corridors—herself, the president, and Dominic Doerr—and Gabriella was struggling to keep up with the two men in her impractical high heels.

"Of course," she said, digging awkwardly into her folio, searching for the document while trying to maintain stride. She already knew Doerr hadn't read his copy, and the president, asking for it now, just a minute before stepping into the room with Roman, wasn't going to be doing its fifteen pages much justice either. It didn't matter that her office had worked through the night to get it ready, or that it had been compiled from disclosures that had only been obtained over the vehement—one might almost say hysterical—objections of both Roman and his agent, Margot Katz. This mission marked the first time ever that Roman Adler had successfully been forced to turn over the details of an active operation, and one could be forgiven for thinking he'd been asked to desecrate his own mother's grave.

And yet, no one had bothered to read any of it.

Gabriella pulled out her copy and handed it to the president.

"Look alive," he said to her, snatching the report and pushing open the door to the meeting room.

Gabriella followed, with Doerr so close behind her he was almost stepping on her heels. "Do you mind?" she muttered over her shoulder.

"Sorry."

"You're not going to be left behind."

"I know," he hissed.

Then why are you tripping over me, she wanted to say, though she held her tongue.

The meeting was taking place in the Secretary of War Suite, the very nerve center of American power right up until the creation of the Pentagon. Some had said that it was in its four walls that American exceptionalism took root. Gabriella just thought of it as Roman's domain.

It was where he and the president held all their meetings—at Roman's insistence—and she suspected there was more to it than just discretion.

When the room was first built, America had been little more than a distant outpost in the minds of European statesmen—a former colony without a navy, on its knees after one of the deadliest civil wars in history, struggling to subdue the scattered forces of the Sioux, Comanche, Cheyenne, and Apache. It was an afterthought, a second-tier power, scarcely worthy of the name.

Looking at Roman now, hurriedly pulling his feet from the museum-quality coffee table, Gabriella found it hard to believe that he wasn't acutely aware of that history—and the luster it lent him. It was in that room that America became the world's undisputed hegemon, capable of bringing all the old empires to heel. By the time it was vacated after World War II, American dominance—military, economic, cultural, even moral—was complete.

The first time she'd sat in on a meeting there, Roman had more or less told her as much.

She'd arrived early, only to find him already there—dressed as always in his policeman's uniform, sitting like a figure carved from the room itself. Later, she'd learn he was always early—sometimes by hours.

That day, as she laid out her notes under his watchful gaze, he'd told her that it was aboard the *Arabella* in 1630, somewhere on the Atlantic between Southampton and Massachusetts, that John Winthrop first uttered the words, *city upon a hill.*

Then he'd looked around the room, the faintest sparkle

in his eye. "But it was in this room," he said, "that the promise became real."

Even then—before she knew all that she later would of Roman Adler, before she'd even heard of the *Bookshop*—she sensed that he believed the words. Truly believed them.

Washington was a city of cynics. Most, if they'd heard the phrase at all, dismissed it as a fairy tale for elementary school children.

But not Roman Adler.

To him, America wasn't just another empire.

It was a nation with a destiny ordained by Almighty God Himself.

It was a *city on a hill*.

And he was willing to die for it.

19

Toko woke in the dark to the vibration of his cell phone. Not a call—just a message from Morozov. The Toyota had been linked to last night's operation. He'd arranged a replacement.

Toko got up, turned on the coffee maker, and stepped into the bathroom. It was bitterly cold—the window had been open all night—and he avoided looking at the bathtub. He couldn't face the shame. Not again.

After freshening up at the sink, he shut the door firmly behind, then, as an added precaution, lay towels along the bottom of the door. He wanted to keep as much of the cold air out of the room as possible. The last thing he needed was a housekeeper coming in to investigate.

The TV in the bedroom was on. He'd left it running to cover the soft hiss of the police scanner—and he watched the local news as he dressed. They'd found the dead cop, washed up against a railway bridge a mile downstream. The report didn't say if they'd found the police car or not, but from the helicopter news footage, he could see that floodlights had been set up around the bridge and a major investigation was being rolled out. There was no mention of the explosion at the dam.

In any case, none of it worried Toko. They'd piece together what he'd done, but he fully intended to be out of the country by the time they did. Morozov had assured him a plane was fueled and waiting at Teterboro, just outside New York. If everything went according to plan, he'd be in Mexico City in time for dinner.

He packed his things, switched off the TV, and left the room, flipping the *Do Not Disturb* sign on the door as he went. Down in the lobby, he had to use the phone at reception to wake the concierge, who took a few minutes to arrive. Toko told him he'd be keeping the room for another two days and that no one was to enter under any circumstances. The kid nodded.

"There should be a Hertz drop-off," Toko said. "White sedan. Came during the night?"

After a moment's searching, the kid found the keys in an envelope on the desk.

Toko exited the hotel and found the car using the button on the fob. It was a modest compact, and he drove it to Richmond International Airport as instructed. There, he left it in long-term and picked up an Alamo jeep with a new ID and credit card. The paperwork claimed the jeep was equipped with off-road tires, though Toko doubted it when he saw them. In any case, it was the best they had available.

From the airport, his orders were to make the sixty-mile drive southeast following the contour of the James River, as far as an old historical landmark known as Bacon's Castle.

Before leaving the city, he hit a McDonald's drive-thru and got a huge coffee—sugar, cream—three egg-and-cheese biscuits, and two hash browns. He ate them on the road, passing through towns he'd never heard of, like Petersburg,

New Bohemia, and Disputanta. At a place called Waverly, he stopped at a gas station and picked up jerky, cigarettes, soda, and the most detailed local maps they had for sale.

He drove cautiously, the road conditions as abysmal as they'd been the day before. The storm was continuing unabated, and the sky was as black and pitiless as any he'd ever seen over the Sea of Okhotsk. He stayed on the highway as long as possible, only leaving it when he reached the village of Wakefield. From there, he was on windy county roads that passed through woods and farmland as desolate and barren as any Russian taiga.

He reached Bacon's Castle two hours before dawn and found a stately brick mansion shrouded in darkness. It had once been the site of a rebellion against the English, according to a sign at the entrance. There was a parking lot for tourists and school buses, though everything was currently shuttered up for the season.

Alone in the lot was a single white Mercedes Sprinter van, right where Morozov had said. Toko had no idea how long it had been there, though it was long enough that its tracks had been covered in fresh sleet. He pulled up next to it and got out of the jeep. The key for the van was hidden on its right rear tire, and he found it and unlocked the back.

Inside—a small amount of industrial grade nitroglycerin, two five-gallon jugs of water, and ten kilos of grocery store sugar in paper bags. In a black carryall—a pistol and suppressor, a rifle and scope, tools, a flashlight, rope, and even a pair of night-vision goggles. There were also insulated pants, winter boots, another parka, and cold-weather combat gloves.

Everything had been thought of. Redundancies on redundancies.

He moved everything hurriedly from the van to the jeep,

locked it up, and placed the key back where he'd found it. Then, he drove the jeep extremely delicately, given the nature of his new cargo, out of the lot and back onto the road.

The full scope of this operation had never actually been spelled out to Toko, but he didn't have to be Sherlock Holmes to read between the lines. There'd been signs for the Dominion Nuclear Power Station since before he'd left the highway, and Morozov had made reference more than once to cyberattacks being coordinated with the bad weather.

In any case, Toko's part in it was simple. He was a foot soldier. He didn't need to see the big picture.

He followed the GPS along a narrow company road slick with ice. It was lit by sodium tubes, not unlike those outside Russian industrial plants, and he was glad for the light they gave. He drove slowly on the concrete, the whole time worried he'd see the headlights of an oncoming car.

About four kilometers short of the plant's entrance, and before its first security checkpoint, there was supposed to be a turnoff leading to a fuel storage facility. Driving at a crawl, he peered into pitch black forest, searching for the opening in the trees. When he was sure he'd gone too far, he turned and doubled back. Time wasn't exactly on his side—to the east, when he got a clear view of the sky, he could already see the first signs of the impending dawn. He looked at his watch and figured he had an hour tops before it started to get bright.

And then he saw it, a turnoff onto an unpaved logging road.

He'd been told it would be open, but he saw now that his access was blocked by a boom. He climbed out and examined it. There was a chain with a lock on it, but no cameras, no lights, no electronic sensors. Presumably, the plant had some sort of decent security, but here, there was nothing more than a chain you might use to lock a bicycle.

He could have rammed it, but the boom was the same height as his headlights, and he wanted to avoid breaking those if he could. Instead, he put the suppressor to the pistol and shot the lock. It took three shots to get a good hit, but when he did, the lock fell to the ground with a thud, followed by the chain. He tried to pull the boom then, but ice buildup had frozen it in place. He tried dislodging it by force but couldn't, so he got the tool bag from the jeep, praying that no vehicles passed by. He worked deftly with a hammer and chisel, chipping away at the ice until he was able to swing the boom up using only his body weight.

Once it was open, he drove the jeep through, then got back out and closed it behind him before proceeding along the dirt road. It was tough going. The ground was covered in ice, but it hadn't frozen solid. The result was a mess of slush and semi-frozen mud that proved too much for the jeep. He managed to get about a hundred yards before coming to a halt. Any farther and he risked getting stuck, which wasn't an option. Walking out of there in that weather would have been ugly.

He glanced back toward the road and could just about see the boom. Driving past, no one would see the jeep unless they stopped to look for it.

He doubted that would happen. He also doubted there were overhead drones patrolling the forest. If there were, the trees would have to mask him. It was his only option.

He killed the engine and killed the lights.

20

Gabriella stepped around the president, putting space between herself and Doerr, who was close enough that she could feel his breath on her neck. Impatience radiated off him like static before a storm. Now that he'd seen Roman's blood in the water, he was circling for the kill. When he got his chance, he would strike.

"Mr President," Roman said, rising to his feet.

"Roman, sit, please. I've brought Gabriella and Doerr."

"I see that," Roman said.

That any of them were there was a major concession. Roman guarded his autonomy as jealously as his secrecy. Ordinarily, none of them would have had any idea what was happening at the Bookshop. Now, they were all over it. Roman's worst nightmare—his precious protocols in shambles—and only himself to blame. He'd been a naughty boy.

Gabriella studied his face, the lines around his eyes. He was tired, agitated, and she knew this could get messy. His agent was elite—trained by Roman himself to perform the most difficult missions in the most hostile environments—

but what she was not trained to do was take orders from a committee.

Yet here they all were.

Another sign that in the battle between Roman Adler and Dominic Doerr, it was Doerr who was gaining the upper hand. Roman and his ilk were fast becoming the endangered species. Their time was coming to an end. All the arguments that had been lain at the president's feet— that the Bookshop was a dangerous anachronism, an unsophisticated dinosaur, as likely to spark a war as prevent one —were taking root. Roman had gone too far, and this was the result.

"Can we get more coffee?" the president said, taking the seat facing Roman.

Gabriella and Doerr were the only others there, but she didn't need to look at him to know the job fell to her. She went out to the corridor and caught the first usher she could. "Three more coffees," she said, raising three fingers.

Back in the room, Doerr had taken the last seat. "Where's the agent now?" he said, eyeing Roman's phone, which was face up on the coffee table. "I thought you were supposed to have her on the line already."

"Technical issue," Roman said.

"*Technical* issue?" Doerr said, glancing at his watch with theatrical disapproval—tactful as a linebacker.

"The masking hardware's acting up."

"*That's* a bad start."

"It's nothing."

"Hardly nothing," Doerr pressed. He really had no idea when to pick his battles. Or maybe he did. Maybe he knew something she didn't.

"Could it be a sign she's in trouble?" the president said.

Roman shook his head. "Absolutely not."

"Well," Doerr began. And Gabriella thought—not for the first time—that for all his supposed genius, he was constitutionally incapable of not coming across like a complete prick. "She *is* in Moscow," he continued. "Trouble sort of comes with the territory, doesn't it?"

"There's no trouble," Roman repeated stiffly.

"I'm just saying it's a *possibility*," Doerr said.

Gabriella had always remained neutral between them. If the two men were North and South Korea, she was the thirty-eighth parallel. Checkpoint Charlie.

The truth was, she wasn't sure which vision of the future terrified her more—Roman's shadowy world of spies and assassins or Doerr's surveillance empire, powered by ever-more-sophisticated quantum chips and neural nets.

HUMINT versus SIGINT. The oldest debate in espionage.

Doerr's world was clean, clinical, sanitized. Scrapers, fiber-optic wiretaps, billion-dollar data centers.

Against that, Roman's world was positively medieval. It reeked of sweat, blood, piss, and shit. Of renditions, zip ties, piano wire, and people falling from balconies.

In short, his was *human*, and came with all the mess that entailed.

It was also—according to some voices Gabriella greatly admired—the only thing that had prevented the Cold War from slipping into Armageddon.

Which may be why, despite all better judgement, she suddenly found herself weighing in on his side.

"If you'd read my report," she said, looking pointedly at Doerr, "you'd know that Ms Katz arrived in Moscow without incident. She's at the *Romanov* as we speak. If Roman says she'll call, she'll call."

"Thank you, Gabriella," the president said, looking at

her slightly askance. Gabriella didn't make a habit of sticking her neck out—for Roman or anyone. But this wasn't tactical. It wasn't ideological. She wasn't Roman's ally. Not really. It was just that there were worse things than ghosts—worse things than secrets—and when she looked at Doerr, she got the distinct feeling she was looking them in the face.

"Would it be too much to suggest," she said, glancing at the phone, "that *we* call her?"

Roman shook his head. "That's a no, unfortunately. The way the hardware's set up, we have to wait."

The president looked like he was about to say something, but a knock on the door stopped him. It was the usher with a tray of clinking china cups. They all watched as he came in and set it down, but when he started to pour, Gabriella stepped in. "Let me do that," she said impatiently.

The usher left, and Roman made room for her on the sofa. "Thank you," she said, taking the seat.

She handed the president a cup of coffee, and he took a sip. "All right, Roman," Westfahl said, "this is your show."

Still his show, but for how long?

"Well, *Hummingbird's* back in contact," he began. "That obviously changes the situation."

"We drop the ambassador thing?" Doerr said.

"I think that goes without saying," Roman said, and from the strain in his voice, Gabriella could tell he was just barely holding back. They were discussing *his* operation, weighing *his* agent's actions, as calmly as if choosing new curtains for the embassy drawing room. And all the while, her life was on the line.

"It's too late for reticence, Roman," the president said. "Spell it out for us. You got us into this mess. Now explain how you'll get us out."

"Foxtrot should have sent over everything we're doing."

The Honeytrap

"We received the files," Gabriella said, holding up her copy of the report.

"We've been updating the disclosures hourly," Roman said, before adding under his breath, "as ordered."

Gabriella glanced at the president to see if he'd picked up on the tone. If he had, he made no sign of it.

After the fiasco of yesterday's meeting, the president had taken the unprecedented step of ordering Roman to turn over his file—six hundred pages of documentation that Gabriella and her office had spent the night sifting through. When Felix woke her up that morning, she'd only had two hours of sleep. It was those six hundred pages that she and her staff had managed to distill into the fifteen-pager that Doerr and the president had so casually failed to read.

"So?" Doerr said. "Let's hear it, Roman. What's the plan?"

"If you'd read the file," Roman started, as Doerr and the president began belatedly flipping through their copies of the report.

"Perhaps it's best," Gabriella interjected, "if I summarize for everyone's benefit."

"Please do," the president said, looking up from the document.

"My office has gone through all of it," she said, clearing her throat. "Honestly, at this point, I think I know the case better than anyone."

"Great," the president said.

Gabriella turned to Roman. "Shall I proceed?"

His jaw was clenched as tight as a clamp. "By all means," he managed.

"All right," she said. "There have been a few developments since the last meeting, but the only one that concerns us now is that *Hummingbird* has indeed re-established contact. It means we can call off the meeting with Zubarev. That was always going to be risky, and now it's no longer needed."

"So if *Hummingbird* sent a message," the president said, "then what the hell did it say?"

"Well," Roman said, stepping in, "*message* might be a generous term for the crumpled cigarette packet she left on a bench in the middle of the night."

Gabriella nodded. She knew the protocol as well as if she'd written it herself. She'd spent the night memorizing every detail. "The cigarette packet was left at *Manege Square*," she said. "A well-known square near the Kremlin."

"I know it," the president said.

"By the glass dome," she added, reaching into her folio for the photos. One showed the fountain at the center of the square. On top was a sculpture depicting the emblem of Moscow—Saint George slaying a dragon—and around it were a number of concrete benches. "The signal required *Hummingbird* to sit on one of these benches and smoke a Prima cigarette—not her usual brand—then crumple the packet and leave it on the ground behind her."

"It means she's willing to meet with Margot," Roman said.

"A face-to-face," Gabriella added.

"So this is good news," the president said.

All eyes were on Roman, but he remained silent. That surprised Gabriella. It *was* good news. The only reason he'd brought them in was to get Margot and *Hummingbird* in the same room. Now they were going to meet.

"Forgive me," the president said, "but wasn't this the biggest emergency in the world for you yesterday? I mean, that's what you said, right? I'm not imagining that?"

"You're not imagining it, sir."

"You said something worse than an invasion was coming and that only *Hummingbird* knew how to stop it."

"I said something like that."

"Then why the long face, Roman? I mean, this is what you wanted. This is why we sent Margot over there."

"It is," Roman said.

"Well, excuse the expression, Roman, but you look about as pleased as a fat kid who just dropped his ice cream cone."

"No, it's good news, sir. Definitely. It's just—"

"Too easy?" Gabriella said. Her voice was quiet, but the question lingered like cigar smoke.

The president looked at him. "Is that it? You're worried?"

"I'm always worried."

"You smell a rat?" the president said.

Roman didn't blink. "Not a rat. Something else. And it reeks."

Gabriella thought back to the previous day. The revelation that *Hummingbird* was Irina Volkova—Chichikov's mistress—had been a bombshell. The kind that shook even seasoned operators. It certainly shook the president.

Recruiting such an asset crossed a bright red line—one that had been in place since the days of Stalin that prohibited targeting the leader's own person or family. It was the closest thing the Cold War had had to an absolute rule. That and the doctrine of Mutually Assured Destruction.

And Margot Katz had traipsed right over it. Some girls in a nightclub restroom putting on lipstick, and the next thing, the entire Council was in Chichikov's pants.

And all that without the slightest clearance from Washington—strike one.

Keeping it from the president over a period of years—strike two.

The president categorically should have been told. Recruiting Irina Volkova was the espionage equivalent of entering a nuclear reactor. One wrong move and it would be game over for everyone. Margot Katz may have been simply doing her job when she made the initial approach, but Roman—with his decades of experience and near-daily contact with the president—absolutely should have known better.

To say Westfahl was pissed was the understatement of the century. What Roman had done was a usurpation. He'd made a decision that was the president's, and the president's alone, to make. It could be argued it constituted treason. Indeed, that very argument had been made, and not just by Doerr. The Attorney General, Kathleen Holman, had called not only for Roman and Margot's immediate resignations, but their arrest. And there'd been no shortage of calls for the Bookshop's disbandment.

What Roman had done was a power grab, plain and simple. And he'd kept it secret because he knew the president would have put the kibosh on it the instant he found out.

That it had worked barely mattered. In the first brutal weeks of the Ukraine invasion, Westfahl himself had credited *Hummingbird* with stopping the Kremlin's thrust for Kyiv. Gabriella had looked up the transcript just to make sure she wasn't misremembering. It was there in black and white.

Without *Hummingbird*, Chichikov would be sitting in the *Mariinskyi Palace* right now.

Westfahl had said that, and more than once. *Hummingbird*—and by extension, Roman—had stopped the Russians from taking Kyiv.

And he'd kept it under such a tight lid that no one guessed how he'd done it, not the White House, and not Chichikov. An unmitigated success, tactically speaking.

And that he'd kept *Hummingbird* alive, online, ready to do it all over again, was nothing short of a miracle.

When Chichikov's invasion faltered in Ukraine, he'd reacted by going on a full-blown killing spree. He purged not only the top echelons of the military, but many of his closest personal connections—other mistresses, favored prostitutes, friends dating back decades, even a son-in-law. His paranoia became so intense—with literally hundreds of secret executions daily—that there'd been talk of a return to Stalin's darkest days.

And through it, *Hummingbird* kept singing.

Kept chirping her pretty tune.

Taken purely on its own terms, *Hummingbird* was a master stroke. It was perhaps the most significant operation in CIA history. It had altered the course of the invasion. It had altered history. And had been pulled off flawlessly.

But all of that was being overshadowed by Roman's decision not to tell the president. Gabriella winced when she remembered Margot saying the words. The moment was seared into her memory.

Everyone had sensed something was coming. Roman had shown up with an agent none of them had ever laid eyes on before. That set alarms ringing before she'd even said a word.

"Who have you got here?" the president said when he saw her.

"I didn't realize it was take your daughter to work day," Doerr added snidely.

"Margot Katz," the president said, reading the name from a communiqué in front of him. It was hard to believe it was just twenty-four hours ago. Until that moment, none of them had ever heard the name Margot Katz. "It says here your job is *handler*."

"That's correct," Margot said.

"She's not just a handler," Roman said. "She's the one who reeled in *Hummingbird* in the first place. She's the reason *Hummingbird* exists."

At that point, everyone in the room, including Gabriella, was still operating under the assumption that *Hummingbird* was a man. A government functionary. A normal target. Fair game.

"I see," the president said cautiously, uncertain where Roman was going to take things. "So *Hummingbird's*...."

"Got a *handler*," Doerr said, and Gabriella noticed the way his gaze lingered on Margot as he said the words. "Lucky guy."

"Try to keep your tongue in your mouth," Gabriella said.

"Not to be rude," the president said, "but why are you here, Ms Katz?"

Margot glanced at Roman, then cleared her throat. "Mr President...."

"Yes?"

"*Hummingbird's* been a very reliable source."

"You can say that again," the president said. "He's the one who kept Kyiv out of the Kremlin's hands."

"Right," Margot said.

As well as Gabriella, Doerr, and Holman, the others present included the Secretary of Defense, Charles 'Chuck' Austin, the Joint Chiefs Chairman, General Vance Poynter, and CIA Director Jake Hawke. Every one of them wanted to know why this young woman was standing before them.

"Well," Margot said, looking at each in turn, "*Hummingbird* is now saying something worse is about to happen. An attack on US soil."

The words hung in the air like fallout.

No one spoke.

21

Oksana jolted awake to her phone alarm. She silenced it and lay still. She hadn't slept—she knew that—but it still felt like she'd been dreaming.

She got up and pulled on the thick robe hanging on the back of the chair next to the bed. Old and faded, worn thin at the elbows, it was one of her most treasured possessions. It had belonged to her mother, had even made the crossing with her from Russia, and Oksana vividly remembered her wearing it.

The room was cold enough that she could see her breath in the air, and she went straight to the propane heater, held down the valve with one hand, and clicked the igniter with the other, like lighting a barbecue. It took a few tries to catch. She also opened the window a crack. It was freezing outside, but a sticker on the heater warned vociferously of carbon monoxide.

She sat on the bed then, blanket over her knees, waiting for the room to warm.

Apartment was too generous a term for the tiny garret she

rented from Mrs Chen, a Chinese lady who smoked incessantly and carried two chihuahuas with her in a canvas handbag. Their heads poked out the top like passengers in a sidecar, and she brought them everywhere, including when she collected Oksana's rent—four hundred dollars weekly, paid in cash.

It wasn't the Ritz, but it was hers, and the price was right.

It consisted of one room and a tiny bathroom, a sofa that doubled as a bed, a table, two plain chairs, a kitchenette with a hotplate, a sink, a microwave, and a fridge. Above the sofa was a large window leading to a fire escape.

The building was as dilapidated as the New York City Fire Marshal would allow, and sat on a lively stretch of 125th near the Apollo. Not the quietest part of town—the sirens were a near constant—but it wasn't far from the apartment on 95th Street she'd shared with her mother as a child. Maybe it was a subconscious thing, choosing a place so close to those memories, maybe not.

As well as Oksana's apartment, the building contained, on the ground floor, a Chinese takeout place that served the most amazing noodles. On the second floor was a *'nail spa'* that received more than its share of middle-aged gentlemen callers. None of them seemed to have particularly well-manicured nails, Oksana noted, though she didn't care what they got up to in there. No one bothered her and that was all that mattered.

If the building had a best feature, apart from the noodles, it was the fire escape. In the summer, the apartment got swelteringly hot, but by climbing over the sofa and out the window, Oksana could get onto a breezy metal platform that overlooked miles and miles of Manhattan skyline, as well as the hustle and bustle of Harlem on the street below. She never tired of it, and even slept out there when the heat got to be too much.

When the room had warmed enough that she could no longer see her breath, she got off the bed and turned on the coffee maker. Then, she switched on the small television on the counter and watched the local news while waiting for the coffee to brew. She drank it at the table, staring vacantly at the television. The news was all about the weather—the storm of the century battering the East Coast, a Nor'easter to remember, so many inches of sleet and snow. After twenty minutes, she threw on some jeans and a gray *Columbia Swim Team* hoodie and headed out. She wasn't a member of the swim team, but she'd found the hoodie in a locker, and when she tried to hand it in, they told her not to bother—they had three identical ones in the lost and found already.

Columbia's fitness facility was large, if dated, and she walked through a deserted Morningside Park to get to it, entering the campus through the 116th Street gate. The pool was just opening when she arrived, and she scanned her student pass and went up to the changing room. There was no one else there.

Oksana had always liked swimming, but since the incident with Proctor, it had begun to resemble something of an obsession. She went every morning, sometimes for hours, swimming back and forth in endless repetition, trying to clear her head. What she liked most was the solitude. No one ever talked to her in the pool, and there were no phone calls, no messages, no notifications. Just her, the muted sound of the water, and the repeating tiled pattern of the pool floor slipping by underneath.

This morning she swam for ninety minutes, then took a long, hot shower before getting dressed. The changing room wasn't as empty as when she'd arrived, but it didn't bother her. After the swim, she'd intended to go to the library before class, but instead found herself walking toward Joe's.

Joe's was a diner just off campus that she used to go to daily. For some reason, she'd stopped going after the incident. She couldn't have said why, exactly.

It was owned by an older black man named Baldwin—he'd owned the place for the better part of three decades but claimed not to know why it was called Joe's. Oksana had been there so much that over the course of years he'd become something of a father figure to her, or perhaps grandfather figure was more accurate. She hadn't admitted it to herself, but that was the reason she hadn't been back. She was ashamed. She was afraid Baldwin might somehow intuit what had happened to her. She couldn't bear the thought of him knowing.

When she reached it, she paused, then took a deep breath and pushed open the door. A bell chimed above her head and Baldwin looked up from the grill. When he saw her, his eyes widened. She raised a hand in greeting. He just stared.

A moment passed. Oksana swallowed. She couldn't speak, so he broke the silence. "I'd be lying if I said I wasn't starting to worry," he said.

Oksana nodded. She'd hoped her absence might have gone unnoticed—or at least unmentioned. So much for that.

"I know," she said quietly, taking her usual seat at the counter. "Sorry."

"Sorry?" Baldwin said, eyeing her closely. "Where've you been?"

"Busy," she said, breaking eye contact.

He looked at her for another few seconds, then turned

back to the grill and began scraping it vigorously. "Busy," he said to himself. "The world's a busy place, I suppose."

Oksana shifted on her stool, staring at the back of his head. She wasn't sure what she'd been hoping for, but she was fighting back the urge to get up and walk out.

"You'll have your usual, I presume?" he said, stirring a big pot of chili that had been sitting on the flattop.

"Sure," she said.

"That hasn't changed."

"Of course it hasn't."

"It's just been so long."

"Stop it," she said, picking up yesterday's *Times*. The crossword page was untouched.

Baldwin put a mug of black coffee on the counter in front of her and she took a sip.

"You want to tell me where you've been?" he said. "Or to shut up and mind my own business?"

She looked up at him, and when she saw his eyes, she knew that she had to give him something. He wasn't just prying, he cared about her, and he'd been worried. Of all people, she wasn't one to discount a thing like that.

"There was a..." she started. "I was at...." She groped for the words that might say enough without saying too much, but was spared when the only other customer in the place, a man in work boots and a safety vest, came up to the counter.

"Ready to settle up?" Baldwin said to him.

"Yes, sir," the man said.

Baldwin gave her a meaningful look, handed over the pen from behind his ear, then went to cash out the customer. When he got back, she'd started the crossword.

Baldwin sighed, but she continued staring at it fastidiously, refusing to look up. "All right," he said, "I won't bug you, but if there's something you want to say—"

"I can't," she said, cutting him off.

He nodded again, then turned to the grill and began cracking eggs for her order. She watched him, looking away every time he glanced back. They'd done the crossword together a thousand times. "Black cats and comets," she said, eyes on the paper.

"What's that?"

She hit the paper with the back of the pen. "Black cats and comets."

"Let me think," he said, putting some chili in a bowl. He scrambled her eggs with the side of the scraper, then dished them on top of the chili. "Cheese?"

It was a question he'd asked her a thousand times. Usually, she said no. "Sure."

He looked up. "Really?"

"It won't kill me."

"No, it won't," he said. "You must have lost ten pounds since I saw you last."

"Is that a compliment?"

"Not from a grill cook, it's not."

She smiled, then looked back at the crossword. He sprinkled cheese on the chili and brought it over to her with a side of toast. "Does *omens* fit?" he said.

"What?"

"Black cats and comets."

"Oh," she said, looking at the puzzle.

Baldwin nodded as she inked it in. "Omens, indeed," he said.

Oksana didn't reply. But the word stayed with her.

22

Gabriella eyed Roman's cell on the table. Why hadn't it rung? Was the delay a tactic?

The president was restless, too, and she knew why—this call could well end up being one of the defining moments of his presidency.

The transcript would be classified—buried deep in the archive, along with the UFO sightings and Kennedy assassination theories—but it would surface eventually. And when it did, it would be noticed. Gabriella knew the president lost sleep over such things. He couldn't take a leak in the morning without one eye to his legacy.

He'd already tasked Gabriella with seizing yesterday's transcripts.

"For accuracy," he'd said.

She'd obeyed, combing through them for most of the night. When she'd arrived back at the White House that morning, he was doing the same thing—striking thick red lines with a sharpie through everything he wanted erased.

She looked at Roman, sitting next to her on the sofa in

his overstarched policeman's uniform. A condemned man. Or was he already dead in the water?

Again, she thought back to the moment that had done it to him. Margot's stance. Her words. The bomb she'd dropped.

An attack on US soil.

The impact had been immediate. General Vance Poynter—whose sonorous voice had always reminded her of James Earl Jones voicing Darth Vader—spun around in his chair like he was manning a gun turret. "An attack? Where?"

"When?" SecDef Chuck Austin added.

Margot, like a deer in headlights, "That's the problem. I don't know."

Another silence, and everyone turned to the president. Westfahl chewed his lip, then said, "You didn't think to ask for details?"

"We lost contact," Margot said. "That's why we're here."

"When exactly did he go dark?" the president said.

"Five days ago."

"You've been sitting on this for five days?"

"What was our option?" Roman said. "We have nothing concrete. The source broke contact."

"You couldn't reestablish?" Doerr said.

Margot shook her head.

"Pay him a visit?"

"*Hummingbird's* not an ordinary asset," Margot said. "Their position's *sensitive*."

"Everything's *sensitive* in your line," Doerr said snidely.

"The reason *Hummingbird's* survived this long," Roman said, ignoring the comment, "is a blanket ban on all digital comms. All direct access. Everything's a process."

"Telegram and Ghost were hacked just this month," Hawke said.

"Hence the insistence on analog," Margot said. "*Hummingbird's* an ex-surveillance specialist. No shortcuts."

"All right," Poynter said. "But there's still a way to talk to him, right?"

Margot glanced again at Roman. He gave her a nod. "*Hummingbird's* father was a radio operator during the Soviet war in Afghanistan," she said.

"Oh no!" Doerr interjected. "This is *too* good."

"Shut up," Margot said.

"I can see it already. He's using his father's shortwave!"

"That's right," Margot said, jaw clenched.

"You're kidding, right?"

"It's worked, Doerr," the president said. "The man's still breathing when a lot of others aren't."

Roman cleared his throat. "Messages are sent using Cold War methods. Every night at 8:45 Moscow time, a pre-recorded broadcast goes out from an unmanned transmitter east of Berlin on 5.933 MHz."

"Shortwave can be picked up by anyone," Hawke said. "It's about as private as a front page ad."

"Sure," Roman said, "but all they hear is a series of five-digit numbers from a robotic voice."

"No code is perfect," Doerr said.

"We use a one-time pad," Margot said.

"And how do you share the keys?"

"They were agreed long ago. Taken from a specific edition of Gogol's *Dead Souls*. Each day, we flip the page and use the new characters to encrypt."

"Shortwave is *recipient-untraceable*," Poynter said.

"Yes," Margot said. "The signal bounces around the ionosphere, mixing with thousands of others. No one knows who a given message is for."

"All right," Hawke said. "But how does he talk back? A broadcast is a hell of a lot harder to hide."

"That's the problem," Margot said. "Center 16 started sweeping Moscow for unauthorized broadcasts five days ago. *Hummingbird* knows this, which must be why they went dark."

"And there's no other way of reaching him?" Hawke said.

"There are ways," Margot said. "But they require me to fly to Moscow."

"More fun and games," Doerr said.

"There are protocols for in-person messaging—pre-agreed locations, pre-agreed actions."

"If you need to be in Moscow," the president said, "then why are you here with us? What do you need?"

"The ambassador can get us into a room with *Hummingbird*," Roman said. "That's why we're here. All he needs to do is call a meeting at the *Sovbez* and bring Margot as his translator. We'll handle the rest."

"So *Hummingbird's* in the *Sovbez*?" Doerr said.

Roman gave him a thin smile—the kind that said he'd spill the name, but only over his own dead body.

"Really," Doerr said. "Who is he?"

"That's not why we're here?" Margot said.

"Then why are you here?" Poynter said.

"I'm sure we can guess," Doerr said, not bothering to hide the leer.

"I'm here to provide dimension—" Margot began.

"Sweetheart," Doerr said, "the only dimension you're supplying here is your bra size."

Margot's eyes flashed, but she held her tongue. Everyone watched, waiting. Then she leaned forward, planting her hands on the table, giving Doerr—and the rest of them—a front-row view down her blouse.

The effect was immediate. The temperature in the room dropped ten degrees.

And Gabriella finally got why Roman had brought her.

She wasn't there for *dimension*.

She was a weapon.

"What bra?" she said.

And just like that, she'd sucked the oxygen out of Doerr's lungs. He seemed visibly to shrink, and Gabriella had to hand it to her. She'd walked into the most powerful chamber on earth and, with a single gesture, taken complete control.

The silence that followed was heavy, and it was the president who broke it. "Miss Katz," he said. "Who's the source?"

She glanced at Roman.

"Don't look at him," the president said. "Look at me."

"Margot," Roman said. "You can leave."

"She's not going anywhere," the president said.

Everyone stared at her—still standing, defiant, silent.

"Time to cough up," Poynter said. "Who's the mark?"

"The *mark*?" she echoed. "That's what you think this is, isn't it? A good-old-fashioned dick-sucking."

"Margot!" Roman barked. "Remember where you are."

"We're not in kindergarten," she said. "Are we, ladies and gentlemen?"

Doerr smirked. "This is your game, not ours."

"This is *not* a game," she said flatly. "Not on my side of the transaction."

"Ms Katz," the president said. "You're right. You keep the geese laying, right? Keep getting us their golden eggs? That's what you do."

She held his gaze. They all thought they knew what she was. Thought they had her pegged. But they were selling her short.

What none of them appreciated was that she wasn't just a tool, she wasn't just a tactic—she was a precision-guided missile, as lethal as any carrier strike group or low-orbit satellite array.

Because the world had changed.

Power had changed.

The old rules no longer applied.

The despots in Moscow and Beijing no longer feared American hardware, American military might. And they sure as hell didn't fear sanctions. What was another zero to men who'd already plundered entire nations? They had more wealth than they could spend in a thousand lifetimes.

No, the only thing to wield against men like that, men who would have sacrificed the lives of every last citizen if it kept them in power, was the frailty of their own bodies. Their own desires. It was the Bible that said *the flesh is weak*.

And it was true.

That was why Roman Adler wielded the power he did.

Because on the new battlefield, sex was the super-weapon. The warhead that couldn't be stopped.

And the woman standing before them—five-foot-nine, top three buttons of her blouse wide-open—embodied it.

"You can drop the act," the president said. "I asked you a very simple question. Who's the source?"

She looked at Roman. At some point, he'd pulled out his ungodly bottle of Pepto-Bismol and was unscrewing the cap very deliberately. They all watched him take a swig, and when he spoke, he addressed the president directly. "You'll be signing a death warrant. If you force us to reveal. Destroying years of painstaking work. Once the name's out of the box, we can't ever put it back in."

What the president said next was one of the lines

Gabriella knew he'd been erasing with the sharpie. "I don't care, Roman. Cough it up."

"The most valuable asset we've ever had," Roman said. "More actionable intel than any other source in CIA history. Not just data—but *context*. The vodka-fueled rants of the generals. The fears keeping Chichikov awake at night. You really want to throw all that away?"

Everyone was quiet, eyes darting from Roman to the president. The two titans, facing off. *Godzilla vs Kong*. Gabriella had never seen anything like it. Seconds ticked by in slow motion.

And just when it looked like Roman was about to speak, the president turned to Margot. "You tell me."

She didn't miss a beat. "I take my orders from Roman Adler."

Gabriella winced. Insubordination? Treason? She no longer knew what she was looking at.

But Roman did, because that was when he said to her, "It's all right, Margot. Tell him what he wants to know."

"Roman—"

He raised his hand. "It's gone on long enough. We need what we need. This is the price."

But even then, she didn't say the name. She said nothing.

"That's it," Doerr snapped. "Call security."

"No," Roman said. He would have spilled the name himself then, but Margot spared him the pain.

"*Hummingbird's* not a man," she said.

"What's that?" the president said, turning slowly to face her.

"She's a woman."

The president's face remained blank but he replayed the facts in his head. Everything he'd been told. Center 16, a surveillance background, a father in Afghanistan, radio tech.

Suddenly, he went pale. In a voice barely audible, he said, "Irina Volkova."

"That's right," Margot said.

"The girl."

"*Woman*," Margot said flippantly.

"I met her," the president croaked. "He brought her to Yalta."

It was only then that Gabriella remembered her too—the lithe blonde in a gold bikini, lounging poolside like a Bond girl with a secret. The summit had been just after the invasion. Margot had already been running her then.

"Who's Irina Volkova?" Doerr said. Everyone ignored him.

"You've crossed the line," the president said. He looked like he'd just aged ten years. Pale. Gaunt. Wrecked. "Chichikov had a lovechild with her."

"No," Margot said. "He didn't."

"You've gone for the jugular."

"She's the reason Ukraine still stands," Margot said.

But the president was no longer hearing her. "This will be war," he said.

23

"It's me," Margot said into the phone. She was still in the bathroom, shower running, and just as pissed off as when she'd hung up. She needed another *tête-à-tête* with the Council like she needed a hole in the head.

"Margot," Roman said. "Everything all right?"

"Copacetic," she said tersely.

"Comms issue sorted?"

"What comms issue?"

"Good," Roman said, pivoting. "Listen. I've got the president, Gabriella, and Doerr in the room."

"How lovely," she said.

"They just want to—"

"I know what they want."

"To make sure—"

"I don't shit the bed."

"I wouldn't put it that way," Roman said.

"Oh? And how would you put it?"

Roman hesitated. Then came the voice that grated like glass—Dominic Doerr. "I think you'll understand, Ms Katz, if we've decided to take a more active role on this one."

"Great," Margot said. "What op doesn't need a bunch of bureaucrats chiming in?"

"You lied to the president, Ms Katz. You're lucky you aren't in prison."

"*I* didn't lie to anyone," she said, "and I'm not the enemy. Don't treat me like one."

"No one's calling you the enemy," Gabriella said. "We're just here to—"

"Limit the damage," Doerr said.

Margot bit down hard on the words she wanted to say.

"We're getting sidetracked—" Roman started, but Margot cut him short.

"Let's keep this real simple. You tell me where to meet her, I'll do the rest."

The president came on the line, but he wasn't speaking to her. "How does she know *Hummingbird* made contact?"

"She guessed," Roman said quickly.

The president muttered something—he wasn't buying it —but Margot didn't give a rat's ass.

Then Gabriella—"*Hummingbird* used the *Manege Square* protocol, Margot."

Gabriella chaired the Security Council and advised the president directly. It was no surprise she was in the room, but it was still off-putting to hear her speak so fluently on *Hummingbird* protocols. She'd done her homework, but those protocols had been built by Margot and Irina over the course of years. Quietly. Without oversight. Not even from Roman.

Now, they were being bandied about like the score of a Nationals game.

"It means a face-to-face," Gabriella added. "At the Café Pushkin. Tonight."

"I think I know what it means," Margot said stiffly. "I only wrote the thing."

"Café Pushkin?" the president said. "Isn't that a little conspicuous?"

Margot had always wondered what it would be like to sit at the adults table. Now she knew. She might as well have been watching kindergarteners finger-painting. "It won't be conspicuous," she said, "because it's not literally a face-to-face."

"It says here," Gabriella's voice again, "that the Pushkin is a small café off *Nikitsky Boulevard*. Twelve tables. Staff and owners pre-vetted—no known ties to Russian security."

"Doesn't mean someone won't be listening," Doerr said.

"No one will be listening," Margot said, "because we won't talk in the café. Her message is a distress code. She wants a meet, but she's scared. She needs precautions."

"Spare us the tradecraft," Doerr said.

"Gladly," Margot said. "If it were up to me, we wouldn't waste another second of your precious time—"

"If it were up to you, none of us would have the slightest clue what you were up to."

"And safer for it," she shot back.

"Margot," Roman said, voice tight.

"Look," she said. "The front window faces the street. She'll clock me arriving, see I'm alone, confirm I'm not followed."

"She doesn't trust you?"

"It's the FSB she doesn't trust. Once she's sure I'm clean, she'll give the signal."

"What signal?" Doerr said.

"There are two restrooms in the café. There'll be a note behind the mirror in the women's. The location will be written on it."

"So she gets to see you," the president said, "but you don't see her?"

"She's the asset," Margot said. "She calls the shots."

"These protocols are *Hummingbird's*," Roman said. "They've kept her alive this long, and she's never let Margot down yet."

"*Yet*," Doerr echoed.

Margot didn't miss a beat. "Real helpful, Dominic."

"Bottom line," Roman said, "*Hummingbird* pulls the plug if she doesn't like what she sees. She'll trail Margot to the final site if she wants. If not, she cuts loose."

"It means I better be damn sure I'm clean before I get to the café," Margot said.

"And lose any FSB tails without raising flags," Roman added.

"If she has any," Doerr added.

"They'll be there," Roman said. "And if they think for one second she's slipped them on purpose—it's game over. They'll flood the zone."

"Which scares off *Hummingbird*," Margot finished.

"Now, the real meeting site?" Doerr said. "Not just scrawled on a napkin or something, I hope."

Margot exhaled hard. "Jesus."

"Margot," Roman's voice, warning.

"*Hummingbird* and I have a pre-agreed list. Over two dozen sites—underpasses, abandoned train platforms, CIA-owned safe houses. It's all in the disclosures."

"Dominic didn't read the disclosures," Gabriella said.

"The point is," Roman said, "there are too many locations for Moscow Station to monitor continuously."

"So she *doesn't* trust us," Doerr said.

"She doesn't trust anyone," Margot snapped, mentally adding a *dipshit* for completeness.

"Play nice, Margot."

"Why are we explaining ourselves to him like we—"

"Like you overstepped? Crossed a line? Lied?" Doerr said.

"We didn't—"

"You lied," Doerr cut in. "You risked everything. And this is the result. We're in a containment op now—we're here to stop you from triggering World War Three."

"All right," the president said. "That's enough. Roman, this protocol, showing up for the meeting, that's one option, correct?"

"Mr President, as far as we're concerned, it's the only option."

"There's always another option," Doerr said.

"And what are you suggesting, Dominic?"

"I'm suggesting we walk."

"Excuse me?" Margot said, stunned.

"He's only saying it's an option," the president said.

"And you're backing him up?" Roman snapped.

"Roman, I don't know."

"This is what we wanted," Roman said. "This is the whole reason we sent Margot over there."

"You've changed your tune," Doerr said.

"What tune?"

"Right before she called, you said the whole thing was a trap."

"I said no such thing."

"You said you smelled a rat."

"I said I smelled—"

"Admit it," Doerr said. "You're so desperate for this you're willing to throw your own agent to the wolves."

"Dominic!" Roman snapped.

"It's the truth," Doerr continued, "and frankly, I'm

surprised I'm the one bringing it up. This shitshow could go south so quickly that—"

Margot cut him off. "Listen. I'm not leaving Irina to dangle in the wind. I'm showing up for the meet."

"She knew the risks when she signed on," Doerr said.

"Dominic!" Gabriella said, her voice sharp as a whip. "That asset is risking her life to get us information about an imminent attack."

"We *think* she is. We don't actually *know* anything."

"Doerr, what are you saying?" Roman said.

"I'm saying, how much do we trust this *mistress*?"

"Don't do that," Roman said, his voice suddenly as hard and sharp as flint.

"Do what?" Doerr said.

"Rewrite history."

"I'm not rewriting anything."

"You were about to," Roman said. "But let's remember this. Everything is obvious in hindsight. Before Ukraine, Chichikov had two hundred thousand men massed on the border. Thousands of vehicles. Over a thousand tanks. They weren't hidden. Our own satellites could see them from space."

"Exactly," Doerr said.

"But you weren't there, Dominic," Roman pressed. "You don't remember the debates. What's obvious now, wasn't so obvious then. Chichikov had done the same before. All our agencies were convinced this was another feint. Even the Ukrainians, staring across the frontier at the build-up, were screaming at us not to overreact."

"I remember that," the president said.

"But not Irina," Roman said. "She told us what the build-up meant, gave us the precise deployments, explained their intentions, how to counter them. Her intel made the difference. It gave Kyiv what it needed."

"That's right," the president said.

"So forgive me for taking offense when you call her a *mistress*, Dominic."

"You're all too close to this," Doerr said. "This is one life versus millions. Am I the only one who hasn't lost my head?"

"You can't seriously be suggesting we walk away now," Margot said desperately. "She's got something for us. Something big. I know it."

"If it was so important, she'd have figured out a way to get it to us already."

"She can't," Margot said. "The protocol—"

"Yes, yes. The precious protocol," Doerr said. "Look, Mr President, if there's actually anything here, my people will get it for you."

"From their keyboards and computer screens?" Margot spat.

"Is that so hard to believe?"

"If this could be googled on an iPhone, Dominic—"

"And if *Hummingbird* really had something so big," Doerr responded, "like everyone keeps saying—"

"All right," the president said, stepping in.

Margot glanced at herself in the mirror. She was being too loud, running the risk of being overheard by the suitcase. She took a breath, then said, "We don't leave assets behind. That's the line, isn't it?"

"Look, Mr President," Roman said. His voice was tight, dangerous. Margot had heard the tone before—it never ended well. "This isn't the time for this. Doerr's made his case. But we're talking to an agent in the field. She can't be hearing this kind of doubt when she's supposed to be focused on staying alive—"

"*Doubt?*" Doerr interjected.

"*Hummingbird* re-established contact," Roman continued. "That's what we wanted. Now, we need to act on it. Not run away."

"Listen," Margot said. "I've worked this woman for years. I know what she values. How she thinks. She wouldn't risk all this unless it was absolutely real."

There was a moment's silence, and Roman said, "Mr President?"

The president sounded very tired. "If this blows back, I'm the one explaining body bags to the nation."

"It won't come to that," Roman said.

Another beat, then the president added, "That's your assessment, then, Roman? We need this badly enough to risk triggering Chichikov?"

Margot waited for Roman's response but all she heard was more deafening silence. At last, she said, "Hello?"

"We're here," Roman said.

"I thought the call dropped."

Gabriella's voice cut through. Cool. Unyielding. "If we walk now, we don't just lose *Hummingbird*—we tell every asset we've ever run that we don't keep faith."

"Remember who we're talking about," Margot added. "Without her, who knows where the Russian Army would be right now. Warsaw? Berlin? Budapest?"

The president's voice. "It's your call, Roman."

"Margot," Roman started, "if this costs your life—"

Margot hung up. Final. Like a guillotine.

24

Toko tapped a nervous rhythm on the wheel with one hand, flipping his phone in the other like a gambler shuffling a deck. The engine was off so he wouldn't be spotted, and it was cold enough that he could see his breath in the air. When the phone buzzed, it startled him.

"What the hell's taking so long?" he growled. "It's almost daylight."

"It's the Moscow guys."

"Trouble?"

"They've disabled the security cameras at the fuel yard, and they think they've disabled the fence."

"They *think*?"

"Best to double-check before touching it. There's a multimeter in the bag."

"Why don't you tell Moscow to sharpen their pencils. We wanted this done while it was still dark, right?"

"They're watching by satellite. They say it's clear."

"And God knows they've never made a mistake."

"Am I detecting sarcasm?"

"I just wasted thirty minutes for no reason. I mean, everything at the plant depends on the same guys, right? This isn't just about spoiling some diesel fuel."

"Of course it isn't."

"Then they better have their shit together."

"Just focus on your own job, Toko. Easy as pie."

Sure—if pie was laced with C-4.

"You could do this in your sleep," Morozov added.

"Flattery. Now I *know* I'm in trouble."

"Place the triggers. One in each tank. Moscow will take care of the rest."

"That's the way you want it done, then? Not the sugar? Not the nitroglycerin?"

"Moscow says triggers. That's all they need, and it gives them control over the timing."

"The timing of what?"

"One other thing," Morozov said, ignoring the question. "The waitress from the diner—local cops have a report out—"

Toko killed the call. That memory was already locked away where he wouldn't see it.

He stepped out of the jeep and breathed in the icy air. The sleet had finally stopped, but the temperature had dropped too. It was causing a thin mist to rise from the ground like a miasma. He slipped the pistol into his coat, slung the rifle over his shoulder, grabbed the carryall, and set off into the trees.

The fuel yard was a mile from where he'd parked and the sky brightened as he pushed through forest and undergrowth. By the time he reached the fence, he didn't need a flashlight.

He tossed the carryall down and eyed the chainlink. Yellow signs every twenty yards showed a lightning bolt and the words *Danger of Death* in block letters. What was less clear was whether or not it had been disabled.

He eyed it cautiously. There were simpler ways to test a fence, but they weren't recommended while standing in a pool of water, which he was, and Morozov had said there was a multimeter in the bag. He took it out and turned the dial to the voltage setting. Standing on a rise slightly less sodden than the rest of the ground, he shut his eyes and touched the probe to the wire.

Nothing happened. The world didn't end.

The multimeter read zero. Either it was broken, or the Moscow boys had done one thing right.

He pulled on insulated mitts, grabbed the bolt cutters, and snipped through the wire of the fence. No sparks. No fireworks. He quickly cut a two-foot opening and squeezed through, pulling the bag behind him.

Another fifty yards of undergrowth, then the forest opened onto a wide clearing. The floodlights were still on, though there was light enough to see without them. What they illuminated was exactly what he'd been told would be there—a fueling yard with three large diesel tanks, as well as an assortment of vehicles, forestry equipment, and two corrugated steel storage sheds. There was no sound, no sign of any workers or guards. The vehicles were all off and the doors to the sheds were shut and locked.

Silent.

In his experience, silence was often the sound of ambush, right before it happened.

From what he could piece together—not that anyone had told him—these tanks fueled the plant's backup cooling system. They weren't a primary system, but rather, fueled a series of backup water pumps that were capable of operating in an emergency independently of the grid. Sabotaging them, if Toko was reading between the lines correctly, would give Moscow the ability to take out the plant's cooling system while the river was high. And with the storm and the damaged dam, he was guessing the river was high.

As far as he could tell, the only reason to do all of this was to cause a core meltdown.

And a core meltdown was the big one. The kaboom. A mushroom cloud. It was what people imagined when they thought of nuclear reactors exploding.

Toko didn't know exactly how far Moscow was willing to take it—actually trigger a meltdown, or just threaten it. He didn't know whether the intent was leverage, or mass murder.

What he did know was that if meltdown really was the goal, it would dwarf everything that had come before. Ukraine would be a footnote. The Twin Towers and Pearl Harbor would look like traffic accidents.

Toko's name would be in the history books, right next to Gavrilo Princip and Osama Bin Laden. Men who'd pushed over the dominos that made history. Men who'd sparked wars.

It was enough to get his heart racing.

As the mist cleared, he saw that around the perimeter of the yard, serious-looking military-grade security cameras sat on top of tall poles, protected by a ring of razor wire halfway up. Toko had no choice but to take Morozov's word that they'd been disabled.

Seeing no sign of any other presence, he moved quickly into the clearing, running at a half-crouch. When he got to the first tank, he stopped. Standing with his back to it, he surveyed the yard again. No movement. No sound. All clear.

Each tank was a massive steel cylinder on a concrete pad, filled with twenty-five thousand gallons of diesel. There was a metal ladder running up the side, the rungs encased in ice. He climbed with the carryall on one shoulder and the rifle on the other. Twice, he almost slipped but held on. Once on top, he kept low to avoid creating a silhouette.

The tank was accessed by a round, carbon steel hatch with a corrosion-resistant, x-shaped handle protruding from the top. Next to the handle was an analog pressure gauge, and next to that was an electronic security indicator. The light on the indicator was blinking red—hopefully thanks to something Moscow had done.

He first checked the pressure gauge and, using the relief valve, brought the pressure inside the tank down to a safer level. Then he turned his attention to the hatch. Ordinarily, it would be locked, but putting his trust again in Moscow, he grabbed hold of the handle and heaved against it. It didn't move. It didn't even seem like it could be moved. He tried a second time, again to no avail, then dug into the carryall for a pipe wrench. He attached the clamp of the wrench to the handle, and, using all his might, drove his weight against it. This time, it budged, and when he rocked on it, it budged again, then opened all at once with a loud whoosh of air. He almost lost his footing but steadied himself.

He took off the unwieldy mitts and began setting the detonator. Handling it like a nervous waiter holding a laden tray, he affixed it to a hook on the inside of the hatch so that it would rest just a few inches above the fuel.

Satisfied, he closed the hatch, twisted the handle until it locked, and re-pressurized the tank. One tank rigged. Enough diesel to drown a small town. Whenever they wanted, Moscow could blow the whole thing to smithereens. He repeated the process at the two other tanks, everything identical, but just as he was finishing, he heard what he'd been dreading the entire time—the sound of an approaching engine.

He lay down flat on the tank, out of view, and pulled the rifle from his shoulder. The scope was a Leupold, basic but up to the task. He aimed at a white pickup truck bearing with the logo of the power company. It pulled up to the gate and stopped, engine idling, headlights on. A beat passed.

Toko remained deathly still, sleeve over his mouth to hide his breath. When the gate opened, he kept his sights on the truck's windshield, driver's side, tracing it as it rolled slowly into the yard.

It came to a halt where Toko's tracks from the forest crossed its path. Another pause. Toko's finger caressed the trigger.

The door opened, and a man in bright orange coveralls stepped out, eyes fixed on the footprints. His eyes followed Toko's path from the forest toward the tanks. The clockwork of his mind was visible as he reached for the radio at his waist.

Toko squeezed the trigger.

One shot dropped him. A second to the head finished it. Two unsilenced cracks in the night air. Impossibly loud. Then quiet.

Toko climbed down the ladder, ran over, and dragged the body ten yards into the undergrowth, a pink trail of blood staining the snow behind him. Nothing he could do about that now.

He took the man's radio, then climbed into the truck. The key was in the ignition. He turned it, revved once, and took off.

25

They called it *getting black*, and it was tradecraft 101.

For Margot, it meant reaching the Pushkin without a tail and, more importantly, without the FSB realizing she'd given them the slip on purpose. That was the crucial part, the element that separated the rookies from the pros, and if she couldn't manage, she could kiss any meeting with Irina goodbye.

The slightest whiff that she was up to something and the FSB would flood the zone with agents. And if that happened, Irina would go to ground for sure. She'd never risk a meet under those conditions.

So Margot steeled herself before leaving the hotel room, focused, concentrated on the task at hand. Even now, hours before she made her move, she was preparing.

She left the room without her luggage, dressed in the flamboyant Balenciaga coat and ski goggles. When she caught her reflection in the elevator doors, she felt more like an extra from *Zoolander* than an active spy. She tousled her hair, and, despite her better judgement, liked it.

When she reached the lobby, she scanned every face,

certain she'd see some of them again later. The FSB didn't mess around when it came to surveillance of foreigners. Even a translator would be assigned a team.

"Checking out?" the concierge said from behind his desk.

"Actually, no," she said, wondering if he was one of them. "I'll keep the room another night."

"I'll make a note."

"And call me a cab, would you?"

He picked up the phone. "Where to?"

She eyed him carefully. Would a concierge ask that? "The embassy," she said.

"American?"

Now, he was overplaying it. She'd checked in with an American passport. "How'd you guess?" she said.

He looked down at his screen.

At the embassy, she had a meeting with a woman named Clarissa Grey. Foxtrot had found her—she wasn't CIA—but she was a near-perfect match for Margot's stats. Height, weight, coloring, facial features, the works.

"It's a very short walk," the concierge said.

"What's that?"

"The embassy."

Margot looked out at the Garden Ring, the ten-lane ring road that served Moscow's central core. The morning traffic was heavy and fast-moving. Speeding buses sprayed slush right up onto the sidewalks.

"I think a cab," she said.

She crossed the lobby to the entrance, where the bellhop ushered up her car and opened the door. She knew it was probably a plant—but that didn't matter. Not yet. She was still doing the expected. Laying the pattern. Playing it straight.

The cab joined the rush of the Presnensky traffic, which included more than its share of federal security vehicles, and Margot kept a close eye out for her tail. At this point, she would have been more worried if she didn't spot one.

"Everything okay?" the driver said when she looked out the rear window for the fifth time.

"Fine," she said, finally spotting the regulation three-series.

This game of cat and mouse felt new but it wasn't. She was too young to remember the Cold War days, when every foreigner in Moscow could safely assume they were being tailed from the moment they stepped off their plane at Sheremetyevo until the moment they got back on board to fly home. In those days, Central Moscow was the ultimate denied area, and everyone, from the man smoking *Troikas* at the bus stop to the girl buying a magazine at the newsstand, was a potential KGB agent.

Dry cleaning, the art of shaking tails, was elevated to a high art in those years. The CIA came up with all sorts of tricks—from prosthetic noses and silicone masks to daring maneuvers like the bailout, the jack-in-the-box, ghost cars, and false trails.

Legend maintenance—making them believe you were who you pretended you were—was a matter of life and death.

Now, those days were back. All the old tricks were being dusted off and repurposed for a new generation. Margot knew that if she was going to survive, she would have to get creative.

Hence the Balenciaga coat, the bleached hair—and now, the body double Foxtrot had found for her in the consular section. And all just to get to a coffee shop without being tailed.

The Honeytrap

The cab exited the Garden Ring onto a small side street and pulled up in front of the embassy's main gate. Ahead of them was an imposing fortified entrance, protected by large concrete blocks that forced vehicles to stop and maneuver awkwardly to get through. Entering the compound required cars to pass a twelve-foot retractable gate, submit to a security check in a tight sally port overlooked by armed marines, then pass the second gate.

Short of an all-out assault, no one was getting through.

"Pull up here," Margot said, pointing to the pedestrian entrance a hundred yards farther along.

She got out, walked up to the guards with her false credentials in hand, and was met by a fresh-faced marine lavishly doused in what she recognized to be Calvin Klein cologne.

"Hold on, hold on," he said as she hurried up.

"I'm American."

"Yeah, so was the Unabomber."

He led her into the reinforced security post, where she was patted down and scanned by an airport-style metal detector, as well as a more elaborate millimeter wave scanner. Her purse went through an X-ray machine.

"All right," another guard said, taking her credentials and scanning them. He held up the passport, checking the photo against the one on his screen, and said, "You're expected, but it says here you're to check in with protocol first."

"What's the problem?" she said, giving him what she hoped was a flirtatious smile, though it probably came across as more of a facial spasm. "Can't you just give me the pass? I'm kind of in a hurry."

He looked at her, then down at his keyboard. "I'm sorry, Miss...."

"Please, call me Peggy."

"Peggy," he said, clearing his throat.

"Just sign me in as a guest."

"It says here you're a translator."

Another voice then, though she didn't immediately see where it was coming from—"Something the matter there?"

A face appeared from below counter-level, belonging to a very short man who'd just stepped up onto a platform behind the terminal. "I'll take it from here, Johnny."

Margot recognized him immediately—a nemesis from a previous visit—Napoleon Bonaparte. Not his real name, obviously, but what he went by in her mind.

"Great," she muttered.

"What's that?" Napoleon said.

"Nothing," she said.

He began typing officiously on the keyboard, clacking the keys like little hammers. Then he examined her credentials very closely. What he knew, and the previous guard hadn't, was that the name she was traveling under was different from the one she'd used the last time she'd visited the embassy. "Will you be staying with us long, Miss *Pechvogel*?"

He knew she had CIA credentials, though the secrecy of her mission meant she wasn't there under Moscow Station jurisdiction. He also knew that she probably had no idea how long she'd be staying, and likely wouldn't be using the lodgings he was about to assign her. "I don't know," she said tersely.

"Well, I need to put something on the form."

"Put '*don't know*' on the form."

He squinted. "'*Don't know*' isn't one of the options."

"Put a week then. I don't care."

"Will it *be* a week?"

She smiled at him, giving him the same squinted expression he'd given her. "If you want it to be."

He chewed his lip, then filled out the rest of the form, pounding the keyboard with his stubby fingers. Eventually, he printed her a pass and lanyard.

"Does Clarissa Grey live on-compound?" she asked.

"Clarissa?"

"Grey."

"Spell Grey."

He had to know. Headcount at the embassy had been reduced from almost thirteen hundred, to just over three. It wasn't that many names to remember, and Grey wasn't exactly a hard one to remember. Nevertheless, she spelled it out.

He typed it into his computer and said, "No, she has an apartment off-site."

"Perfect," Margot said, attaching the lanyard to her purse strap. A moment later, Calvin Klein was leading her through to the compound proper. They crossed a concrete courtyard before getting to the main building, known sensibly enough as the New Office Building to distinguish it from its predecessor. The old one had been so riddled with bugs and so irradiated with microwaves that Gerald Ford's ambassador reportedly started bleeding from his eyes during his posting. He later died of leukemia, along with a number of his staff.

His fate pretty much summed up Margot's view on US-Russia diplomacy, which was to say, the whole thing was a sham. A farce. A game of make-believe.

There was one language, and one language only, that the superpowers understood, and that was the language of mutually assured destruction. That was the unspoken subtext to their every interaction, and it hadn't changed since the days of Stalin. They each had their red line, and if the other party ever crossed it, the ultimate recourse wasn't diplomatic, it was the complete destruction of both civilizations. That was the backstop. The final word. The backup plan for resolving grievances.

It had been that way since before Westfahl or Chichikov ever drew their first breath. And they weren't young men. It was what rendered all other aspects of the relationship—all treaties and conventions and summits—utterly moot.

That was why Margot always felt conflicted when she entered the embassy. She was smart enough to know that in an ideal world, people like her wouldn't exist. She'd read the history books. When the Founders framed the Constitution, they'd never envisioned anything like what she did. They'd dreamed of a future in which nations ordered their affairs through the noble practices of statecraft and diplomacy, and they'd intended for America to be foremost among them in virtue.

The possibility of war was foreseen, but as a last resort.

And there categorically was no third option, no *tertio optio*.

No legal and moral *demimonde* of subversion, assassination, extraordinary rendition, and targeted killing. Such things were *unAmerican*, unworthy of the world's newest, bravest democracy.

Their idealism, if it ever truly existed, died its death in the Second World War.

Death camps, industrial extermination, millions of people turned to ash, and the looming specter of a still worse future war against a nuclear-armed Soviet Union meant the ideals of men in wigs could no longer trump necessity. The yawning gulf between the world of the diplomats—with their *démarches* and ambassadorial notes—and the world of GIs being blown to bits on beaches, and civilians being shoved into crematoria, could no longer be denied.

The world wasn't a concert of nations. It was a pit fight—and no one got out until someone hit the ground.

It was in the shadow of Auschwitz, of Stalingrad, of Hiroshima and Nagasaki, that the ideals were finally laid to rest and America's intelligence agencies were permanently constituted.

Margot knew it wasn't the diplomats who kept the wolves at bay. It wasn't the politicians and the handshakes for the flashing cameras.

It was her. And Roman. And Foxtrot.

Their ilk. Their people.

"This is as far as I go," the marine said when they reached the lobby. "You can take it from here?"

"If I run into trouble," she said, "I know where to find you."

26

Oksana slipped into her Russian literature class fifteen minutes late. Professor Dillon Bennet caught her in the act and looked almost pleased to have an excuse to pounce.

"Ah, Ms Tchaikovskaya. How nice of you to join us."

"So sorry," she said, squinting toward the stage lights in the otherwise dark auditorium. The entire class turned to look back at her.

"Trouble sleeping?" he asked, feigning concern.

She said nothing. Bennet was young for a professor—maybe a decade older than she was—and easily one of the least shabby members of Columbia's humanities faculty. With rimmed glasses and an elbow-patched blazer, he pulled off the GQ-academic look annoyingly well.

She gave him a thin smile, thinking he might let her be, but then he said, more to the students in the front row than to her, "Late night, I imagine."

There was a smattering of laughter and Oksana felt a flush of embarrassment rise to her cheeks. She knew what he was doing—and why. More than once, she'd bumped into him on the campus bar circuit. She liked to drink alone. He, on the other hand, was more of the chatty type, especially when he was half in the bag. He also wasn't one to let the university's strict student-faculty dating policy prevent him from making a move. He came on so strong she'd been forced to tell him, in no uncertain terms, to back off. It was fair to say that things had been frosty between them ever since.

The auditorium wasn't small, it could have held over a hundred students, but this class only had thirty. They were clustered in the first few rows, within the catchment of the lights overhanging the podium, and Bennet said, "Let's not have you back there in Siberia, Oksana. Come join the rest of us in the light."

By now, the lecture had well and truly lost its momentum, and the rest of the students watched her, eager for a little drama. They were all Russian majors and had spent the better part of the past three years in the same handful of classes with her. They knew her. They knew her temper and sharp tongue, too. This time, she was determined not to give them a show. "I'm fine back here," she said tersely.

But Bennet wasn't ready to let it go. "Really, I insist."

Oksana looked at him, then at the faces of her classmates. They weren't a bad lot. That she had no friends among them said more about her than them. She sighed, knowing resistance would only drag it out, and made her way down to the fourth row.

"No, no," Bennet said, indicating a seat in the center of the front row. "Here's a better spot."

She hesitated again, then complied. Half a dozen students had to stand to let her get by, and when she was finally in her seat, Bennet gave her a satisfied look.

"Comfortable, are we?" he asked, like a dentist admiring his own handiwork.

"Sorry about this," she muttered to no one in particular, opening her backpack.

"Maybe next time, if you don't show up so late—"

"I won't," she said.

He shook his head, letting his gaze linger on her like he was trying to think of something more to say. She stared back defiantly until he turned his attention to the presentation screen behind him. "Okay, as I was saying before we were so rudely interrupted, this story is going to come up in the final, so you need to be thinking about it now."

The students returned to their note-taking and Bennet proceeded to hold forth on the deeper meanings of Turgenev's short story, *Mumu*, which they'd been working on for weeks. Oksana tried to listen, but her mind kept wandering back to the art gallery. She wasn't just nervous. She'd cased harder targets. But something about this one—the setup, the stakes—was off. Like the stillness before a trap snaps shut. She knew she should walk. But it wasn't just a job.

It was that most Russian of dishes.

Revenge.

"What's Turgenev trying to say here about Russian society?" Bennet said. "What's he telling us about the cruelty of the Russian social order under the tsars?"

His eyes landed on Oksana, and she thought she would have to speak but she was spared when the girl next to her said, "It's a story about powerlessness."

"Powerlessness?" Bennet said.

"The serf...."

"Gerasim," Bennet offered. Gerasim was the story's protagonist—a serf who'd been forced to kill a beloved dog.

"Right," the girl said. "Gerasim is deaf. He's mute. Those disabilities symbolize his powerlessness. The powerlessness of all serfs."

It was a familiar theme. The story's political symbolism was well-trodden ground—the reason it had been required reading in Soviet times.

But Oksana wasn't thinking about Turgenev. She was thinking about the gallery, the alarm system—cameras, motion sensors, glass-breaks. Modern security systems weren't her thing. Give her a tension wrench and a stubborn old safe and she was in her element. But circuit boards? Not so much. If she couldn't disarm it, her only option would be to outrun the alarm.

A dangerous proposition when Muldowney's meatheads —with their kevlar and carbines—were on the job.

"What about you?" Bennet said to a student in the row behind Oksana. "What's your take?"

"I think it's a story of submission," the student said. "Gerasim loves his dog. It's the only thing he loves in the world, the only pure thing he has in his entire life, but when the rich lady orders him to kill it, he obeys her."

"The ultimate act of submission," Bennet said, his eyes locking on Oksana's. "To kill what you love most."

Again, Oksana held his gaze. If he was looking for an act of submission, he wasn't going to find any from her.

"Gerasim submits," another student added, "but then he rebels. He breaks free. It's not submission, it's rebellion."

"Rebellion?" Bennet said skeptically, still looking at Oksana. "Do you really think Gerasim manages to escape his *boyar* masters?"

The woman who forced Gerasim to kill his dog was a member of the class, and a symbol of it.

"At the beginning of the story," the student continued,

"Turgenev calls Gerasim an ox. At the end, he calls him a lion. There's a triumph in that transformation."

"Maybe," Bennet said, "but let's not oversimplify. The story was written during a time of major upheaval—the serfs were about to be emancipated. There's class struggle in every line. But Turgenev wasn't just a social critic. He was a chronicler of the human condition. Our job is to see these characters not just as symbols but as people. To ask what their struggles tell us about ourselves."

He was looking directly at Oksana now, as if his words were solely for her. "You believe in literature, don't you? You wouldn't be in this room otherwise. So let me ask you this—do you really believe in the soul of someone like Gerasim? Can you wear his skin? Feel his blood in your veins. Or are you just pretending?"

Their eyes locked, and, despite herself, Oksana blurted, "Of course I believe in him."

Bennet held her in his gaze. "Oh?" he said. "You sound very sure of that."

"You're seriously asking if I can know the soul of a man who must sacrifice the one thing he loves? Who of us couldn't relate to that? Who of us couldn't relate to a bitter old widow or any of the other characters in the story? Would any of us even be in this room, studying two-hundred-year-old literature, if we didn't believe that our own souls had something in common with the characters in these stories?"

Bennet couldn't prevent a smile from crossing his lips. "Perhaps," he said, "as the only real Russian in the room—"

She felt a flash of anger. "Surely you're not suggesting that the location of a maternity ward has anything to do with—"

She stopped mid-sentence. He'd been baiting her since the moment she'd entered the room, and she was biting.

"Don't stop now," he said. "You were just getting started."

She looked at him and found herself wondering if there was more to him than she'd initially thought. Maybe she should have gone home with him after all.

"Go on," he prodded. "Say what you're thinking."

"No," she said.

"Afraid you might say something you can't take back? Something you're not ready to admit?"

"What are you talking about?"

There was a look on his face, simultaneously intriguing and infuriating. "Drop your guard, Oksana. Say what you're feeling. Put it on the line. For once."

Her jaw clenched. She couldn't help herself. "All right," she said. "I'll tell you what I'm thinking. They're alone. They're all alone."

"Now we're getting somewhere."

"Gerasim, the widow, Tatiana, every one of them. It doesn't matter if they're rich or poor, powerful or weak, none of them has anyone to love. The widow lost her husband. Gerasim loses his dog. He falls for Tatiana but she refuses him, she's afraid of him, and then she marries someone she doesn't love. They're all alone. All in the same pot, and it's slowly coming to a boil."

"*Coming to a boil?*" Bennet said, enunciating the words as if he'd never heard them before.

"We're alone," Oksana said. "We're born alone. We live alone. We die alone. That's not literature. That's life."

Bennet leaned back, satisfied with the performance. Every student in the room was staring at her.

Oksana rose and slung her bag over one shoulder. "If we're done playing Socrates, I've got somewhere to be."

27

Morozov stood in his thirteenth-floor office and looked out at the sprawling American metropolis. He liked New York, sure—but he'd never been one of those Russians who bent over backward to keep a foreign posting. He'd take a Moscow penthouse—with Beluga Gold vodka and a gaggle of Tverskaya prostitutes—over the charms of Manhattan any day.

There was a knock on the door from his secretary. He'd hired her for her looks, though it had been an online hiring process. She'd been in Moscow at the time, and he'd had to interview her via video call. She'd looked better on the computer, he thought. She'd been friendlier, too. She'd only been in New York three weeks and had already turned down his advances more times than any God-fearing secretary had a right to. What was he going to do with her? He had no need of a secretary who didn't know how to bend over a desk. He'd just have to wear her down like he'd done with all the others, he supposed.

"We just received this," she said, handing him a printout. "It's marked urgent."

He brushed her hand deliberately. "Thank you, Nadia."

She nodded and was already retreating from the room when he said, "It says here it was received fifteen minutes ago?"

"I'm sorry, sir, we were—"

"Don't they teach you what *urgent* means in secretary college?"

"They do, sir."

"Maybe you need a little discipline," he said, his voice oozing like motor oil. "A proper secretary knows how to take instructions."

She remained where she was, chin raised slightly—just enough to register contempt—then turned and walked out without a word. He had half a mind to chase after her, but he unfolded the notice instead.

It was from the Office of Countersurveillance, and he couldn't remember the last time they'd sent him anything even remotely urgent. In his estimation, they had the easiest job in the Mission.

In Russia, the FSB had 170,000 active agents, not counting the *Sluzhba Kontrrazvedki*, the DKRO, or the 12th Directorate's tech teams. Thousands of eyes watching Americans every minute of every day—tailing cars, tapping phones, hacking emails, and bugging hotel rooms and embassy toilets. If an American ordered pizza in Moscow, an FSB plant delivered it. And if they even tried to leave the city —well, there was no way. It simply wouldn't happen. They did not roam freely.

America, on the other hand.

Take Toko, for example. He'd entered the country on a false passport, but it was still a Russian document. He'd met a known Russian operative a block from the Mission without the slightest effort to hide the fact. And the FBI?

Not even a single man in a Crown Vic had been tasked with the job.

Did they even want to win?

As usual, for all their big talk, they weren't wearing any trousers. They still hadn't faced up to the most basic tradeoff in all of politics. Freedom vs control. Democracy vs security. They thought freedom was a strength. He knew better. There was no way they could compete with a full-blown police state.

It never ceased to amaze Morozov that they'd apparently thrown in the towel. They simply weren't playing to win anymore. They'd used to when he was younger. But not now.

Their diplomatic presence was supposed to be reciprocal, too. Tit for tat. But Russia still had two consulates outside DC, as well as the Mission in New York, while the US consulates in Vladivostok and Yekaterinburg had long since been strangled out of existence.

Staffing levels at the Moscow embassy had been reduced from over a thousand to just a few hundred in the space of five years. They didn't even have enough marines for their security. They supplemented with Russians.

While in the US, the FBI didn't even know how many Russians were in the country.

And there were a lot.

All of which was to say, Morozov lost very little sleep worrying about the reports of his Office of Countersurveillance, even with an operative like Toko running amok.

As he scanned the printout, however, he saw that it wasn't about the FBI. It was about Gabriella Wintour—the US National Security Advisor. That was something new. They rarely concerned themselves with cabinet officials. The report noted that she was a Russia hawk, though that hardly meant anything. Everyone was hawkish these days. It also contained information on her Secret Service detail, including the identities of the agents likely to be serving on it, the name of her driver, and schematics of her vehicle, her office, and her home. Additionally, it contained profiles on her ex-husband, her ex-husband's new wife, her teenage daughter, and even her elderly housekeeper.

Morozov didn't like it.

Politics—and blood.

Never a good mix.

On a yellow sticky note on the cover, his secretary had written a phone number. He stared at it a moment. Moscow.

Trouble.

He dialed, and the call immediately began working its way through re-routing procedures that would make its ultimate destination untraceable, including to Morozov. More secrecy.

That was another thing that was bothering him about all this.

He still didn't even know where Toko's operation was originating from. He had Toko roaming the country, sabotaging infrastructure, playing with nuclear plants, and none of the orders had come to him through official channels. All he really knew—and this, he'd divined from the format of the authorization codes rather than from anything he'd been told—was that the entire operation was originating not in Yasenevo or *The Forest*, as he'd told Toko, but from the *Sovbez* itself. That made it all the more sensitive, and all the more political.

"This is Morozov," he said when the phone finally picked up.

"Ah," the voice on the other end said. "So you received my little parcel?" The voice was being distorted through a modulator, another unusual precaution that was raising Morozov's already heightened suspicions still further.

"I'm looking at a report from the Office of Countersurveillance," he said, "if that's what you're referring to."

"It's Gabriella Wintour's personal security detail."

"Right," Morozov said, feeling distinctly disadvantaged by the asymmetry of information. He didn't like taking anonymous orders, and something told him this wasn't just a briefing. It was a setup. And he was the one being led in. "What do you want me to do with it?"

"Surely you don't want me to spell it out."

"I think you'd better," Morozov said firmly.

"Well, you can see that there are multiple options for a strike, but we think the house makes for the softest target. The property backs onto a wooded area. There's no one watching it there. She's also divorced, which means there won't even be a man in the house."

"You're not suggesting I break into the home of the National Security Advisor?"

"That's exactly what we're suggesting."

"I don't... I can't...."

"You can't what?"

"I don't have the manpower. This kind of thing takes weeks of—"

"Your man in Virginia has proven to be efficient. What's his name?"

"Toko?"

"Yes, Toko Gromovich Sakhalinsky. It says here he's done everything on our list. The power plant disruptions are going better than planned. Our cyber warfare team has confirmed that the water levels on the James River are higher than at any point since the plant's construction. And the fuel for the backup pumps has been—"

"Toko's a hundred miles away from Washington. He's already heading for a private jet that will extract—"

"The jet's in New Jersey, is it not?"

"It is, but—"

"Well, he'll be driving right by DC then."

"Yes, but he has to get out now. He's compromised."

"I know about his nasty habit," the man said. "The waitress in New York. The Punjabi cab driver. I know he can't help himself."

"That's why I need him out."

"We're hardly going to reward him for this disgusting behavior, are we?"

"I'm not talking about rewarding him. I just want him out of the country so his shit can't blow back on us."

"On you."

"On the entire Committee."

"No, no," the man said. "Nothing's going to blow back on anyone. Toko's going to do this last job, then he can get on his jet. To be honest with you, he'll probably enjoy it. There's a daughter involved. His profile says he has a proclivity for—"

"What is this job, exactly?" Morozov said. "It says here you have the cell phone of the daughter's boyfriend?"

"Yes, she's smitten. She's going to leave some doors unlocked. Some lights turned on. That sort of thing."

"So Toko can get into the house?"

"Now you're catching on. Honestly, I don't see why they say you're slow, Morozov. You seem perfectly sharp to me."

"Who says I'm slow?"

There was some laughter then, a throaty guffaw that sounded positively evil through the modulator, like the leader of the *Decepticons* in the children's cartoon. Then it cut off, replaced by a sudden seriousness. "Now, Morozov, this visit he's going to pay Wintour, it's not all fun and games."

"I never thought it was," Morozov said.

"Her office distributed a memo last night. Something for the Security Council only. Top Secret."

"And you got your hands on it?"

"It mentioned a mole, Morozov. A mole close to Chichikov."

Morozov didn't blink. But inside, something shifted. Something very close to fear.

"Did it say who the mole was?"

"Only a codename."

"I'm listening?"

"*Hummingbird.*"

Morozov stood very still. The room felt colder somehow. Outside, the city blinked like nothing had changed—but it had.

28

Sheryl Cassidy hadn't left bed all morning. The television had her in a trance—unshowered, still in pajamas, oblivious to the rising chaos downstairs.

"Mom!" her five-year-old son called from the kitchen. "Harley spilled Cheerios."

Harley, her eight-year-old daughter, was usually the tidy one. If she was being ratted out for spilling, it was a sign things were getting out of hand.

"Did not," Harley shouted. "I cleaned it up, Mom!"

"I'll be down in a minute," Sheryl cried, even now distracted by the footage on the TV. "I'll make waffles."

On the screen, a field reporter for the local news channel was struggling to deliver a story from a windswept parking lot. She was holding an umbrella in one hand and a mic in the other, and with each gust, the umbrella threatened to take flight. It wasn't even pretending to keep her dry.

—I'm coming to you live from the Emergency Operations Center here in Newport News, and it has been a night of absolute bedlam down here. There are reports of widespread flooding and power outages. People are already calling it the storm of the century. I'm being joined by Chris Whittaker, the city's Emergency Management Coordinator, to get the latest.

The camera panned across a squat, brick building with the words *Public Works* printed above the doors. There were two fire trucks in front of it, and emergency responders were hurrying in every direction. A local official with a winter coat pulled inelegantly over his suit stood next to the reporter, holding the hood of the coat to prevent the wind from blowing it off his head.

—Mr Whittaker, there have been reports of absolute chaos from every department. There's flooding, power outages, car accidents, road closures, and now they're saying that emergency responders can't get where they're needed most. What can you tell us about that?

—Well, look, Cathy, our first responders are doing a hell of a job out there, and that's what they've been doing through a night that—frankly, if I can say so—has been hell for them.

—But what have you got to say to residents who can't get through on the emergency lines. I mean, the operators are down, they're calling 911 and no one's picking up. The system seems to have completely collapsed at the most basic level.

—I don't want to downplay it, Cathy. We've had issues.

—*Issues*? With all due respect, we're in crisis

mode. People can't leave their homes, if they even have a home that hasn't been flooded or cut off from power. There are evacuations in some areas, and what about these reports that there may be some sort of cyberattack?

—A cyberattack?

—We've had 911 operators saying their systems are down because of a massive, coordinated cyberattack. What's the story there?

—Look, Cathy, I'm afraid that's above my pay grade. What we need now are cool heads so that our responders can get out there and do their jobs.

—Well, these reports are saying the attacks are hitting strategic emergency response systems across the city and have been coordinated to create as much chaos as possible.

—All I can say is that we're stretched very thin, and we're doing our utmost, our absolute *utmost*, to keep the residents of this city safe during an extreme weather event that struck without warning and that's wreaking havoc on our flood controls, and on systems across multiple states.

—Right, flood controls, and what about reports that all three bridges over the James River have now been shut to traffic and that Interstate 64 northbound is so jammed that nothing's moving? People can't get out. They're just sitting there in their cars for hours.

—Look, I can't advise on road closures at this juncture.

—Are we in danger of being cut off here, Mr Whittaker? Are we going to be stranded in a city that's flooding, that's losing power? On Christmas Eve?

"Mom!"

Sheryl looked up to see her sandy-haired son, Kevin, staring at her from the doorway. There was chocolate around his mouth and chocolaty finger marks on his pajamas. "Kevin, what did you get into?"

"Nutella," he said with a grin.

He'd been named after Kevin McCallister in *Home Alone*, and for a brief second, she imagined him left behind in something far worse than a suburban burglary spree. "Come here," she said. "Let's get you cleaned up."

He looked like he was going to come to her, then his face turned to mischief and he disappeared, feet thumping down the stairs.

"Tell your sister I'm going to make breakfast," Sheryl called after him, catching a glimpse of herself in the mirror.

She looked a fright—like her hair had lost a fight with an electrical socket. It got that way when she'd had trouble sleeping. She'd tried calling Harry at the plant over and over during the night. Under normal circumstances, she'd be embarrassed by the number of messages she'd left him, both on his cell and at the front desk. He'd called to tell her he was being kept overnight—not unheard of for a nuclear safety engineer—but never before had she had this much difficulty getting hold of him. She was forcing herself not to let her fears take over.

At least he'd messaged, she told herself. She'd received two short text messages during the night, one at 3.42 AM and one at 5.19 AM. She felt like she hadn't slept a wink, but she must have been asleep when those came in because she hadn't heard them, and she certainly hadn't left her phone on silent. They weren't reassuring. If anything, they echoed the chaos she'd just seen on TV—glitches, malfunctions, technical jargon.

But at least she knew he was alive. She picked up the phone and tried calling him again. It went straight to voicemail. Maybe his battery had died. She tried calling the plant too—not the official line but the receptionist's direct number. That also went to voicemail.

She let out a long, fraught sigh, then put on her robe and left the room.

"Mom!" Harley said when she got to the kitchen. The TV was on in there too, cartoons, and Kevin was watching them. Harley, on the other hand, was not. She was watching her mother. Quietly. Like she knew something was wrong but hadn't figured out yet what it was.

"One second, sweetie," Sheryl said to her. "Mommy's got to make one more phone call, then we're going to have the best breakfast ever."

Ignoring spilled milk and cereal on the floor, she went straight to the refrigerator, where Harry's work schedule was stuck to the door with the aid of a magnet advertising a lawncare company. Jack Priesenhammer was on the night shift. She punched Jeanine Priesenhammer's name into her phone and hit dial before she could talk herself out of it.

"Sheryl, I was just thinking about you."

"Have you heard from Jack?"

"Jack's right here."

"He came home?"

"No, he never made it last night. He got in a fender bender and had to go to the hospital for an X-ray."

"Oh no, is he all right?"

"He hurt his neck, but he'll live. We're on our way to the plant now, though."

"I thought the bridges were closed."

"We're going around, Sheryl."

"What do you mean, going around?"

"Believe me, I'm as flummoxed as you are, but Pete Porter called six times during the night. I had to pick Jack up from the hospital and take him directly to the plant. We went all the way to Richmond to get on the 295. It's a mess out here."

"What in God's name is going on?"

"Pete Porter's losing his head, that's what."

Sheryl heard Jack's voice in the background. "Sheryl. Can she hear me?"

"I can hear you, Jack."

"She can hear you."

"They've had crews working overtime through the night," he said. "Something to do with the cooling loop."

"The cooling loop?" Sheryl said, trying to keep the fear from her voice, if only for her daughter's sake.

"The pumps aren't responding," Jack said. "Some of the guys are whispering cyberattack. But you didn't hear that from me."

"Tell me straight, Jack," Sheryl said, lowering her voice. "Is this looking to you like a...."

"Like a what, Sheryl?"

"A BBDA, or whatever you call it?"

"BDBA," Jack corrected. "Beyond Design Basis Accident."

"Well, is it?"

"Sheryl, let's not get carried away. Anything like that, and we'd all be—"

"A Site Area Emergency?" she said, grasping for every phrase and acronym she'd ever heard as the wife of a nuclear safety engineer.

"Absolutely not, Sheryl. Anything like that, anything

even remotely like that, and we'd perform a SCRAM. A full reactor trip. Lights out."

"A shutdown?"

"Yes. Or an RSD. There are procedures upon procedures to avoid disaster, Sheryl. We'd turn the whole thing off long before any real harm was done."

"That's what you'd do?"

"Me?"

"All of you? If things were getting out of control?"

"Sheryl, we haven't looked at doing a thing like that in fifty years."

"But if worst came to worst?"

"If worst came to worst, then yes, absolutely we'd shut down the reactor. Of course we would."

"If there was a cyberattack?"

"Gosh, Sheryl, look, it's a bad storm. That's what it is. It's ice on the pump sensors, if I had to guess."

"You said the cooling loop."

"It's all the same water flow."

"But it's flooding. High water should help cool things, right? The river's freezing."

"It's more complicated than that. When the water's high, it backs up. We have to pump it out to keep it moving."

Jeanine cut in. "Sheryl, honey, none of us like these situations, but this is what we signed up for. We have to let them do their job now."

"I'm sorry, Jeanine."

"Yeah, you just need to speak to Harry. Hear his voice."

"I think so," Sheryl said, suddenly feeling a wave of emotion. She turned toward the sink, pressing the phone to her chest so no one would hear the catch in her breath. "Sorry," she said then.

"I'll tell him to call as soon as I see him," Jack said.

"You hear that, Sheryl?"

"I heard, Jeanine. I'm sorry. I'm just getting a little worked up."

"Listen," Jack said, "first thing I do, I'll get Harry to call you. First thing."

"And SCRAM the reactor," Sheryl said.

Jack let out a little laugh. "Sure, why not? SCRAM the reactor, while I'm at it."

They hung up, and Sheryl composed herself. She turned toward the counter. Harley was staring right at her. "You okay, honey?" she said to her daughter.

"Where's daddy?"

"He's at work, sweetie. Mommy's just being silly. Come on. Let's get that waffle iron plugged in. We're going to have a little breakfast party." She knew she had a can of whipped cream in the refrigerator and she reached up to the cabinet where she kept the special treats. "I've got M&M's and Reese's Pieces. What do you think—rainbow or peanut butter?"

Outside, another siren wailed—closer this time.

29

Margot stepped off the elevator onto the fifth floor—the consular section.

"Pechvogel," she said to the receptionist. "Here to see Clarissa Grey."

"Ah yes," the receptionist said, eyeing Margot's flamboyant fur coat, bleached hair, and oversized sunglasses. "We received a note from Washington a few hours ago. Ms Grey is in her office."

"Could you point me in the right direction?" Margot said, looking across the cubicles in the open-plan office.

"Of course," the receptionist said. "Just follow me."

She led Margot past a photocopier and water cooler, up to a glass-walled office with Clarissa Grey's name on the door. Inside, Margot could already see Clarissa sitting at her desk, speaking to someone on the phone.

"Thank you," she said, giving the door a light knock. "I'll take it from here."

Clarissa hung up the phone and beckoned Margot in. She entered, and then the two of them stood awkwardly for a moment, staring at each other. They could have passed for twins—same height, same build, same shoulder-length hair. The only difference was that in place of Margot's bleached white hair, Clarissa's was a more natural, sandy blonde.

"You must be Clarissa," Margot said, extending a hand.

A little less certainly, Clarissa stood up and shook it. Then they both sat, still staring at each other.

"What is it?" Margot said.

"If I'd known the gig came with a bleach job, I might've asked for hazard pay."

"Will it be a problem?"

Clarissa laughed once. "Hard to answer when you haven't met my sister."

"Is that a yes?"

"She's getting married in London in three days. I'm maid of honor."

"Ah," Margot said.

"She'll think I'm trying to steal the show."

Margot smiled. "You could dye it back," she suggested.

The woman let out a sigh. "To be honest, she was always the attention whore. Maybe I'll keep it."

"That's the spirit," Margot said.

Clarissa picked up a printout from her desk—something Foxtrot had sent ahead—and said, "So, this is CIA?"

"Yes," Margot said.

"But I'm not allowed to speak to the Station Chief?"

"You're not allowed to speak to anyone except me and the driver. The Station Chief will be read in on what he needs to know, but not by either of us."

"And you know I've never done anything like this?"

"I do," Margot said. "I'll walk you through every step."

"And it won't be dangerous?"

"Who told you that?"

Clarissa held up the printout.

"It shouldn't say that," Margot said.

"It says I'll just sit in the car."

"And look pretty," Margot added. "While helping a CIA officer disappear into the night on Russian soil."

"But it's true I'll only be a decoy?"

"Sure," Margot said. "You'll be in the car, we'll pick up a tail, and at some point, I'll jump out and the tail will stay on you."

"And I'll lead them back to your hotel."

"Yes," Margot said, "and if the Russians find out you helped a CIA officer evade surveillance, it won't end well."

"Well, the file doesn't quite spell all that out."

"It should," Margot said. "You'd be taking a risk. No doubt about it."

"I appreciate your being honest."

"And I appreciate your taking the time to hear me out."

"I don't suppose you're going to tell me what the mission's about?"

Margot smiled again. "Afraid not."

"And can you tell me what will happen if I refuse to help?"

"I'll find another way."

"You won't force me?"

"Of course not," Margot said. "That file didn't try to force your arm, did it?"

"No—it was polite. But there's volunteer, and there's *volunteer.*"

"That's right," Margot said. "So choose carefully. If you decide this isn't the job for you, we'll understand. No one's going to force you to do a thing like this, and no one's going to put a black mark on your file if you don't. We'll do it another way, and you'll never hear of it again."

"But your first choice is to go with me?"

"Yes, it is."

"And you think the plan will work?"

"You'd be surprised how easily trained surveillance teams can be tripped up. We're betting they'll follow the coat and not the woman wearing it. The plan's not any more complicated than that, and it will probably work."

"They'll follow me to the *Romanov*?"

"That's right."

"And I just wait in the room?"

"And you can't bring a cell phone, a computer, anything with Internet access."

"Right."

"You could watch the TV, I suppose."

"I don't watch Russian TV."

Margot didn't say anything. Just waited.

"I could bring this," Clarissa said, holding up a tattered Grisham paperback.

"Sure," Margot said.

"And how long do I have to stay there?"

"An hour should be enough. The Station Chief will send a driver to pick you up. You'll come back with him, and this will all be over."

"And the Russians will be none the wiser."

"If everything goes to plan."

"Now you're making me nervous."

"Good," Margot said. "You should be nervous. Means you'll be careful. You don't want to get into something like this without both eyes open."

Clarissa said nothing. The silence hung over them.

"So you'll do it?" Margot said.

Another beat.

Then, with a quiet nod—less to Margot than to herself—Clarissa opened a drawer in the desk. "Yeah," she said, pulling out a small mirror and studying her reflection. "I'll keep the hair for the wedding, too."

30

Toko pulled off the highway near Arlington and found the lot Morozov had told him about. He'd been none too pleased when Morozov gave him the assignment, either.

"Fuck this, Morozov. You told me to get to the plane."

"*The Forest* owns that plane."

"And they told you to give me this shit?"

"It's one small thing."

"It's a suicide mission."

"Look," Morozov said. "The job's over when they say it's over. No point arguing with me over it."

Toko had more he could have said, but Morozov was right—there was no point. He was arguing with the messenger.

He drove up and down the aisles of the lot, squinting through the snow for a dark blue Grand Caravan that was supposed to be waiting, fully loaded with the weapons, tools, maps, and plans necessary for the job. When he found it, it was a total heap—rust-eaten, tires bald as cue balls.

For a job this high-risk, it felt like a bad joke.

He parked next to it, slipped the pistol and silencer into his pocket, and got out. In the Dodge, a pale, sharp-eyed man sat behind the wheel, just as expected. Toko gave the window a sharp rap, catching him off guard.

The man rolled it down, exhaling a stream of smoke. "You're late."

Toko didn't bother explaining himself. "Here," he said, handing him the keys for the pickup.

"What are those?"

"What do they look like?"

"I'm coming with you," the man said flatly.

Toko stared at him, trying to place the accent. "Who told you that?"

"Morozov."

"Morozov knows I work alone."

The man shrugged. "Call him if you want."

Toko narrowed his eyes. He didn't like it. Not that a second man was a bad idea, given the mission parameters, but Morozov hadn't mentioned it. Probably because he knew what Toko's response would be.

Leaning against the Dodge, he said, "You have the briefing?"

The man passed a folder through the window and Toko tore it open. There were more details inside—drawings of Gabriella Wintour's home, a plan of the property, specifics of the security system and the Secret Service detail likely to be on-site.

"It says here there's a cell phone?" Toko said.

The man nodded. "I've got the phone. Morozov's guys are sending the messages remotely, but we can read the conversation."

"A daughter and a boyfriend?"

The man nodded.

"And you took care of the boyfriend?" Toko said, scanning the document.

"That's how we got the phone."

"When did you get him?"

"This morning. Right before I came out here."

"Killed him?"

The man nodded.

Toko tapped the folder against his palm, thinking. Reckless. Premature.

"You got a problem with that?" the man said.

"What did you do with the body?"

"Dragged him into a ditch. Parked the car. We're good."

"Oh, we're good? That's your professional opinion? Leave the corpse in a ditch and hope for the best?"

The man exhaled more smoke. Said nothing.

"How long until they find the body?"

Again, no answer.

"Take a guess," Toko said impatiently. Everything hinged on the boyfriend's body not being discovered. If it was, the job was a bust before it even started.

"We've got time," the man said. "Some hours, at least. It was a quiet place."

Toko sighed. He didn't like being dropped into a mission already in motion, and he didn't like going after such a high-profile target with so little planning. "Get out," he said.

"I already told you, I'm—"

Toko cut him off. "I'm driving."

The man hesitated, then got out, grumbling like it was a big pain in his ass.

Toko got into the driver's seat and took one of the man's cigarettes from the pack on the dashboard. The man sank heavily into the seat next to him.

"You got a light?"

The Honeytrap

The man handed him a plastic lighter.

"Stinks in here," Toko said, lighting the cigarette.

The man opened his window, and Toko threw the car into reverse. "You're Hungarian," he said as they left the lot.

"That okay with you?" the man said, lighting himself a cigarette.

They closed their windows when they got on the highway and Toko said, "You're one of Orbán's guys?"

The man sucked on his cigarette but didn't answer.

"How long have you been in the US?" Toko said.

"What does that matter?"

Toko shrugged. It didn't, he supposed. He'd been in the country himself scarcely twenty-four hours.

"No more small talk," the man said.

Toko stubbed out his cigarette against the dashboard. "Fine by me."

They drove on in silence, crossing the Potomac into a leafy, forested neighborhood north of the city. The road was windy and lined with multi-million dollar homes on both sides, set back from the road behind fences and high gates. They pulled over at the entrance to a hiking trail and looked out at their surroundings.

"This is it," Toko said, looking down the trail. "We walk that way about a mile, then cut through the woods to the back of Wintour's property. There's a fence we need to hop, then it's a clear run to the house."

"I've seen the plans," the man said.

"Then you know that we need to confirm with the daughter first."

The man pulled out the boyfriend's cell and opened the text message thread with Gabriella Wintour's fourteen-year-old daughter. On another phone, he sent a message to Morozov's computer guys saying they were in position.

The messages began flowing back and forth a minute later, showing up automatically on the screen.

> You're sure no one will see me?

No one will see. No one watches the back.

> The alarm's definitely off?

Yes!

> And the housekeeper?

In the living room. Honestly, a herd of elephants could come in, and she wouldn't notice. Just come through the garage.

> It's definitely not locked?

Oh my God! It's not Fort Knox! Just get to the garage and I'll meet you.

> Sorry. Just being paranoid.

Stop worrying. The Secret Service are out on the street. They'll never see you coming in the back.

> All right. I'll be there in fifteen. Be ready in the garage.

"Looks like we're all set," the Hungarian said.

Toko nodded. "Ever danced with the Secret Service before?"

The man said nothing.

Toko added, "It's not a contest."

"I've done similar work."

"You read the specs of the security system?"

"The girl said it's off."

"Motion sensors," Toko said, "motion-activated cameras, tamper detection on the fence, sensors on all points of entry."

"And the girl says it's off," the man said again flatly.

"She's fourteen years old," Toko said. "We need to be prepared for a surprise."

"How will we know if it's not off?"

"We won't," Toko said. "Until it's too late."

"The brief says there are only two Secret Service guys on-site."

"Right," Toko said, "but the slightest sign that something's wrong, the *slightest*, and we abort."

"Two guys. I think we can take them."

"No," Toko said, "if they know there's an intrusion, we'll be looking at a full-blown CAT within minutes."

"CAT?"

"Counter Assault Team. You sure you're ready for—"

"I'm ready."

Toko looked at him for a moment. "You know what they say in this country?"

"What do they say?"

"They say fuck around and find out."

The man nodded. "They say that in my country also."

"Then you understand. If there's a problem, we abort."

"I can't abort."

"What are you talking about?"

"Morozov has me over a barrel. He said either we find out the name of his rat, or he finishes me."

"Forget that," Toko said. "He has something on everybody, but we won't be doing him any good if we got shot up by an assault team."

"I can't abort," the Hungarian said again.

Toko looked at him a moment. He wasn't going to budge. "Suit yourself," he said. "If shit hits the fan, it's every man for himself."

"Every man for himself," the Hungarian repeated, cracking his knuckles.

Toko nodded, eyes on the treeline like he'd already seen how this whole thing played out. Two disposable pawns. That much was clear. And if he came back alone, he was fine with it.

He turned to the Hungarian. "That's how we'll play it, then. Let's go."

31

Margot stepped away from the mirror. Clarissa's reflection stared back. Two hours of makeup, a dye job, the Balenciaga coat, the Fendi sunglasses.

"We really could be twins."

"Yeah," Clarissa said quietly. "No kidding."

Margot, meanwhile, had swapped into the business suit Clarissa had worn to work—dark gray pencil skirt, blazer, long black coat, and knee-high leather boots. The boots were sensible. Flat-soled. She could run in them.

They'd spent the day drilling the plan with the driver—supplied by the Station Chief and sworn to secrecy. Every inch of the route had been memorized. The driver, Steinhauser—around thirty, born in Boston with the accent to prove it—seemed to know his stuff. He also seemed to have stepped straight off the set of *The Departed*. Margot kept wanting to ask him to say things from the film—*What's the mattah smaht ahss? Don't know any Shakespeah?*

She resisted, but it wasn't easy.

Still, he was solid—CIA-trained in evasive driving, close protection, and he knew Moscow like the back of his hand.

"You two *shaw* you're ready for this?" he said in the elevator, dropping 'R's like they were going out of fashion.

Margot just smiled at Clarissa.

They descended to the embassy's underground garage. The car was waiting—a marked government sedan with diplomatic plates and ballistic glass. No deception in the vehicle—the point was to be seen.

"This is it," Clarissa said, climbing into the back.

She took the seat behind Steinhauser and Margot slid in next to her.

"Let me move this for you," Steinhauser said, leaning over to the passenger seat.

It lurched forward, making room on the floor for Margot to crouch out of sight.

She looked up at Clarissa—Fendi sunglasses on her forehead, platinum hair glowing in the cabin light. "That look works for you."

"I was due a makeover."

"Sit tall. Don't hide. We want them to see you."

"Like bait," Clarissa said, trying to sound flippant—and failing.

Margot's stomach twisted. She'd been straight with her about the risk, had made it clear from the start. But if anything went wrong—if Clarissa was burned, captured—Margot would carry it.

Clarissa sat up straight as Steinhauser brought the car up the ramp. Once out of the lot, they headed straight for the checkpoint.

Embassy security was a patchwork of diplomacy and deterrence. The Kremlin had refused enough visas for a full Marine detachment, so a hybrid system had emerged—

Americans within the perimeter, Russian contractors beyond. This checkpoint, though, was pure US Marine Corps.

The Marine contingent was thirty strong, technically under Marine Corps command, though in practice they took their orders from the RSO, a diplomatic post answerable to the ambassador.

Their mandate was simple—protect classified material, hold the perimeter, secure evac routes if things went to hell. One thing that wasn't up for debate? Their jurisdiction ended at the embassy gate. If they ever spilled off-compound, it wouldn't just be a breach of protocol, wouldn't just be an *incident*. It would be an act of war.

Once out in the city, they'd be on their own.

Margot had coached Steinhauser on what to do at the gate—make small talk, keep it casual, give the FSB a nice long look. Steinhauser dutifully cracked a limp joke about the Patriots. No one laughed, but it was natural enough. The guard waved them through, never noticing Margot curled up on the floor, and Clarissa, following instructions perfectly, pretended to be on the phone to partially block her face.

They rolled out into the heart of darkness—the capital of the evil empire.

"All right," Margot said as they cleared the gates. "From here on out, assume every car behind us is a tail."

"I always do," Steinhauser replied.

The key was to act naturally—no glancing in mirrors, no nervous corrections, no erratic decisions. Just another American town car joining the late-night traffic.

And Steinhauser did well. Steady hands, dead expression, no mistakes. He could have been driving them to the grocery store.

"Nice and easy," Margot murmured. "We've got all the time in the world."

She tracked their progress by feel—the turns, the angles, the braking pattern—every shift in speed mapped against the exact route etched in her mind. They'd rehearsed it endlessly, but this was no dry run. Her heart was pounding.

"Passing the White House," Steinhauser said.

Not *that* White House—but a modernist hulk of marble and concrete that had once been called the House of Soviets. It had been the site of a violent coup attempt after the Soviet collapse. Tanks opened fire killing nearly two hundred. First tank rounds fired inside Moscow since the October Revolution.

As a result, it had been ground zero for FSB surveillance units ever since.

Crawling with security.

Which made it—ironically—perfect for what Margot was about to attempt. The FSB wouldn't see it coming. Who'd try something so reckless right under their noses?

That was the bet, anyway.

"Turn one," Steinhauser said coolly, turning onto a narrow side street. "Ready?"

"Ready," Margot said.

Clarissa glanced down at her. "Good luck. I mean—break a leg. Not literally."

Margot felt the car accelerate, then cut left.

"Turn two," Steinhauser said, less cool.

Another jolt of speed, a hard right. Steinhauser jammed the brakes and Clarissa leaned over and popped the door.

"Go, go, go!"

Margot didn't look. She jumped.

The car had slowed to a crawl, but the cobblestones didn't care. She hit hard—shoulder first—and rolled. One, two rotations. A stab of pain in the shoulder. Her breath left her.

Then she was still, tucked against a wall in a narrow alley between two buildings, Steinhauser and Clarissa already gone.

The alley was pitch black, but she was exposed.

She scanned it for the dumpster that was supposed to be there.

But it wasn't. Just cold cobblestones and the cover of darkness.

She pressed herself flat against the icy ground and remained still.

A Land Cruiser appeared. Big, gray, familiar. An FSB staple. It rolled past, not ten feet from where she lay, and she saw the silhouette of a man in the backseat smoking a cigarette. The butt was flicked out a crack in the window and she prayed the vehicle didn't stop.

Black against the snow, she wasn't hard to spot. Seconds passed like an eternity.

The Cruiser rolled on.

But that didn't mean she was in the clear. There was never only one tail. The real threat was the one that held back. Out of visual contact. Lying in wait.

She held her breath, watching for the glow of the second tail's headlights.

Whoever caught her now—FSB, SVR, GRU—made no difference. Everything would be over. No deals. No extraditions. No headlines.

She would be alone. Disavowed. No one would ever come for her.

She wouldn't be PNG'd—no *persona non grata,* no escorted military flight back to Washington, no press, no protest. Just—gone.

The Lubyanka was a good bet. Or some nameless dungeon.

And she'd never be heard from again.

It would be as if she'd never existed.

Doerr had been right to be cautious. If he'd gotten his way, she'd be at home in Washington right now. And it wasn't just her safety that was at stake. Every ounce of intel she'd ever absorbed, every sliver of insight, conscious or otherwise, over years of operations, would be extracted from her brain like entrails being pulled from a carcass by vultures. They'd flay her to within an inch of her life, then bring her back, just to do it again. Days would pass. Weeks.

And she would crack. Everyone cracked.

And when she did, everything she'd ever loved would burn.

Roman. Foxtrot. The Bookshop.

The whole network—ash.

Burned to a cinder.

And then, when there was nothing left to harvest, they'd put a bag over her head and shoot her with all the ceremony you'd give a rabid dog.

She remained absolutely still, breath shallow, shoulder throbbing, the cold seeping into her like an illness. But nothing came.

She lifted her head. No headlights, no footsteps, no shadows creeping in the dark.

She stood up, wet and shaking. But she was clear. Clean. In the black.

In the sky above, she searched for the shimmer of a drone, the whir of rotors, a flashing light. But the sky was empty.

The alley was silent. The city held its breath.

Moscow had lost her—for now.

32

Gabriella's phone buzzed. She looked up distractedly from the document in her hands and unlocked the screen.

> Mrs Wintour, it's Cassie. She won't come out of her room.

The message was from the housekeeper, Mrs Koeffer. Gabriella fired off a quick reply.

> She had a late night. She's probably resting.

"What's that?" Westfahl asked. Gabriella was on the settee, documents spread across the table in front of her. The president stood at the window, watching dusk fall like a curtain.

"Sorry, sir. Just my housekeeper."

"Everything okay?"

"You've had teenage daughters," she said. "You know what it's like."

"That I do," he said. "Anyone who thinks *this* job is hard, I tell them I raised four girls. That shuts them up quick."

Gabriella looked back down. The update from Moscow Station confirmed that Margot had left the embassy to meet *Hummingbird*. She'd taken no electronics, no phone. They wouldn't hear from her again until after the mission.

The president let go of the curtain. "If Doerr's right—"

"He's not right," she said too quickly.

"*If* he is—and if Chichikov finds out we've been flirting with his *lady friend*—"

"We can't think like that. We have to trust Margot now. That's the play."

Westfahl looked at his watch. "I wonder how it's going. Any word from Roman?"

"He's running point from the Bookshop, but he's sent no updates. I think the best thing you could do right now, sir, is get some rest."

Her phone buzzed again. She felt embarrassed when the president noticed.

"Go on," he said. "Pick it up."

She glanced down—another message from Mrs Koeffer.

> I'm sorry, Mrs Wintour. She's texting that boy again. You told me to let you know.

"Everything all right at home?" the president said.

"I'm sorry, sir. I'll shut it off."

"No, no," he said, looking again at his watch. "You're right. There's nothing more for us to do. Why don't you go home? Eat dinner with your kid. I'll have dinner with Martha. This might be the last calm we get."

"What if Roman—"

"Roman knows how to run his agent. He'll let us know when it's done."

"You're sure?" Gabriella said, picturing Cassie at home on her bed, texting that infernal seventeen-year-old.

"I'm positive. It's Christmas Eve. I dare say the *Free World* will survive a few hours while we remind our families we still exist."

Gabriella might have objected—if only for appearances—but she was too worried about Cassie to turn down the offer. "Thank you. I'll be back in a few hours."

"You didn't drive in, did you?" he added, looking out the window again.

"No, no. I used the service."

"Good," he said. "Looks like *The Day After Tomorrow* out there."

She gave him a blank look.

"The movie."

"I haven't seen it."

"It's good."

She looked at him again for a moment—he really did look like he'd aged ten years—then turned and made for the door. By the time she got to the exit, her car was already waiting. A flurry of snow buffeted her as she ran out to it, the wind catching the door and slamming it shut behind her.

"You okay?" the driver said.

He was more than a driver—he was an armed Secret Service detail officer. And—breach of protocol though it was—he was more than *that*, too. A lot more. "I'm okay, Cole. Just get me home. We'll be coming back in a few hours."

Cole radioed ahead, passing the guard booth and turning onto Western Executive Avenue. "Roads are rough," he said.

Gabriella wasn't listening—she was busy texting Mrs Koeffer.

> Be home in a few minutes.

Mrs Koeffer replied with a thumbs-up emoji—not her usual style. New phone, maybe, Gabriella thought, already beginning to nod off.

The next thing she heard was Cole's voice. "Ma'am, we're home."

She gasped awake, like she'd been holding her breath underwater. "Goodness, Cole!"

"Sorry to startle you, ma'am."

"Out cold," she muttered, wiping her mouth. She felt like she'd been out for hours, though it had been all of twenty minutes since they'd left the White House. "Ugh. Was I drooling?"

"You're all right," Cole said, getting out and opening the door for her.

"And what did I say about calling me *ma'am*?" she teased, stepping out.

"Roger that," he said, grinning.

She smiled, touched his hand. "Want to come in? It's freezing."

Cole looked down the driveway at the black sedan containing two more Secret Service officers. Under ordinary conditions, they wouldn't have been there, but the threat level had been raised by the president after the Council meeting. "I'd better not," he said.

"Ever the professional," she said, feeling a tinge of rejection. "Well, don't wait around here. Go get some rest—I'll need you later."

"*Will* you?" he said playfully.

"For work, dummy."

He sighed, and she punched his arm, then hurried up the steps and pushed open the front door. Inside, she kicked the door shut behind her and glanced around. The lights were all out. The house was cold.

"Mrs Koeffer?" she called, flipping on the hall light.

Nothing.

"Cassie?" she tried, louder this time.

She paused at the foot of the stairs, listening. Silence.

A cold draft crept down the hall, as if a window had been left open.

Something wasn't right.

33

Oksana arrived at the *Tsaritsa* before seven and immediately saw she had a problem. Instead of winding down for the night, the whole place was lit up like a Christmas tree. Speakers by the entrance thumped with electronic music, and a red carpet, flanked by velvet ropes on stanchions, stretched from the gallery doors to the sidewalk.

In front of the entrance, three Muldowney security guards stood like nightclub bouncers while a woman with a clipboard meticulously checked names against a guest list.

Out on the street, a police officer directed traffic as limousines rolled up, their doors swinging open to reveal partygoers in flamboyant sequined gowns and impeccably tailored tuxedos. Paparazzi cameras flashed, lending the scene the panache of a Hollywood premiere.

Looking at the spectacle from across the street—dressed in black with a scarf and hat concealing as much of her face as possible—Oksana considered calling the whole thing off. She couldn't disable the alarm. Her plan hinged on letting it trip—then getting in and out before the guards could respond. Heavy traffic on the Queensboro was a key part of that calculus, and this *soirée* didn't look like it was going to wrap up any time soon.

She ducked into the same recess as the night before and dropped the duffel bag. Inside were her tools of the trade: lock picks, bump keys, a pry bar, flashlight, suction cups, even a tungsten carbide glass cutter. She waited for someone to exit, caught the door with her foot, and slipped inside. There was no one in the lobby, and she went straight to the third floor, picking a lock to get to the staircase.

From the window, she watched as the party guests continued to arrive across the street. Inside the gallery, they mingled and admired the art, grabbing fancy *hors d'oeuvres* and champagne flutes off silver trays carried by waiters.

It was a disaster, she thought, and was just deciding to call it off when an armored truck—more military than private—rounded the corner from Park Avenue. It pulled up behind one of the limos and came to a halt.

It wasn't a Muldowney truck—formidable as those were —but something decidedly more serious. The logo on the side, written in both English and Cyrillic script, read *Novoguard*. Oksana had never heard of the company, though a quick Google search told her it was based in Moscow, with offices in London, Paris, New York, and Dubai. It specialized in the secure import and delivery of '*high-value objects originating in Russia.*' Photos showed a truck—identical to the one she was looking at—outside Moscow's *State Tretyakov Gallery*. The *Tretyakov* was one of the foremost art depositories in all of Russia, and near the top of Oksana's list of places to visit if she ever made it to Moscow.

There was only one reason a truck like that would come from there to here. And Proctor was mixed up in it.

Breaching sanctions came with some pretty hefty penalties, she mused. And a guy like Proctor would be real popular in prison.

Real popular.

Two armed guards got out of the truck and retrieved a package about the size of a phone book from the back. It was wrapped in bubble wrap and additionally protected by a wooden frame. Ignoring the glitz and glamour in front of the gallery, the guards—both of them, even though the package could easily be carried by one—brought it into the building using the lobby's main rotating doors.

Whatever they were carrying was Oksana's new target. She didn't know what it was yet, but it mattered. Enough to require Moscow muscle.

She wanted it, and *badly*.

The desire wasn't monetary—the paintings Proctor dealt in fetched millions at auction—but not if they were stolen. Without proper paperwork, paintings were about as marketable as mineral rights on the moon. There was a black market, to be sure, but Oksana had no desire to be mixed up in that world of cutthroats. Whatever she took wouldn't be worth a penny to her.

And that was fine.

Make them pay, Ksyusha.

That was what she'd been taught, and that was what she intended to do.

While the gallery's ground floor was thronged with people, the upper level was empty, off limits to the partygoers. Oksana figured that someone would have to go up to let the *Novoguard* men in, and, sure enough, someone soon appeared on the staircase.

Through a pair of high-powered Zeiss binoculars, she recognized that figure as Proctor. Whatever was being delivered was important enough to drag him away from his guests. He reached the top of the stairs and ambled to the door to receive the package. He signed some papers, took the package, and brought it directly over to the enormous Diebold Nixdorf safe.

That wasn't good. Given enough time—thirty to sixty minutes, perhaps—Oksana could have cracked it. But she wasn't going to have thirty to sixty minutes. She would have five, tops.

Proctor was just beginning to turn the dial on the safe when another figure appeared on the staircase. He immediately stopped what he was doing and went to the desk, shoving the package into a drawer and locking it with a key from his pant pocket.

The figure on the stairs was female, possibly the woman from the night before in the polka dots, though tonight she was wearing a decidedly more provocative leopard print number that left precious little to the imagination. When she reached the top of the stairs, Proctor stepped away from the desk as if to hide what he'd been up to. The two of them talked then, or maybe they argued, and after a few seconds, the woman marched over to him and slapped him on the face. Proctor drew his hand back to return the favor, then thought better of it and grabbed her by the wrists instead. There followed what appeared to be a struggle, which ended with him bending her over the back of the velvet sofa—the same one etched irrevocably into Oksana's memory. The sofa faced the window—faced Oksana directly. She fought back the bile in her throat as she watched what happened next. The woman, hands splayed on the backrest, held herself up while behind her, Proctor pulled up her dress and gyrated like an over-eager Jack Russell. His face contorted—half ecstasy, half something darker.

Oksana wanted to look away. But she couldn't. She stared, transfixed, her hands clenched so tightly it hurt.

The business took Proctor all of sixty seconds, at which point he stepped away and did up his pant zipper. The woman turned to face him, but he left her, hurrying back to his party without so much as a word.

Oksana watched the woman straighten her dress, fix her makeup. Maybe she wiped some tears, maybe not, Oksana couldn't be certain. She couldn't even be certain of what she'd just witnessed—was it consensual? An assault? Degradation? Whatever it was, it made her want to kill him all over again.

Proctor, for his part, went on to become the life of the party, knocking back a truly eye-watering amount of vodka, which was being served from crystal bottles shaped like skulls. Caterers brought out silver trays piled high with fresh oysters, caviar, and shellfish on mounds of crushed ice. At one point, Proctor began groping one of the male waiters. The man shoved him away, sending him crashing to the ground. It did nothing to slow him down, though, and he pulled himself up and kept drinking and laughing, his behavior growing ever more boisterous and unpredictable as the evening progressed. Finally, he was carried out of the building by two security guards and loaded into one of the waiting cars.

For better or worse, he'd never made it back upstairs.

Oksana watched through the binoculars, checking her watch as the evening dragged on. It wasn't *that* late, but the rush-hour jam on the bridge would have definitely thinned.

When the caterers were done clearing up and the last of the guests had left the premises, the guards came out and lingered on the sidewalk, smoking and chatting, waiting for something.

Inside, the woman in the leopard print was the last one standing. She locked the front doors, switched off the lights, then poured herself one final drink. Oksana watched her by the window, looking out at the security guards until they were picked up by the next Muldowney patrol. As soon as they'd disappeared from view, the woman downed her drink and went straight for the stairs.

Oksana watched on, more curious by the second, feeling a strange sense of kinship with this woman. A kinship made stronger by the suspicion she was up to something.

The woman reached the top of the stairs and began riffling through Proctor's desk. She tapped the keyboard, glanced at the monitor, then got down on her hands and knees and checked underneath the desk. She tried the drawers, some opened, some did not, then went over to the Diebold Nixdorf and stared at its thick steel door. Whatever she was considering doing, she thought better of it because she went back to the desk, straightened up everything she'd disturbed, and activated the electronic alarm.

Then she turned off the remaining lights and hurried out. A moment later, she came out through the revolving lobby doors, nearly tripping as she descended the steps. She looked up and down for a cab, gave up, and staggered off into the darkness.

Whatever she'd been looking for, she hadn't found it.

34

"Mrs Koeffer?" Gabriella called again, uncertainty in her voice.

Still no answer.

"Hello?"

Cole's headlights were already retreating down the driveway. Was it too late to call him back?

A white lace curtain stirred in the living room. Definitely a door or window open somewhere.

"Cassie?" she called. If that girl had snuck out again, so help her.

And where on earth was Mrs Koeffer?

Her phone began vibrating in her pocket and she pulled it out. It was the office. "Yes, what is it?" she said. "Is there a problem in Moscow?"

"Sorry, no, Ms Wintour, nothing like that."

"What then?"

"I'm calling about the background check you requested this morning."

"Background check?" she said, trying to recall the dozens of issues she'd juggled since morning.

"Cody Richards? Seventeen years old. Summer Heights Road—"

"Ah, yes," she said hurriedly. "What about it?"

"He's dead, ma'am."

Gabriella's blood ran cold. Her body knew before her mind did.

"Local police found his body in a—"

The phone was already falling to the ground.

She lunged for the door—and never made it. Something exploded from the shadows and knocked her to the floor. Kicking and screaming, her mind reeling, she realized a man was on top of her. Heavy. Powerful. She struggled for the door, slapping her hands against it uselessly.

"No," she gasped. "Help!"

Hands clawed at her face—calloused fingers tearing at her eyes, prying at her mouth. She bit down with the force of a pit bull, tasting blood as he yelped in pain. He struck her head, once. Twice. A third time. Her face cracked against the wooden floor. Something broke. His hand came free, but not without leaving a chunk of flesh behind. She spat it out—his blood, her blood, shards of her shattered teeth.

"Bitch," he growled. "She bit me."

Then—another shadow.

A second man, his silhouette passing over her like an eclipse. She saw only his hand, reaching to grab her shattered phone from the floor. Then she heard his voice.

"Gag her," he said, "before she makes any more noise." His voice was calm. Too calm. Slavic. Russian. Cold as ice water.

Before she'd processed the words, the other man was stuffing a rag into her mouth.

She cried, gasping for breath, her mouth full of blood.

"The bitch bit me," he said again, still on top of her.

"Shut up," the second man said.

"Did they hear us? On the phone, did they hear us?"

The second man went to the window and peered out between the lace curtain, gun in hand. "Doesn't look like it," he said. Then he came over and grabbed Gabriella's wrists, yanking them painfully behind her back. He caught them together in one enormous hand while the sharp grip of a zip tie cut into her flesh.

Then, he flipped her onto her back to get a look at her.

She struggled against the zip tie. Flailed and kicked. She couldn't breathe. The rag was so far down her throat she was choking on it. Choking on blood and her own shattered teeth. She tried to reach for it but the zip tie stopped her.

"Look at her squirm," the first man grunted, then he kicked her in the gut so hard her vision blurred.

"Easy, we need her," the second man said, pulling the rag from her mouth. "Don't scream, or it goes back in."

She coughed and gasped, spitting up blood and mucus. "Cassie!" she screamed. "What have you done with her? Where's my—"

Immediately, the rag was back, shoved in even further than before. She struggled against it in a frenzy of terror, unable even to think, shaking her head back and forth as if force alone might dislodge the rag.

"Calm down," the man said, grabbing her face and slapping it hard with an open palm. "You're going to choke yourself to death."

She stared at him, eyes wide with terror, struggling with all her might against the zip ties. Then her eyes darted to the other man, the one who'd jumped her. He'd wrapped his hand but blood was already seeping through where she'd bitten him.

The second man, crouching over her, put a finger over his lips and pulled the cloth again from her mouth. She gasped for air.

"Don't scream," he said. "I mean it this time."

She breathed deep gulps, her vision focusing. He was Asian, but his accent was Russian. And he was definitely the one calling the shots.

"Your daughter's alive," he said.

Gratitude flooded her veins like morphine. Numbing, dizzying. Too much, too fast. Despite everything, she could have kissed his hands for saying that.

"Where is she?" she whispered.

"Upstairs," he said, glancing toward the ceiling. "Her and the nanny."

"They're alive?" she cried, eyes filling with tears.

"They are."

"Why are you doing this?"

He smiled. "We'll get to that," he said. "But first, I need to set some ground rules. Time is tight, and there are armed guards at the end of the driveway, so let's get one thing very clear. Any more screaming, any interruption by the Secret Service, and your daughter eats a bullet. Do you understand?"

Gabriella didn't know if she understood or not—what mother could?

But she was nodding frantically. Nodding, crying, spitting. That was her reality now—raw, reduced, consumed by terror. There was nothing else.

"That's it," the man said, nodding. "Nice and calm."

Inside, she was screaming, but on the surface, she was deathly quiet.

"Now," the man continued, "do I need to go over all the terrible, ugly, brutal things that my friend and I will do to your girl if you don't tell us what we want to know? Do I need to waste time talking about those things?"

"No," she gasped, tears streaming.

"Because I will if you force me to. My friend is a terrible degenerate. He's a deviant. A pervert. Hurting girls... that's what excites him."

"No," she cried again. "Take whatever you want. My jewelry is upstairs. Cash... there's a safe. I'll give you everything I have."

He smiled again—wolfish, satisfied—then said to his colleague, "Go upstairs and get them."

"What?" Gabriella cried, trying to get to her feet, trying to pull her hands free so that she could leap on this man and claw his eyes out. All she succeeded in doing was slamming her back painfully against the floor.

The other man went up the stairs while she continued struggling desperately.

The man in front of her said, "Remember what I said. If your guards hear us, if they come sniffing, your girl eats a bullet."

She nodded emphatically, though she forgot everything when the other man reappeared at the top of the staircase. In front of him, like two hostages from a terrorist scene, were Cassie and Mrs Koeffer. Their hands were bound behind their backs, and they were gagged and blindfolded. Both of their faces were bruised and swollen, and there was blood on Mrs Koeffer's dress.

But Gabriella didn't scream.

She looked from them to the man and let out a sound she barely recognized as her own. From where it came, she didn't know. "Why are you doing this?" she gasped. "Why are you hurting them? What do you want from us?"

He crouched and put the gag back in her mouth, then

gave a signal to the other man, who raised a gun and fired a single, silenced shot.

The bullet struck Mrs Koeffer's temple and disappeared inside her skull. There was a split second when nothing happened, then a spray of blood and brain flew from the other side of her head, hitting Cassie's white cotton nightie like a splash of crimson paint.

Cassie—blind, gagged, bound—dropped to her knees in horror.

Gabriella fixated on the lace gown, oddly anachronistic now, like something from a painting.

Her mind reeled, unable to process.

Images flashed and vanished. She wasn't in control.

And Mrs Koeffer's body didn't fly into the air. It didn't do anything. Just crumpled lifelessly like a dropped marionette.

Seconds passed, perhaps minutes, before she realized that the man in front of her was slapping her face, demanding her attention.

"Hey," he said. "Right here. Look at me. Not them."

She focused, and he said, "I'm going to take away the gag again, and when I do, you're going to remain silent. Otherwise, your daughter gets the same fate."

At the top of the stairs, Cassie, on her knees, was whimpering and sobbing through her gag. She knew Mrs Koeffer was dead. She was blindfolded but she knew. Her nightie was smeared red, as if it was she who'd been shot. She knew her mother was there, too.

"It's all right," Gabriella gasped. "It's all right, baby."

"Not a word," the man said.

Cassie was pulled to her feet and led slowly down the stairs. When the man put his gun to her head, Gabriella felt as if she might pass out in terror.

But he never pulled the trigger.

They reached the bottom of the stairs and stopped, but he kept the gun pressed to her head.

"Don't hurt her," Gabriella wailed. "Please don't hurt her!"

Why wasn't he lowering his weapon? Why was it still pressed to Cassie's head?

"Calm down," the man in front of her said. "Think very clearly about what you want to happen next."

Gabriella locked eyes with him and brought everything into focus.

Then Cassie bolted—straight into a wall. The thud was sickening. She collapsed like a ragdoll.

The man with the gun laughed, then reached down and grabbed her by the ankle, pulling her away from the wall like he was pulling a dog to heel. Cassie struggled, but he just held her by the ankle and laughed.

The other man then said, "As you see, she's in a very vulnerable position. What happens next depends on you. On what you choose to do. Whether or not you choose to help us. Like I said, my friend, he's a deviant."

Gabriella forced herself not to give in to the terror. Somehow, she managed to conjure the presence of mind to understand one thing and one thing only. That she had to get through this. She had to handle these men and give them what they wanted. For Cassie.

The voice, the accent—Russian or Eastern European—she focused on that. She'd need it later. She'd need details.

That was how she'd survive. She'd gather information. She'd remember everything. Not Mrs Koeffer's blood dripping down the smooth steps of the staircase, not the crimson stain on Cassie's nightdress, but these men. Their voices. Their faces.

Their faces.

He was looking right at her.

Was he waiting for her to scream? She wouldn't.

He took her chin and forced her to lock eyes with him. "I thought Americans loved Christmas," he said. "You don't even have a tree."

She said nothing.

"I'm disappointed."

"What are you going to do to us?" she stammered.

"I'm going to ask you one question. One time. If you lie, if you try to hide anything, I'll know, and my friend and I will take your daughter into the next room and we'll absolutely *ruin* her." His voice lingered on the word with a terrible fondness, like it was the name of a cherished lover. "And you'll be in here, listening. You understand?"

Gabriella's mind threatened to reel out of control again, and she forced herself to listen to the voice. His breathing. His dark brown eyes, almost black.

"Tell us about the report," he said.

"What?" she gasped.

"No games," he said, glancing at Cassie on the floor.

"I don't know what you're talking about."

"The report. *Hummingbird*. The mole."

"*Hummingbird*?" she gasped. "That's why you're here?"

The man looked at his colleague, who pointed his gun again at Cassie.

"All right," Gabriella said. "All right."

"Who is it?"

She looked at the man again, then at her daughter, then back at him. "You're not wearing any masks," she whispered.

The thin smile that followed told her everything. She understood, in that moment, how this was going to end.

Gabriella wasn't a hero. She'd never served on the front

lines. She'd never seen the shock of battle or tested her will against the enemy.

But she'd always told herself she'd die for her country. If she had to, she told herself, she would do it. If it came to it.

And maybe that was true.

Maybe she'd have taken what she knew to the grave, through whatever untold tortures these men inflicted on her. Maybe she'd have suffered any pain. Any humiliation.

But not for Cassie.

That was the limit.

Patriot. But mother first.

"I know what you want," she said, as calmly as if speaking to her child. "I know who *Hummingbird* is. I'll give her to you, but you have to let my daughter go. You have to let her live. She's blindfolded. She doesn't know a thing. She's not part of this. You have to let her live."

The man leaned in closer to her, so close that she could smell the cigarettes on his breath. "Don't lie to me, now," he said. "Tell me the truth, and I'll let the little one live."

"Unharmed?"

"You have my word as a professional."

She could hear Cassie struggling to scream through the gag in her mouth, but she blocked it out. She thought of Margot Katz—pictured her in Moscow, her operation already in motion. This would be a death sentence for her, too.

"A life for a life," she whispered.

35

Margot sat rigid in the café, tapping the menu against her water glass in a staccato rhythm that betrayed her nerves. Streetlamps bled through the lace netting on the window, casting the room in a dim amber gloom.

She'd positioned herself to be seen from outside, and the few nighttime pedestrians hurried by on the street, their coat collars turned up against the cold.

"What can I bring you?" the waitress asked, her white apron starched stiff over a light blue dress.

"A Raf Coffee," she said, praying her accent didn't give her away.

The coffee arrived in a porcelain cup. She tested it with a sip, added sugar, and stirred, her eyes moving methodically across the room. The place felt subdued, conspiratorial, like a hideout for thieves, informants, and cutthroats. The other patrons spoke in hushed tones, as if they too were flying below the radar.

She looked up as the door opened, letting in a gust of cold air. A heavyset man in a wool coat and cap stepped in.

He looked around the café, his eyes lingering on Margot a fraction of a second too long. She broke eye contact, then risked a glance. Watching her. Not watching her. Hard to tell.

The café had once been grand—Baroque paneling, ceiling lights with velvet shades—but the grandeur was long gone. It smelled now of boiled cabbage and stale smoke.

She watched the newcomer find a seat and order borscht and a glass of beer. She checked her watch, careful not to seem like she was waiting for someone. Another man was looking her way. A chill traced her spine. Had she been followed? Everywhere she looked she saw hostile glances, hidden daggers. She looked at the clock above the door, the table in front of her, the coffee, anywhere but at the other patrons—apart from the waitress, they were all men. The one by the door kept his gaze on her before finally taking a newspaper from his satchel and opening it up.

Margot forced herself to breathe deeply. She sipped the coffee and touched her shoulder. It was tender from the fall but nothing serious.

Unbidden, a memory of Roman came to her mind. "There'll come a time," he'd said to her once, "when you're going to be asked to give something of yourself. Something no one has any right to ask."

"I'm not a schoolgirl," she'd said. "You can speak plainly."

"You'll want to believe you're in control. That's the lie. Control's what they strip from you, inch by inch. How much you give, and to whom, is for you to decide."

"I know that," she'd said.

"You don't," he said. "But you will."

"Okay," she'd said carefully.

The Honeytrap

"You'll be on enemy territory, in some foreign city, and it will be for you alone to decide what happens next."

"Understood," she'd said, though she hadn't been quite sure what he was trying to say.

"When that time comes," he'd added, "protect yourself. Protect your own soul. Put that first."

She wasn't sure what exactly about this night was bringing those words to mind. *Protect yourself. Protect your soul.*

She glanced again at the man by the door and caught him a second time looking her way. He looked back at his newspaper. She couldn't help noticing the headline. *Roskomnadzor* was calling for criminal charges against the editors of *Sobesednik*—Russia's last free paper.

Sobesednik had already folded, but still, they wanted blood.

She checked her watch again. Subtly. Ten minutes had passed since her arrival. That was it. That was the limit. She had no idea if Irina had been one of the pedestrians who'd passed by on the sidewalk—it was a blustery, frigid night and everyone had a scarf up over their face—but she'd done her bit. She'd shown her face. Now she just had to trust that Irina had done hers.

She drained her coffee and raised a finger to the waitress.

"Everything all right?"

"Fine," Margot said, already standing. "How much?"

"I'll get the bill."

Margot was suddenly very aware of the eyes on her. "Where's the women's restroom?" she asked, though she knew exactly where it was.

The waitress pointed it out and Margot went. It was a small room with a single toilet and sink. She locked the door, flushed the toilet, then ran her fingers around the frame of the lone mirror.

Nothing. No slip. No note. Just her reflection—and a sharp, audible inhale of panic.

That was it then. The link was severed. The protocol broken. Irina was gone. Lost in the wind. There were steps that could still be taken. The meeting with Zubarev would be resurrected. Margot would likely be put back on the attendance list. But those were desperate measures. The truth was, whatever Irina knew, she'd either lost her nerve— or lost her life.

Margot glanced at her reflection in the mirror, then pushed her way out of the restroom. She went to her table and dropped cash on it without looking at the bill, then slipped out into the night. It had been snowing again and there was a thin layer blanketing the cobbled street. She walked to the corner of *Nikitsky Boulevard* and waved at a passing taxi. It didn't stop. She turned and looked for another—her absolute priority now was to get back to the embassy, the lone safe haven, and stay there.

And that was when she saw her.

For an instant, she doubted her eyes. Then she knew. Tucked into the shadow of a shuttered store not twenty yards away stood Irina, her face flushed from the cold. Her breath hung in the cold air like smoke from a spent match.

For a brief second, Margot felt a flood of relief. It was instantly replaced with fear.

Why was she there?

Why hadn't she followed the protocol?

Why hadn't she left a note?

Margot fought back the urge to rush over to her. She remained where she was, her hand still raised for the passing taxis. Another one sped by.

She lowered her hand.

What was going on?

What was the play?

Irina seemed to be asking herself the same questions.

For a terrifying instant, Margot thought she was going to walk away, then she flashed an almost imperceptible sign—thumb and two fingers. Alternate site. Safe house. North of the city. The signal was unmistakable.

Margot gave no sign of having received it, but turned away immediately, walking briskly down *Nikitsky Boulevard* in the direction of the embassy. She kept a steady pace and continued, in vain, to try and hail a passing taxi. She never looked back, though the urge was overwhelming.

Eventually, a cab stopped. She told the driver to take her to *Mayakovskaya* Metro Station. The place wouldn't be busy at that time of night, but the trains were running and that was what mattered. Once she was out of the cab, she took counter-surveillance precautions—a box route, as well as crossing a raised pedestrian bridge and watching to see if anyone followed. No one did.

At the metro station, she killed some time at a little bar, sipping flat beer from a chipped glass.

The safe house was located in a drab, concrete apartment building not far from the *Khovrino* Station, the last stop on Moscow's *Zamoskvoretskaya* line. Margot had never been there before, though she'd studied the location on paper. She knew the surrounding streets, the surrounding neighborhood, where to lie low, and where to catch local transport.

She got off her train two stops early at *Rechnoy Vokzal*, the old terminus of the line, and waited on the platform. It was all but deserted. When the next train arrived, a single commuter got off, a tired-looking man in a shabby business suit. Margot waited, watching him, making sure he cleared the platform before stepping on board.

Two stops later, she got off with a small handful of other passengers. Any one of them could be a cut-out. A tail. A noose in a long coat disguised as a commuter. She committed each one to memory, and hung back so that she was the last one to get on the escalator. *Khovrino* was the nearest station to Sheremetyevo Airport, a factor in the safe house's selection, and outside, there were a number of tram and bus stops.

Margot hurried past them, across a plaza, toward a hulking apartment block. Normally, a detached house would be chosen for this type of thing—but in Moscow, empty ones were rare, and suspicious. As far as she knew, all safe houses in the city were apartments.

She sat on a bench a hundred yards from the entrance and checked her watch again—heart thudding, breath steady, eyes sharp as razors.

36

Oksana went through the ritual of checking each item in her duffel.

When she was done, she zipped it up, slung it over her shoulder, and left the building, telling herself to walk away. It was too late. The streets were too empty. The bridge would be too quiet.

No job was worth dying for.

But another voice was louder. This was the night—the only night—and the package in Proctor's desk was the one thing that would make him pay.

Outside, the night air was frigidly cold. She waited before crossing the street, counting off the minutes until the next Muldowney drive-by. It wasn't long before the vehicle rounded the corner and slowed down. Oksana pulled her hat low over her eyes and the neck of her turtleneck up over her mouth. The patrol moved on, and she gave it time to clear the area.

Then, she crossed the street to the building. The main doors weren't locked, she'd known they wouldn't be, and she pushed her way inside, careful not to look in the direction of the numerous cameras. She moved quickly past the elevators to the end of the corridor, where a set of fire doors led to an emergency stairwell.

There, she set the bag down, took out an industrial-grade magnetic disc, and snapped it to the doorframe—a foot from the ground, just beneath the infrared sensor.

It took fifteen seconds to pick the lock, then she took a breath and opened the door.

No alarm.

Good.

She slipped into the stairwell and bounded up three flights of stairs, praying that no one was monitoring the lone camera overlooking each landing.

On the third floor, she placed a second magnet on the fire door—there was no need to pick the lock—and pushed it open. It led to the same raw, concrete corridor she remembered from the night she'd been drugged by Proctor.

Drugged.

Not *raped.*

She told herself to call it what it was, but the truth was too much in that moment.

There were two more cameras, and again, she could only pray that the guards weren't watching. She walked briskly down the corridor, following it parallel to 57th Street behind the backs of the south-facing retail units. She passed the elevator and made note of the stenciled number three on the wall opposite. From there, she counted the identical doors, all bearing the same 'Staff Only' sign, until she got to the one that she knew belonged to the gallery. She scanned the corridor a final time before crouching down and examining the door's old pin tumbler lock from eye level. It was solidly built, probably top of the line when the building was constructed in the forties, but no match for Oksana.

She'd calculated that a Muldowney response unit would take five minutes to arrive on the scene, so she set the timer on her watch now to three minutes and thirty seconds, though she didn't start it. She took a tension wrench from her bag and, working with the fluid precision of a professional, slid the wrench into the keyway, applying the smallest amount of pressure in the direction of the key turn. Very carefully, she coaxed the pins into place with her pick. She started with the binding pin, pushing it toward the shear line, then worked her way through the rest, waiting for the almost imperceptible click of the mechanism that told her they were in place.

When she was sure she had it, she took a deep breath and, extremely slowly, increased pressure on the wrench. If it snapped now, the lock would jam and there'd be no getting past it. Proctor would know someone had tampered with it, and the whole thing would be replaced and upgraded before she ever got back to finish the job.

She twisted the wrench. Nothing happened. She increased the pressure. Still nothing. It was stuck. She adjusted the position of the pick, applying more upward pressure, and then—snap. The lock gave with a single, clean click.

She started the timer—three minutes and thirty seconds—then grabbed the bag and pushed open the door.

A soft beep—like a bedside clock. Harmless. But deadly. The moment of no return.

A signal had just been sent to Muldowney's dispatch center across the river. If she was still there when they arrived, she was dead meat. Adrenaline hit her bloodstream like a jolt.

Her mind snapped into gear, propelling her forward.

But the instant she stepped into the gallery, the memories slammed into her like a wave. She looked at the green sofa—obscene in its unchanged familiarity, like it had been waiting for her—and her stomach lurched. The texture of the velvet, the sickly mess between her legs, the pain, all came rushing back in a torrent.

Every instinct screamed at her to run.

Instead, she doubled over and retched, wasting seconds.

She slapped herself hard. Twice. A third time. Then checked the watch. Thirty seconds gone. She scanned the loft for threats, for movement—there was none. The lighting was just enough to make out the contours of the space. Swallowing her fear, she dashed over to the desk and began working the lock on the drawer. Her fingers moved deftly, but it was trickier than the door lock and took almost a minute to pick.

She put the lock pick and tension wrench in her pocket and slid open the drawer.

The first thing she saw inside was a gun—a sleek, compact pistol with a steel frame and checkered wood grip. She was no expert, but this one had a manufacturer's mark etched on the barrel.

Walther—Made in W. Germany.

She considered it—she knew how to use a gun, and the guards would be coming fast—but she didn't touch it. Instead, she grabbed what she'd come for, the bubble-wrapped package next to it. It was light in her hand, scarcely a pound in weight, and she tucked it into her coat, left the carryall, and ran.

37

Roman Adler sat behind a modest desk in a modest room above a Dupont Circle bookshop. The office was less than a mile from the White House, with buses running by outside every ten minutes. That was generally how he traveled between the two. The trip to Langley was more of a slog—metro to Rosslyn, then a long bus ride, but he made that journey far less frequently. For the most part, this was where he conjured his magic, the place from which he ran his *fiefdom*, as he'd heard the president call it. It was all executed with Foxtrot's unwavering assistance—and, like everything Roman touched, was understated to the point of invisibility.

If federal auditors had suspected for a second that one of the most powerful, most secretive organs of the deep state was operating from this shabby bookshop, with its three-thousand-dollar-a-month rent and ordinary home security system, they'd have blown a gasket. That, or they simply wouldn't have believed it, which, of course, was the point.

The whole place followed Roman's old-school ethos of hiding in plain sight. The store was open to the public, and attracted precisely the clientele it should have been hiding from. And yet, it had managed to remain completely off the radar. No one knew it was there, even within the Agency, and if anyone ever came across it, for whatever reason, all they'd find was a fully functioning bookstore, with Foxtrot behind the cashier's desk, a cozy seating area where prospective buyers could pour their own coffee for a two dollar donation, and, of course, row upon row of well-stocked bookshelves.

The subject matter was somewhat specialized, with a focus on politics, and, especially, geopolitics. Foxtrot chose the books, and did such a good job that the store actually had a reputation among DC's foreign policy clique as the go-to place. She was a devotee of the canon—Mahan, Mackinder, Spykman—alongside modern voices like Kennan, Mearsheimer, and Brzezinski. Many had done readings at the shop, their signed hardbacks tucked between collector's editions that sold for hundreds of dollars.

And it wasn't just books. She kept up subscriptions to every serious periodical. She curated the shelves with surgical precision—dense on doctrine, light on fluff.

And then there was her guilty pleasure, the fiction section. She stocked every spy thriller ever written by an ex-official, ex-general, ex-president, or ex-spook. The usual suspects were all there—Le Carré, Maugham, Greene—plus the Beltway names who couldn't resist cashing in their credentials for a publisher's advance—Clinton, Gingrich, Comey, Carter. Both she and Roman, despite his strenuous objections that such things were frivolous, read every one of them, cover to cover.

Who would have guessed that beneath all that curated calm—within a hair's breadth of the coffee maker, the geopolitics, the spy paperbacks—was the nerve center of the country's most covert op?

At the back of the store, accessible internally as well as from a private door in the adjacent alley, was a rickety old staircase leading to Roman's office. The office looked exactly as one might expect from a reclusive, old-fashioned bookshop owner—grimy, curtained windows, a threadbare sofa, a reading lamp, and an old wooden desk with a deceptively secure filing cabinet tucked inside.

Two monitors sat on the desk—unremarkable to anyone who might see them. No one would guess that they were wired to one of the most powerful computing arrays on the planet, hardlined to Langley, Fort Meade, and the NSA's Utah Data Center. There was also a direct patch to satellite feeds from Keyhole, Orion/Mentor, Overhead Persistent Infrared, and Project Maven.

The office was one of the most connected locations on earth, with real-time access to the highest-resolution satellite imagery in existence, and full-spectrum battlefield telemetry from every US and NATO unit equipped to provide it.

It was also cloaked—visually, thermally, electromagnetically, and on all digital signatures. Outfitted with the same tech as the E-4B Nightwatch—the Air Force's airborne command center—it could, in theory, mirror the functionality of the Emergency Ops Center beneath the White House. A president, if the need arose, could maintain continuity of government from within its shabby walls.

Needless to say, Roman had built it all *off the books*, under the radar—quietly, methodically, across multiple decades and administrations. No single agency knew its full extent. No government department had any inkling of its scope. Even the utility providers were in the dark. Its power consumption and data flow were off the chart, but they were so meticulously disguised that local energy companies couldn't ever figure out where the resources were going. They routinely dispatched technicians to investigate the anomaly, without success.

It was an open secret among the crews—whatever was wired to that feeder pulled more load than a Tier IV data center. And no one knew what it was.

Roman sat at his desk, gazing out the grimy window at the evening traffic, hugging the hot water bottle he always kept close.

He'd just intercepted an urgent dispatch from the Nuclear Regulatory Commission—flashed to the White House, Homeland, FEMA, and the Nuclear Security Administration. That it hadn't been sent to the Pentagon, US Northern Command, or NORAD was some small comfort, but the message was grim.

Extreme weather had battered a Dominion-operated nuclear plant in Surry, Virginia, fifteen miles from Newport News and barely a hundred-fifty from where Roman sat. The plant's main cooling loop was buckling under the floodwaters of the James River.

Worse—there were whispers of cyber interference hitting state and municipal flood controls, emergency lines, and backup systems.

It was worrying, but it wasn't Roman's responsibility, and there was something more urgent on his mind. Margot hadn't reported. He looked at his watch and counted the hours since her meet with *Hummingbird*. It was the middle of the night in Moscow, and she should have checked in, even if only to report trouble.

He reached into the drawer of his desk and pulled out an old-style Rolodex. It contained thousands of contacts, written in a simple cipher of Roman's own devising, and he found the number he was looking for. It was a number he'd called only very occasionally over a period of three decades, but it had yet to fail him.

"*Tsentr Taxi*," a man said in Russian when he picked up. The voice was gruff, like it belonged to someone who'd spent a lifetime smoking unfiltered Russian cigarettes, which it did.

"Dmitry, it's your old American friend," Roman said, speaking Russian.

"I don't have any American friends," Dmitry said suspiciously.

"Yes you do," Roman said. "A very old, very loyal friend."

"Ah," Dmitry said, suddenly lowering his voice. "I see. How are you, sir? Are you back in our beautiful city?"

"I'm not," Roman said.

"Your number shows as local."

"Well," Roman said, "I have a little favor to ask. Something easy. Nothing risky."

Dmitry laughed. "Everything's risky these days."

"Fair enough," Roman said, "but payment will more than make up for it."

"What did you have in mind?"

"Do you know the Café Pushkin?"

"I meant in terms of payment," Dmitry said. "Our banks are very picky now. They report all foreign wires."

"I can pay in bitcoin," Roman said. "I recall you're set up for that sort of thing."

"I am. Can I send the payment instructions to this number?"

"Of course," Roman said. The system he was using masked calls, rotated numbers, and made them untraceable, but it could still receive messages. He saw on his computer screen that a text from Dmitry had already been received. It contained a screenshot of payment instructions from the crypto app he was using. "That was quick."

"I'm sitting in the car."

"I see your prices have gone up."

"What can I say? Times are tough."

"Two grand for a cab ride—"

"This isn't a cab ride."

"It's less. No pickup. Just a drive-by."

"And what's the location? The Café Pushkin, you said? The one off *Nikitsky Boulevard*?"

"That's the place," Roman said. "All you have to do is drive by. Tell me if you see anything unusual."

"And what counts as unusual?"

"Police, security services, ambulances, broken windows, injured people, fire, smoke—"

"Sounds like you're expecting a party."

"I hope not," Roman said, setting up the fund transfer. He hit send.

"I'm just around the corner," Dmitry said. "I can call you back on this number?"

"You can," Roman said, hanging up.

Thirty years ago, Dmitry had given Roman a cab ride from Vnukovo Airport to Central Moscow, and at the end of the ride, Roman had asked for his personal number. He'd been using him for jobs like this ever since.

He looked out the window again. In the summertime, the circle was a lively place, full of kids feeding pigeons and old men playing chess by the fountain. Tonight, it was cold and deserted. Even the Christmas decorations had a desolate feel to them.

The phone started to ring and he picked it up immediately.

"I'm outside your café now," Dmitry said.

"And?"

"Nothing."

"Nothing at all?"

"It's completely normal," Dmitry said. "It's late, and it's closed, but what do you expect?"

"No police? No broken glass, cordons—anything?"

"Nothing," Dmitry said.

Roman sighed. "All right," he said. "Thanks, Dmitry. Take care of yourself."

"I always do," Dmitry said. The line went dead.

Roman looked at his computer screen, where another intercepted dispatch had been flagged. This one was from the Surry County Office of Emergency Management, and repeated the warning that emergency response systems within the power plant's Emergency Planning Zone—an area that extended ten miles from the plant and included parts of Newport News, Williamsburg, and the I-64—may have been the target of a coordinated cyberattack.

He forwarded the dispatch to Foxtrot downstairs—she would be at her desk for as long as this operation with Margot was ongoing. Then he picked up the phone and dialed the number of the CIA Station Chief in Moscow—a man codenamed Boreal, whose real identity was known only to a select few within the Agency. In Moscow, his cover was as a senior ambassadorial aide, and as far as Roman knew, the Russians were still buying that story. His real name was Levine, and Roman was not his biggest fan.

"Hello?" Levine said, his voice sounding every bit as hoarse and rough as Dmitry's had.

"This is the Bookshop," Roman said, pulling up a live CCTV feed from inside Levine's office in Moscow.

"My word," Levine said sarcastically, "what an honor."

Levine was pale, pudgy, and distinctly unhealthy-looking, with a penchant for flannel shirts and pleated slacks. He also had some pretty strange political ideas. He'd made his fortune in Silicon Valley, like Doerr, and had gotten caught up in some of the transhumanism stuff that seemed to be making the rounds out there. He was definitely more of a natural ally to Doerr than Roman. "I hope I didn't wake you."

"You know you didn't," Levine said, glancing at the camera. "I take it this is about your translator."

"It is," Roman said. "I haven't heard from her."

"Well, as you know, I wasn't read in on the particulars of the operation."

"I like to keep my circle small."

"I know you do."

"Did the driver get back?"

"Yes, and so did the decoy. She spent an hour at the hotel, then got picked up as scheduled."

"I see," Roman said.

"Tell me you haven't just pissed all over my patch?" Levine said.

Levine didn't know who Roman was, though the two had spoken before. He knew nothing of the Bookshop other than its name. However, like most Station Chiefs, he was fiercely protective of his *patch*, as he'd called it, and didn't appreciate Roman's interference.

"I haven't pissed on anything," Roman said.

"You've made a mess, haven't you? That's what this is. You need me to clean something up."

"I just want to know if you've heard anything. Any local chatter? Anything from Moscow police?"

"I don't have sources in the Moscow police."

"I really hope that's not true."

Levine sighed. "Where was she going?"

"Café Pushkin, but you already know that." The driver had been sworn to secrecy, but Roman wasn't naive enough to believe that would extend to his own boss.

"And I would have advised you against going there," Levine said. "Whatever mess you've made could have been avoided if you'd only included me."

"I'll keep that in mind. Anyway, if she got in trouble, it wasn't at the café."

"Then what do you want from me?"

"The café wasn't her final destination. Her contact was going to give her another meeting place."

"And you know where that is?"

"I've got a list," Roman said. "I'll send it over."

He sent it and waited.

"This is twenty locations," Levine said incredulously. "Just how big an operation have you been running under my nose?"

"It's not as big as it looks."

"You've got to be kidding me. I don't have the men to check all these."

"Start with safe houses. Call me when you've got something."

38

Margot entered the apartment complex, coat collar high against her cheekbones. The entrance was brightly lit, and she was surprised by an old man in the hallway. He had a small dog on a leash. Evidently, they were on their way out for a late-night walk.

"They're out of order," he said when she pushed the button for the elevator.

"Right," she said, avoiding eye contact. The building contained 360 apartments on twelve floors—enough that residents wouldn't necessarily know one another—but it was still unnerving to see him, or anyone. She glanced at the dog, a Russian Toy Terrier with enormous floppy ears and little insulated boots on its feet.

"She gets restless at night," he said in explanation, as if one were required.

Margot nodded, then made for the stairwell. Nine flights and not a soul in sight. Thankfully.

When she reached the ninth floor, she stopped and waited, listening. An advantage of the elevator being out was that this was the only way anyone could follow. The disadvantage was that it was her only way out. When she was satisfied no one was behind her, she went out to the corridor and found the apartment. The door had been fitted with an electronic lock, and she opened it with a four-digit code. She rapped gently as she pushed it open. If Irina was inside, she didn't want to startle her.

The apartment appeared empty. The air was stale and musty, as expected for a place that likely hadn't been entered in months. And it was a good thing, she told herself, that Irina wasn't yet there. She'd looked panicked when Margot spotted her on the street, and this meant she hadn't rushed. She'd taken precautions. That was the hope, at least.

She shut the door, switched on the lights, and quickly scanned the other rooms—bathroom, single bedroom, and a connected kitchen-living room. She'd left the embassy unarmed, so she headed to the bedroom where she knew a weapon was stashed. She found an M11 pistol—a compact version of the familiar SIG Sauer P226—and confirmed that it was loaded. It was, with thirteen rounds of 9x19mm Parabellum.

Gun in hand, she went back to the living room. At the window, she pulled back a faded curtain to reveal the sprawl of Moscow's northern fringe. Endless apartment buildings, all identical, and the red and white lights of the snaking highway. It intersected the MKAD in a complicated knot of ramps and overpasses that were almost hypnotizing to look at.

A sound.

She spun, gun outstretched.

It was Irina.

"Margot!" Irina gasped, eyeing the gun.

Margot lowered the weapon, watching carefully as Irina shut the door behind her. "Something's wrong?" she said.

"I don't know," Irina said, eyeing Margot as if she expected her to point the gun again.

Margot put it in the pocket of her coat. "You're all right here. We're safe."

Irina didn't believe it and moved further from the door, her gaze flitting around as she hurried through to the bedroom, the bathroom, clearing the apartment as Margot had.

"We're not safe," she said, satisfied the place was empty. "My name's been flagged. The FSB is looking for me."

"Flagged? When did that happen?"

"Right before I got to the café," Irina said. "The system screwed up and sent me the general alert. If I'd been home when it happened, I'd be dead already."

"What does it mean?"

"It means they know," Irina said desperately. "What I've been up to. Maybe even what I stole."

"I'm sorry," Margot said.

"Your harebrained scheme," Irina said, "to meet at Zubarev's—"

"I know," Margot said quickly.

"It would have been a death trap."

"I'm sorry," Margot said again. "My people wanted to force your hand. You'd broken contact, and they needed—"

"Broken contact? I'm fighting for my life here. I paused contact because Chichikov raided my offices. Dozens of my colleagues were arrested. They're clamping down on everything. I couldn't use the radio because Center 16 launched new monitoring protocols across the capital. It was only a matter of time before they locked my broadcasts."

"I'm so sorry, Irina. I fought them on it. I tried to buy you more time."

"It doesn't matter," Irina said, shaking her head. "Nothing matters now."

"That's why you broke protocol at the café," Margot said.

Irina shrugged. "When I saw the alert, I was going to cut and run. I was going to run as far and fast as I could. You'd never see me again."

"What changed your mind?"

"I watched you. In the café. I trusted you, and I remembered what you told me the first time we crossed paths."

"What I told you?"

"In any case, we have to finish what we started. We can't let Chichikov win."

"We need to get you to the embassy."

Irina shook her head. "Let's not kid ourselves, Margot. The embassy won't take me in. They know my history with Chichikov. The personal angle. It could trigger war."

Margot was going to protest, but the look on Irina's face told her there was no point. They both knew it was true. Irina was on her own now. And with the Kremlin on her tail, well…. The odds weren't good.

Irina returned to the door and peered through the peephole. "You never received my card, did you?" she said.

"What card?"

"I sent a postcard to the embassy. *Ten' Stalina*?"

"*Ten' Stalina*?"

"You didn't get it, then?"

"That was the message?"

"A warning. Hidden in plain sight."

"I didn't know."

"It doesn't matter now. I have the files with me."

"Files?"

Irina reached into her bag and took out a small portable hard drive. "This is everything I could get," she said. "Encrypted files, schematics, drawings, cyberattack code."

"This is the attack, then?" Margot said, looking at the hard drive before putting it in her pocket. "This is what you were talking about in your final message?"

"Yes, but it's encrypted—I couldn't break it. Your people will have to."

"What can you tell me about the attack?" Margot said. "How much do you know? I need everything. My people need everything."

"Only what I told you before," Irina said. "An attack on the US homeland. But combined with what we know of Chichikov, and the fact that he said it would be bigger than Ukraine—"

"Okay," Margot said, nodding. "We need to get these files to the embassy."

"Not *we*," Irina said. "*You*."

"I'm not leaving you, Irina. We're in this together."

Irina looked out through the peephole again. "You know there's no running from Chichikov. He'll chase me to the ends of the earth. Even if I made it to your embassy, he'd go to war to drag me out."

"I'm not abandoning you," Margot said. "We'll figure it out."

Irina's voice was soft, almost bitter. "Don't say things we both know you can't deliver."

"After all you've done for us, for *me*—"

Irina shook her head. "I didn't do it for you. I did for my country. The Russian people will lose everything if Chichikov isn't stopped. I'm willing to pay the price for that."

The Honeytrap

"Wait here. I'll take this to the embassy, then come back. We'll get out—together."

Irina gave her a thin smile. She opened her mouth—

Then they heard it. A sound in the corridor.

"They're here," Irina hissed, leaning to the peephole again.

Then, the door exploded inward.

A flash of light.

A roar of splintered wood.

39

Oksana sprinted down the corridor and slammed through the service door. The magnet held—no alarm, no siren. Just silence. She leaned over the rail to see down the stairwell and immediately drew back.

"Hey!" a voice echoed from below. "Someone up there?"

Oksana checked her watch—one-hundred-twenty seconds since she'd triggered the alarm. No way Muldowney was on the scene yet. A door somewhere below slammed, followed by footsteps and the crackle of a security guard's radio. She made sure the lower half of her face was still covered, then darted up the stairs and pushed through the fire doors.

The alarm shrieked to life—an old mechanical bell howling through the stairwell like a ship's horn in fog. The lights dimmed, and a strobe flashed, but she hardly noticed as she rushed along another corridor. She'd expected the same layout—but this floor was all wrong. Instead of running east-west, following the line of 57th Street, the corridor ran north-south, parallel to Madison Avenue and the building's west façade. Also, instead of raw brick and a concrete floor, it had carpet and a commercial drop ceiling.

She moved fast, past doors for other businesses, uncertain where she was headed but acutely aware of the ticking watch on her wrist. The cameras overhead meant it was only a matter of time before security caught up to her. Moving almost at a run, she reached a large freight elevator, just as the watch on her wrist began to beep. That marked three and a half minutes since she'd triggered the silent alarm. Muldowney would be on the scene any second.

There was another fire door next to the elevator, leading to another set of emergency stairs, but she wondered if the elevator would be a better option—if it even functioned during a fire alarm. If she could take it to the basement, there might be a way out that way. She jabbed the elevator button twice—nothing.

A voice barked from down the hall. "You there—stop!"

She saw the guard—barreling toward her, not Muldowney, just building security—and bolted through the fire door. Leaping down two flights, she got to the second floor and shoved her way through to another corridor.

Panic closed in. The building's security team was onto her. The fire alarm was blaring. It was only a matter of time before Muldowney's team was on the scene.

She ran, disoriented now, past delivery bays for retailers. She sped past bays 201 to 204 and rounded a corner. Behind her, she heard the crackling of a two-way radio.

"Muldowney, on site."

"Level two," the guard responded. "Requesting back up."

She was running out of time, and hiding wasn't an option. She had to get out, and now.

The only way to do it was through the retail units. She went first to 205, slamming against the door. It had an electronic lock, accessed by swiping a fob, and when she tried the door—it was solid as a brick wall. Same story with 206 and 207, but the last one, 208, had the same old-school mechanical lock that the *Tsaritsa* staff door had. She dropped to a crouch, tools already in hand. The tension wrench slid into the keyway—her fingers trembling so badly she could barely hold the pick. It slipped. Fell to the floor.

"Hey, stop!" the guard shouted as he rounded the corner. "Stop, or I'll shoot."

She glanced his way. The game was up—but he wasn't coming for her, not alone, and his weapon stayed holstered. He was waiting for backup, she thought, and that gave her one final chance. "Visual on intruder. Level two," he said into his radio, then to Oksana, "I mean it. Stop what you're doing."

She snatched the pick from the floor, jammed it in, felt the pins align—and the lock gave. She burst through.

"Hey!" the guard cried as she slammed and locked the door behind her.

She was in a retail space—dark, save for the fire alarm strobes and the light spilling in from the street. The store contained luxury clothing, and as she moved toward the stairs, she realized she'd been there before.

Versace. Of course. The one she used to window-shop. Back before she became this—thief, fugitive, ghost. Whatever she was now.

As she reached the stairs, she passed a window and scanned the sidewalk below. There was nothing there. All clear.

She hurried down a sweeping staircase to the ground floor, passing displays of silk in bold patterns. Behind her, the guard pounded on the door like he meant to break through.

She reached for the street entrance—it unlocked from the inside—but just as she was about to shove it open, a cruiser slid into view, moving like a shark in shallows. It pulled up to the corner and came to a halt. The siren wasn't wailing, but its lights were flashing. An officer got out and scanned the street. He said something into his radio, then wandered out of sight along 57th.

Oksana didn't wait for him to come back. She pushed through the door and was immediately engulfed in ice-cold air. The fire alarm was blaring, and strobe lights flashed along the length of the building. She knew the cop might come back any second but didn't dare look in that direction. She didn't look at the cruisers tearing down Madison either, sirens screaming, blue lights bouncing off every windowpane.

She turned north and marched—forcing herself not to run. Behind her, the building howled.

Under her coat, the package weighed nothing—and *everything.*

40

The door blew inward just as Margot yelled, "Take cover!"

It hurled Irina across the room and, a second later, something small and metallic clattered across the floor. Then, the smoke bloomed.

Margot grabbed Irina and pulled her behind the kitchen counter just in time to avoid a spray of bullets.

"Stay down!"

Bullets pelted the other side. Margot raised her gun over the top and fired two shots blindly. "Come on," she cried, trying to drag Irina behind the solid steel of the refrigerator. But Irina didn't come. She didn't respond. Blood trickled from her mouth.

"Irina," Margot breathed, horrified.

She checked Irina's body—then drew back her hands, slick with blood. Irina had been hit, and more than once. And she was trying to say something. Through the blood in her throat, it came as a pained gurgle.

As the smoke thickened, Margot leaned in close and placed her ear to Irina's mouth.

"*Ten' Stalina,*" Irina gasped.

Margot held her, looked at her face, then locked eyes with her. Her mind flitted to the moment they'd first met. "This will cost you your life," Margot had said.

"Both our lives," Irina had answered.

Another burst of bullets ripped into the room, submachine gun fire, and Margot fired two more blind shots at the door. "Irina!" she gasped. "Don't do this. Don't let go."

Irina mouthed something else, blood rising in her throat, strangling her. Margot heard a single word. "Run!"

She stared as the last of Irina's life faded from her eyes. She'd seen this moment in nightmares. Now, it was real. As Irina took her last breath, Margot had a sudden, overwhelming realization. They would both be proved right.

Then she was moving. She rolled—no time to stand, to think—just muscle and instinct as she dove for the steel bulk of the refrigerator, bullets shattering the room behind her.

It was getting harder to breathe in the smoke, impossible to see, and she fired another shot at the door as more submachine gun fire shredded the kitchen cupboards.

Bullets tore into Irina's body.

She was already gone.

A pool of crimson blood spread around her.

Margot fired again, though she could see nothing now, then dashed into the living room, diving behind the sofa.

More gunfire, still directed at the kitchen, and Margot scrambled along the length of the sofa and made for the wall of the room. Then, hugging the wall, she crept to the front door and waited, holding her breath. There was a break in the gunfire, and she didn't dare move, didn't dare breathe, forced her eyes to remain open through the pain of the smoke.

The instant a man appeared in the entry, she grabbed his arm, bent it backward, and pumped two bullets into his torso using his own gun. He was wearing kevlar, and the bullets didn't penetrate, but he felt their punch. In his confusion, she pushed him back out to the corridor, where he was immediately gunned down by his own guys.

There were voices in the corridor then—two men—debating whether they should wait for backup. She dashed across the room, tripping over shattered glass and broken furniture as gunfire tore past her. She reached the narrow hallway leading to the bedroom as another spray of bullets shattered everything behind her.

In the bedroom, she went to the weapons stash and ejected her magazine, replacing it with another. She grabbed a flash-bang and crouched in the corner behind a large wooden dresser.

She guessed this was an FSB or GRU advance unit. The alarm had been raised and somehow they'd tracked Irina to this place. Perhaps they'd been following her all along, waiting to find out who she was meeting. If it really was just three men, then backup wouldn't be far behind. She knew how they operated. They wouldn't be allowed to sit back and wait. They'd press their attack.

She heard them then, trouncing through the living room, tripping in the smoke, and announcing their positions like three-year-olds playing hide and seek. A single gunshot. The final insult to Irina.

The *coup de grâce*.

Then, the sound of padding feet, creaking floorboards, two-way radios. They were coming her way, and they would come together.

She saw the beam of flashlights in the smoke but resisted the urge to throw the flash-bang. She counted the seconds as they inched closer. Then it came, another smoke canister. She took a deep breath and forced herself to stare into it.

When she saw the shadow of the first man in the smoke, she threw the flash-bang and covered her eyes. Bang!

Then she fired. She saw the vague outline of the man she'd hit and adjusted aim. A headshot, and before his body hit the ground, she'd rolled across the bed to the other side of the room. The third man wouldn't get a clear shot at her without entering, and she waited again in silence, listening to his footsteps, his hesitation, his request on the radio to pull back.

She didn't wait. She rounded the corner and leaped—straight into him. She slammed into him shoulder-first, pain lancing through her body. He staggered back.

Too late—she realized her mistake. There was a fourth man behind him.

He opened fire, and the third man took the rounds meant for her.

As she fell, she raised her weapon and fired.

One to the chest.

One to the skull.

The fourth man crumpled, and everything went quiet.

Through the smoke, she scanned the living room, the kitchen, the doorway leading out to the corridor. There was no one there, though the light in the living room was now flickering as if from a sudden lack of electricity. The effect was amplified by the smoke, giving the room the strange intermittent glow of a lightning storm in clouds.

Something on the floor caught her eye. She bent, cautious, and lifted it. A black battery pack, duct-taped tight. A red light blinked. Coiled wires. Duct tape. A voltage step-up. She dropped it like it burned.

Whatever it was, it didn't belong.

She checked that she still had the hard drive, then slipped out of the apartment, scanning the corridor as she went.

The door of another apartment opened a crack, and a woman peered out.

"Back inside," Margot hissed.

The door slammed shut, and Margot began running.

41

Oksana slouched low in the backseat as a flurry of police sirens tore past.

"What the hell's going on?" the driver muttered, watching the chaos unfold in his rearview. There were at least six cruisers back there—lights flashing, sirens screaming—and multiple fire trucks.

"No idea," Oksana said quietly.

She'd wanted to go home—to her bed, her comforter, her little gas heater—but she didn't dare. Instead, she asked to be taken to the Port Authority Bus Terminal. She sat low, shielding her face as they passed still more police cars.

The break-in had been a mess. Her heart jackhammered like it wanted out of her chest. She'd gotten her prize—the unseen painting tucked in her coat—but it hadn't been clean. She'd triggered every alarm in the building, kicked the whole hornet's nest. Police and firefighters had swarmed, as well as Muldowney and the building's own security.

Dozens of cameras must have caught her—entering the building, crossing the street, waiting in the cold. They'd know where she'd waited before the job. She'd kept her face concealed, but what if she'd slipped up? What if some angle caught enough for a composite? What if she'd left a fingerprint on the tool bag? What if she was—that very instant—being captured on some grainy cab camera?

Paranoia.

But there was no pretending—it hadn't been a clean job.

A clean job required perfect control, and this had been about as controlled as a junkie swinging a crowbar in a Rolex store. A smash and grab. And she hadn't left the scene on her own terms, in her own time. She'd bolted like a two-bit shoplifter.

"Here we are, lady," the driver said.

She got out and headed straight for the subway, turtleneck still pulled high. She caught the A Train to Washington Square, switched lines, and rode the G train into Brooklyn. At Fulton Street, she got off and started walking—no plan, no destination. Just motion.

She didn't see any cameras, but that didn't mean they weren't there. These days, they were everywhere—doorbells, cellphones, ATMs—lurking in every corner like roaches. She kept looking over her shoulder, half-expecting sirens and handcuffs at any moment.

This wasn't like her other jobs. They hadn't left her like this.

There was no exhilaration—only panic.

She crossed onto Schermerhorn and, spotting a Holiday Inn, decided it would have to do. Anything beat stalking the streets, twitchy and paranoid, attracting attention.

The entrance was locked. She buzzed. A heavy click and the lock gave.

She entered, and behind the front desk, a concierge watched her approach. "Checking in?" he said.

"Is that okay?"

"Reservation?"

"No."

He tapped at his computer. "That's fine. I've got a room for you. I'll just need ID and a credit card."

Oksana hesitated—showing ID now felt like a bad idea—but she told herself she was being foolish. She'd created as much distance as she could from the gallery, and if anyone was looking for her by name, then she had bigger problems to worry about than checking into this hotel.

She took the cheapest room—a twin without breakfast for $279 plus tax—and went straight up, locked the door, and shut the curtains.

She sat on the bed and stared at the bubble-wrapped package. Her hands were shaking. She clenched them in her lap, willing them still.

A minute passed, and another, and she still hadn't looked at the painting. Part of her didn't want to—as if not knowing could keep the danger suspended, unreal. She almost hoped the package contained nothing of value at all. Something cheap, something worthless.

But then she thought of *Novoguard*, the pictures on their website, the truck outside the *Tretyakov*. They didn't seem like the type to deliver postcards and utility bills. No, they delivered high-value packages. Life-and-death packages. Packages worth killing for.

She swallowed and told herself that was what she wanted. That was the whole point. She'd promised to make Proctor pay—for the rape, and for the power he still held over her.

That required leverage.

On the counter by the TV was a wine bottle opener, and she used the serrated blade on the back to cut open the bubble wrap, careful not to damage what was inside. She couldn't believe how light it was, how insubstantial. All that chaos—for something that weighed less than a sandwich.

Inside, she found a ten-by-twelve-inch panel. She held her breath as she looked at it, examining the back first.

The canvas was coarse, glued to birchwood with rabbit-skin glue. The kind of rough mounting you only saw on Russian works from a certain era. It was frayed slightly at the edges, and she inhaled the dusty smell of ground linseed oil, lead white, and gray pigment. It was definitely old.

She turned it over, her first glimpse at the front, and forced herself to breathe. And then—relief. And disappointment.

One glance and she knew—this was not the type of painting that anyone would kill for.

That wasn't to say it was worthless—there was a market for it—but she'd passed up paintings worth millions for a niche item, of interest only to a few specific collectors. If she had to guess, it would be lucky to fetch thirty or forty grand at auction. Maybe.

Would losing it be enough to harm Proctor? A modest financial hit—depending on his insurance. And a break-in was never ideal in his line of work.

But ultimately, no. A painting like this was not going to be the ruin of him. If anything, it would be an inconvenience. It was not going to make him pay in the way she'd set out to do. Even if it had been imported illegally, she couldn't see anyone going to jail over it.

It was a bust.

That said, it was also unlikely to get her murdered in her sleep.

She took a breath and tried to make sense of it. Relief

that she was still breathing. Rage that Proctor would keep breathing, too. And he'd tighten his security like a noose, shutting her out for good. There would be no second chance. This had been her shot to make him pay. And she'd blown it.

She held the picture to the light. It was mundane to the point of insult—a trite propaganda piece—a barge passing through a canal lock. On the banks of the canal, workers under a red banner watched the barge as disinterestedly as Oksana now was. The palette was muted, tones of black and gray and blue, and it was the brushwork, if anything, that gave the painting what little expression it possessed. Even that, though, given the painting's small size, might be said to be overdone. Overall, it was a drab, unremarkable rendition of the Socialist Realist style, and she'd seen dozens of works just like it, churned out under Stalin's iron fist.

There was no art in it, only fear. In those years, artists bowed to the state—or disappeared into the monstrous Gulag that swallowed twenty million souls. That was all this painting was.

An act of obedience.

Not art—propaganda.

Submission to the totalitarian power.

Paint or starve. That was the compact Stalin made with his artists.

Paint—or vanish into the machine.

This painting was a relic from a time when truth carried a death sentence. And this one wasn't even of anything momentous. By the looks of it, it was a canal opening. Stalin had paraded his *achievements*, and canal openings were certainly among them, but it could hardly be described as anything earth-shattering. One little barge in a narrow canal. A hundred huddled onlookers. A stark, hellish landscape in the background.

She studied the onlookers now, wondering if they were prisoners. That would explain their blank, joyless faces. Perhaps they weren't celebrating at all, as the banners suggested, but were inmates, dehumanized and starving, forced to watch the fruit of their suffering drift past.

Whatever it had once meant, the painting was dull, dead, and empty—like her revenge.

42

Roman paced the bookshop like a caged animal, picking up books only to discard them moments later, while Foxtrot watched from behind her desk, visibly tense. The shop had shut for the night, and outside, the sleet had finally given way to snow.

"You're making me nervous, Roman."

"We should have heard something."

"Traipsing around, messing up my displays isn't going to help."

He forced himself to stop pacing and glanced at his phone—still no updates, no messages, nothing. The Council meeting had been postponed pending an update from Margot, but there wasn't one. He picked up another book, a Lance Spector thriller, and put it back on the shelf.

"Sit down, for crying out loud," Foxtrot said.

"You should go home," he said back to her, then added feebly, "Christmas."

"You know I have nowhere to be."

He nodded, then poured some of her burnt coffee into a

styrofoam cup. He stirred in some powdered milk, took a sip, and winced.

"Not up to your usual standards, Your Highness?"

He dropped onto the sofa with a groan, the weight of everything pressing in. "We should check again with Boreal."

She hit some keys on her keyboard and picked up the phone. Roman watched like a hawk as she waited for Boreal to pick up. She put down the receiver.

"No answer?"

"It's late over there."

"God damn it!" he snapped as coffee sloshed down his shirt—for the second time that day. It was the same shirt he'd spilled coffee on that morning, and he decided it was time for a change. "Tell me there's a clean shirt upstairs."

Foxtrot looked at him over the rims of her glasses. "I hope you're not suggesting I get it for you."

With an exaggerated sigh, he rose to his feet and went upstairs. There, he found a clean shirt, still in its Neiman Marcus packaging, and put it on. He was doing up the buttons when Foxtrot called out from the bottom of the staircase. "Roman!"

"Yes? Is it her?"

"You'd better get down here."

"What is it?" he said, hurrying down.

She was back at the desk, her eyes glued to the computer monitor.

"What's happened?"

Her voice was flat when she spoke, reading blankly from the screen. "An emergency bulletin from Homeland."

"What does it say?"

She glanced at him, about to speak, but stopped herself.

Returning her gaze to the screen, she read the words verbatim.

"Alert! Alert! Principal down. National Security Advisor, Gabriella Wintour."

Roman stiffened, knuckles whitening on the arm of the sofa. "My God," he said quietly. "Is she...."

"Dead?" Foxtrot said.

"Well?"

"It doesn't say."

"Contact the White House. Find out everything—now."

She tapped rapidly at her keyboard and said, "I'm in the Continuity Comms system."

"And?"

She looked up. "Roman, they're saying she's dead."

"Dead?" he rasped, a knot catching in his throat like a stone. "How?" He stared at her, waiting.

"Execution-style," she said at last. "Gunshot to the head."

Roman stood absolutely still, as if his body were made of granite. He heard Gabriella's voice in his head—calm, ruthless—just as it had echoed in the meeting room. *If we walk now, we show them we don't keep faith.* She'd deserved better.

"Roman? Roman?"

"Call me a cab," he said, already grabbing his coat. "I need to get to the White House." He was halfway to the door, coat half-on, when Foxtrot's phone rang.

They both stared at it for a second before she snatched it from its base. "Hello?" she said. "Boreal?"

Roman stared at her as she listened. It took an eternity.

"Understood," she said at last, then put down the phone.

"What?" Roman said eagerly. "What did he say?"

"There was a shoot-out in Moscow."

"A shoot-out?"

"One of our safe houses. The apartment building by *Khovrino* metro."

"Okay," Roman said, swallowing, trying in vain to clear whatever was caught in his throat. "What else?"

"The GRU is in control of the scene."

"Not local police?"

She shook her head.

"And Margot?" he said, his voice betraying a quiver of emotion.

"He didn't say," Foxtrot said, typing furiously on her keyboard. "That's all he gave me."

"Get into SORM."

"I'm trying, Roman."

SORM was the GRU and FSB's shared domestic surveillance system, wired into all Russian internet service providers, phone companies, and online chat apps. The Russians used it to track everything, and Foxtrot had a back door.

"Here," she said, leaning closer to her monitor. "GRU advance team. Safe house near Khovrino. Extended shootout. Two female targets. Multiple fatalities."

"What else?" Roman asked, his voice thin.

"One of the targets was killed."

"Which one?"

Foxtrot shook her head. "I don't know."

"Was it her?" he said again, louder. "Was it Margot?"

Foxtrot looked him dead in the eye.

"If it's her...."

He stopped, unable to finish.

"Roman. Pull it together."

He pressed the heel of his hand into his eye, trying to grind away the rising dread. "Sorry," he said. He knew she was as worried as he was.

The Honeytrap

"The description says, one female casualty," she said.

"All right," Roman said.

"It also says that the FSB has called in hundreds of additional officers for a city-wide manhunt."

Roman looked at Foxtrot. Her face was pale. She was in as much shock as he was. She just hid it better. He wanted to comfort her—he knew she needed it—but the impulse faltered. Something held him back. Maybe fear. Maybe he was just too worn down to try.

"I have to go," he said.

He already knew the next chapter of this disaster was being written without him. And probably against him.

43

By the time Margot exited the metro, an hour had passed since the shootout at the safehouse.

By some miracle, she'd made it out.

She'd reached a patch of scrubland near the highway and crept to a dark, unwatched parking lot beneath an overpass, its rusted chainlink fence sagging inward. A handful of vehicles sat inside, shrouded in shadow. Crouching low, ducking the sweeping flashlight beams, she found an unlocked van and slipped inside.

She stayed hidden as the area swarmed with FSB and police.

Dozens of cruisers.

Dozens of men.

Canine teams.

Helicopters slicing the night sky with searchlights.

The search was frantic but sloppy. Dogs barked. Lights swept overhead. Within ten minutes, they'd widened the perimeter—and she slipped away.

She walked two kilometers to an unobserved bus stop, where she managed to get on a late-night bus as far as the metro. From there, she caught one of the last trains to *Krasnopresnenskaya*, where she now was.

She took in her surroundings, trying not to flinch every time a car passed. The traffic on *Barrikadnaya* was surprisingly steady for the hour, and she walked at a steady clip. At the corner of *Konyushkovskaya*, she spotted the brick wall of the embassy compound a few hundred yards further down the street.

A gated sally port guarded by armed marines—tantalizingly close.

She could almost smell the ambassador's Fabreze. Thirty seconds at full sprint. That was all it would take. But it might as well have been thirty years.

Outside the gates, eight Russian cruisers and an armored personnel carrier blocked the road. Her hand clenched the reassuring steel of her pistol, but shooting her way through wasn't an option. For one thing, her own side wouldn't countenance it. Even if she made it through, she wouldn't be safe. That wasn't how diplomatic immunity worked.

She had to find another way. A quieter way.

If she was smart, she wouldn't try to get in at all, she would get on a train and slip out of the city, then across the border and out of Russia entirely. She had the hard drive. As close as she was, she had a better chance of reaching the embassy in Warsaw or Berlin than this one.

But there wasn't time for that. She needed to get the drive to a CIA tech team—and urgently. They would copy it, back it up, and, most importantly, send its contents securely to Roman, who could get it decrypted and find out what the hell was on it. Every minute she held it was a minute closer to capture—or death. But it was also a minute closer to the attack.

She pulled the drive from her breast pocket—the case smeared with blood—and studied it.

It seemed sturdy enough. She considered simply throwing it over the wall, praying it survived the fall. Agents in her situation had done worse—with mixed results.

Another option was to get someone from inside to come out and meet her. The problem with that was that they'd be facing the same problem she was—getting back inside without being intercepted. It didn't look like anyone would be getting into that embassy any time soon without being thoroughly searched by the FSB.

She crossed the intersection, moving at a steady pace, every nerve taut, resisting the urge to look over her shoulder. At the Garden Ring she would be able to turn in the direction of the embassy. That road was busier than *Konyushkovskaya*, more than five lanes in either direction, and there'd be enough traffic to let her blend in.

She ducked into a small park, careful of the slick pavement. She'd been there before, in the summertime, and it was a lot prettier at that time of year, with trees at the center dripping blossoms into an enormous fountain. Now, the bare branches of the trees seemed to reach out for her like clawing fingers.

The far side of the park was flanked by a shopping center, shut for the night, and to her right was an enormous high-rise apartment building. It was one of Stalin's Seven Sisters—the original Soviet skyscrapers built in the fifties—and it dominated the sky above.

On its sixteenth floor, Roman had a safe house, intended for precisely this type of situation. She'd thought about leaving the drive there—or at least contacting Roman from its phone, but she saw now that that wasn't an option either. Four police cruisers were parked in front, their lights flickering, and uniformed cops stood around the entrance as if waiting for someone.

She adjusted course—head down—and turned into the narrow street that curved around the side of the building. It abutted directly against the back of the compound and there was another entrance there. It was a long shot, but—

"Hey! You!" a cop barked from the steps of the apartment building.

For a split second, she froze, a thousand thoughts flashing through her mind at once. Then she was running.

"Hey! Halt!"

She sprinted toward the embassy, praying she didn't slip on the ice. She didn't dare look back, but she knew they were there, hot on her tail.

"Stop!" a cop shouted. A gunshot rang into the air.

It missed.

She didn't know if it had been fired as a warning or aimed to kill.

Either way, she kept running. The perimeter came into view. She was close enough now that she could make out the barbed wire, the security cameras. She spotted the service entrance—a small guard post standing next to it like an old telephone booth. Inside, she could see a marine's face, staring wideyed, already aware he was watching a disaster unfold.

She was close enough she could almost throw him the drive.

The post abutted the perimeter wall, and a door inside it lead into the compound proper. If she could just make it, she'd be inside the wire.

But she had no illusions—nothing about this would be clean.

She kept running, heart hammering, speed building on the downward slope, fighting to keep her footing.

She was fifty meters from the post. Forty-five. Forty.

"Help!" she cried, gasping, staring at the faces of two marines now. They watched in horror, frozen, every ounce of their training screaming not to leave their post.

A second gunshot.

This one struck the wall of the compound, mere feet in front of her. Definitely aimed to hit.

Twenty five meters—close enough to make out the marines clearly, their faces wide-eyed with the blank expression of men who had no idea what they were supposed to do. No one had trained them for this.

A revving engine. She glanced over her shoulder.

She saw the grille a split second before impact.

Then everything went dark.

The car hit her like a freight train, flipping her, weightless, over the roof. A red-blue strobe of light. Pavement. Ice. Pain.

But she focused.

Skidding to a halt with a scream of brakes, the car came to rest between her and the guardpost. The driver's door opened.

Behind her, two cops who'd been chasing on foot slowed down, breathless, guns drawn. They approached like men sent to put down something rabid.

"Game over," one of them gasped between breaths.

Margot tried to get to her feet, but the same man yelled, "Stay down!"

She remained where she was, coiled like a spring.

"Hand over the drive. We know you have it."

She eyed them, then the cop by the car. Three against one, and they were armed and willing to kill. In the guard post, the two marines watched on. She met their eyes, pleading without words. Neither moved a muscle.

They knew the rules of engagement. Everything in their training told them not to intervene. Their jurisdiction, their right to exist, began and ended at the walls of the compound. Within those walls, they were Americans on American soil. Outside, the very moment their boots hit the pavement, they were a two-man ground invasion. An act of war.

They knew it.

The cops knew it.

This would remain three against one.

The cop by the car spoke. "Don't make this any harder on yourself."

She remained silent, catching her breath.

"Silly bitch," he added, then to the other two, "Move in."

"Okay," she said, rising slowly to her feet. "You got me."

She made sure the two behind her kept their distance, then faced the third. He was closest, though not by enough to matter. She had her hands out in front of her, palms down, fingers splayed open.

"The drive's in my pocket," she said.

"No sudden moves," he answered. "Give us the coat."

She slowly untied the belt at her waist.

"Get it from her," he said to the other two.

Margot glanced over her shoulder.

They were younger, and timid. "Dispatch said she's dangerous," one of them said.

Margot remained as still as a statue, every muscle in her body coiled like a spring, ready to strike. She let the coat fall off her shoulder, though not to the ground.

"Don't you move," a cop said, inching closer.

He took a tentative step, then another. She slowed her breathing. Kept loose. Waited for his next step—then struck.

Like a cat, she spun, grabbing his head and following through with the momentum, swinging herself behind him.

Wild gunshots.

She snatched his weapon and returned fire, pelting the Kevlar vest of the cop by the car and forcing him to stagger backward. The other fired three times, and all three bullets hit the man she was holding.

She fired twice more, once at the man nearest, once at the man by the car. She hit both in the forehead, then let go of the man she was holding.

He slumped to the ground at her feet, gurgling and choking as he struggled to breathe. Her hands were covered in his blood. She wiped them on his uniform, then looked at the two marines in their post. They had no idea what they'd just witnessed, but they did know one thing—they weren't going to let her in.

The American government didn't kill Russians on the embassy doorstep—and it didn't shelter fugitives who did.

Margot ran—into exile, into the cold, into whatever came next.

44

Roman got off the bus at Lafayette Square, hurrying through the park as an ice-cold wind cut through him. He flashed his pass at the Eisenhower Building's northeast gate, went through security, and was scanned and patted down.

Once through, it was an elevator ride and an interminable series of corridors. The walk gave him time to think, though he tried not to. Outside the meeting room, a young aide with a fashionable blonde bob stood by the door, a black leather folio in her hand. Roman gave her a brief nod and said, "Is the man inside?"

"He is, sir," she said, knocking lightly and holding the door for him.

"Roman," the president said, rising to his feet.

"Mr President, please don't get up."

The fireplace was lit, and the president sat in the same chair he'd occupied that morning. It was hard to fathom that it was still the same day. The president didn't even look like the same man. His face was ashen with grief.

"Are you all right, sir?"

"Roman," he said again, his voice cracking as he tried to speak. He motioned for Roman to sit, extending his hand.

Roman clenched it tightly. "I'm so sorry, sir. I truly am. I know how close you two were."

"Thank you, Roman. You've lost a friend too. Don't think I don't know it."

"And the nation has lost a true warrior."

The president nodded, looked down at the whisky glass in front of him. He picked it up and took a sip, then said, "I just keep going over it in my head."

"Over what, sir?"

"We were together not three hours ago. In my office. I told her to go home."

"You couldn't have known—"

"Where are my manners?" he said suddenly, cutting him off. "Gracie," he called.

The door swung open.

"Bring my friend a drink," he said. "He takes it neat."

Roman watched the president carefully. The grief on his face was raw and unfamiliar. The two men had known each other a long time. They'd lost friends before. This was different.

The aide returned with a fine single malt on a tray. The president took it from her and poured Roman a generous measure. She hesitated, waiting for him to return the bottle to the tray. When it became clear he meant to keep it, she withdrew silently.

The president raised his glass. "To Gabriella," he said, "one of the good ones."

"To Gabriella," Roman said quietly, picturing her next to him on the *chaise*.

They both drank, the fiery liquid burning in Roman's

throat, and when he put down his glass, the president immediately topped it up. He refilled his own, too.

"When's the meeting?" Roman said, eyeing the president's glass.

"They're on their way," the president said. "The whole damn lot of them."

Roman nodded, thinking ruefully of what was coming. "I take it," he said, "that we're working under the assumption the Russians did this?"

"Leave all that to the FBI," the president said. "Tell me what the hell's going on in Moscow?"

Roman leaned forward. "I think we need to mount a search operation."

"So you've really lost her?"

"She's missing, yes. Missed her check-in. Irina Volkova—"

"Is dead."

"Yes," Roman said, taking another sip.

"But you can't mount a search operation in Moscow without Hawke. Without the Station Chief. You need their people, right? You don't have your own."

"Boreal has about fifteen agents in Moscow."

"Including sleepers?"

"Yes, and I think this warrants activating them."

The president stared into the fire, chewing his lip, thinking. He said nothing, and Roman wasn't sure where his mind was as he drained his glass again.

"I think Gabriella would have wanted us to remain focused on the mission," Roman said tentatively.

The president nodded, then looked Roman dead in the eye. "You haven't seen the Secret Service report, have you?"

"From Gabriella's home?"

"The account from the scene?"

"I haven't seen anything," Roman said. "Only the NCCS alert."

"So you don't know?"

Roman sighed deeply. He gathered from the president's tone that more bad news was coming. He felt a vibration from his phone but ignored it. "Know what, sir? The Continuity System said Gabriella was found with a gunshot wound to the head. Killed execution-style."

"It didn't mention Cassie, then, or the housekeeper?"

"It did not, sir."

"Cassie Westport, Gabriella's daughter. Fourteen years old. She's dead too."

Roman blinked. The air in the room seemed to vanish. His mind scrambled for meaning, for someplace to file the horror—but there was none. Just a blank, sickening silence. "Why would they do such a thing? This isn't how...."

Roman's words trailed to nothing. The president was at a loss, too, and a moment passed in complete silence.

Then the president said, "A woman named Gertrude Koeffer was there, also. Gabriella's housekeeper."

"It's barbaric."

"Yes, it is."

"It doesn't make sense."

"It makes perfect sense," the president said grimly.

"Fourteen years old?"

The president sipped from his glass again. He was staring at Roman. "It gets worse."

"Worse?"

"They weren't just executed," the president said, speaking like each word was a shard of glass in his mouth.

"I'm not sure I follow—"

"There's no doubt it's connected to Moscow," the president said. "To what's happening with Margot. Her safe house being found. Irina being found."

"Gabriella was tortured?"

"Worse than tortured," the president said. "They made her watch."

"Watch what?"

The president shook his head again, as if his mind recoiled from what needed to be said. He drank again. "Gabriella's daughter was found..." he began. "Fourteen years old. And Gabriella was forced to watch."

"I can't...," Roman stammered. "Their MO, Moscow, that's not how they operate...."

"It is now," the president rasped, his voice suddenly dry.

Roman locked eyes with him. For all the battles they'd fought together, all the grisly bloodshed they'd witnessed, this was different. They were on untested ground. Unsteady. "This just isn't how they operate," Roman said again quietly.

"So," the president continued, clearing his throat, "I mean, when I say Gabriella was a good soldier...."

"Absolutely," Roman said. "Best of the best."

"But they broke her, Roman. It's a certainty. Anything she knew, anything she was privy to, Irina's identity, Margot's cover, the list of safe houses...."

"I see," Roman said. In his mind, he'd written off everything in Gabriella's memo the moment she'd distributed it. He'd known it was only a matter of time before it found its way into Russian hands. What he hadn't written off just yet, however, was the information not written in her report. That included Irina's name, Margot's current cover, details on protocols, safe houses, emergency procedures. "This is why I didn't want to share my—"

"Yes, yes," the president said testily. "Your treasured

secrecy. I know, Roman. Save it for when the others arrive. You'll have plenty of time to explain yourself then."

"Right," Roman said gravely.

"They'll be out for your blood, Roman. You know it as well as I do. And, honestly, this time, I don't know that I'll be able to hold them back."

"I understand," Roman said.

The president took another drink, then looked back into the fire. "Tell me this was all worth it," he said quietly.

Roman said nothing. That was answer enough. He wanted to excuse himself, but there was a knock on the door.

"Yes?" the president said.

The aide appeared in the doorway. "Mr President," she said, coming in and handing him a tablet, "there's something you need to see."

"What now?"

"The Moscow embassy, sir. Recorded literally seconds ago."

The aide hit play, and Roman leaned forward to get a view of the screen.

Grainy, green-tinged footage from a night-vision security camera. The marker identified the location as the laneway behind *Kudrinskaya Park*. The street was still and dark— until, from off-frame, a woman burst into view, sprinting toward the embassy. It was too dark to identify her—but he knew instantly it was Margot, alive and crying for help.

She came down the slope at a dead sprint—then bang— she was floored by a speeding police cruiser. The car hit her, and she rolled right over the roof before landing hard on the ground.

"Oh no," he gasped.

Three cops closed in. Words were exchanged. One of

them approached cautiously. In a blur of motion, Margot disarmed him. Gunfire cracked the air—and within seconds, all three cops lay sprawled on the ground, unmoving.

Roman and the president sat quietly for a moment, staring at the screen.

"That's your little lady," the president said at last, his voice as dry as dust.

"Yes," Roman said, then to the aide, "where is she now?"

The aide shook her head.

He looked at the president, who seemed to be in shock.

"Sir," he said hesitantly, "I know this is bad."

"She just executed three Russian cops on the very threshold of the embassy."

"I don't know what to say, sir."

"It could be war, Roman—with Russia."

Roman met his gaze.

"War's already begun."

45

Sheryl Cassidy almost dropped the casserole on the way to the table, her hands trembling with exhaustion. It should have been a day of sugar cookies and last-minute gifts. Instead, she'd spent it glued to the television, watching the world fall apart. It was so stressful she'd taken one of the pills her doctor had prescribed—something she almost never did—and it had knocked her straight out.

That there was dinner at all was a small miracle, possible only because the kids shook her awake when it got dark, hunger finally prying them from their screens.

"Mom! MOM!" Kevin had cried, jumping up and down on the sofa.

She'd spoken to Harry in the morning—Jack Priesenhammer had made him call—but that felt like a lifetime ago, and he was unreachable again. It was insane—more than twenty-four hours, and still no word. No ETA. No reassurance. Just silence. She was beginning to wonder if he'd be home for Christmas at all.

She'd called Jeanine while the casserole cooked—but it

was no different at their house. Since dropping off Jack, she hadn't heard hide nor hair of him, and that was despite the fact he'd been in a car accident. Something very serious was going on, and it was made worse by the complete lack of communication from the plant. Everything she knew, she'd learned by compulsively scanning the news channels. They kept mentioning flooding, water levels, and glitches with the county's emergency response system, but nothing about why plant engineers weren't being allowed to leave the site.

"Harley, Kevin," she called. "Dinner's ready."

She still had the TV on in the background, something she usually tried not to do during dinner, and she hit the mute button on the remote.

"Finally!" Kevin said, throwing himself into his chair. "I'm starving to death."

Sheryl was skeptical, given the amount of Dorito crumbs she'd seen on the living room floor, but she hoped it was true.

She dished him a bowlful, and he said, "When's daddy coming?"

"Soon, honey. He's stuck at work because of the rain."

Another worry—were the roads even passable anymore?

Harley wandered in with her iPad, and Sheryl didn't have the heart to make her turn it off.

"Put it here, sweetie," she said, propping it up so she could continue watching *America's Got Talent* auditions while they ate.

The three of them picked tentatively at the Chef Boyardee extravaganza she'd concocted.

"What's this?" Kevin said, more confused than complaining.

"A new recipe."

"I like it," he said, raising his fork high above his plate to break a string of melted cheese.

"I don't know," Harley said, more skeptical, but she put a spoonful in her mouth as the iPad showed another girl walking onto the stage to sing *Frozen*.

On the TV, the screen flickered. The news chyron scrolled across the bottom of the screen—Assassination in Washington.

Sheryl blinked, then grabbed the remote and unmuted.

I'm standing here outside the home of President Westfahl's longtime political ally and National Security Advisor, Gabriella Wintour. We're still not clear on what happened, but preliminary reports suggest she was the victim of a home invasion that resulted in multiple homicides. It's believed that Gabriella Wintour is one of the deceased, as well as her fourteen-year-old daughter. The circumstances of the attack are unclear, and there's been no statement from the White House, but commentators are definitely raising the specter of a potential national security link—

She turned off the sound. She couldn't take it. It was one thing after another, and her nerves were already worn to threads.

"Mommy?" Harley said. "This meat's gross."

"Can you eat around it, honey?"

"It's inside the pasta. I can't eat around it."

Ordinarily, Sheryl might have put up more resistance,

but not tonight. "How about a grilled cheese?" she said, trying to keep her voice light.

Kevin looked up from his plate. "*I* want a grilled cheese."

"All right," Sheryl said, feeling a tightness in her throat and across her chest. She knew what it was, the onset of a panic attack, and she positively could not afford to lose her cool now in front of the children. "Why don't you both go back to the living room? I'll call you when it's ready."

As soon as they were out of sight, she rushed to her purse and dug out another of the heavy-duty pills from her doctor, swallowing it dry.

She was worried about Harley. It wasn't like her to be picky with food. It was a small crack in a child's armor, and Sheryl saw it.

Kevin was oblivious, but Harley knew enough to be scared—and she bottled it up. The parenting manuals—of which Sheryl had read too many—called it a type C personality. She would have to come up with something to tell her if Harry wasn't home very soon, and it wasn't a conversation she looked forward to.

She picked up her phone and tried him again. A little red number by his name reminded her that this was her seventeenth attempt without answer. She waited until just before his voicemail came on—she knew exactly how many rings—then hung up and dialed the plant's front office. This one answered immediately, but it was the same prerecorded message about technical difficulties she'd already heard a dozen times.

She put the phone down and started buttering bread for the sandwiches. She'd just opened the fridge when the TV jumped to breaking news. She snatched the remote and unmuted.

> We're coming to you live from the Chippokes Creek Campground here in Surry County, and as you can see behind me, things have taken a dramatic turn, folks.

Behind the reporter, a thick, black plume of smoke rose beyond the trees, stark against the night sky.

Sheryl's knees buckled. She recognized the ridge. It wasn't far from the south gate.

> —Word from the plant is that this is not related to core nuclear functionality, but rather an explosion at a backup fuel storage yard more than a mile from the reactor. I want that to be very clear, Percy. There's been an explosion, but it's absolutely *not* nuclear-related.
>
> —And what have you got to say to the families of plant workers? They've got to be terrified watching this.
>
> —All I can say is my heart goes out to them, and to reiterate, this was an explosion at an unmanned fuel yard. That smoke is not coming from the plant itself.
>
> —You're saying the storage yard is unmanned. Can you confirm whether there have been any casualties or injuries?
>
> —As of now, the plant's press office has issued a statement saying there are no casualties related to this accident, but they are searching for one worker who's unaccounted for. He was involved in Facility Mainte-

nance, according to the statement, and that's all they've said.

—So, one missing worker?

—Unaccounted for, Percy. Not missing. And let me say this again, because I've been asked to emphasize it for public safety. Right now, critical nuclear functioning at the Surry Plant is not impacted.

—They're very eager to get that across.

—Absolutely, they are, and with good reason.

Dizziness swept over Sheryl. She staggered, grabbing the counter to keep from falling. Her elbow struck a water glass, knocking it to the floor with a crash.

"Mom?" It was Harley, her voice high and scared, standing in the doorway. "What's wrong?"

"Honey—" Sheryl choked. "How long have you...."

"What's going on, mom?"

"I'll tell you what's going on. Go get your coats. Yours and Kevin's."

"Why? Where are we going?"

"Grandma's."

"What about daddy?"

"He'll meet us there, sweetie."

Harley hesitated, her small hands fisting the hem of her sweatshirt. "Mommy, you're scaring me."

Sheryl's heart broke. "We're all right, honey. We just need to get to grandma and granpa's. Go get your brother."

46

Margot was seated in the window of a second-floor hotel room near the *Kievsky Railway Station*. It was a run-down hotel in a rough neighborhood not too far from the embassy, and a place she knew well. It was also crawling with illicit nighttime activity. That, she hoped, would make someone like her—a single female with a trace of an accent—a tad less conspicuous.

The place wasn't on any CIA lists—no pre-mission surveillance, no backup plans, nothing. After what had happened, safe houses weren't an option. She didn't know what had gone wrong—whether she'd been followed, or Irina had—but it didn't matter anymore. What mattered was that she had the drive. And she needed to get it home.

The room was a dingy place—threadbare carpets and a flea-bitten mattress you couldn't have paid her to sleep on. Out on the street, there was a surprising amount going on, with hookers on the corner wearing long fur coats that they flashed open to reel in a customer. Cars crawled the curbs as if lining up for a drive-thru.

In the lobby, the manager—a big guy in a leather jacket

with a cigarette glued to the corner of his mouth—told her she'd have to pay extra for each visitor she brought up.

"I won't be having visitors," she'd told him, trying her damnedest not to give away the accent.

"Shame," he'd said, cigarette dangling precariously.

He gave her the creeps—she didn't trust him as far as she could throw him—but roaming the streets wasn't an option. Also, he'd accepted cash for the room and hadn't asked for ID.

She looked out the window at a black BMW crawling the curb. It was a three-series—a model she knew all too well—but when two women climbed in, she exhaled, though the coil of tension in her chest held firm. Every car could be the start of the next firefight. She watched it drive away, then looked at the clock by the bedside. She couldn't waste much time. The hard drive wasn't where it needed to be, and she still didn't have a real plan to get it there.

Perhaps someone coming to her was the better idea after all.

She couldn't call Roman, but she'd have to find a way to check in soon. Most likely, he was well aware of her status—the embassy had scores of security cameras, her mishap wouldn't have gone unnoticed—but he knew nothing of the drive.

And the drive was the whole point.

Maybe he'd tell her to just get to a computer and transmit the files in the clear. She wouldn't be able to decrypt them, but she could at least transfer them to Langley. The problem with that was the high probability Center 16 would intercept the data. They might even be able to corrupt it before Langley picked it up, and no one would know it had been done. That risk alone would render the data unreliable.

The best option was definitely to get the drive to a CIA analysis team, and the only team within a thousand miles was inside that embassy.

She scanned the room, her mind flitting from one option to the next.

What would be the political blowback, she thought, of what had happened outside the embassy? There wasn't much she could do about it now, but it weighed on her.

Wars had been started over less.

It also meant—if she made it to the embassy at all—that any respite would be short-lived. The Russians would demand she be handed over.

Focus, she told herself. Shut out distracting thoughts.

She'd placed the gun and hard drive on the sill next to her. No phone. No electronics of any kind. She was as certain as she could be that she hadn't been followed. She'd crossed the river at the *Borodinskiy Bridge*, a broad concrete span wide enough for eight traffic lanes. On this side, she sheltered in a small park, keeping the bridge in sight and watching for followers.

There were none.

Nevertheless, she refused to sleep.

There was a television in the room, which she didn't use, and an electric kettle, which she did—after checking inside for cockroaches. She made tea using a hotel tea bag, then turned off the light and sat back down by the window, leaning against the glass, angled so that she could see through a gap in the curtain without being seen herself.

Her mind wandered again—over what had happened, what was happening now, what would happen next.

How, she wondered, had the safe house been discovered so quickly? She herself hadn't known they'd be using it until Irina told her outside the café. And why had the Russians sent such a small team? One possible explanation was that the Kremlin had gotten access to the full list of safe houses—two dozen potential locations in all. With that many, they would have had to divide and conquer.

That would also mean the leak was in Washington. She thought back to Roman at the Council, fighting tooth and claw not to share his file. He'd seen this coming. He'd seen many things. She still held her grudge—he'd lied to the president, and she'd paid the price—but he'd been right, too. Widening the circle put everything at risk. She had no doubt, if he'd told the president about *Hummingbird* when he was supposed to, she'd have died years ago.

Thinking of Washington led her to Bryce. Was he with Cynthia right now, screwing her brains out, lying on his back blissfully with a cigarette in his mouth? It wasn't impossible, she thought. The cigarette was invention—but why not the rest? Cynthia could certainly offer him a better life than she ever could. Pretending otherwise had always been a lie.

The things she did for the job, the things she had to be prepared to do, were incompatible with having a true relationship with a man. That was another point, she thought ruefully, that Roman had been right on all along.

She was beginning to doze, succumbing to exhaustion, when she was jolted awake by a vehicle rounding the street corner. It was a lightly modified Lada Vesta—an unarmored civilian compact often used by Russian police. This one was painted in the Russian Military's *Izlom* fractured camouflage pattern, the preferred pattern of *Spetsnaz* units.

Here for her, then.

From what she could see, it wasn't accompanied.

Two men got out wearing black tactical gear and carrying PP-19 Bizons. One also carried a GM-94 grenade launcher. The Bizon was a submachine gun developed by *Izhmash* specifically for the MVD. That meant these two were probably counter-terrorism. Their backup, if it wasn't already watching from the shadows, wouldn't be far behind.

She considered opening fire on them from where she was, but the grenade launcher gave her pause. She was literally a fish in a barrel.

She grabbed her gun and the hard drive, then slipped out of the room. The corridor was empty, and she crept along it away from the staircase, ducking into a small alcove ten yards further down. The alcove held a vending machine on one side and an ice machine on the other. She tucked behind the ice machine, giving herself a dim view down the corridor in the reflection of the vending machine's glass.

A moment later, she heard footsteps on the creaky staircase leading up from the lobby. They must not have known for sure she was there, or they'd have waited for backup. She guessed the hotel manager had tipped them off, possibly in response to an FSB bulletin sent out to hotels. She'd known that was a risk.

They appeared in the corridor and went straight to her door, where they adopted a standard assault position—the breacher behind the wall, while the second man stood behind him, offset so he had a sightline to the door.

The second man fired a spray of bullets at the door's lock. When he stopped, the breacher stepped forward and kicked the door hard. It stuck on something and required a second kick before flying open on broken hinges. He ducked aside then, and the spotter went in first.

Her moment.

She swung out and fired. The shot landed clean. She was past him before his body hit the floor.

The second man whirled around, but he was too slow by

a fraction of a second. Her bullet struck him in the temple, making his head jerk backward as he crashed onto a small coffee table in the center of the room, shattering its glass top.

She snatched his Bizon, found the vehicle key in his pocket, and was at the window in seconds. Already, she could hear the sound of approaching sirens.

Slinging the Bizon over her shoulder, she opened the window and climbed out, lowering herself over the ledge before dropping to the street. She hit the ground as a police car careened around the corner, almost skidding into the building.

She raised the Bizon and pulled the trigger, spraying it with bullets. The windshield shattered, and one of the bullets must have hit the siren speaker because the wail suddenly dropped an octave, coming out as a low, electronic whimper. She got into the Lada and fired it up, revving the gas as the bellowing thrum of a helicopter shook the air.

She didn't look up.

She slammed the car into gear and hurtled down the narrow street. The car was a 1.8-liter manual with 122 horsepower—no stallion, but tuned for acceleration. It leaped off the mark. When she reached the river, she yanked the handbrake, slammed the clutch, and drifted onto the *Borodinskiy Bridge*. Traffic was all but non-existent, and she opened the throttle and sped over the bridge.

She had zero overhead cover, and it took only seconds for the gunfire to start raining down.

She saw the pocks of dust on the road before she heard them—a hundred bullets sparking off concrete. She swerved, dodging the gunfire—but slammed hard against the steel rail dividing the lanes. The car lost speed, but she jammed it into second gear and slammed her foot down, sending it into an accelerated lurch that almost lost her control a second time. Somehow, she stayed on the road, swerving onto the Garden Ring and opening a gap between herself and the pursuing chopper.

It was then that she saw, coming right for her, two more police cars, lights flashing and sirens screaming. She had no choice but to hold her ground, and she floored the pedal, accelerating directly at them. She hurtled forward blindly—at some point she shut her eyes—and in the final second, they swerved to avoid collision. In her rearview, she saw one crash into a lamppost, while the other fell into a violent, rubber-burning spin. At the same time, another cruiser rounded from a side street and took up the chase. She kept her foot down as it gained on her—the helicopter closing in overhead.

The American Center loomed in front of her—a massive modernist fortress of barred windows, locked gates, and a high metal fence. It marked the east-most edge of the embassy compound, and she gunned the car toward it, closing the distance in a blur. At the last possible second, she flung open her door, slammed the brakes, and leaped out. She managed to clear the vehicle right as the trailing police car smashed into its back, sending both skidding into a concrete barrier.

She hit the pavement hard. Pain exploded in her ribs. She tumbled, breathless until everything was still.

It was the helicopter that brought her to her senses. It had overshot but was already banking back. She pushed through the pain and scrambled to her feet, scanning the fence for an entry point. There was none.

She made for the narrow side street that led toward the embassy entrance, limping and running as best she could, every muscle screaming in protest. The helicopter was coming in hard and fast, but it couldn't follow down the narrow street without rising over the rooftops. She dashed a hundred yards, and when she saw the Marines at the first guard post, she almost burst into tears. One of them was out on the sidewalk, gesturing madly for her to run faster.

Behind her was another cruiser. She heard the siren, then the engine, then saw the glow of its flashing lights on the wet tarmac. It didn't matter. She was close enough that it could no longer stop her.

Ten yards.

Five.

One.

She'd made it.

Then the bullet struck—clean and sharp—and the world faded to black.

47

Roman stood in his office in the Eisenhower Building, jaw clenched, temples throbbing. It was a room he'd never truly moved into, and with its bare walls, government-issue desk, ergonomic chair, and empty filing cabinet, it had always felt more like a cell than an office.

Today only confirmed it.

The Council was already in session. Its members—the full *plenum,* minus him and, of course, Gabriella—had been seated around the big circular table for nearly an hour.

Even Ethel Sinclair, the NSA Director, who'd attended the previous meeting remotely, had flown in at the last minute from her Montana ranch.

And it wasn't the power plant they were discussing, though that situation was increasingly dire.

It was Margot. The mission. *Hummingbird.*

He'd never seen anyone iced out of a meeting like this—like a recalcitrant schoolboy outside the headmaster's office. It wasn't just humiliating, it was dangerous.

He'd been watching the reports from Surry County as

closely as anyone. It hadn't been confirmed yet, but to him the signs were clear.

It was an attack.

An act of war.

But instead of dealing with it, Doerr and Hawke had staged some sort of procedural *coup*, citing obscure rules that allowed the rest of the Council to decide his fate without his being present to defend himself.

He could see the writing on the wall. The president hadn't intervened. Gabriella—his only real ally—was gone. That left only wolves.

His title—Director of Clandestine Services—was a relic from a time before the current hierarchy existed. That ambiguity had always made him an outsider, a threat to their order. Now that they had the chance to neutralize him, they were going to take it.

He glanced at his watch.

Right on cue, the aide with the blonde bob appeared in the doorway. "They're ready for you now."

He nodded, straightened his uniform, and summoned what dignity he could muster as he followed her down the corridor. At the door, he took a deep breath before entering.

Inside, Jake Hawke was speaking animatedly, but snapped his mouth shut the instant Roman entered. Every eye turned to him. No one said a word. He scanned for a single friendly face. There wasn't one.

"Sorry I'm late," he said, aiming for humor and missing.

Hawke smiled facetiously. "You're a busy man, Roman."

It was the same table they'd been seated at when Roman and Margot had dropped their bombshell about *Hummingbird*, but to Roman, the entire world had shifted in the intervening hours.

And Gabriella's seat was empty.

As he looked at the grim faces, he knew the verdict was already in. They'd decided his fate.

"Why don't you take your seat?" the president said.

Roman sat down, and the president picked up a single page of typed text. "I need to read this into the record, Roman. It's the resolution we passed in your absence."

"Go ahead," Roman said, forcing calm.

The president cleared his throat, buying himself a few seconds, then began. "Be it resolved that the actions of the Director of Clandestine Services—in his decision not to inform the President about the *Hummingbird* operation—usurped the power of the Commander in Chief. His actions—exacerbated by those of his agent, Margot Katz—have brought the United States to the verge of war with its greatest foe. In addition, they contributed to the chain of events that culminated in Gabriella Wintour's brutal murder."

Roman remained mum, though inside he was seething. He had a dozen things to say—chief among them, a defense of Margot.

But he didn't.

"Anything to say?" the president said.

Roman waited, took a deep breath, then said, "The only thing I would add, is that this Council's order to circulate the *Hummingbird* file contributed greatly to the current threat environment. For all we know, it was that order, which blew open the lid on an operation that had been proceeding in perfect secrecy for years—"

"Oh, come on," Hawke protested. "I told you he wouldn't swallow his medicine. His status should be rescinded immediately."

"If you hadn't forced me to disclose my file, my protocols, my safe houses, the details of my operation—"

"All right, all right," the president said. "Your comment will be added to the record. Anyone else have anything to say before I shut the file permanently?"

Roman leveled a cold stare at them, daring someone to speak. He felt the sting of betrayal—no allies, no lifeline—and looked at Gabriella's empty chair.

She would have said something. She always had.

He was tempted to walk out. To hell with it. He could still deny them the pleasure of watching him squirm.

Then, a voice broke the silence. It was Ethel.

"As a point of fact," she said, "my agency intercepted two illegal drones over this very building in the last twenty-four hours. The initial analysis suggests they're Russian."

"So they're watching us," the president said. "Right here in our own house."

"Yes, they are," Ethel said, "and from their chatter, we know that they've identified every member of this council other than Roman Adler."

Roman studied her. He'd always thought of her as an intensely elegant woman, with a muscular build, sun-browned skin, and a western drawl that evoked the glamor of old westerns. What he hadn't viewed her as was a potential friend.

"What are you saying?" Hawke said.

"I think it's only right that the record reflect that Roman alone takes precautions to conceal his identity when attending Council meetings. He takes public buses. Wears a disguise. If Gabriella was targeted because of something here, he's the last person it should be pinned on."

"Well," Doerr interjected, "if we're deciding what should and shouldn't be pinned on Roman Adler—"

"That's enough," the president said. "Everyone's had their say."

"Let the record also show," Doerr went on, "that Roman's *tradecraft* put us in bed with Chichikov's mistress in the first place. So when cabinet members start dropping dead, then yes, it very much can be pinned on his—"

"I said enough," the president repeated.

"Thank you," Roman said to Ethel.

She nodded. "I just think the record should reflect the facts."

"The fact is," Hawke said, "Gabriella circulated her *Hummingbird* memo, and hours later, she and her daughter were bound, gagged, and gang—"

"Hey!" the president snapped.

Hawke cleared his throat.

"Have some decency," the president added.

"Sorry," Hawke said with mock contrition. "But those are the facts."

Kathleen piled on. "And let's not forget the unprecedented *clusterfuck* that's happening in Moscow right now."

"Could someone play the footage for us?" Doerr said.

"I think everyone's seen it," Roman objected.

"No," Doerr said, already pressing the call button. "Let's watch it again."

A moment later, the green-tinged CCTV footage of Margot killing Russian police was playing on a loop on the room's enormous high-definition screen.

"Is this really necessary?" Roman said. "We have deniability. She never showed her face—"

"Give me a *break*!" Doerr said. "They know she's ours, and they're going to raise absolute hell for it. You know it as well as any of us."

"I thought your job was to prevent World War Three," Hawke added. "Not kick it off."

Roman stared at the screen, the footage of Margot

playing over and over to maximize its shock value. "Look," he said, "we sent Margot over there for a reason."

"Not for this, we didn't," Kathleen said.

"No, but we need to finish the job. She wouldn't have tried to get to the embassy if she didn't have something to give us. And, honestly, I'm beginning to worry it might be related to this nuclear plant in Virginia."

That got their attention. The power plant was the elephant in the room—the threat they should have been worrying about all along.

No one spoke for a moment, and the screen, still looping the footage, gave everything a ghoulish green glow.

"Can we turn that off?" Roman said to the aide, who instantly got up to shut it off.

It was Hawke who spoke next. "This is classic Roman," he said. "Always trying to deflect—"

"This isn't a diversion," Roman said. "If you want to fire me for what I've done, so be it, but if Margot's information has anything to do with that power plant, then there's your World War Three trigger right there."

"There's no evidence—" Kathleen started, but the president raised his hand to stop her.

"It's not looking good," he conceded. "We all know it. Deliberate sabotage of flood controls. Cyber interference across multiple counties. And now, three fuel tank explosions. It's not a coincidence. Someone's pushing that plant toward catastrophe."

"Those fuel tanks are directly responsible for cooling the plant," Roman added. "If we don't get a handle on the situation, it will be the biggest attack on US soil in history."

"Everyone's working on it," Hawke said. "The president's got a call with the Virginia governor, the nuclear watchdog agency, the lead engineers at the plant—"

"I hope you're going to order a SCRAM," Roman said, locking eyes with the president.

"Let's not get ahead of ourselves," Doerr said. "We're a long way from a meltdown, and the engineers are doing everything they can to get the systems back online. The exploding fuel tanks affect that calculus, but—"

Roman couldn't believe his ears. "Are you kidding me? The *calculus*? You all saw the explosion. The fuel tanks blew your *calculus* to hell, Dominic. We need to SCRAM that plant right now."

The president turned to Ethel. "What is NSA saying?"

She glanced at Roman before saying, "My people have been on this since the alarms started sounding yesterday. They're concerned about foreign interference, but they're still saying a SCRAM would be premature."

"They want to keep watching the temperature rise?" Roman said. "Watch it go up and up until it reaches the point of no return?"

"Excuse me," Kathleen said, raising a hand. "But am I the only one who has no clue what SCRAM means?"

"SCRAM, is the backstop," Roman said. "The last resort."

"It's the rapid shutdown process built into all nuclear plants," Poynter added. "It drops control rods into the core, instantly absorbing neutrons and halting the fission reaction."

"Meaning the plant won't explode?"

"Exactly. It neuters everything."

"Which is why we have to do it now," Roman said.

"However," Doerr interjected, grasping for control of a conversation miles beyond his depth, "a SCRAM also drops power output to zero. Which, frankly, makes this not just a safety issue, but a political one."

The Honeytrap

"Did you seriously just say that?" Roman gasped. "A *political* issue? You know, that's what the *politburo* thought when Chernobyl started to spike."

"Come on," he said. "That's not what I meant. I'm just saying, cutting power to half of Virginia during a massive storm—"

"Chernobyl's not the comparator here," Hawke said. "Just more of your theatrics, Roman."

"I just think," Roman said, forcing himself to keep his voice level, "that it would be prudent not to let ourselves get into the danger zone on this, given the stakes, and the signs of interference."

The president looked at Roman for a moment, his face softer than it had been, and said, "Roman, listen, I agree with you. I do. That's why, if the engineers say to SCRAM, I'll order them to do it. The last thing I want is to be the president that brought Chernobyl to Virginia."

The aide looked up, touched her earpiece, and whispered something to the president. He visibly paled.

"What is it?" Roman said.

"Something on the screen," the president said, voice taut.

They shifted their attention as the aide hit some keys on her keyboard and pulled up fresh footage. "This is happening now," she said as another green-tinged feed filled the screen. Roman's heart lurched. He recognized the street in front of the embassy, and he could see multiple Russian police and FSB agents outside the entrance.

"What are we looking at?" the president said.

"This is the southern edge of the Moscow embassy compound," the aide said. "The street is called *Bolshoy Devyatinsky*. It's a narrow lane, as you see."

"What happened?" the president said, voice dripping with dread. "Why are there Russians at the gate?"

"I'm going to jump back to just a few minutes ago," the aide said.

A clock in the corner of the frame counted backward from the current time to just six minutes ago, then rolled forward again.

They saw the same scene, the entrance, the branches of the trees rustling in a light breeze, then suddenly, multiple vehicles sped by at the end of the street. More seconds passed, a helicopter flew by, and then a woman appeared. She was running directly toward the camera.

"That's not Margot Katz," the president whispered—like saying it might make it true.

The aide said nothing, but everyone in the room knew it was her. She was injured, limping—but still running. Above her, the helicopter came back into frame.

And then came a police car. It careened around the corner, skidded to a halt, and a cop got out and drew his gun. Margot kept running, and a Marine—out on the street—shouted for her to run faster. She reached him, but just as she did, a bullet struck her in the back.

Roman felt it like a punch to the gut. He flinched visibly.

Margot collapsed and the marine caught her, pulling her into his post.

"She made it," Roman gasped.

"She made it?" Doerr said incredulously. "That's your takeaway?"

"This is a disaster," Poynter said, dumbfounded.

"Mr President," Austin said. "This situation's out of hand. The Russians will respond."

"What if that bullet hit the Marine?" Poynter said. "A US

Marine shot by a Russian bullet? What's the response to that?"

"Agreed," Kathleen said. "This is beyond the pale. We need to be ready for blowback. We need to evacuate that embassy."

The president's eyes widened. "Evacuate the embassy? Is that necessary?"

"I don't know," she said, "but we need to be ready for anything. I mean, look at that!" The screen had reverted to the live feed. Two dozen police and federal security agents surrounded the guard post, shouting threats, guns drawn. "That's a tinderbox," she said. "Ready to blow."

"Agreed," Hawke said. "This is a bomb—and we need to diffuse it."

"There's no diffusing this," Roman said grimly. "Not anymore." He almost held back then, knowing what his words might mean for Margot, but he added, "Sir, you need to send a directive to European Command and Strategic Command right away."

"Telling them what?" Hawke said.

"Telling them to brace for fucking impact," Roman said.

STRATCOM—Strategic Command—controlled America's nuclear deterrent. Telling them to *brace* was not something to be done lightly. It meant shadow wars became real.

"Have you lost your head, Roman?" Hawke said.

"Roman's right," Austin said.

"General Poynter?" the president said.

"I agree with Roman and Austin. DEFCON Three, sir. Immediately."

The president hesitated only a second, then said, "Very well, General. Defense Readiness Condition Level Three. My order."

It was a significant decision. It meant bombers fueled on

runways and submarines rising to launch depth. Armed forces across the globe would have to be ready to deploy within fifteen minutes. There would be an immediate flurry of activity on bases across Europe.

"The Russians will notice," Roman said. "DEFCON Three, and they'll notice. They'll match us."

"This is what your *vigilantism* has gotten us," Hawke said to Roman. "Chichikov's mistress is dead, Margot Katz is running around Moscow like she's Jason fucking Bourne, and now we're on a war footing."

"Chichikov," Doerr said, with a strange adrenaline-fueled frenzy in his eye, "is going to make us hand Margot over. That's what comes next."

"Over my dead body," Roman said.

Hawke let out a brief, mirthless laugh. "That won't be up to you, Roman."

"Handing Margot over would be a grave mistake," Roman said to the president. "I'll get her out of there. Give me one hour."

"Is she operating as a NOC?" the president said.

"No," Roman said immediately. "She's under diplomatic cover."

"Damn it," Doerr said. "Who's idea was that?"

"Mine," Roman said.

"She can still be disavowed," Doerr shot back.

"No," Roman snapped.

"Roman," the president said quietly. "Anyone can be disavowed."

"One hour," Roman said again. "I'll get her out. I swear it."

The president shook his head. "Roman, she was shot. Even if you did—"

"I'll make her disappear," Roman said, desperation

The Honeytrap

rising in his voice. "No one will ever hear her name again." He'd trained her to vanish. Now, he was going to order her to do it.

"I don't like it, Roman."

"You'd risk the entire embassy, war even," Doerr said, "for one agent?"

Roman scanned the room. Everyone agreed with Doerr. Even the president wouldn't meet his eye. "If the Kremlin gets its claws into Margot..." he started, but trailed off, unable to finish the thought.

"Surely, you're not considering this?" Hawke said. "One agent's life against the lives of—"

"*Please*," Roman gasped.

"Roman, stop," the president said, tension crackling in his voice. "They're right. If she's still inside when the request comes, we hand her over."

Roman didn't say a word.

Turning to Austin, the president said, "I want plans for a full evacuation. Files destroyed. Sensitive data erased. All personnel out. We leave no one behind. No skeleton crew. No Marines. I'm not waiting for Chichikov to make the first move, and I'll be damned if I give him hostages to hold over us."

Austin nodded as the president turned to Kathleen. "See if State can draw up a list of every US citizen currently in Russia."

"On it, sir."

"Tell them a crisis is coming. They need to get out. If they can get to the embassy, we'll evacuate them."

"Very good, sir."

"And get a meeting with the congressional leaders. Both sides. If this spills over, I want the nation behind me."

48

"You're hit!" the marine cried, dragging Margot inside his post and slamming the door with a firm kick. The cop who'd fired the shot crashed into it a second later, pounding on it with both fists.

"Don't open it," Margot gasped. "They'll take me away."

"No one's taking you anywhere," he said. His hands were covered in her blood and he looked for the wound.

"It's my shoulder," she said. "Bullet's still in there." She caught a whiff of cologne. Same scent. Same guard. "I remember you," she murmured, then everything went black.

When she came to, she was looking up at him. "I think you saved my life."

He smiled. "You need the medic."

Another two marines appeared behind him, crowding the post. "Give her room," he said. "Let her breathe."

One of them cracked open a first aid kit. "We need to stop the bleeding."

Margot felt the sting of alcohol as they hastily patched her up.

She was wounded, trapped, and one request away from being handed over to the Russians. She told herself she'd survive—though she had no idea how.

But she had the hard drive. Whatever else happened, that was what mattered.

"All right," a marine said when the wound was covered. "We need to get her inside."

"The medic's already waiting for her."

"No," Margot said. "There's no time for that."

"You ready to stand?"

She nodded, then winced as they pulled her to her feet.

That was when she saw the mayhem on the street. Right outside the post, two officers of the Russian Ministry of Internal Affairs were holding their credentials up to the bulletproof glass. There were a dozen others behind them.

She glanced nervously at the marines.

"Don't worry," Calvin Klein reassured her. "If they want you, they'll have to get through me first."

"Come on, Romeo," one of the others said, slapping him on the back of the head. "Let's go."

They were about to leave when she said, "Hold on."

A black 7-Series BMW skidded to the curb, its headlights sweeping over them. A man in a sharp, navy blue suit stepped out and walked up to the guard post, reaching into his jacket. His body language made all of them flinch, bracing for a grenade—or something worse.

If it had been a bomb, a few sheets of bulletproof glass wouldn't have saved them. They were in a six-by-six metal box in the heart of an empire that assassinated critics, invaded neighbors, and committed atrocities with impunity. If the Russians chose this moment to pick a fight, they were done for.

But he hadn't pulled a bomb—just the same duct-taped device she'd seen at the safe house. He held it to the glass now as if taunting her with it, and immediately, the lights began to flicker. The screen on the computer flashed red, then green, then settled on a blank blue before going dark. Even the street lights flickered, their glow quivering ominously. His eyes locked on Margot's, and a sneer crossed his face. He'd won, and he knew it. Instinctively, she put a protective hand on the drive in her pocket.

"What's he doing?" one of the marines said.

Something unsettling about the man's face made her look away. "It's an EMP."

"A what?"

"Come on," she said. "I need to get out of here."

The marines helped her, taking her weight as they led her through the courtyard. Above, the helicopter hovered low, its blades whipping the snow into a raging maelstrom.

It wouldn't dare open fire, she thought.

Not here.

Would it?

"The medical unit's this way," Calvin Klein said, leading them toward a side entrance.

"No," Margot said. "I need the seventh floor. It can't wait."

It was shorthand for CIA—those top floors built entirely with American labor, American concrete, and American paranoia, all flown in on Boeing C-17 Globemasters

The marines hurried her through the main entrance, but as soon as they hit the lobby, a night-duty guard got in their way.

"You were just shot," he said.

"You don't say," Margot said patronizingly.

Red lights blinked all over his control board, and he was

scrambling to catch up with events. The buildup of police outside was plain to see on the monitors.

"You need authorization to get through," another guard said. He seemed to be in charge.

"I've got authorization," Margot said, though she wasn't carrying anything to prove it. "Check with the Station Chief."

"It's the middle of the night."

"Yeah," Margot said, eyeing the chaos on the monitors, "I think it's safe to say he's awake."

The guard looked torn.

"Go on, call the seventh floor. Believe me, you'll be making a big mistake if you don't."

A medic burst into the lobby carrying a first aid kit. She forced Margot to sit, and Margot didn't have the strength to argue with her.

The woman removed the field dressing and brought out a pair of sinister-looking forceps.

"Tell me those aren't for the bullet," Margot said, wincing.

"It'll hurt like hell," the medic warned, dabbing antiseptic. "Better than blood poisoning."

"Looking forward to it," Margot said dryly, then to the security guard, "Did you reach the Station Chief?"

"Working on it," he said, a phone at his ear.

"Well, work faster," she snapped—then screamed as the forceps found the bullet. "Holy hell!" she cried, almost fainting.

"You all right?" the medic said.

She nodded, though her ears were ringing and her eyes brimmed with tears. "Son of a bitch."

"I know," the medic said, handing her a bloody mess—a 9x18mm Makarov.

"Full metal jacket," Margot muttered.

"You were lucky. This could have been a lot worse."

"Just patch me up," Margot said. "I'm running out of time."

More marines flooded into the lobby, lining up in front of the glass façade. The police helicopter still prowled outside, its spotlight slicing across the courtyard like a prison yard light.

"It's only there to intimidate us," Margot said to the detachment commander.

"It's working," he said back. "They just ordered us to form a defensive line while DoD prepares an evacuation."

Margot blinked at the speed of the decision. "Under whose order?" she said.

The man shrugged. "Hell if I know."

Margot peered through the glass. "Throw smoke grenades," she said. "That'll get the chopper to back off."

She felt a surge of pain.

"Sorry," the medic said. "Almost done."

"I really need to get upstairs."

"Just one more second," she said, applying the finishing touches to her work. "I'm going to give you these pills. Doxycycline. Take two every twelve hours."

"Will do," Margot said, taking the bottle from her.

"And I'm obligated to advise you, though I know you'll ignore me, that you shouldn't be on your feet. It could upset the wound's—"

"Thanks, doc," Margot said, swallowing two pills dry and getting to her feet. She went straight to the security desk and said, "Are we good? Am I authorized?"

"No," the guard said. "They told me that there is no Station Chief."

"Did they?" she said. "And do you really believe that?"

He hesitated.

"Right," she said. "I'm going up. I'm not kidding when I say it's life and death."

"Let her up," the marine commander said from across the lobby. "Whatever she's up to, the Russians just shot her trying to stop it."

Reluctantly, the guard hit a key on his keyboard and waved her through. Margot hurried into the elevator and punched the button for the seventh floor, leaning against the wall for support. Stepping out, a wave of dizziness nearly toppled her. There was a water cooler, and she stumbled toward it, reaching out to steady herself. A woman—about thirty, with a tight ponytail and round-rimmed glasses—rushed over as the cooler fell to the ground.

"Oh my God," Margot said.

"Don't worry about it," the woman said.

They both stared at it, glugging water onto the carpet.

"You're Pechvogel," the woman said.

Margot nodded.

"That was you out there. I saw the whole thing."

Margot looked out the window—a dozen cruisers, armored vehicles, the helicopter. "Looks like I kicked a real hornet's nest."

"Yes, you did."

"The ambassador will be pleased," Margot said, smiling slightly. "Is he on his way?"

"A car just left for the residence. I'd guess you have thirty minutes, tops."

Margot nodded—sizing her up, wondering if she could trust her. "You're CIA?"

"I am. Gina Hartwell, Operations Officer."

"You're working late."

"This is Moscow Station. Someone's always on duty."

"Did they tell you anything about my operation?"

Gina shook her head. "Not much. Clarissa made it back, though. Steinhauser, too."

"That's good," Margot said. "One less thing."

"And your hotel room was raided. A few hours ago, after Clarissa had already left. I wouldn't go back there."

"And the embassy? Will it be evacuated?"

"The order just came down from the White House."

"So it's really happening."

"They also raised the Defense Readiness Condition," Gina said. "It could be precautionary—"

"Or they could be preparing for war."

Gina nodded.

"And it's all my fault."

"I hope it was worth it," Gina said. "Whatever you were up to."

"So do I," Margot said, looking across the office at the empty desks. "Boreal isn't here, is he?"

"No, but the entire team has been recalled. All hands on deck for the evacuation."

"And upstairs?" Margot said, glancing at the ceiling.

The eighth floor was the most sensitive section of the entire embassy. It was where the technical analysis and digital forensics hardware was located.

Gina didn't immediately answer, and Margot looked at her intently. "Just tell me if anyone's up there."

"There's a skeleton crew."

"Can they clone a hard drive? Get it to Langley and Fort Meade?"

"They could," Gina said.

Margot took the hard drive from her pocket and placed it in front of Gina.

"That's what all this is about, then?" Gina said.

Margot nodded. "Can I trust you to get it to the tech team?"

Gina looked at her. "You know what I say?"

"What's that?"

"Sometimes, a hornet's nest needs a kicking."

Margot nodded. "As long as we don't get stung."

"Good luck with that," Gina said, picking up the hard drive. "I'll take this up right away."

"Tell them the National Security Council is waiting for it."

Gina nodded, punching the elevator button. "They'll know what to do."

Margot looked at her, praying the EMP hadn't destroyed every byte of information on the drive. "Tell them to be careful," she said. "For all I know, it could be booby-trapped."

Gina nodded.

As she waited for the elevator, Margot added, "Oh, and one more thing."

"Yes?"

Margot smiled tiredly. "I don't suppose you know where a girl could find a bottle of black hair dye?"

49

The robbery replayed in Oksana's mind on a constant loop—camera angles, fingerprints, every possible screw-up. She went to the window and opened the blind a crack, peering out at the street.

Nothing unusual.

She went into the bathroom and, to calm her nerves, took a long, hot shower. Still, she couldn't shake the feeling of dread. She toweled off and got back into the same clothes as before, then made coffee and sat on the bed.

She turned on the TV for background noise, but soon, she was flicking through news channels, unable to focus. No art robberies—just traffic updates, a shooting in the Bronx, and extreme weather wreaking havoc on everything from bus timetables to power grids. There was a lot of talk about a nuclear power plant in Virginia, with the two anchors in the studio debating rumors that it had been the target of a cyberattack. Locals were trying to get out of the region in advance of a big power outage, but they were being thwarted by the weather and road closures.

She turned up the volume.

—Here with the latest is NBC12's Amy Wyant, reporting live from the ground in Virginia. Amy, what can you tell us?

—Well, this plant is a major provider for this part of Virginia, Bryan. They're saying an outage could impact half a million homes.

—That's a lot of people's Christmas plans up in smoke.

—Which is why they're doing everything they can not to disrupt the supply. The outage would affect Williamsburg, Newport News, the Hampton Roads Region, and potentially even Richmond, fifty miles away.

—And what about this talk of explosions? Cyber-attacks?

—We're waiting for a press conference with the governor. Hopefully, we'll know more soon. For now, they're begging people to sit tight and stay off the roads.

—We'll leave it there, Amy. It looks like that storm is really giving you a run for your money.

Oksana watched the reporter struggle with her umbrella, then switched off the TV. She'd propped the painting on the desk, and she turned on the lamp and studied it, taking a few photos with her phone.

She'd intended to do a reverse image search—but stopped. Instinct kicked in. No searches from her phone. Instead, she wrapped the painting in the bubble wrap, put it in a cloth laundry bag she found in the closet, and gathered up her things.

Down in the lobby, the concierge was surprised to see her. "Everything all right with the room?"

"Perfect," she lied, uncertain if she'd return. She hurried outside and hailed the first cab that passed.

"Where to?" the driver said over his shoulder.

"Columbia," she said. "Butler Library."

Her student card gave her twenty-four-hour access, and she entered past a bleary-eyed librarian at the front desk. Inside, the place was all but empty, and she went straight to a computer and logged in. She emailed herself the photos from her phone. She also did a quick search for burglaries in Midtown, on 57th Street, anything tying back to the *Tsaritsa* or Proctor Sifton.

She got a hit, and a shiver ran down her spine.

It was a report in the online edition of *The Daily News*, and she quickly scanned it.

Police were searching for a white female, slender build, unknown hair color, unknown age, who'd broken into a famous gallery specializing in Russian art. The gallery had hosted a gala fundraiser for the People's Promise Initiative—a registered non-profit that had come under scrutiny in the past for its connections to the Chichikov regime. Police were alerted when the gallery's alarm was triggered. No one had been hurt, but a single painting had been stolen.

There were grainy CCTV stills—just a figure in the corridor. Unrecognizable. But Oksana knew it was her.

She took a deep breath and opened the email she'd sent herself. As she clicked on the photo attachments, she instinctively glanced over her shoulder. Then she pulled them into Google and ran the search.

There were hits.

Her stomach flipped. The painting had a name.

In fact, according to an entry on the Russian Art Archive,

it had been displayed for decades in the *Tretyakov* before being sold off after Stalin's death.

She looked around. Her heart was pounding. The librarian was drifting silently between rows of dimmed screens, making sure the computers were off, and Oksana waited for her to leave before reading on.

According to the archive, the painting's title was *Ten' Stalina, Stalin's Shadow*, and it depicted the first barge to pass through the famous—or infamous—White Sea Canal.

Built in the nineteen-thirties, the canal had been hailed as one of the landmark achievements of Stalin's first Five-Year Plan. He'd put such stock in it that its official name had been changed from *Belomorkanal*, meaning White Sea Canal, to *Kanal imeni Stalina,* meaning *Canal in Honor of Stalin*.

Putting his name on it gave it immense symbolic importance—not just as a showcase of Russia's industrialization but as a testament to the brutal efficiency of the Gulag system, which by that point had swallowed up two million souls. The Gulag's stated purpose was *re-education*—turning undesirables into productive citizens—and the canal, built in record time, was supposed to be proof that it worked.

Stalin had demanded the canal be finished by the end of the Plan—forcing tens of thousands of prisoners to carve a 118-foot-wide trench across 141 miles of Precambrian granite. Not only did they have to do it in just twenty months, but tools were in such short supply—even shovels, picks, and barrows—that they often had to dig using just their bare hands.

The result was a hellscape. Without adequate food or clothing, in weather that frequently dipped below negative forty, a hundred thousand godforsaken prisoners gave up their lives to carve that blood-soaked trench across the land.

But it was finished on time.

Oksana took a breath. It didn't feel like history. It felt like a warning.

The librarian came over. "We close early tonight for the holiday."

"Oh," Oksana said. "I'll just be another minute."

She quickly finished reading the entry. The painting had been created as part of an official state delegation to the canal led by Maxim Gorky. A picture of it had even been included in a ceremonial volume presented to Stalin in honor of the achievement.

The artist's name was Zoshchenko, and while he must have been in favor at the time of the delegation, he later vanished into the Gulag himself, for reasons unknown, where he eventually starved to death digging a ditch in the Kolyma.

That was the end of the entry.

As she'd suspected, the painting was one more artifact from the torrent of propaganda Stalin's regime had churned out during those dark years.

But there was a footnote—small, almost missed.

It linked to the blog of a late art professor from Lomonosov University who'd been somewhat obsessed with Zoshchenko. It seemed that, unlike Gorky, Zoshchenko had never fully bowed to the regime. Instead, he'd hidden acts of rebellion inside his paintings—so subtle they'd escaped detection for decades. That was why they'd been allowed in state galleries.

The professor had spent his career uncovering these hidden messages, and in this painting, he'd found a stark commentary on Stalin's recklessness.

The canal had been rushed to provide the Soviet Navy with a secret corridor between the Baltic and White Seas, allowing new submarines to slip between theaters unseen. But Stalin's haste had come at a cost—the canal's depth was slashed to twelve feet—too shallow for most vessels and, critically, too shallow for the new *Dekabrist* and *Leninets*-class submarines it was built to serve.

In the painting, if you looked closely, the cargo on the barge wasn't timber—as would be expected—but one of these new submarines. It had been hoisted onto a shallow-draft barge because that was the only way it could traverse the channel.

That was the flaw. The fatal irony.

A canal built for submarines—too shallow to let them pass.

A small act of defiance. Almost invisible. Seen only by those who knew where to look.

Which Oksana did.

A tap on her shoulder made her jolt. She fumbled to close the tabs, hands suddenly clumsy.

"Sorry to startle you, miss. We're closing the section."

"Of course," Oksana said. "Just leaving." She managed a smile, but her hands were still shaking.

"Merry Christmas," the librarian said.

50

Harry dialed. No tone. Just dead air. He tried again. And again. The fourth time—finally—a voice.

"Hello? Hello, Harry?" It was Sheryl, panicked and crackling through the static.

"Honey, it's me."

"Harry?" she gasped, bursting into tears.

"I'm sorry. It's chaos down here. We're barely hanging on."

"I saw the explosion. They said someone was missing." Each word was a struggle, dragging fresh sobs from her. "I was afraid it was you."

"I'm okay, honey. What about you? The kids are all right?"

"Of course. They're frightened, though. They know something's not right."

"I need you to get them into the car."

"What? No!"

"Honey, listen."

"We're at my parents' house," she blurted. "It was brutal

getting here. Flooding everywhere. Roads were closing behind us."

Harry shut his eyes. Of course they were. The whole state was seizing up like a choked engine.

"Honey, get back in the car. You, the kids, your mom and dad. All of you."

"What are you talking about?"

"There's going to be a state-wide blackout. It could last days. I need you to head for Durham—my sister's place. You remember the guest house?"

"Durham?"

"I'm going to call now and tell her you're coming. She's got that guest house."

"What are you talking about? That's three hours away. I'm not getting back on those roads."

"The window's closing, honey. If you don't leave now, you might not leave at all. You have to get on the road before the governor makes his announcement. Once it's public, every highway in the state will be gridlocked."

"What announcement?"

"They're going to SCRAM the plant."

"Oh my gosh."

"It's nothing to be afraid of. I just want to know that you and the kids are well outside the EPZ."

"How am I going to get my parents into the car at this time of night? You should have seen how hard it was just to get here. And the kids, they're sleeping."

Harry wiped the sweat from his palms onto his pants. "Please, Sheryl. Don't argue. Just do it."

"If you want us safe, come get us yourself."

A hand clamped down on Harry's shoulder. "They're ready for you in the control room."

"Just a minute, Jack."

"Harry, the President and the Governor are on the line."

"All right," Harry said. "Sheryl, I've got to go."

"I love you, Harry Cassidy."

"I love you too, honey."

He clung to the silence a second longer, then hung up. It might be the last time he ever heard her voice.

He climbed the metal stairs to the control room, each step heavier than the last, like he was walking down death row. He'd been at the plant thirty-six hours straight, and other than a few snatched hours of sleep in his chair, there'd been no let-up. No shower. No change of clothes. For sustenance, only vending machine snacks and a steady flow of coffee and energy drinks.

He was nearing his breaking point—and he could feel it.

He entered the control room and looked around—too many new faces. Too many suits.

The Plant Manager. The safety engineers. The control room supervisor and both senior reactor operators.

Behind them, a wall of suits, stiff-backed and sour-faced. Those were the officials from Dominion, representatives of the Nuclear Regulatory Commission, and state officials from Virginia Emergency Management.

Even more chilling—the phone lines were live with the President, the Governor, their staffs, intelligence officials, and a dozen federal agencies.

The control board was lit up like a Christmas tree. Everything was flashing—main pumps, backups, cooling loop intakes, temperature and pressure monitors, rod controls, hydraulic systems, electromagnetic relays. Even the radiation monitors were beginning to twitch off baseline.

The plant was groaning under the strain.

Warnings flickered. Systems stuttered.

If no one made the call soon, it wouldn't just fail—it

would blow. The five-hundred-year catastrophe they talked about in the training manuals would be upon them.

And it was Harry's job to stop it.

"Listen up," Pete Porter barked, his voice filling the room. "You all know how serious this is. If you didn't, we've got the Governor and the President on the line to remind you. Eyes of the nation are on us. Let's get this right, people."

Someone muttered agreement.

"Harry Cassidy, our lead safety, is here to make his recommendation."

Harry cleared his throat. "Mr President. Governor Atwater. Members of the board. My recommendation is to SCRAM this reactor. Immediately. Over the last twenty-four hours, we've had critical failures across every major system. Our cooling loops are unstable. Our sensors are glitching. The reactor's pressure and temperature are rising. And we can't control it."

"With all due respect," one of the corporate flunkeys piped, "your job, Mr Cassidy, is to keep the plant running, not pull the plug."

Harry's jaw tightened. Another suit, another set of polished shoes, another man whose family wasn't inside the EPZ. "I know you don't like it," Harry said. "And I know it won't look good for any of us, but I've been here all night, and trust me—there's never been a nuclear plant on US soil this close to meltdown. We need to kill this reactor—now."

"There must be something we can do short of a full SCRAM," the suit said.

"Six hundred degrees Celsius," Harry said. "That's when the fuel rods in this reactor melt. Now, please take my word for it when I say we do not want our fuel rods to melt. That's Chernobyl. That's Fukushima."

"You say six hundred," someone else said. "And we're at?"

"We're at three-eighty-seven. But anything above three hundred is bad. Over four hundred is critical. And we're climbing. Fast"

Harry paused. Looked around the room. Nothing. Not a breath. Not a word.

"That's problem one," he said. "Problem two is the pressure level. When things start to boil, they create gas, and gas in an enclosed space creates pressure. The containment dome is airtight. Built to hold in hell itself. Under ordinary conditions, the pressure inside the structure should be below 2000 PSI. If that goes up to 2200 PSI, we start seeing alarm bells flashing."

"And what are we currently at?" the same suit said.

"We're at 2300 PSI, and as the temperature keeps going up, that pressure will rise exponentially." He paused again. Silence. "At 3000 PSI, the dome doesn't crumble. It detonates."

"This is insane," the suit snapped. "You're trying to scare us into overreacting. There's still time to contain this."

"Not in my assessment," Harry said.

"And if you shut down this plant," the suit continued, "the entire East Coast grid collapses. Not just Virginia. Half the country. You want to take credit for that on Christmas morning?"

The man blinked hard, sweat glistening on his upper lip.

Harry stared him down. "Let me make this real simple. If I wait, and you're wrong, you get to be the guy who vaporized Richmond."

"With all due respect—"

Harry cut him off. "The numbers are climbing. I can't

stop them. No one can. If we don't SCRAM, we're going into meltdown. It's a certainty."

"I don't think that tone is appropriate—"

"This plant has two EPZs," Harry continued. "EPZ stands for Emergency Planning Zone, but you can think of them as death zones. First zone is the Plume Exposure Pathway, extending ten miles in every direction. This is where people need to start choking down potassium iodide to stop their thyroids from melting. My family's inside this zone. Do I tell them to start choking down pills now?"

"Of course not, but—"

"The second death zone? Fifty-mile radius. That's Richmond, Newport News, Williamsburg. Hundreds of thousands of people—"

Harry stopped talking because the phone operator was in front of him, waving the handset. "Harry," a voice said, "this is the President of the United States."

"Mr President," Harry said, scarcely able to believe it.

"You're saying it melts down within hours?"

"Correct, Mr President."

"I thought we had more time than that."

"These problems feed each other, sir. Coolant evaporates, temperatures spike. Gas forms. Pressure builds. Everything feeds on itself faster and faster. We're hitting the point now where these forces take on a life of their own, feeding their own momentum. If I don't SCRAM, the plant will do it for us. Only it'll be a lot uglier."

"There's absolutely nothing, in your opinion, that can be done to prevent this SCRAM?"

"Sir, I'm a patriot. If the president orders me to wait, I'll wait. But the moment pressure in the dome hits 2700 PSI, or temperature breaches 500 degrees, the plant shuts itself down automatically. And it won't ask our permission. The question isn't whether or not to SCRAM, but whether I do it now, at 387 degrees, or the plant does it automatically at 500. And believe me, sir, we're all a lot safer if we shut her down at 387."

"It will result in power outages across half the country?"

"The grid's not as flimsy as our friend suggested," Harry said, eyeing the suit, "but it won't be pretty."

"Mr Cassidy," someone else said on the phone. "This is the DNI, Dominic Doerr. What's your take on the reports that this failure is the result of a cyberattack?"

"I'm sorry, Mr Doerr, but I'm not here to hypothesize about attacks. I'm here to advise the president to SCRAM. Now."

"Then there's nothing else to say," the president said. "You all heard the man. SCRAM the plant."

Pete Porter gasped in relief. "Very good, Mr President. Look alive, people. We have an order to SCRAM. Harry, you have all necessary codes?"

"I do," Harry said, as certain of the words as he'd been on his wedding day. He punched in the codes, flipped the safety, and said, "What I'm about to do is called a Full Manual. It's the Lead Safety's last Hail Mary. If you pray, now's the time."

"You're not suggesting—" the suit stammered, voice cracking. "I mean, it's got to work, right?"

Harry looked at him, dead-eyed. "This is a last-resort failsafe to prevent a nuclear reactor meltdown. It's the most dangerous thing a nuclear engineer has attempted since Trinity."

The man looked like he was going to throw up.

"We're all with you," the president said. "Godspeed."

"Thank you, sir," Harry said, then flicked a switch. "Electromagnets, manual."

There was an audible hum as another engineer confirmed the command. "Electromagnets, manual."

"The rods are held in place by electromagnets," Harry said. "This lever cuts power to the magnets, causing the rods to drop under their own weight. The chain reaction will stop in seconds."

"Let's do it," Porter said.

Harry gripped the lever, heart hammering. In his mind, he saw his children, their mother. He mouthed the words '*Hail Mary,*' and yanked down hard.

A split-second of silence.

Then, a deafening alarm erupted, rattling the control room as if a freight train was suddenly blasting by.

"What the hell is that?" someone shouted.

Harry stared at the control panel, feeling his stomach drop.

The rods hadn't moved.

"SCRAM unsuccessful," he choked. "Trying again."

He shoved the lever back up and ripped it down again, harder. The steel of the lever slapped the steel of the baseplate.

Nothing.

The rods didn't budge an inch.

"Deactivation failed," he repeated, louder again. "SCRAM unsuccessful."

For a heartbeat, no one moved.

Harry's eyes dropped to the gauge.

391.3.

391.7.

392.1.

It was accelerating.

51

Margot peeled off the flimsy plastic gloves that came with the hair dye and threw them in the trash. She'd just applied the concoction—a Russian over-the-counter product that Gina had rustled up for her, Licorice Black Crème Supreme—and she shuddered to think what it would do to her hair. It was already burning her scalp, and she peered at herself in the mirror, dabbing any spots where it made contact with her skin.

She was sitting on the counter in the women's seventh-floor restroom, the only person there, and she turned when the door opened. A pudgy man of about fifty-five, with thinning hair and unflattering slacks, entered without knocking.

"Excuse me," she said. "This is the—"

"*Boreal*," he said, extending a hand.

Margot indicated the toxic waste in her hair. "You don't want to shake my hand right now."

"Of course," he said, nodding awkwardly.

She stared at him, dressed in her camisole, the stench of ammonia filling the room. "Well?"

"So. You're fleeing."

"Yes," she said stiffly.

"Your work here's done, I suppose." His tone left no doubt as to his thoughts on the matter.

"I didn't mean to cause all this."

He took a step closer. "You know how long the CIA's been operating in Moscow?"

She shrugged, checking the mirror to make sure she wasn't staining her skin.

"Since 1947," he said. "As long as it's been in existence."

"Right," she said.

"And not even during the darkest days of the Cold War did we see a clusterfuck like this."

"I'm sorry," she said. "It wasn't my intention—"

"Intentions are irrelevant."

She felt the sting, even if he was right. She was about to respond, but he steamrolled ahead.

"This could have been avoided if you'd come to me. I could have told you there was a spike in chatter before you left the compound."

"You know it wasn't my decision."

"Right," he said, "and now I've got to track down every US citizen in Moscow and get them to Sheremetyevo. That's every single citizen. A full evacuation, diplomatic, military, civilian."

"Look," she said, "I followed my orders. I pursued my objective."

"Your shadowy, unvetted objective bypassed the entire chain of command, bypassed all legitimate channels—"

"I don't write the rules, Boreal. You know that."

"Your agency—if we can call it that—the *Bookshop*," he said, practically spitting the word, "just precipitated a diplomatic catastrophe. A disaster. There's talk of war."

She didn't flinch, but her stomach lurched. "War?"

"Have you looked out the window? There are soldiers lining up outside this very minute."

Boreal chewed his lip, waiting for a response. When he saw he wouldn't get one, he reached into his pocket.

"What's that?" she said.

He tossed a Belarusian passport onto the counter as if glad to get rid of it. Then came a matching license, bank cards, PINs, cash in three currencies—and an embassy security pass.

Margot picked up the pass first. "What's this for?"

"Not from me. From your boss," he said, handing her a cell.

"Secure?"

He nodded. "My advice to you is to get the hell out of this compound before the ambassador realizes you're still here."

She watched him leave, then picked up the phone and dialed the series of numbers needed to reach Roman.

He answered instantly. "Margot, thank God."

"Miss me?"

"I saw you take a bullet."

"I'm sure it looked worse than it felt."

"Will it slow you down?"

"Only if I pass out."

"Listen, you need to get out of the embassy pronto."

"So I keep hearing."

"The Russians have issued a note. They're demanding we hand you over. The President's going to fold."

"No one's willing to go to war for me?" she said.

Roman let out a brief laugh. "Believe me, if it were up to me, the carrier groups would already be entering the Black Sea."

"Thanks Roman, but I'm the most wanted woman in

Russia. Even if I get out of the embassy, how the hell do I make it to the border?"

"Foxtrot's already on it."

"Scrambling?"

"Cooking the whole damn breakfast," he said.

Scrambling eggs—that was Foxtrot's term for her facial obfuscation protocol. Instead of deleting Margot's data, which would raise flags, she'd warp it just enough to generate false matches all across Russia.

"That's something. Might buy me a mile or two."

"Scrambling you. Laying false trails. Cutting feeds."

"I appreciate her help."

"Did Boreal give you an embassy keycard?"

She glanced at it. "Yes."

"All right, you remember that storage garage near the center of the compound?"

"Of course."

"The keycard grants access. Get inside without being seen—by them or by us."

"You've got someone there to meet me?"

"Your guy from earlier. Steinhauser. Boston accent?"

"Of course."

"He'll have a van."

"And the ambassador knows nothing about it?"

"For now."

"And then what? Where's he taking me?"

"Your best bet is *Belorussky Station*. Head west. Smolensk. Make for the border. Easiest crossing."

"Okay."

"But you really need to go now."

"I've got dye in my hair."

"Just go," he said, ignoring the comment. "I'm sorry we couldn't do more for you."

"Did you get the files? The hard drive?"

"Tech team's working on it as we speak. We should have them any minute. Langley and Fort Meade, too."

"Roman, they used an EMP."

A beat of silence, then "What?"

"I saw it at the safe house."

"How do you know it was an EMP?"

"I held it in my hand."

"That's definitely what it was?"

"I mean, it was coiled wire. Lights flickered. They had it outside the embassy, too. The guard post lost power."

"Well, if they brought an EMP, it confirms there's something valuable on that drive."

"If it's fried, Roman... all of this was for nothing."

"Don't say that."

"They were ahead of me every step of the way. They knew everything—where to find us, what we were doing, what to bring."

"Margot, listen—"

"They breached the safe house before we even stopped talking. That's not a coincidence. The Council's as leaky as a sieve, Roman."

"Margot, there's something you haven't been told."

"What is it?"

"Bad news."

"Well, don't keep me waiting."

"It's Gabriella."

Margot went cold. "What about her?"

"She dead. Murdered in her own home."

"What?"

Silence, then, "Along with her daughter and housekeeper."

"My god," she whispered. "When did it happen?"

The Honeytrap

"Just before your meeting with Irina."

"That's how they knew. The whole thing's a nightmare. We're still blind to what Irina was trying to tell us."

"Well, there's been a development there, too."

"What are you talking about?"

"Did Irina say anything about a power plant?"

"A power plant?"

"Dominion Power. Surry County, Virginia?"

"Nothing like that."

"A cooling loop? Sensors? SCRAM procedures?"

"She said there were schematics on the drive. I didn't know what to make of it, but they could be related to a power plant. Drawings, too, and something about cyberattacks. Computer code."

"That could be it. Schematics. Diagrams. Code. It all fits."

"A plant's been attacked?"

"Yes. Multiple systems crashed at once. The core's overheating, and the SCRAM failed. They can't shut it down."

"What happens if they can't shut it down?"

"It's a runaway train."

"Meltdown?"

"In a word."

"Oh, God. How much time before that happens?"

"We're in the red, Margot. Core temp's rising fast. If we don't stop it very soon—"

Margot thought she was going to throw up. "If the code was on that drive—and I let them wipe it—"

"Don't go there," Roman said. "Was there anything else she said that could be useful? Anything at all?"

"I don't know. She mentioned a postcard. Said she sent it to the embassy, but I never received it. Something about *Ten' Stalina?*"

"*Ten' Stalina*?"

"Stalin's Shadow."

"What the hell is that?"

"Roman, we're fumbling in the dark—and we're running out of time."

52

"Well, well, well," Baldwin said, looking up as the bell over the door chimed. "Twice in one day. To what do I owe the honor?"

Oksana smiled, almost surprised to see him still there—and glad. "Sorry to come so late," she said. "I know you're shutting down."

"Nonsense. Come right in. Let me cook for you."

"You sure it's no hassle?"

"No hassle," he said, cracking some eggs over the grill. "You'll take your usual, I presume?"

She nodded, and he said, "If I didn't know better, I'd say you were getting sweet on me."

She smiled. "It's not that, Baldwin."

"People will start to talk," he said, teasing her.

"I assure you, I'm here for the chili."

"You keep telling that to yourself."

She took her usual seat. "Long day for you," she said, placing her bubble-wrapped package on the stool next to her.

"Every day's long when you're my age," he said, then went to the coffee machine and put on a fresh pot.

Oksana picked up the newspaper and opened it to the crossword to avoid having to make too much small talk. Baldwin put a cup of coffee in front of her. "Thanks," she said without looking up.

He went back to the grill and she watched him scramble the eggs. He had a way of slicing and flipping them with the side of his scraper so they seemed scarcely to touch the surface of the grill. "Cheese?"

"Always," she said, chewing the end of a pencil she'd found.

"Give me a clue," he added. He'd poured himself a coffee, too, and he stirred it as he leaned over to see the paper. "A tough one."

"I just started."

"One question."

She sighed. "Eye for an eye outcome."

"Hmm," he said, taking a sip of coffee.

"Starts with 'R'," she added.

The eggs were done and he turned back to the grill and scooped them up with the scraper. He laid them out on top of her chili, then sprinkled cheese on it. "Retribution," he said, setting the bowl in front of her.

"What's that?"

"Eye for an eye outcome."

"Oh," she said, checking if it fit. It did, and she penciled it in.

"You thought I meant something else," he said, and from the look on his face, it was hard to tell if he was joking or being very serious. He went to the door and flipped the sign. Then he shut off some lights, bathing the diner in a sudden, intimate gloom.

The Honeytrap

He looked at her again.

"Maybe I did," she said, setting the puzzle aside so she could eat.

He studied her for a moment, then said, "You look different."

"Different?"

"From this morning."

"In what way?" she said, taking a bite.

He shrugged. "I don't know. Something in your eyes. A look. *Electricity*."

"Electricity?" she said, giving him a smile. "I have no idea what you mean by that."

"Sure you do. Your old spark."

"My old spark? Returned since this morning? That's a lot to ask of a single day."

"Well, like you said, it's been a long one."

"Maybe," she said, looking away from him. She'd come precisely for this—the connection she had with him, the feeling of being understood. *Seen*. Because as much as she hated it, she needed it. Needed him. Just for a moment. Just to remember that she was still a person.

He was right. There was a difference in her. For one thing, she was scared. She'd broken into the gallery and she hadn't heard the last of it. Of that, she was certain. But she also knew that wasn't what he was talking about. Electricity —her old spark—that didn't come from fear.

She took another bite of chili. Maybe it wasn't justice. But it was something. A small measure of control in a life where she'd had none.

"Maybe I did something for myself," she said.

"What kind of something?"

"*Retribution*, if you like."

He raised an eyebrow but said nothing.

She took another bite of chili.

"You never get tired of that," he said.

"Retribution?"

He gave her a look. "Chili."

"Oh," she said, laughing. She thought for a moment, then said, "It reminds me of something from my childhood. Something my mother used to make."

"I thought your mother was Russian."

"Russians can't make chili?"

He nodded, looking at her intently. She looked back, wondering what he was thinking, and there was a part of her that wanted him to pry further, to probe deeper, to force her to say more about her mother. There was a part of her that wanted to tell him everything because, really, and as sad as it was to admit, there was no one else in her life she could talk to about it.

But it was she who broke eye contact first, picking up the newspaper again. She wasn't ready for any of that.

She looked at the package on the stool beside her. She'd stolen it to hurt Proctor—but hadn't even managed that. He was just a dealer. He didn't own the painting. The real owner, smuggling art out of Russia, might come after him. Or maybe not. Especially if it was insured.

Getting him in trouble with the law was probably still her best bet. She was nearly certain it had come into the country in breach of sanctions. All she needed was the right agency to care—and the right way to make sure they did.

An anonymous tip to a reporter. A stolen Russian painting turning up in a newsroom—what journalist could resist that?

Baldwin refilled her coffee and she sipped it while he cleaned the grill with a pumice brick. On her phone, she pulled up the pictures she'd taken of the painting and deleted them, one by one. Whatever she did next, she needed to be careful.

She did a quick search for *Tsaritsa Robbery* to see if there'd been any updates.

There was. A new story. Her thumb trembled as she clicked the link.

And then her blood ran cold.

Renowned art dealer Proctor Sifton was found dead in his Upper West Side home just hours after his Midtown gallery, the *Tsaritsa*, was the target of a high-profile robbery. The *Tsaritsa* has been a pillar of New York's art trade for decades but has also been the subject of numerous allegations, including alleged links to Russian organized crime. Police declined to comment in detail, though a spokesperson did confirm that they're treating the death as suspicious and have opened a homicide investigation.

Oksana stopped reading. She shut the tab on her phone and put it down.

"You all right?" Baldwin said, his eyes darting over her. "You look like you just saw a ghost."

"I have," she said, putting a twenty-dollar bill on the counter.

"What happened?"

"I can't explain," she said, picking up the painting, "but thank you for the food. I've never told you this, but I'd be lost without you."

She pushed out of the diner, gulping the cold night air, then paced hurriedly down the street. She couldn't have said why, exactly—but she was headed in the direction of Proctor's apartment. Something told her that her life could depend on it. If his death was related to the robbery, and she found it hard to imagine that it wasn't, then whoever had killed him would be willing to kill her, too.

She raised her hand at an approaching cab and climbed in, giving the driver Proctor's address. As the car made its way downtown, her thoughts spun out in every direction. She should have been happy. Proctor had raped her. She'd fantasized about killing him herself a thousand times. But now that it had happened, all she felt was terror.

She got out a block from his address and every instinct told her to turn back. But she didn't. Something pressed her onward. She had to know more.

There were multiple police cars on the street, as well as a small group of reporters and onlookers huddled around the entrance of the building. She walked toward the police tape, fingering the cash in her wallet. Just in case.

"What happened?" she asked a reporter near the tape.

He didn't even look at her. "Get your own story."

Oksana watched the cops and detectives going in and out, then looked around. There was a guy in a doorman's uniform leaning against the wall of the adjacent building—smoking a cigarette, uniform ruffled, face drawn. She still had the cigarettes she'd used as a prop outside the gallery, and she went up and asked him for a light. He took out a box of matches and sparked one for her.

"Quite the story," she said, cupping his hand as he lit the cigarette. She added, "Kelly Weiss, *World Daily News.*"

"No comment," he said immediately.

She smiled. "Don't worry, I'm off the clock."

He nodded, and they stood there, smoking, until he

threw his butt on the ground and made to leave. She grabbed his hand, squeezing it gently.

"What the hell?" he said. Then he realized she'd slipped him some money. "What's this?"

"Just tell me what happened."

"This could get me fired."

"Come on," she said. "It'll all be public soon enough."

He looked at her, at the money in his hand, and let out a long sigh. Then he lowered his voice. "You didn't hear this from me."

"Of course," she said, nodding.

"I'll lose my job."

"Totally off the record. Promise."

He looked at the money again, a crisp hundred, then said, "Fine, if you want to know, it was a bloodbath."

"What do you mean?"

"Whoever broke in wasn't messing around. They tied him to a chair, cut him up, burned him with cigarettes."

"Tortured him?"

"Tortured him, interrogated him, whatever you want to call it."

"You saw this with your own eyes?"

"I did not, thankfully, but I heard it from the super. He doesn't make shit up."

"All right, thanks," she said, already walking away.

"Hey," he called after her as she climbed into another cab, this time back to the Holiday Inn.

"Anyone come looking for me?" she said to the bellhop in the lobby.

"No, were you expecting someone?"

"Maybe," she said.

He looked at her inquisitively, and she said, "An ex." The

bellhop nodded knowingly, and she added, "He doesn't take no for an answer."

"I know the type."

"Do me a favor," she said. "If anyone comes by, call me immediately. Don't send them up, and don't confirm that I'm here."

"You got it," he said.

She got in the elevator and pressed the button. Her hand was shaking.

In her room, she sat down on the bed and wondered what the hell she was going to do next. If she'd been nervous before, she was positively panicked now. She needed to calm down. She told herself that no one knew she had the painting, and if she got rid of it pronto, no one ever would. She focused on that, on what she needed to do next, but the thought of Proctor being tortured and murdered kept flooding her mind. They'd killed him, she thought, and if they found her, they'd kill her too.

She unwrapped the painting and stared at it like it was a death sentence. She was tempted to destroy it right then and there. She didn't need it to hurt Proctor.

But something told her not to ditch it. Not yet. If she got rid of it, she needed whoever was looking for it to know.

Dropping it anonymously with the police, or even at an FBI field office, might do the job. That information would get to the press eventually. But giving it to a reporter directly would get it out even faster. They'd print the story by morning, she thought, and anyone searching for it would know the thief no longer had it.

She didn't know how to get it to a reporter, but she would figure it out. Before it got her killed.

She picked up the painting, then saw it—something she hadn't noticed before. The canvas, ever so slightly frayed, was coming away from the birchwood panel at the corner. She wondered if it had been tampered with at some point in the past and, as she looked more closely, realized there was something there, beneath the canvas, between it and the wood. She dug her fingers under the frayed edge. The canvas tore slightly. Her nail snagged something hard—plastic. No bigger than a fingernail.

A microSD card.

This was it. This was why Proctor was dead.

And now they'd come for her.

53

Veronica Bailey, aka Foxtrot, tapped her foot nervously against the leg of her chair. She'd been staring at gibberish on her screen, shoulders locked with tension. She leaned back, rubbing her eyes.

On the second screen, the temperature and pressure gauges crept ever higher at the Surry plant—numbers blinking red, edging toward meltdown.

"Gah," she muttered, the sound bouncing back at her from the empty room. She'd never felt so powerless in her life.

She began shutting down the terminals on her screen—staring at them any longer was pointless. No, it was worse—it was torture. She still had no idea what she was looking at. She'd been told that Ada 83—the archaic programming language behind the plant's controls—was *human-readable*. That was a goddamn lie.

"I might as well be looking at cuneiform," she muttered, glancing at her watch. If she didn't get home soon, her cat would start eating the house plants.

In any case, other than her abject uselessness, two

things had become very clear to her. First, the plant had most definitely been hacked. There was little doubt now that the code had been corrupted by a hostile actor. And second, there was no easy fix. The only solution the experts had come up with was to recompile the entire operating system from scratch, rebooting all the controls. There simply wasn't time for that.

The temperature gauge on her screen was at 428 degrees already, and rising fast. It updated, a jump from 428 to 432, and she felt her pulse quicken.

She got up from her seat and went to the door, where she flipped the sign and began locking up. She was about to shut down the computer when she saw a notification in the corner of the second screen. She told herself to ignore it. Just a general notice. Nothing for her. But she clicked it anyway. It opened a live television feed—a cable news network—showing the prelude to the Virginia Governor's press conference.

Governor Atwater stood at a makeshift podium, flanked by a nervous gaggle of bureaucrats and state officials. Someone had printed the state seal on plain printer paper and taped it to the podium, while behind, the American and Virginian flags tilted at awkward angles. It looked like a school assembly. Hardly confidence-inspiring.

They were broadcasting from the Virginia Emergency Operations Center in Richmond, and a staffer in a headset rushed past the camera. Then the flags tipped over and collapsed to the floor—just as the camera zoomed in on the seal.

"Good grief," Veronica murmured as an official bent to pick them up.

The ticker text changed. "Virginia Governor Addresses

State," became "Emergency Evacuation Order: Nuclear Incident at Surry Power Plant."

Someone called for order. The governor stepped forward and gripped the podium with both hands. Cameras flashed, the assembled reporters hushed, and then, in a flat, steady voice, he began to speak.

Fellow Virginians, as I speak, sirens are sounding across the ten-mile Emergency Zone around the Surry Nuclear Power Station.

The situation is rapidly evolving, and while there has been no confirmed release of radiation at this time, the risk of a core meltdown is real.

This is not a test. This is not a drill.

Immediate action is required.

If you live in Surry County, Isle of Wight County, James City County, or the designated portions of Newport News—you must evacuate now. Law enforcement and emergency teams are already mobilizing. Shelters in Richmond, Norfolk, and Petersburg, stocked with food, water, and medical aid, are open.

Let me repeat. If you are within the ten-mile EPZ, evacuate immediately. Take only essentials. Follow posted routes to the nearest shelter. Do not delay.

If you are not in the EPZ, remain calm. Stay indoors. Keep the roads clear.

Potassium Iodide tablets are being distributed through shelters, emergency checkpoints, and mobile teams. Those teams will go door to door. You do not need to leave your home to access tablets. Shelter in place.

Let me be clear. Your safety is our highest priority.

No one wanted this—least of all on Christmas Eve—but every agency involved, from the Nuclear Regulatory Commission to FEMA to Virginia Emergency Management, is working around the clock to resolve this crisis.

Updates will continue via Wireless Emergency Alerts, radio bulletins on 97.3 FM and 102.5 AM, and local television interruptions.

I will speak to you again in one hour.

Until then, stay safe, stay calm, and do what needs to be done. We will get through this, and we will do it together.

May God protect us all.

The screen shifted to a map of the EPZ, dotted with little red house icons marking shelters. The newscaster came back on, speculating on whether this was the result of a cyberattack, whether it was connected to Gabriella Wintour's murder, and whether the President would address the nation.

Veronica was lost in thought. The gauge jumped to 433.

Then came the bang on the door.

It was Roman trying to get in. He pushed the door again, then rapped on the glass with his knuckles.

She hurried over. "All right, calm down," she said, opening the door. "It was locked."

"I know it was locked."

"Well, don't get fresh with me, Roman Adler."

Roman went straight to the seating area and sank into one of the chairs. He had that look on his face that he got when at his wit's end, and she said, "What's happened?"

He threw up his hands. "Where to begin."

"The meeting?"

"Yes, the meeting."

"He's not going to stand us down, is he?"

"They passed a resolution in my absence. It basically blames us for Gabriella's death."

Veronica stood over him, arms crossed. His coat was wet from snow, his pants stained from slush, and, overall, he had the look of a drowned cat. "You really need to get out of that uniform," she said.

He shrugged, shoulders slumping as if he'd been punched.

"Why don't I make tea?" she said. It had calmed him before.

He said nothing, and she went over to the kettle and filled it. She'd lost track of how many hours he'd been up but she could tell he was reaching the end of his rope. "You look like hell. You need sleep."

"Sure," he said. "I'll take a nice nap while the nation watches a nuclear power plant blow up. Great idea!"

"I told you not to get fresh."

"Sorry," he said, then threw up his hands. "What are we even doing? This whole situation is devolving into chaos."

She brought the tea over, along with two cups, sugar, and a little pot of milk from the refrigerator. As she poured, she said, "Try not to be so worked up. It won't do any good."

"It wasn't just a slap on the wrist," he said. "They're going to follow up with more than a resolution."

"They're actually pulling the trigger?" she said, handing him his cup.

He smiled, thin and tired but real, and for a moment, they were just two people, alone together. Too soon, the moment passed. She looked away. She knew where glances like that led. She'd made her choice a long time ago.

Not with him.

"They're going to pull the plug, Veronica. I can feel it."

She stopped stirring her tea. He rarely said her name, and she couldn't help but feel a flicker of pleasure at hearing it. "It wasn't our fault," she said.

He shook his head.

"I mean Gabriella," she added.

"I know what you mean."

"And you know it's true."

"They think we're off the leash. Doerr and Hawke, especially. They're saying we've gone too far, and maybe they're right."

"They're not right," she said. "They're sycophants. They say whatever gets them ahead."

"Yeah, and they're saying we failed in our one job—preventing war."

"Preventing war with a country that's provoking us at every turn. At a certain point, prevention becomes appeasement. I'm sorry to say it, but it's true."

"Well, no one else sees it that way."

"They've had it in for you since day one, Roman. All of them. They see a chance to take you down, and they're jumping on it."

"Maybe this time they'll get their wish."

"Then Calvin can enjoy Hawke and the *wunderkind* sucking up to him 24/7. Let's see how long that lasts."

Roman took a sip of tea. "It won't go well for Margot," he said, "if we're cut off."

"Good thing I've already scrambled the system."

"You got it all done?"

"Breakfast is cooked," she said with a slight smile. There were still things she could do—track Margot on satellite, tap into Russian systems—but the main task was done. She'd corrupted the data in the Russian facial recognition system. "Once I know which way she's headed," she added, "I'll plant a decoy. Make sure the Russians look for her in all the wrong places."

Roman nodded. "And Dmitry? Did you manage to get hold of him?"

"I did, though he was inordinately reluctant. Honestly, I'm not sure he'll follow through."

"He'll do it," Roman said. "He's never let me down yet."

"I told him the back of the travel agency."

"Good," Roman said. "And the hard disk? Anything?"

She shook her head. "Nothing. And they've stopped trying."

"The EMP obliterated everything?"

"Yes, it did."

"And the plant?"

"Four-thirty-three and climbing. Governor just went live."

"You saw it?"

"The entire country saw it."

"How'd he do?"

She nodded. "Fine. Ordered the evacuation of the ten-mile zone."

"He'll need to expand that."

"Yeah, but fifty miles covers two and a half million people. It'd be the biggest evacuation since... ever?"

"It's been done," Roman said.

"Well, it would be pointless to make that order if the roads can't handle it."

"They'll stagger it. Ten-mile zone's first."

"And how do we stop it?" Veronica said.

Roman sighed, took another sip of tea. "You'll be wanting to get home," he said, dodging the question.

"Nonsense."

"*Sooty.*"

She smiled. "Sooty will understand."

"I've got another job for you. Something you can do from home."

"What is it?"

"I need everything you can possibly find on *Stalin's Shadow*."

"*Stalin's Shadow?*"

"Or the Russian, *Ten' Stalina*. Margot said Irina mentioned it."

"Before she died?"

"Right before."

"Any idea where to start?"

"Afraid not," he said. "You'll have to run the gamut."

"*Ten' Stalina*? Sounds like a code name. It might take some time."

"Go through Internet traffic, messaging apps, Facebook posts, classified advertisements, eBay listings, bank transfers, customs shipments, the works."

"Barbarossa. The purges. *Holodomor*. The *Gulag*. You could say the whole twentieth century was in Stalin's shadow."

"This will be something specific," Roman said. "Something concrete. I'm sure of it."

"If it isn't...."

"If it isn't," he said, "we're staring at a meltdown."

She nodded once, then grabbed her coat. "You should get home, too," she said.

If he heard her, he made no sign of it. "I probably don't have to say this," he added, "but no calls. No favors. We're on our own now."

She gave him a long, pointed look. "When have you ever known me to ask for help?"

54

Margot tore down the corridor, past offices where staffers were frantically stuffing documents into boxes. The sun was just cresting the skyline outside, but already, the embassy pulsed with panic—shouted orders, slammed drawers, shredders screaming through the halls. It reminded her of war films—soldiers torching files before the enemy stormed the gates.

Through a wide window, she glimpsed a Sikorsky Black Hawk dropping fast, its rotors whipping the courtyard into chaos. Three smaller Moscow Police helicopters circled warily, giving it space.

In the lobby, someone nearly knocked her over with a cart stacked high with boxes. She swerved around it—then slammed into someone rounding the corner. They both hit the ground.

It was Napoleon.

"You!" he barked, eyes wide.

"Sorry," Margot said, getting to her feet.

"You don't think they'll make us hand you over?" he gasped. "Think again."

"I don't have time for this," she said, hurrying away.

"Of course you don't—more havoc to wreak."

She ignored him and shoved through a fire exit. The alarm screamed—but who cared anymore?

She was outside, at the edge of the courtyard, and through bare branches, she could see the Black Hawk as it made contact with the ground. Staffers sprinted toward it, their carts piled with classified cargo.

Margot skirted the courtyard, ducking through more trees, shielding her face from the circling choppers.

She headed straight for a squat service building marked by ventilation slats below the eaves. There was a garage door, but she went for the side entrance. The keycard Boreal had given her granted her access, and she slipped in quickly, praying she hadn't been noticed.

Inside was a raw, concrete floor and sixteen-foot-high steel roof. One wall was stacked with broken boilers, tanks, air conditioners—hardware awaiting repair. The rest of the space was large enough for three or four light-duty vehicles, though there was currently just one—a large, black van with civilian plates and the logo of what appeared to be an ordinary Moscow plumbing company on the side.

Her ride. A one-way ticket.

She slipped into the van's cargo bay and found a crate big enough to hide in. The lid was loose and inside, it was lined with shredded packing paper. She climbed in, pulled the lid up over her head, and waited. Several long minutes passed before someone climbed into the front and started the engine. She stayed quiet.

She heard the garage door open, then the van began to move. She tracked their path in her mind—through the courtyard, past the screaming Black Hawk, then out of the compound through the freight gate at the back.

The van picked up speed and she held her breath, unsure it was him—until the voice came. "You can come out now."

She raised the lid slowly, peering out cautiously before rising to her feet. "You knew I was here?"

"I knew," the driver said—Steinhauser. "Just wasn't *shaw* I should say."

Margot crouched low behind his seat, eyes on the road ahead. Police cars sped past in the opposite lane.

"Are we being followed?" she said, glancing back.

"Not that I can tell."

"Where are we going?"

He passed her a small metal key without looking. "Not far. A shop with a reinforced door. That's the key."

"What kind of shop?"

"Front for something. Travel agency, supposedly."

"Have you been there before?"

"Never. Didn't even know it existed."

"And it will be empty?"

"As far as I know. Your instructions are to let yourself in, lock the door behind you, then go to the basement. It's connected to the building behind via an old World War Two bunker."

"Then what?"

"There'll be another car waiting on the other side. A cab. The driver's name is Dmitry."

"That's it?"

"You should try to get to the cab as quickly as possible."

"Right," she said. It wasn't the most sophisticated plan she'd ever heard, but it was what it was. "Let me know when to jump."

"It's right up here," he said, taking a sharp corner. The

van jerked to a halt outside a row of old tenements. "This is it," he said, already shifting gears. "Go now! Fast!"

She leaped out as the van stopped. A black sedan was already swinging around the corner behind her. She didn't wait to find out who it was. She ran. Straight for the derelict travel agency. Key in hand. Heart hammering.

As the van peeled away, she darted inside, slamming the door behind her. It had two deadbolts and she slapped them home with a metallic clunk. A window next to the door was papered over. She prayed it was also reinforced—otherwise the deadbolts bought her nothing.

She hurried through a deserted office, eyes adjusting to the gloom. Old travel posters lined the walls—a black and white shot of the Coliseum, another advertising Crimea's beaches, pre-2014. She rushed by, knocking over a dusty swivel chair, sidestepping a rusting desk and cabinets. Then she found a wooden door.

It was locked, but a few firm kicks cracked the frame and it swung open. So much for stealth. She rushed down some old stairs to a pitch-black basement and groped at the wall until her fingers found a switch. A bare bulb flickered on, trembling from years of disuse, to reveal a basement of raw stone that was clearly older than the rest of the building. At the far end stood an iron door. It was unlocked and led to a passageway.

There was no light ahead. No phone. No flashlight. She stepped into the darkness, the bulb light fading behind her as she stumbled forward over uneven earth.

Somewhere behind her, metal clanged. A door being rammed? Or just her imagination? She kept moving.

She crashed blindly into another door. It was locked and she rammed it with her good shoulder. It budged, leaking a sliver of dim light. She threw her weight against it and slowly, inch by inch, it cranked open. She squeezed through, gasping. Her shoulder throbbed. She touched the bandage —bleeding again.

The door led to a second basement, dark but for some streaks of daylight bleeding in through filthy windows near the ceiling. A short flight of steps led up to another door.

She ran up the steps and the door, miraculously, was unlocked. She slipped out into a narrow alley. At the end of it was a waiting Moscow taxi cab, engine running.

Her hand brushed her pistol as she ran to the cab, yanking open the door.

"Dmitry?" she said, still breathless.

"*Da.*"

She climbed in. "Go, go, go!"

She didn't look back.

55

Veronica walked home briskly. The snow had finally stopped, and the night streets were quieter than she'd ever seen them. Her apartment was on the second floor of a grand Federal-style townhouse off 18th Street Northwest. Her phone buzzed as she turned onto the quiet, tree-lined block.

It was a message from Roman confirming that Margot had successfully fled the embassy. She exhaled in relief as she climbed the stoop. Through the window, she could see her neighbor's beautifully decorated Christmas tree. She slipped inside quietly, then hurried up the stairs to her door.

As soon as she stepped inside, Sooty was underfoot, nearly tripping her. She bent down and picked her up. "Good girl," she cooed. "Mummy's home."

She carried Sooty into the kitchen and gave her some food, then wondered if she should prepare something for herself. It was late, but she wouldn't be going to bed anytime soon, so she decided to eat something. Being English—and no Michelin chef—she settled on a simple omelet. Eggs, milk, salt, and pepper. She whisked the eggs, melted some butter in a pan, and poured it in. She was careful not to overcook it—as an avid Julia Child fan, she knew that much—and gave it just a minute on each side. She made some toast and brought it to the counter on a tray.

Then she opened her laptop. Sooty leaped onto her lap as she typed the words "Stalin's Shadow" into her search terminal in both English and Russian. She hit enter, querying not just public engines but proprietary NSA and CIA systems—AI-enhanced tools that trawled petabytes of data: private messaging apps, email servers, financial records, phone transcripts, shipping logs, and more. Laws technically limited domestic surveillance—but loopholes and foreign partnerships rendered them meaningless.

While the search ran, she ate her omelet. When she was done, she rinsed her plate and went rummaging for something sweet. She found what she was looking for. Technically, they weren't cookies—they were biscuits, imported from a specialty grocer on 14th—and she brought the pack to the counter.

On her screen, the algorithm had flagged a Russian shipping company—and its recent communications with a US citizen named Proctor Sifton. She let the search continue while she put on the kettle and made herself a pot of strong, black tea. The teabags were British, too, bought at the same specialty store, but the tea was never as good as back home. Something to do with the water, she'd been told. In any case, it was better than the dirty dishwater that passed for tea in America.

When she sat back down, the search was still running. She left it on in the background while opening the first few results. There were plenty of false positives, unsurprising given the breadth of Stalin's impact—and the literal and figurative shadow he'd cast over the twentieth century. She was still sifting when her phone vibrated.

She answered immediately—Roman.

"Anything?" he said.

"I only just started the search. It takes time."

He sighed—tired, frustrated, and still awake.

"Are you still at the bookshop?"

"Yes."

"I told you to go home."

"I can't do that."

"Exhausting yourself isn't going to help anything."

"Yeah," he said, letting out a long yawn. "But the search is running?"

"It's running and you might as well be asleep while it works its magic. Let me do my job."

"Stalin's Shadow," he said, almost wistfully. "Sounds like one of your Cold War paperbacks."

"Oh, they're *mine* now, are they?"

"You're the one who keeps bringing them in."

"I buy them for you, Roman."

He sighed again. But she could tell—despite everything—he was starting to lower his guard. Maybe he'd even close his eyes. "Ever hear the story of the plucked chicken?" he said.

"Roman, at least one of us should be taking this opportunity to get some rest."

"It's a story about Stalin," he continued. "Stalin's *shadow*, you might even say."

"Is that so?"

"Maybe it's apocryphal. Some say Aitmatov made it up to make the monster more vivid."

"Aitmatov?"

"Kyrgyz author. Chinghiz Aitmatov. Wrote about Stalin —among other things."

"I see," Veronica said, as Sooty leaped back onto her lap. "Our reading lists may be less similar than I thought."

"In the story," he continued, "Stalin calls all his lieutenants into a room, and when they get there, they see that he's holding a live chicken."

"Stalin is?"

"Yes, and he begins plucking its feathers," Roman said.

"Alive?"

"Right there in front of them."

"That can't be true."

"Feather by feather."

"Is that even possible?"

"I don't know, but that's how the story goes."

"And the moral?" Veronica said. "Because I sense there's one coming."

"You tell me."

"Stalin was a psychopath?"

"He tortured it. Then threw it to the floor—"

"Where it died?"

"No. It didn't die. It screamed and thrashed and ran around, leaving a trail of blood on the floor while it searched for some way to escape the room. But there was no way out."

"This is a horrible story."

"Yes. And you want to know the worst part?"

"Not particularly," she said, sipping her tea, "but you're going to tell me anyway."

"The worst part is that by the end of the meeting, the chicken was shivering in fear, quivering in pain, but it was huddled between Stalin's feet."

"Lovely. Just the thing to hear alone in a dark apartment."

"Supposedly, Stalin took some corn from his pocket and fed the chicken. They say it ate right from his hand."

"It's obviously a made-up story, Roman."

"Maybe. It doesn't matter. What matters is that decades later, people still tell it. You and I are talking about it. In the USSR, everyone knew it. They believed it. Even senior Soviet officials referred to it in cables. The closer they were to him, the more they believed."

"And what's the moral, Roman? That we're all just bloodied birds, begging the man who hurt us most for protection?"

"The point I'm trying to make, I suppose, is that this is what we're up against. This is what we're fighting. The same darkness. The same menace. Millions fleeing their homes in a blizzard before Christmas. It's the same suffering—Ukraine, Georgia, Belarus, Russia, God-knows-where. We're the chicken. All of us. The whole world."

"We're all in Stalin's Shadow, you're saying?"

"Stalin told his lieutenants, as he fed the chicken from his hand—*This is how we rule. The more they suffer, the more they cling to us.*"

"He's been dead seventy years, Roman."

"But the ghost lives on, Vee. The earth is still scorched. He destroyed life at the root and it hasn't grown back. We're still reaping from that salted earth. Still harvesting the fallout. This all goes back to him."

Veronica's computer dinged. She leaned forward, scanning the result that had been flagged.

"Hang on," she said, clicking through. "The computer found something."

"What is it?"

"Obscure," she muttered. "A painting. *Stalin's Shadow*. It depicts the construction of the White Sea Canal—was in storage at *Tretyakov Gallery* sometime in the fifties."

"Doesn't sound promising."

"Don't interrupt." Her eyes scanned faster now. "Intercepted Telegram traffic suggests a New York art dealer's been discussing the risks of importing it in breach of sanctions. Customs seizure, criminal liability, who'd eat the loss."

"Was it imported?"

"There's talk of the commission—bumped for the added risk."

"Who was sending the painting?" Roman said.

"I said don't interrupt," she said sternly, then, "It was shipped using a company called *Novoguard*. Roman, it was delivered to a New York art gallery. Tonight."

"What?"

"Less than six hours ago."

"Are you kidding me?"

"A gallery in Midtown Manhattan called the *Tsaritsa*."

"And the painting's called—"

"This is it, Roman! This is it!" Her voice spiked. Sooty bolted.

"I need to get to that gallery," Roman said. "Immediately."

"There's more," Veronica said. "According to this, *Novoguard* is a Kremlin-connected high-value transportation firm. They got it through JFK—likely by bribing officials."

"Vee! Get me a chopper."

She was already opening a fresh terminal. The familiarity of it—the urgency. He ordered. She obeyed. It came like muscle memory.

She commandeered a Bell Boeing V-22 Osprey already

stationed at Joint Base Andrews as part of HMX-1. Overkill, but with vertical landing capability and a 310-mph top speed, it was the fastest way from DC to New York. "Can you get to Andrews?"

"I'm already on my way," Roman said, and she could hear him shuffling hurriedly out of the bookshop.

"The dealer's name is Proctor Sifton," she said. "Gallery's the *Tsaritsa*. Sending it all now. The Osprey can put you down on the roof of the Four Seasons on 58th Street in forty-five minutes if you get to Andrews fast enough."

"Taxi!" Roman barked. "I need a cab."

"Oh my God!" Veronica whispered.

"What?"

"The gallery," she said. "It was robbed. Tonight."

"Tonight? When?"

"The report I'm reading was published an hour ago."

"Send me everything," he said. "I'm already heading to Andrews."

56

Veronica opened a direct link to the NYPD database to check if the gallery burglar had been caught. As she scanned the report, her eyes widened in shock.

Not only had the gallery been burgled, but the owner, Proctor Sifton, was dead. His body had been found scarcely an hour ago at his multimillion-dollar home. According to the report, he'd been tied to a chair and tortured before being finished off with a bullet to the head. The apartment had been ransacked, too, as if the intruders were searching for something.

The painting.

She typed rapidly, navigating the agency data streams.

No footage from the home. But the gallery? That was a different story. The robbery was captured by multiple cameras—building, gallery, and external feeds on 57th, Park, and Madison. Veronica scrubbed through them—first at double speed, then at normal. Three facts.

One: female.

Two: alone.

Three: deliberate.

She watched the footage closely—a sleek woman in black, moving with the precision of someone who knew exactly where to go and what to take. Even the escape—which hadn't gone to plan—was a measured, controlled affair in which no one panicked, no one was hurt, and no one was caught.

The operation had been old-school, using traditional methods and a traditional skill set. Unlike at Proctor's home, the gallery's surveillance hadn't even been touched.

There was no question the burglar was a pro. Not military. Not *Spetsnaz*. Something older. More elegant. Veronica felt a faint chill. Whoever it was, she hadn't come to make a scene. She'd come to make a statement.

"Who are you?" she murmured, watching her prowl down a corridor—*Julie Newmar* as *Catwoman* reborn. She picked the lock in seconds—clearly, she'd known what to expect—then slipped inside and took one thing, and one thing only. A single, small canvas.

By contrast, the attack at Proctor Sifton's apartment was an entirely different affair. Scanning the police report, she saw instantly that it reeked of violence and brute force. No finesse, no signature. Veronica didn't need the grainy traffic camera footage from outside the residence—showing two men forcing their way into the apartment building—to know that the home invasion had been pulled off by a different outfit.

For one thing, there'd been a blackout of the security system at the apartment, knocking out the cameras and suggesting the assistance of a sophisticated hacking operation. For another, while the thief at the gallery appeared unarmed, the home invasion was much bloodier, culminating in an execution.

If anything, Veronica thought, it had more in common with the Gabriella hit. Blunt force. Scorched-earth. Dead body.

And then there was the ransacking. At the gallery, the thief knew exactly what she was after and, apparently, where to find it. She'd been in and out in less than three minutes. The search at Proctor's home was chaotic, messy—and took longer.

Veronica rewound the exterior footage from the gallery and watched the burglar slip out through the Versace boutique like she owned the place. No rush, no glance back —just a little package tucked inside her coat.

She cross-referenced the *Ten' Stalina* specs—a ten-by-twelve-inch birchwood panel—with what was on the screen.

Close enough.

She also noted that there'd been far more valuable paintings inside the gallery—some worth millions. The burglar hadn't even looked at them. The *Ten' Stalina*, according to the intercepted messages, was valued at between thirty and fifty thousand dollars.

Why that one, Veronica wondered. Why not a million-dollar canvas?

She scrolled through all of the CCTV footage, then widened her search to include traffic cameras on the surrounding streets, as well as nearby transit stations. The MTA operated cameras in all subway stations, and she requested the feeds from Fifth Avenue-53rd Street, 59th Street-Columbus Circle, and 57th Street-Seventh Avenue.

A Madison Ave cam caught the burglar hailing a cab—throwing up her hand like a Manhattan native. "One cool customer," Veronica muttered, chewing her biscuit like a detective with a cigar.

She created a tracker for the cab—it would flag all

further sightings of the vehicle—then shifted her attention to some of the other search results, narrowing the parameters to show only matches from New York City in the past two hours.

Then she saw it.

The slip-up.

The jackpot.

Someone had performed a reverse image search using a public terminal at Columbia's Butler Library—uploading a photo they'd just taken on an iPhone.

The photo was of the *Ten' Stalina*.

The metadata placed it at a Holiday Inn on Schermerhorn in Brooklyn.

She cross-checked the location—just a few blocks from the G Line at Fulton Street Station. She began acquiring security footage from that station, too, along with every train that had passed through since the robbery.

She ran a second query for footage from inside the Butler Library—and there she was.

Bingo.

Blonde. Early twenties. Dressed in black and moving with the coiled grace of Catwoman in the sixties.

Or a ballerina.

She pulled up the guest list from the Holiday Inn and scanned the names.

Then—

There it was.

Oksana Tchaikovskaya.

Her heart gave a jolt.

She stared. Pulled up the ID used to check in. Ran the match.

Twenty-four. Dates aligned. Russian Literature major at Columbia.

She glanced back at the footage. Lithe. Precise. Graceful as a cat.

Then, back at the ID.

A face from deep in the CIA vault.

A name she hadn't heard in years.

Tchaikovskaya.

Not just a match.

A ghost.

57

Strapped into a V-22 Osprey, Roman gripped his seat like his life depended on it. The pilot, Captain JD Harlan, sat beside him, his face locked in concentration as he threaded the aircraft between buildings. Outside, the twin Rolls-Royce turboshafts roared like NASA rockets on takeoff. The Osprey was the fastest ride from DC to New York short of hijacking an F-22 Raptor—but riding it felt more like having a fistfight with gravity than flying.

Roman held on, staring at Harlan's shoulder patch, trying not to look outside. Harlan flew with HMX-1, the elite Marine unit tasked with presidential transport. That was why he'd been sitting fueled and ready on the tarmac at Andrews when Veronica made the call. His original flight plan would have brought him to the Virginia Emergency Ops Center in Richmond—but only if the meltdown was fully averted.

Harlan glanced at him, his voice coming through the earpiece in the flight helmet. "Brace for touch down."

Roman leaned forward to see the helipad below, its red beacon lights flashing the letter H in the mist. Thirty minutes prior, he'd been looking down at the Washington Monument.

They were landing on the roof of the 58th Street Four Seasons—one of the most exclusive hotels in all of Manhattan and, ironically, a place that was inordinately popular with Russian intelligence. Roman had seen with his own eyes the expense claims submitted by GRU and SVR operatives. They charged more rooms to this one hotel than any other in the country. For them, it was a forward operating base with room service. It was even rumored that within its walls, in one of the fifty-thousand-dollar-a-night suites, Chichikov himself had penned the secret agreement with his Chinese counterpart to mark the birth of the Russo-China axis—their *Great Containment Pact* to challenge American dominance.

An axis born in opulence.

That had been years ago, but Roman still used the hotel. It was sometimes a point of contention with Foxtrot.

"You like the danger," she'd said more than once.

He argued that it kept him close to the action, as well as fitting with his policy of hiding in plain sight. However, as a place accustomed to serving the needs of shady foreign oligarchs and billionaires, it was also uniquely disposed toward privacy. Roman knew this because he'd tried more than once to violate it by spying on guests. Never had the hotel acquiesced, and in fact, it was easier to spy on visiting Russian dignitaries when they stayed at their own consulate on 91st Street, or at the UN Mission on 67th Street, than at the Four Seasons.

The helipad's altitude—682 feet above street level—also made it nearly impossible to monitor. And on this occasion, being right next to the *Tsaritsa* art gallery didn't hurt either.

The Osprey touched down, and Roman waited for the

signal before jumping out. He kept his head low as he followed the hotel's security director away from the craft, the downdraft of the propellors whipping them violently. The rooftop was shrouded in low cloud, and they followed a narrow catwalk rimmed with more strobing beacons. It led to a small, opulent elevator lobby, and even before the door slammed shut behind them, the Osprey was rising back into the night sky.

Roman took in the lobby as he caught his breath. He'd been there many times and the contrast with the rooftop couldn't have been starker—Italian marble floor, golden recessed lighting, and art deco elevator doors with gilded trim.

"Your office called ahead," the security director said, eyeing Roman's uniform. "We've got the room ready."

"Room?"

"As well as most of the items that were requested. Given the lateness of the hour, we had to make some substitutions."

Roman had no idea what he was talking about, though it wouldn't have been the first time Veronica had taken the liberty of making arrangements. They took the elevator to the forty-eighth floor, and the director led him to his door.

"None of this happened," Roman said, handing him a fifty.

"Of course, sir."

Once inside, Roman went straight to the window. The view was obscured by a lone super-tall building across the street. He squinted at it, putting on his glasses to see better. Across the way, a man in white boxer shorts and a wide-open robe was standing behind a wall of glass, looking back. In his hand was what appeared to be a bowl of cereal.

Ah, New York, Roman thought, shutting the blind. Where even the voyeurs were watched.

He'd grown up in the city and, despite decades in DC, had never shed the sense that New York—not Washington—was the nation's true beating heart. DC was too prim and orderly—more like the capital of a mid-tier European country than the greatest nation on earth.

He checked the messages on his phone. The latest data put the core temperature at the plant at 471 degrees, just a few hours from total meltdown. He shuddered.

On the bed, he saw the items that had been brought up at Veronica's behest. They felt like a commentary on his wardrobe as much as anything necessary for the mission, but he began undressing all the same. As well as a garment bag for a suit, there was a long black coat, black leather gloves, a gray cashmere scarf, socks and underwear, and a pair of hand-polished Berluti Oxford shoes. He stripped naked, took a quick shower, then opened the garment bag. A dark Tom Ford suit and crisp white shirt tailored to his exact measurements. He put on the underwear, then took out his phone and dialed.

"You've arrived," she said, picking up immediately.

"I have," he said. "Where am I going—The Met Gala?"

"Very funny," she said. "You're going to a bar in Brooklyn, and trust me, if you showed up in your policeman's outfit, you'd blow the whole thing."

He picked up the jacket and held it to the light. The silk-smooth fabric exuded luxury. "The lapels are a bit much, no?"

"You try ordering a suit at midnight on Christmas Eve with thirty minutes' notice."

"I'm not complaining."

"That's exactly what you're doing."

He pulled on the shirt and fastened the buttons, wincing when he saw his reflection in the mirror. What stared back at him was a stark reminder of mortality—tired eyes, hunted eyes. Too much lost sleep. Too many dead friends.

"So, who am I meeting?"

"I don't think you'll believe me when I tell you."

"I just hope they appreciate all this effort," he said, tying the tie.

"Really, Roman. You're not going to believe it."

"Believe what?"

"Are you sitting down?"

"Yes," he lied.

"I'm tracking her cell," Veronica said, still stalling.

"Whose cell?"

"The thief," Veronica said. "The one who stole the *Ten' Stalina* and—"

"Vee! Who is it?"

"It's Oksana Tchaikovskaya."

"Oksana Tchaikovskaya?"

"The daughter, Roman. The little girl. You remember—"

Roman's breath caught. He hadn't heard that name—hadn't let himself think it—in over twenty years.

The past came roaring back—like a T406 twin-spool turboshaft.

"The little girl?" he said quietly, now actually sitting down.

"The little girl," Veronica echoed. "All grown up."

58

Oksana was in a basement dive bar not far from her hotel on Schermerhorn, and she raised her hand to get the bartender's attention. "Another!" she cried, though she was quite sure she'd had enough already.

The bartender was run off his feet—it was surprisingly busy for the night before Christmas—and pretended not to see her.

"Hey," she protested. "I'm talking to you."

She was being obnoxious—she could feel it—but was beyond the point of caring. Back in her hotel room, a MicroSD card waited like a death sentence. Decorum could wait.

"Same again?" the bartender said to her while pouring someone else's drink.

"Make it a double this time."

"You sure?"

She looked at him pointedly, then did a little circular motion with her finger in the air. Some guys across the bar laughed as she gestured. "Put that on my tab," one of them said. He was wearing a Buffalo Bills jersey.

"Don't," Oksana said, though she did glance at the guy, trying to decide what would be worse—going back to his place for the night, or getting strung up and tortured in her hotel room when the murderers found her. She wasn't sure which.

On a television screen behind the bar, the news was all about the nuclear plant. People in the bar, for the most part, were trying to ignore it, though that was getting harder and harder to do when the network kept bringing up an illustrated gauge representing the plant's core temperature. It kept climbing toward a very dramatic 600 number—currently at 487—and the way it was drawn made 600 look like the prize.

The bartender placed a fresh glass in front of her, and as she raised it to her lips, she felt someone sidle onto the stool next to her.

"I'll have what she's having," a man said.

Oksana rolled her eyes. As she turned to see what she was dealing with, her stool shifted, and she almost lost balance. She grabbed the man's arm to steady herself and then, for some reason, held on longer than she might have had she been fully sober.

The man wasn't what she'd expected. He was in his sixties, for one thing—old enough to be her father—and certainly out of place in that dingy bar. He wasn't unattractive. Long black coat, expensive gloves, cashmere scarf—out of place here, but somehow magnetic. She glanced at the Bills fan and thought, if he wasn't careful, this fellow might steal his lunch. "Sorry," she said, letting go of the arm.

"Oh, I don't mind."

"I'm sure you don't," she muttered, trying not to slur.

The bartender poured the man's drink, and the man, looking at the bottle, said, "Ah, Mendeleev."

"What's that?" the bartender said impatiently.

"Russian Standard," the man said. "A recipe developed by Dmitry Mendeleev."

The bartender rushed off to serve another customer.

"The chemist who came up with the periodic table," the man added, speaking now to Oksana.

She shrugged and was about to look away when he raised his glass. "*Na zdorovye.*"

That got her attention. Why Russian? Just because they were drinking vodka?

"What are we drinking to?" he said.

"Oh, *we're* drinking now?"

"Well, aren't we?"

She squinted, trying to get a read, and raised her glass. Was she really that drunk—toasting with a sixty-year-old who'd just started speaking Russian? Then she pictured Proctor Sifton—cops outside, corpse inside. She imagined the body on a chair, tied upright while blood pooled on the floor. How much trouble had she stumbled into?

The man clinked his glass on hers and raised it to his lips.

"*Oderint dum metuant,*" she said before she even realized it. It was a strange choice of words, but that was what came to her when she'd been drinking. She knocked back the vodka and immediately looked around for the bartender.

"Another?" he said when she caught him.

She shook her head. "Just the bill."

He left and she pulled her jacket off the back of her seat.

"*Oderint dum metuant,*" the man said, and she looked at him again, wondering if he'd get the reference.

"Caligula," he said.

She raised an eyebrow—impressed despite herself. "Close, though technically, it was Accius."

"Accius?"

"The playwright. He wrote the line and gave it to Caligula."

"I see."

"But I think it's more an emperor's line than a poet's."

The man nodded. "Let them hate," he said slowly, tasting the words, "so long as they fear."

The bartender put the bill in front of her. She expected to have to fight to pay, but the man didn't offer. His eyes were glued to the television, his face drawn with strain. On the screen, the Virginia Governor was announcing that the evacuation radius had been extended to fifty miles around the plant, putting millions of people on the roads on Christmas. There was footage of miles-long traffic jams on the major highways, then the illustration of the temperature gauge came back up, now showing 489 degrees.

She took out her wallet, and it was then that the man said, "Let me get these."

"No," she said quickly.

"Please." He placed a card on the bill. "It's the least I can do."

She looked at him curiously. Odd way of putting it, she thought.

She put on her jacket, and if he intended to persuade her to stay, he wasn't making any sign of it.

It was then that she got the feeling she'd misread the situation, misread their conversation, brief though it was. He hadn't been trying to pick up. And his being there was no accident. His speaking Russian wasn't, either. Maybe if she'd stopped at two drinks she'd have seen it earlier, but she saw it now.

He was there for a reason. And that reason was her.

She blurted it before she could stop herself. "All right, why don't you tell me what this is about?"

He smiled then, with almost a pleased look on his face, as if the whole thing had been a test. "I'm sorry?" he said.

"Why are you here?'

"Who says there has to be a reason?"

"Come on," she said. "You come in here like Michael Douglas in *Wall Street*."

"Gordon Gecko?"

"No, the other one—where he jumps off a building."

"*The Game*."

"Right."

"You think I look like Michael Douglas in *The Game*?"

"You didn't just stumble in here. That's what I'm saying. There's an agenda."

"What agenda? Can't a guy buy a girl—"

"Me," she said, then felt immediately self-conscious. What was she doing? Losing her mind? Drawing attention to herself when she should have been doing precisely the opposite? She shouldn't have been out. She should have been in her bed, under the covers, lights off. Hell, she should have been a hundred miles away.

"I think—" the man started hesitantly, and she could tell from his tone he was about to beat a retreat.

"No," she said quickly. "You knew I'd be here. Admit it."

"Look," he said. "I don't think this is the place—"

"The place for what?"

He looked around then as if there might be someone in the bar who could help him out. "For a serious talk."

"A serious talk? That's why you're here?"

"That's why I'm here."

A moment passed. She was right—something was up.

Finally, she said, "I think I've had too much to drink."

She turned to leave.

"Oksana."

Her name. Spoken like a trigger. Her breath hitched. She sobered instantly—like a bucket of ice water had been dumped over her head. "What did you say?"

"Don't be afraid."

"Oh, we're way past afraid—"

"*Proshloye—eto reka*," he said suddenly.

For an instant, her mind blanked, then she remembered the phrase. It was something her mother used to say. "The past is a river that runs through us," she said quietly. It had always sounded so poetic, until now.

He nodded, and the bartender came by to pick up the bill. "Put mine on there, too," the man said to him.

"Who *are* you?" she said when the bartender left.

"Let me ask you something before I answer."

"I think you should answer first."

"You're a student of Russian literature, right? Russian history?"

"You seem to know a lot about me for a man without an agenda."

"Here's a river for you. The Czar. The Checka. The GPU. The NKVD. The KGB."

She didn't answer. Just stared. Heart thumping.

"I'm not playing games," he said.

"Sure you're not."

"Let me put it this way. The Czar, Lenin, Stalin, Lavrentiy Beria, Yuri Andropov, Vladimir Chichikov."

"I have to get out of here," she said, turning again to leave.

"You know Chichikov was a KGB officer," he said after her. "Before he was president."

She stopped and turned back to him. "What are you doing?"

"It's all closer than we realize, Oksana. Chichikov—the man in the Kremlin—touched with his own hands the same KGB typewriters, the same documents and files, as Lavrentiy Beria and Yuri Andropov."

"What the hell are you talking about?"

"The same sheaves of papers. The same folders. The same desk phones. The same drawers. Even the same restroom faucets. That's a strange thought, don't you think?"

"I don't know what I think."

"The connection," he said, and something about the look on his face made her blood shiver.

Her chest tightened. She needed air—needed to get out of there, and fast. She didn't fully grasp what he was saying, but one thing was loud and clear—he knew her. Knew she'd be there. Knew something about her past.

"Let me guess," she said, backing away. "Next, you'll tell me we're all just six degrees from Kevin Bacon."

He didn't smile.

She fled.

59

Veronica stepped out of the tub and checked her phone. Still nothing. She crossed to the vanity and squeezed a dollop of lotion onto her hand. Winters in Washington never failed to dry her skin—she blamed the North American heating systems, she couldn't recall English radiators ever having the same effect—and she sat on the side of the tub and rubbed lotion into her legs.

In the bedroom, a news network was showing round-the-clock coverage of the power plant. The entire nation was now watching illustrations of the plant's core temperature, collectively holding its breath as the number inched closer and closer to the catastrophic 600 mark. It created a strange, morbid, communal tension—like waiting for the ball to drop at New Year's. Only this time, for the end of the world.

She killed the feed, tied her robe, and returned to the kitchen.

The laptop was still running searches—trawling every reference to Oksana Tchaikovskaya and her family it could find. Some Veronica had seen before—she'd been around when Roman ran the mother as an asset—but she hadn't been directly involved, and much of what she was seeing was new to her. She hadn't realized how deep it went—how tragic the father's end had been. She'd really only known what came after—the mother and daughter fleeing Russia, Roman bringing them onto the books properly.

She scrolled through the files, saving everything and anything that referenced the child. There wasn't all that much, she'd been little more than an infant, after all. An appendage to the mother.

Collateral. That was how Roman had labeled her in the file.

Funny how collateral grew up.

Roman had kept extensive files on both parents, and had been running the mother as an asset right until the end. The whole story wasn't there, there were too many gaps and redactions to really piece it together, but Veronica was used to reading between the lines. Especially when it came to Roman Adler. And one thing was very clear.

His hands weren't completely clean.

He'd been up to his old tricks again—playing five-dimensional chess with people's lives. She'd have to make sure that whatever she pulled together for Oksana didn't raise any flags in that regard. It would have to be thoroughly sanitized. With the core temperature climbing by the second, there wasn't room for mistakes. Or for ghosts.

Her phone rang. She picked up on the first buzz. "You found her? You spoke to her?"

"I did, and I did," Roman said.

"And?"

"I'm letting her process."

"What did you tell her?"

"Nothing. Just planted seeds."

"You and your seeds."

"I know how to catch flies."

"With vinegar, maybe—not honey."

"*Touché*."

Veronica pulled up the tracker she'd placed on Oksana's phone and requested a ping. "She just left the bar."

"I know she just left the bar. I watched her go."

"Well, looks like she's headed back to her hotel."

"She won't stay long," Roman said.

"You scared her."

"I mean, I wasn't pushy, but I did, you know...."

"*Push*?"

"A little. I brought up Chichikov. The KGB. That sort of angle."

"Fairly vague."

"I also used her name."

"Well, then," Veronica said, surprised he'd been so forward. "How did she react?"

"Shocked."

"And the KGB stuff? Chichikov?"

"About how you'd expect. Like an ordinary American girl."

"There's no such thing."

"Like a Columbia student, then. She didn't show emotion about the KGB angle."

"She's been in this country a long time. She knows nothing of what happened with her parents."

"You'd never guess she'd been born in another country."

"What about her Russian?"

"I didn't hear enough of it to say, but she's wired with that... that *electricity*..."

"*Electricity*?"

"That wired Russian energy. You'd know if you'd been

there. She fought me on everything. Fought me for the sake of fighting."

"She fought you because she's a twenty-four-year-old woman in a bar, and you moseyed over like... some sort of...."

"What?"

"*Prowler*," she said, at a loss for a better word.

"She knew I had an agenda."

"You didn't bring up her parents, though."

"God, no."

"Good."

"Well...."

"Well, what?"

"Something her mother used to say. I used it to...."

"You're going to scare her off, Roman. She's extremely vulnerable right now."

"What does that mean?"

"You don't need to know what it means," she said, thinking of the internet search history she'd uncovered. About a month ago, after having dinner with Proctor Sifton, Oksana had developed a sudden and intense interest in date rape and the law surrounding it. She'd even looked into buying a gun, though she hadn't followed through.

"Of course I need to know," Roman said.

Veronica sighed. "She went on a date with the gallery owner."

"The one who was just murdered?"

"Yes."

"And?"

"And afterward, she went down a rabbit hole in her Google searches."

"What sort of rabbit hole?"

"Rohypnol, GHB, Ketamine, Benzodiazepines—"

"Those are all—"

"Date rape drugs. Yes."

"I see."

"So go easy."

"I wasn't going to waterboard her, Vee."

"Just don't get any ideas."

"As if I would."

"Anyway, what was your read? Did she pass muster?"

"Pass muster?"

"Does she have what we need? And will she give it to us?"

"I think she will if she has anything."

"The gallery owner's murder won't help."

"She's not going to keep *his* secrets if he raped her—"

"Right," Veronica said, cutting him off, "but it also highlights what's at stake. Murder. It shuts people down."

"What's at stake is a nuclear meltdown."

"Not to her."

"I think the information on her mother will push her over the edge."

"That's how you're going to lead?"

"Not lead, exactly. But it's our strongest card. We don't know what she has other than a painting. We don't know how it's connected. She may not even know. We need her to be invested if she's going to be of use."

"*Invested*?" she said. "That's what we're calling it now?"

"She studies Russian literature."

"Yes, Roman. I'm aware."

"She brought up *Accius*."

"Is that supposed to mean something to me?"

"A playwright, Late Roman Republic."

"So, two thousand years ago?"

"Yes."

"I don't believe this."

"What?"

"Don't *what* me. You're quoting *Atticus* now?"

"*Accius.*"

"She charmed you."

"She did not *charm* me."

"You're smitten."

"I'm just trying to get inside her head."

"Interesting turn of phrase."

"Come on."

"You'd like to get inside more than her head."

"I'm trying to get inside her head, Vee. We need to convince her."

"Oh, we *need* to convince her, do we? We need to get her *invested*? There's no other way?"

"What other way?"

"I could send over a bunch of guys right now to knock her door down."

"That's not funny."

"Well, get over there then. Convince her. Get her invested. I'll do what I can from here."

He hung up the phone.

Veronica stared vacantly at the screen for a few seconds, watching the cursor blink. She couldn't help but feel a pang of something—sadness, nostalgia, she couldn't say. She pulled up a picture of Oksana, pulled up her biographical details, her personal history, her transcript from Columbia. She couldn't have invented a woman more likely to get inside Roman's skin. And then there was the connection.

She got up from the computer and put on the kettle. She'd been regarded as a beauty once, too, in her day. It was so long ago now that it might never have happened—except it had, and she remembered it. What was it Oscar Wilde said? *No one is rich enough to buy back the past.*

Nowhere were the words truer, she thought, than for a woman who'd once been beautiful.

She'd been working with Roman for thirty years. But even when she'd first arrived, she'd already been in her forties—too late for him to really notice her.

There'd been moments. Not many. But enough.

Enough to wonder if it had ever crossed his mind.

Enough to know it had crossed hers.

But moments pass.

Old men like Roman liked to think there was honor in restraint. That holding back absolved them. That denial was a virtue.

They were wrong.

Denial wasn't virtue. It was cowardice.

60

Oksana burst into the room, grabbed the painting and memory card, and bolted. In the corridor, she jabbed the elevator button, as if she could will it to come faster. When the doors slid open, she stepped inside and punched the lobby button just as aggressively.

Who the hell was that man?

He'd spoken Russian.

Known her name.

What was all that talk about KGB agents? Vladimir Chichikov?

He hadn't struck her as a threat, exactly—but he hadn't just wandered in off the street, either. It was all connected. The painting. Proctor's death. His sudden appearance.

And that line—*The past is a river*?

Where had that come from? The only other person she'd heard say it was....

No way—*no way*—it was a coincidence.

She shut it down.

That was hallowed ground.

The ding of the elevator barely registered. She stepped

out, rubbing her temples, nerves frayed to the quick. And then—standing by the check-in desk, taking a stack of papers from the receptionist like it was the most natural thing in the world—there he was.

She stopped in her tracks. Her pulse kicked. A rush of adrenaline.

She didn't know whether to run or throw herself at him. She did neither, just froze, caught in the open.

"Oksana," he said.

"You!" she snapped, pulse surging. Fight or flight. She glanced at the exit, half-expecting a SWAT team to be accompanying him.

She was nearer the exit than he was, but he didn't seem the least concerned she'd run. "You're following me," she said.

"I told you. We have something to discuss."

The receptionist cleared his throat. "Miss, if this is the ex that you—"

"God, no," she blurted. "That's disgusting."

"Sorry," he said. "I was only asking."

"I'm her uncle," the man said smoothly. Then, to her— "Isn't that right, dear."

"Don't," she said flatly.

"Come, now," he said, eyeing the package under her arm. "Let's go upstairs."

She shook her head and started for the exit.

"Oksana, please."

She stopped. He hadn't moved, but somehow, it felt like she'd lost ground.

Truth was, she needed him. Someone had killed Proctor. She had a sinking feeling this man knew why. And if he'd found her, how long until they did, too?

"What the hell do you want from me?"

"Just to talk," he said, glancing at the receptionist. "In private."

"Something tells me you want a lot more than that."

"Let's go upstairs. I'll explain everything."

She studied him for a few seconds. "If you're lying—"

"I'm not. Just talk. That's it."

Reluctantly, she turned back to the elevator. They entered together and stood in silence, avoiding eye contact. She used the moment to get another read on him—expensive shoes, expensive suit, everything crisp, precise. Like his words.

Under different circumstances, she might have pegged him as a lawyer, a Wall Street guy. The papers in his hand were rolled into a loose cylinder that he tapped absently against his palm, cool as a cucumber.

"I should warn you," he said as the elevator opened, "this might be one of those conversations you look back on."

"Oh, you mean you're about to change my life?"

"In a word."

"That's what they all say," she muttered, striding down the corridor.

He followed her into the room. When the door shut, the space felt suddenly very small. She felt embarrassed, too, her privacy on display. She'd left the bed unmade, and now, with him there, it felt oddly intimate. Too personal. In the bathroom, her towel lay crumpled on the floor.

"Why don't you sit there?" she said, pointing to the chair by the desk.

He sat down, placing the papers on the desk, then turned the chair to face her.

She shut the bathroom door, then went to the coffee maker and inserted a pod. "Sorry. Just need to clear my head."

"Go right ahead."

"You want one?"

"Do they have milk?"

"They have these," she said, holding up a little plastic creamer.

"Okay," he said. "If you don't mind."

She made them both coffee, then sat on the bed across from him and waited. The painting, still in its bubble wrap, lay on the bed next to her.

"You're good," he said, nodding at the package. "Where'd you learn all that?"

It was probably meant as an icebreaker, but it made her bristle. It was a reminder of the danger she was in, for one thing, but it also suggested a degree of surveillance at the gallery that she hadn't been aware of. He must have noticed her unease because he said, "If it's a sore point—"

"I'm self-taught," she said quickly, cutting him off.

He raised an eyebrow, as if that impressed him, and she said, "Why do I feel like I'm in some kind of a job interview?"

He pulled the lid off the coffee creamer and said, "Nothing as simple as that."

"You tracked me down quickly enough."

"Don't be offended," he said, pouring the cream into his cup. "We have extraordinary resources."

"Who's *we*?"

"I'll get to that."

"How do you know my name?"

"Like I said. Resources."

"Government?"

"Something like that."

"But not police?"

"No, not police."

"FBI?"

"The agency I'm with doesn't matter."

"So that's how you know my name? Some government list?" What she really wanted to ask was where the *past is a river* reference had come from. Instead, she said, "If you know I'm a thief, then you know what I took."

"I know what you took. I know who you took it from. And I know that he's dead."

Her mind leaped to Proctor in a pool of blood. A shiver ran down her spine. "Do you know who killed him?"

"I have a theory."

"Am I in danger?"

"You already know the answer to that."

She said nothing then, and he cleared his throat. He took a sip of coffee, as if to buy time, then said, "I also know why you chose to steal from him."

It took her a moment to catch his meaning, then she felt a hot flash of emotion. The words landed like a slap.

"I'm sorry," he said. "I didn't mean—"

"Something tells me you don't say anything without meaning it."

"There were some very valuable paintings in that gallery."

"Yes, there were."

"But you didn't take those. Instead, you took something far more modest."

He was eyeing the package, and she picked it up. "This is why you're here?"

"I'm here because I need your help."

She touched the memory card in her coat pocket—still there, still warm. Was that what he really wanted?

She handed him the painting, watching his reaction closely.

He set his coffee aside and took it eagerly, then slid on his glasses and removed it from the packaging. She watched his face, but he gave nothing away. He was a blank page.

"Not what you expected?" she said.

"I don't know what I expected."

"Do you even know what you're looking at?"

"It's the White Sea Canal, right?" he said, sounding unsure. He examined the frame, then ran a finger along the frayed canvas where the memory card had been.

To distract him, she said, "There's more to that story."

"Oh?"

"The barge on the canal, it's carrying a submarine."

"So it is," he said, shifting his attention from the frayed corner.

"That's a mistake," she said. "A mistake of Stalin's making. The canal was too shallow for submarines—the very reason it was built in the first place."

"And the painter chose to highlight that detail?"

"Right."

"An act of political resistance."

She nodded. "One the artist was willing to risk his life for."

"And that pleases you?" he said.

She thought for a moment. It did. That was the point. Risking everything, even knowing it wouldn't change a thing.

Her eyes drifted to his, catching the glint beneath his calm. She smiled just slightly. Cleared her throat. She wasn't going to flinch when she said this.

"I think you already know the answer."

61

Roman couldn't help it. It was uncanny—like peering through a fractured window into his own past. That porcelain skin, those vivid sapphire eyes—Anastasia was there, unmistakable, like a ghost flickering behind glass. This girl had her mother's grace—her distinctly Russian elegance—like a tsarina draped in furs, crossing a palace courtyard in winter.

But there was something else there, too, stirring beneath the surface. Something that reminded him—subtly, unsettlingly—of the quiet, coiled intensity of a caged cat.

She caught him staring. He dropped his gaze. But he couldn't help it. His eyes drifted back to her before he even realized it.

He hated having to push. There was a way to do this right, and his instinct told him not to rush. But time was a luxury he didn't have.

He tried to hand her the painting back, but she didn't take it.

"Keep it," she said.

"Keep it?"

She nodded.

"Why?"

"It's why you came, right?"

It wasn't, and she seemed to know it. Which meant she might know why he *had* come, even if he didn't. "I came for you, Oksana."

"Little old me?"

"You know Proctor's dead because of this?" he said.

"Does that make me a murderer?"

He shook his head. "That's not what I'm saying. You need to be careful. What happened to him—"

"Could happen to me?"

"Well, couldn't it?"

That seemed to make her uncomfortable, and she got up and went to the coffee machine. "I'm going to have another," she said, inserting a capsule. "And when it's done, I'm going to leave."

"Okay," he said hesitantly.

"That's how much time you've got. So take your best shot."

"I'm not here to take shots."

"You're sitting there, thinking, calculating, watching me like a cat watching a mouse. We both know you're holding a loaded gun, so pull the trigger."

"I assure you, I don't—"

"The papers," she said, glancing at the documents on the desk next to him.

She was right, of course. But they weren't a loaded gun, they were a hand grenade with its pin pulled. He picked them up and placed them on his lap.

"Okay," he said, still hesitating, still weighing his approach.

"Pull the trigger—"

The Honeytrap

He looked at her and made a choice. There was no path forward without breaking something open. Her past. His silence. Maybe both.

"Your mother—" he said.

Her reaction was instant. Her face drained of color—if such pale skin could. Her eyes filled with tears.

"I know it's a sensitive—"

"Family is sensitive," she said quickly, her eyes dropping to the floor, "when you don't have one."

"You study Russian," he said tentatively, seeking a less emotionally charged path. "The language. The literature. The culture."

"Nineteenth-century literature."

"Right," he said. "Because you're trying to hold onto something. Something from your past."

"What's in those documents?" she said flatly.

"I'm getting to that."

She sipped her coffee. "Get to it faster."

"You grew up in the system," he said. "In and out of foster homes."

She rolled her eyes. "We're not really going to start with the creation myth, are we?"

He leaned forward. "Sorry. I'm trying to frame—"

"You didn't come here to talk about my childhood."

"No," he said. "You're right, but let me ask this. How much do you know of your parents' life in Russia?"

"My father died before we left."

"Your mother told you about that?"

"Of course."

"What did she say?"

"I was with her until I was six years old. Use your imagination."

"Right," he said. He was floundering.

Still, if he just came out with it—if he told her why he was really there—there was no telling how she'd react.

Ordinarily, that was a risk he could take. If she didn't want to cooperate, he had other options. The big guns. The waterboards. The pliers and knives.

It would have been ugly—it would have broken his heart—but to stop a nuclear meltdown, he'd have done it.

But that path took time, and time was the one thing he didn't have. This was a one-shot thing. He needed her to give him what she had. And he needed her to do it on the first ask.

"Did she ever tell you," he said, "anything about her work? About your father's work? About the political situation in Russia?"

"The political situation?"

"The work she did?"

"When I was six?"

"Or before that?"

"Have you ever *met* a six-year-old?"

"Right," he said, collecting himself. "Of course."

"When's the last time you talked politics with a tiny child?"

"Never. That's not what I meant."

"You're wasting my time. And yours."

"You study literature," he said. "Stories."

"You could call them that."

"What do you call them?"

"Windows," she said. "Into the past. Into a world that doesn't exist anymore."

"You think the past doesn't exist?"

She rolled her eyes. "I suppose if you want to get philosophical…"

"I don't. I'm being practical. I want to tell you a story

The Honeytrap

from before you were born. A window into a past that I promise you is still very much alive."

"Be quick," she said, sipping more coffee.

"It takes place in Dresden, East Germany, 1989."

"Okay."

"A modest villa in a quiet suburb—brick wall, iron gate, drab garden, unkempt and gray."

"How exciting," she said.

"The house was the Dresden headquarters of the KGB. Across the street were the headquarters of the *Stasi*, the East German secret police?"

"I know what the *Stasi* is."

"They ruled East Germany for forty years. In that time, they gathered files on more than six million individual citizens. Every whisper. Every doubt. Recorded."

"Okay."

"That's out of a population of sixteen million."

"Right. Almost everyone. I get it."

"When the Wall came down, warehouses were discovered containing over one-hundred-eleven kilometers of shelving for all those files."

"I get it," she said again. "Big Brother's watching."

"Yes."

"And I think I know where this is going."

"You've heard it, then?"

"Are you about to bring in the esteemed Vladimir Vladimirovich?"

"Vladimir Vladimirovich Chichikov. Russian president. But on that dismal December day in '89, he wasn't a politician—he was a KGB agent, stationed at the villa on *Angelikastraße*. And when the protestors appeared, intent on storming the office—"

"He called Moscow, and Moscow didn't respond."

"If you know the story—"

"No, no," she said quickly, "tell it your way."

"Like you said, he picked up the phone. But he didn't call Moscow—not at first. He called the 20th Guards Army, stationed nearby in Riesa, and told them to send tanks."

"And *they* called Moscow."

"Yes, they called Moscow, and that's when they told him—"

"Moscow is silent."

"Moscow is silent," Roman repeated. "That's the story. You know it, so...."

"So, thank you for the little history lesson—"

"There was another call made that day," he said, cutting her off. "December 5th, 1989. From the same *Angelikastraße* KGB headquarters."

"Another call by Chichikov?"

"No," Roman said, and he chose this moment to lean forward and give her the papers. "A nineteen-year-old intern from Moscow."

She paused, then took the papers.

"The intern's name was Anastasia Tchaikovskaya," he said.

For the second time, Oksana's face whitened. Her eyes shimmered with emotion. She remained motionless, the papers quivering in her hand. When she spoke, her voice cracked.

"That's not possible."

"I know it's not what you've been told—"

"It can't be," she snapped.

"There's a transcript of the call in there," he said, indicating the papers. "She called a US military attaché at the American Consulate in East Berlin. A man named Alfred Miller."

"No." Her voice was sharp, desperate. "She would never have worked for them. She hated everything they stood for. She was a ballerina."

"A ballerina?" Roman asked too quickly.

"I mean, my father was in the military, he was a—"

"Your mother worked for the KGB," he said again. "It's all in the file. The contents haven't been doctored—"

"No!" Her voice cracked. "She was a dancer. She was even called to the *Bolshoi*. They said she danced like...." She never finished the sentence.

"Have you seen any evidence she performed at the Bolshoi?"

"Of course not. They scrubbed her record when she fled...."

Even as she said the words, she seemed to hear it herself —how much they sounded like a fairy tale. The *Bolshoi*, a ballerina—it was a story meant for a child.

"She wasn't a dancer, Oksana. She was KGB. And she called us first."

62

Veronica had done all she could.

Along with sending the files on Oksana's mother to the hotel, she'd quietly pulled strings at the FBI's New York Field Office to get the originals brought up from storage. Computer printouts were one thing—but no match for the real thing: the weight of the paper, the smell of it, the truth baked into every smudge, and crease, and tear.

Original police reports.

Lab-developed photographs, still mounted on black archival card stock.

Incident sketches, hastily drawn by a patrol officer on the scene who hadn't known what he was looking at.

Everything had been tracked to an FBI warehouse in Long Island City, packed into a courier's envelope, and signed out under a false case number. Two field agents were already *en route* to Roman's location, carrying the envelope in the back of a Bureau-issued sedan.

But that wasn't all.

She'd also anticipated the next step, and authorized the

agents to carry a basic CIA tech package. It included a hardened laptop, encryption and decryption devices, wireless signal dampeners, and an isolation rig. If Oksana handed over anything—documents, audio, a flash drive—they'd be ready to forward it to the right people.

And though no one had said it aloud, if Roman didn't get something soon—if Oksana didn't hand something over—it would be lights out in Virginia. Meltdown.

She pushed the thought aside and forced herself to focus on Margot.

A train toward Smolensk was the last she'd heard of the extraction plan. She'd already scrambled the facial recognition data, but there was still something more she could do. She could set a decoy.

Ideally, it would have been closer to Smolensk—if the Russians knew which direction Margot had fled, then this would be useless—but she had to work with what she had. And what she had now were personal connections. Favors. Debts.

She went quietly to the entryway, as if even her footsteps here might get Margot killed. The console table by the door was slim and lacquered—a catch-all for keys, mail, the detritus of life. She gripped the second drawer's handle and pulled it open.

Inside, beneath a stack of old envelopes and used-up pens, was a spiral-bound notebook. It was scuffed, dog-eared, the coil warped from years of use. She slid it out carefully, brushing a thin layer of dust from the cover. A log. A ledger. A place to write down what couldn't be trusted to memory—or machines.

She opened it to a page halfway through, the handwriting tight and slanted, done in pencil—easily erasable in a hurry—and stared at it. It was a coded list concealed in a cipher of her own design. Her finger moved down the page—Baltic, Cobalt, Nightlglass. Then she saw it—*Ganges*.

Veronica's last intel put *Ganges* on the Georgian side of the Enguri River, very close to the demarcation line with Russian-occupied Abkhazia. It was a volatile place, where loyalties were fluid, and maps changed based on who was doing the asking. Ganges operated in that gray zone, and her real name was Nino Gelashvili. Next to her codename was the line, 'Wild zebras love lazy zookeepers while bees fight lions.'

A nonsense sentence, except it wasn't.

"Good grief," Veronica muttered, bringing the notebook back into the kitchen and setting it down on the counter. It had been a while since she'd used the cipher system, and she looked at the words now like an archeologist rediscovering a lost language. Wild Zebras Love—WZL. Nine, nine, five. The country code for Georgia. It wasn't just the first letter of each word—there were nine words used to reconstruct the twelve digits of Nino's number—but after a little playing around, she had it—or hoped she did.

She dialed nervously and waited.

The answer came in Georgian, a language Veronica had no mastery of, and she responded in English. "I'm calling to check on a book order."

There was a moment's silence, then a cautious, "*Book order?*"

"Yes."

"I see. You're calling from the bookshop?"

"Yes, I am."

"To collect?"

"I take it you're the right person to speak to?"

Nino—who had never met Veronica, Roman, or Margot—said, "You're speaking to the right person."

The Honeytrap

"And I trust it's not a bad time."

Nino laughed—a flat, mirthless sound. To her credit, she said, "It's no worse than any other."

"I understand it's been some time since you—"

"It's been fifteen years," Nino said. "If you want to know."

"But you'll do me a favor?"

"Depends on what it is."

"Where are you—Zugdidi?"

"Zeda Etseri."

"Zeda Etseri," Veronica repeated, pulling up the location on a map. "That's close enough."

"To the frontier?"

"I'm afraid so, yes."

"What do you want me to do?"

"Not so much," Veronica said. "What I'd like is for you to create a distraction."

"A distraction?"

"If you could make it look like you were expecting someone."

"Who?"

"An asset. Make it look like they're crossing the border—and you're there to pick them up."

"But I'm not?"

"No, they're crossing somewhere else. But your presence would be helpful as a decoy."

"Where are they really crossing?"

"Nowhere. That's not part of it."

"Nowhere?"

"Thousands of miles away. I just want to raise the possibility it's happening there—where you are. A disputed border on the wrong side of the country."

"I see."

"I was thinking something at the bridge?"

The bridge she was referring to was the Enguri Bridge Crossing, one of the principal border crossings between Georgia and Abkhazia. It was closed now, but it had once been an important highway, and there were still frequent illegal crossings there. It was guarded by barbed wire, some half-hearted concrete road barriers, and a few poorly-motivated Russian soldiers.

"Nothing too drastic," Veronica added.

"What did you have in mind?"

"Well, can you park a few hundred yards away? Fly a drone over the post, maybe. Just make them twitch a little."

"A drone?"

"Do you have a drone?"

"I do not."

"Well, you can figure out some way to make a stir?"

"Parking near the bridge won't do much. Smugglers sneak across there all the time."

Veronica thought for a moment. She was aware of what the situation required, but she was also very aware of what she was and was not authorized to do. Not even Roman was aware of this.

She hesitated.

"Do you have a gun?"

63

Oksana stared at the man so intensely that he seemed almost to wither under her gaze. "KGB?" she said, drawing out each syllable. "My mother?"

He swallowed. He was about to answer when they were interrupted by a knock on the door. He didn't turn—he'd clearly been expecting it.

"Come in," he said.

The door opened—despite being locked, supposedly—and two men in suits entered. One was tall and lean, the other stockier, with a sharp jawline and steel-gray hair. They exchanged no words as they scanned the room, scanned Oksana, missing nothing. The taller man's hand brushed the lapel of his jacket—close but not quite touching a sidearm.

"What is this?" Oksana said, rising to her feet.

"Oksana, relax," the man said. "They're with me."

She eyed them cautiously—like two man-eating lions loosed into the room. One remained by the door while the other placed a briefcase on the desk and clicked open its latches. There were electronics inside—a laptop, other devices—but what he took from it was an envelope. It was heavy-duty, like what a courier might use, reinforced with a weave of synthetic fibers that gave it a faint shimmer. Along one edge was a perforated tab.

The man from the bar tore it open in a single motion and looked briefly inside. Satisfied, he passed it to Oksana.

She took them hesitantly. "What am I.... What is this?"

He also handed her a business card. It said, Roman Adler, and included a phone number. "Gentlemen," he said then to the two men in suits, nodding toward the door.

All three made to leave.

"Where are you going?" Oksana said.

"We'll wait downstairs. Call the number on the card when you're ready."

She watched them leave, then peered through the peephole to make sure. Only after the elevator doors closed behind them did she return to the documents. Her hands shaking, she sat on the bed—steeling herself. What she was about to see would change everything she believed about her life. About who she was.

The man—Roman Adler, she read from the card—had already given her documents he'd printed in the lobby. As well as a transcript of the phone call in 1989, they included a report of the car crash.

She looked at it, and it seemed to align with what she'd always been told.

Compiled by NYPD investigators, each page was marked with the initials of whoever had been responsible. The typewritten reports were occasionally interspersed with handwritten notes and corrections, each also initialed. She flipped through pencil sketches—the car's position on the road, the location of skid marks, shattered glass, debris.

Even the positions of the bodies were marked—her mother and the driver. The driver's name, which she'd always known, was Zoran Dragović.

She paged through everything slowly, taking it in. It was the first time she'd seen any of it—anything more than the stock responses from the police and the brief coverage the crash had received in newspapers. Everything in the report aligned with what she'd always been told—bad driving conditions, black ice, a tragic accident.

Two fatalities—one driver and one passenger.

But there was more. The courier's envelope.

It was heavy, and inside it was a second envelope—light manila, soft with age. It smelled musty when she took it out, like the pages of an old book from the library. On the back was a metal clasp, slightly rusty as though stored somewhere damp, and she unhooked an elastic band and tipped the contents onto her lap.

The first pages she saw were typewritten sheets of a report. All original. On top was a cover page with boxes filled in by hand stating the date, a case number, and the name of the responsible officer. In blotchy, blue ink was the seal of the FBI.

Oksana recognized the date. Of course she did.

The day her childhood ended.

A tremor passed through her—a breathless, aching certainty that everything in her life had been leading here. To this. As if fate had conspired to put these yellowed, dog-eared pages in her hands—and that everything that happened from now on would be because of them.

First was a ballistics report.

Her heart pounded when she realized what it was. Crisp diagrams marked with tight clusters of bullet holes, each annotated with precise measurements. The impact patterns on the steel of the car were unmistakable—tight groupings, deliberate spacing, no wild shots. Whoever had fired knew how to shoot. There were equations scrawled in the margins —angles of entry, velocity decay, ricochet probabilities. A trajectory map traced faint red lines across a schematic of the vehicle, converging like a spiderweb from multiple points of origin.

She scanned the conclusion, and her breath caught. Three shooters. Coordinated. High ground advantage. Precision consistent with military or intelligence training.

Her fingers trembled as she flipped the page, forcing herself to keep going.

Lab-developed photos, stark and clinical, with date stamps in the corners and evidence tags scribbled in blue ink. She held them with care, the edges curled with age, a chemical scent still clinging to the paper. The first showed the crash site from a distance—the taxi crumpled against a concrete barrier, its front end folded in on itself like paper. Broken glass glittered on the asphalt like frost.

The next made her stomach lurch.

It was a close-up of the windshield, pierced by a tight cluster of bullet holes. She leaned closer. Through the shattered glass, she could just make out the figure slumped behind the wheel—the driver, his head tilted at an unnatural angle.

In the back seat, blurred but unmistakable, was a woman's silhouette.

The air left her lungs in a cold, involuntary rush. This was the truth they'd buried. The truth they now wanted her to see.

Her mother. Still. Lifeless.

She put down the documents and sat very still. She didn't know if a minute passed or ten, and she reached into her pocket to confirm that the memory card was still there.

That was the point of all this. The *quid pro quo*.

At the bottom of the stack of documents was a map of the city, a red circle drawn in marker around the crash site.

She pulled out Roman's card and dialed the number. "Where are you?" she said.

"Downstairs."

"*Who* are you?"

"If you want to know if that report is true—"

"It's true," she said before she could stop herself. She hadn't meant to say it aloud, but the images—her mother, the bullets, the slumped figure in the back seat—she knew it was all true.

"Yes," he said, and for some reason, she found his voice strangely reassuring.

"What are these lines on the map?" she said, tracing them from the crash site.

"Those," Roman said, "are the likely escape vectors of the attackers."

"Escape vectors?" Her voice caught.

"That's right."

"Of the men who killed my mother."

"Yes. I'm sorry."

"Why was I never told?"

"You were a child."

"This wasn't in any of the media reports from the time."

"There were national security implications."

"Where do the escape routes lead?" she said, following the red lines to the northern edge of the map.

"It was never decisively concluded," he said, "though the most likely exfiltration point was Teterboro."

"Teterboro?"

"A small airport. A private jet. It flew to Moscow."

"My mother was killed by the Russian government?"

"Yes."

"And the shooters? Were they ever...."

"Caught?" His voice dropped, as if what he had to say pained him. "No," he said. "They never were."

The breath she drew was sharp and cold—like something had broken inside her. "You're certain of that?"

"Yes, I am."

"How can you be sure?"

"Because I was working with your mother at the time. She was helping me."

Oksana's chest tightened. Suddenly, all the half-truths and omissions began to align. The way he looked at her. *The past is a river.*

A silence filled the line. Neither spoke, and she suddenly realized that there was far more to this story than what she'd just been shown. This was all just the beginning.

"You knew my mother," she said, breath catching. "You knew me."

He hesitated just a second. "Yes."

"You're CIA."

"Yes."

"Then it was your job to protect her."

More silence.

Why had the CIA been working with her mother?

Why Roman?

Had she betrayed her country? Was that why she was dead?

And what of her father? Of his death?

She wanted to ask everything, but this wasn't the time. She was at the beginning of a path, but if she wanted to get to the end of it, then she would have to play his game. She would have to reciprocate.

She needed to give this man what he'd refused to ask for.

"Are those two guys still with you?" she said.

"They are."

"Bring them back up."

A beat.

"And tell them to bring the laptop. It's time."

64

President Westfahl looked composed, but panic thundered in his chest. His top advisors had gathered in the Oval Office for what might yet be the greatest disaster of their tenure, and the atmosphere was thick with tension.

He leaned on the Resolute Desk, head in his hands, eyes fixed on the ancient wood like the answers lay hidden in the grain. The room was silent. The tick of a grandfather clock filled the void. Every Council member was present—except Roman, holed up in a Brooklyn hotel room, fingers no doubt trembling as he transmitted the data.

"Well?" Westfahl snapped, his voice crackling through the silence like static in a storm.

In the center of the room, a speakerphone had been set up on the table. It was connected directly to the power plant control room, and on the line, along with a tangled chorus of engineers, cybersecurity analysts, and agency liaisons, were the Governor of Virginia, the Speaker of the House of Representatives, and the Senate majority leader.

"Data being transmitted."

"Who was that?" the president demanded. "Whose voice?"

A pause. Then, the same voice, quiet but resolute. "This is Roman, sir."

Westfahl's gaze drifted to the window. Outside, the South Lawn blazed under a sea of light. News crews had swarmed the grounds, staking out positions with tripods, cameras, floodlights, and cables that crisscrossed the snow like trenches on a battlefield. Secret Service agents watched it all warily from behind the fence.

"Now what's happening?" he said.

Everyone stared at the speakerphone.

Doerr, arms crossed over his vest, cleared his throat. "The President asked for an update."

"This is Harry Cassidy, Lead Safety Engineer. We've received the raw data packet and we're waiting for the decrypt."

Kathleen Holman sat stiffly at the table, her expression carved in stone. Chuck Austin and Vance Poynter sat directly opposite, exuding that cold, military calm that seemed only to put everyone else more on edge. Jake Hawke and Ethel Sinclair were by the fireplace, murmuring in low, clipped tones.

The speakerphone crackled. Cassidy's voice.

"Mr President, Governor—the packet has been decompressed and decrypted. It appears to be a complete diagnostic payload—traffic logs, binary diffs, PLC command histories. The full anatomy of the breach."

Kathleen leaned forward. "So it can help?" she asked into the phone.

"It can," Cassidy said, guarded. "It shows us the altered control logic. The subroutines the hackers rewrote. It even contains an isolate-and-restore script."

"A what?" the president muttered.

"A patch tool, sir. A reversal protocol."

"Reversal—as in, undo the breach?"

The president's fingers curled against the edge of the desk.

"In theory."

"In theory?" Doerr echoed, his voice sharp as a whip.

"Someone want to translate this into English?" Holman said.

Roman came through again. "The data maps the logic needed to undo the hack. If it works, we'll be able to run the SCRAM. We'll be able to shut down the plant."

"And avert the meltdown?" Holman said.

"Unless it's booby-trapped," Cassidy interjected. "There's a chance the code is malicious. It could be designed to trigger fail-safes. It could lock us out completely—or worse."

Roman snapped, "What the hell's worse than a meltdown?"

A beat, then the president spoke. "What's the core temp?"

"Five ninety-six," Cassidy said grimly. "If we don't act now, we're done for anyway."

"Run the script," Roman said.

"That's not your call," Doerr snapped. "Mr President—"

Westfahl looked around the room. The fire crackled in the hearth, its amber light throwing shifting shadows, flickering across their faces—Doerr's bearded jawline, Poynter's unblinking stare, Ethel's statuesque calm.

"Do it," Kathleen urged.

"If we wait, it blows anyway," Poynter said in his sonorous baritone. "Better to act."

"Cassidy," the president said. "Can you run the script manually? Line-by-line."

"I can," Cassidy said. "The code appears clean. It's a hash-matched restoration—feedback loops spoofing the core sensors. Break the loop, and we regain control."

"Do it," Roman said. "It's the only shot we've got."

"He can't be sure," Doerr said.

"None of us can," Ethel said softly. "But if we wait, we lose everything."

The President drew a breath. "Run the script, Cassidy!"

"Running script," Cassidy confirmed.

Then—silence.

The longest silence Westfahl had ever endured.

Seconds passed. A minute.

"Report," Doerr demanded.

"Coolant flow stabilizing," Cassidy said. "Temperature curve normalizing. SCRAM signal re-engaged."

"Pull the lever then," Roman burst.

Cassidy pulled the lever without waiting for any more confirmation than that. Nothing followed but an agonizing silence.

"Core temperature?" Roman barked, breaking the silence.

"Five eighty-seven... five seventeen... now four seventy-nine."

Roman exhaled. "It's working."

"Four twenty-three... three ninety-one," Cassidy said, relief flooding his voice. In the background, cheering erupted. "Three sixty-five," he continued. "We've stabilized, Mr President. SCRAM successful. Meltdown averted."

The President gasped for air, his chest rising and falling like he'd just sprinted the length of the South Lawn. The strain on the faces in the room gave way to relief. Poynter clapped Kathleen on the back, and she let a cautious smile cross her face.

Doerr leaned over the speakerphone and severed the connection with the push of a button. A power grab. The president knew one when he saw it.

"We need to talk about Roman," Doerr said.

The president was still feeling the flood of relief, but already the pieces on the board were repositioning. "You're not big on celebrations, Dominic."

"I'll celebrate when the man who caused that crisis has been taken out of play."

Hawke nodded. "Agreed, sir. We have to stand Roman down immediately. There's no telling the damage he could do if he remains in place."

Ethel's eyes flared. "Roman just saved us from the greatest disaster—"

"Exactly," Doerr said. "His part is done."

"Agreed," Hawke added. "We can't afford any more wild cards. Stand him down, Mr President."

Silence again. To Westfahl, even the fire seemed to dim, its light suddenly faltering. He stared at Doerr and Hawke, seeing clearly what he'd long suspected. They'd waited for this moment a long time. The changing of the guard.

And the president wasn't sure he trusted their vision of the future more than Roman's.

But who was he to hold back the flow of time?

He gave the nod.

Just once. Quiet.

And just like that, Roman Adler—master of the dark art of Human Intelligence, hero, liability, wildcard—was erased from the board.

65

"Everyone off!" a woman announced. "End of the line."

Margot blinked awake. "Sorry," she murmured, rubbing her eyes. "I must have dozed off."

The woman, who looked to be in her fifties, wore a flimsy cotton dress and apron. "Happens," she said curtly, wiping down the nylon surfaces of the seats.

Margot shifted—and winced. Her shoulder flared, the wound pulsing with heat. She touched it tenderly, trying to detect any unusual pain, any hint of infection. She didn't think there was any.

"Are you okay?" the woman said.

"Oh, just getting old," Margot said with a smile.

"Hah!" the woman said. "If only you knew."

Margot looked out the window. They must have arrived some time ago because the platform was already empty. A weathered wooden sign read *Smolensk-Tsentralny*, the city's central station, sixty kilometers shy of the Belorussian border. She could have ridden straight through to Minsk, but that was too predictable. The Russians would be on the watch for it. A remote road crossing would be safer, she thought—more opportunity to control the situation, fewer prying eyes. It would also buy her time to find some shabbier, local-looking clothing before making the attempt.

With nothing but her purse, she made her way down the aisle toward the door. She'd traveled third class. A berth might have offered privacy—but also the risk of being cornered. Not that it mattered. She'd slept through half the journey.

She'd never set foot in Smolensk, and as she stepped off the train, the station's deceptive quaintness struck her. It called to mind the Potemkin villages built to deceive Catherine the Great. While unmistakably Stalinist in its bulk, the architects had indulged in classical flourishes that seemed almost mocking in their intent. The building was turquoise—festive to the point of garishness—and it gleamed unnaturally in the cold light. Around it stretched acres of decaying concrete. High above, the city's coat of arms loomed—a cannon emblazoned on a shield—aimed forever outward, ready for what history had already shown to be inevitable. Invasion.

She'd planned to go straight to the border, but exhaustion hit her hard. A few hours of rest would do her good. It would also allow her to make the crossing after dark.

Unlike in most Russian cities, Smolensk's station appeared to be far from the center of town, marooned in some forgotten quarter on the banks of the sluggish, mud-colored Dnipro. There was no welcome here—only cracked parking lots, skeletal pedestrian bridges, and the ghostly outlines of distant housing blocks. Civilization, if it existed, lay well beyond this industrial sprawl.

There was a hotel—if it could be called that—wedged into the far end of the station like an afterthought. Faded signage, curtains yellowed with age, a flickering light above the entrance. It wasn't much, but it would do.

Inside, the lobby was dim and smelled of mildew and stale smoke. She asked the man behind the desk if he had a room. He nodded without speaking, then quoted a price that converted to about fifteen US dollars per night—a figure that told her all she needed to know. She checked in under the false documents given to her by Boreal. The man barely glanced at them, then handed her a heavy key on a battered wooden fob. The number two was carved crudely into the wood.

"Is there a restaurant?" she asked.

"Not here," he said, "but the station has something."

She nodded.

"Cheap," he added, leading her out of the lobby and up a creaking set of stairs. The second-floor corridor was lit by a single weak bulb, humming faintly as if straining for life.

The room was as cold and sparse as expected, with a narrow wooden bed, a lumpy mattress, and a lamp with a crooked shade trimmed in tassels. On the table by the bed was an empty vase on a lace doily. There was a phone next to it, though she wouldn't dare use it. As she stepped inside, she felt the man linger—watching her longer than necessary.

"Television is there," he said, gesturing toward a battered set with a coat hanger for an antenna. "Sometimes it works."

"The bathroom?"

He was already turning away. "Down the hall."

"Of course," she muttered, wondering who she'd be sharing with.

The man left and she shut and locked the door, then turned on the television. Flickering images resolved into her worst fear—the embassy evacuation unfolding in real time.

Footage of the stars and stripes lowering in slow motion played on a loop, and a ticker at the bottom of the screen called it the most humiliating American withdrawal since Afghanistan.

"They're running like dogs with their tails between their legs," a commentator said, her voice thick with disdain. "They're fleeing like the cowards they are."

In the background, a row of buses filed out of the compound, Russian helicopters hovering overhead like buzzards over a battlefield.

Her stomach turned. She'd caused this. Irina in a morgue. A hard drive full of nothing. An operation that was eating itself alive.

There was nothing about her on the news—no photo, no name—but she knew how it worked. Border agents would have her face by now. They'd be on the lookout. The noose was tightening.

She shut off the TV and sat in silence. The old springs creaked beneath her. She rose, unlocked the door, and made her way downstairs—uncertain if it was food she was looking for or just somewhere to disappear.

66

Roman stared at his reflection, scanning his face like a hostile witness—searching for cracks in the armor, for signs that he was still there. The man he used to be.

He was back at the Four Seasons and the lighting was soft—one might even say, flattering—but it couldn't hide this truth. He looked tired. Not the tired that came from a late night—and it was four AM—but the kind that took years to accrete. Like sediment forming a stalactite.

Foxtrot once told him he looked like an eagle. Not anymore.

The suite was opulent—forty-eighth floor, corner room, northwest view. Soft carpets, bronze accents, automated blackout blinds, and a king-sized bed draped in linen so fine it might as well have been silk. On the bedside table was a glass bottle of distilled mineral water, and on the pillow next to it was a small chocolate wrapped in gold foil—a gift from the turndown service that had come and gone hours earlier.

Through the window, Manhattan gleamed like so many glass missiles. It was Christmas morning.

His phone began to vibrate, and he glanced at the screen. No name, no number, just a secure channel identifier. A line reserved for one person.

"Mr President," he said, his voice low and measured.

He was met by silence, long and weighty—the kind that signaled bad news. Behind him, someone entered the room, and he scarcely noticed. His mind was already a million miles away.

"Roman."

Just his name. Nothing else.

It told him everything he needed to know. This was no victory call. The machine had made its decision. No appeals. No pleas.

It was a monster Roman had fed for forty years— through ten administrations, multiple wars, and more burned bridges than he could count. He'd nourished it with the secrets he peddled. With his silence. With bodies. He'd fed it willingly, sometimes with blood on his hands, sometimes with regret, sharp and piercing.

It was he who'd forged its logic, bent its will, carried out its cruelties.

And tonight, it would turn on him.

Not because he'd failed. But because he'd become inconvenient. An embarrassment.

The war he'd fought wasn't over—but the appetite for it was.

And the worst part?

It wasn't even personal.

He walked slowly toward the window, phone pressed to his ear, and stood there in silence, his back to the room.

"Crisis averted," the president said at last.

Roman allowed himself the shadow of a smile. "We live to fight another day."

"It couldn't have been done without you."

Roman glanced over his shoulder. "I had help."

"Oh?"

"A new recruit, if I play my cards right."

That seemed to catch the president's interest, though only for a second. "Listen, this isn't a courtesy call, Roman."

"Then say it."

"The blowback from the Council...."

Roman's jaw tightened. "I see."

"Yes, well, they voted."

"Voted?"

"Of course, ultimately, it's my decision."

"Of course," Roman said.

"But they're pulling the plug. *I'm* pulling the plug."

"On everything?"

"I'm afraid so."

Roman said nothing. It had finally happened. His enemies had gotten what they'd always wanted.

"Are you there?"

"I'm here, Mr President."

"I'm sorry about this. We go back a long time."

"We do, sir."

"But this is final."

"You're certain it's what you want?"

"The opposition is insurmountable, Roman. The entire Council...."

"You're sure you want to abandon my methods?"

"We won't be abandoning them entirely."

"But my outfit is the bleeding edge."

"You've cost us too much, Roman. Have you seen the news? The embassy's being compared to Kabul."

"It's a building, sir. No one's dead."

"Someone's dead," the president said. "Irina Volkova."

"Once this blows over—"

"Margot killed Russians on their own streets, Roman. The media is having a field day. This isn't going to blow over."

"She was defending herself."

"The Russians aren't interested."

"But the Council—"

"I'm sorry, Roman. The decision's been made. The *Bookshop* is dead."

Roman let the silence linger.

The president began, "Any other assets still in play—"

"Margot's still in play."

There was another pause, then, "She's a big girl."

"You're not serious."

"She'll have to find her own way home."

"You're hanging her out to dry?"

"It's over, Roman. Don't do anything stupid."

The line went dead.

Roman kept the phone pressed to his ear a moment longer, as if the silence itself might change the outcome. Then he lowered it slowly. He turned back to the room.

And saw her—

Oksana.

She stood in the corner, beyond the spill of the lamplight, half-hidden in shadow. She looked so much like her mother it hurt. The blond hair, loose, curling slightly inward toward her collarbone. Her eyes, unblinking, absorbing everything, reflecting the dim light like two opals.

She was like Margot—young, cynical, sharp as a scalpel. Both had the same hard-edged calmness, precise, disinterested, conscious of everything. And both had the same steely courage that couldn't be taught, only earned.

She'd made up her mind. He could tell just by looking at her. She'd heard enough.

The air stank of betrayal. Sulfur after gunfire. The *Bookshop* was dead. The plug had been pulled. A lifetime's work had been torn down in the space of a few clipped sentences. But that didn't mean the work stopped.

Roman moved to the edge of the bed and sat down slowly, like a man who'd just read his own obituary. He leaned forward, hands clenched on his knees, spine bent under the weight of everything.

He looked up when he spoke. "You heard all that?"

She watched him carefully, then nodded almost imperceptibly.

"And you're sure you want in? You're sure you're ready for what's to come?"

Another nod. Firmer this time. Almost defiant.

Outside, snow had begun to fall again, light flakes drifting slowly past the window like ash.

"There will be blood," he said. "And compromise. Nothing will be black and white, only endless shades of gray."

She stepped forward, out of the shadow, and into the warm pool of lamplight. She moved like someone crossing a threshold—a Rubicon. There would be no going back.

The light caught her face—the cut of her cheekbones, the intensity of her eyes.

She looked impossibly young at that moment, and impossibly ancient. All of Russia's long, cruel history ran in her veins.

"There'll be no going back," he said.

She didn't blink. "Then we go forward."

Her voice was soft, but it struck him like a gunshot.

She took another step forward, bringing her within a

few feet of him, and he straightened up, as if the weight on his back had just been lightened.

Then she held out her hand—an unspoken pact. An alliance forged in the ashes of something older. Dead men's wars. Her mother's war. "We'll make them all pay," she said. "No matter the cost."

And, for the first time in a very long while, something flickered in Roman's eyes.

Not hope.

But the ghost of it.

67

Margot waited for the last smear of daylight to vanish before slipping out of the hotel. She'd grabbed a few hours of fitful sleep, bought some cheap clothes, and eaten twice at the station's dingy restaurant. She'd also had the man at the hotel print out some grainy photos of a missing girl. A teenager—vanished in Moscow—the photos ripped straight from a police website. She'd tucked them into a flimsy plastic folder along with a typed letter—backdated and forged with the father's signature—purportedly hiring her to investigate.

The ruse wouldn't hold up for long, but it didn't need to. Just something to show the border guards before they waved her on.

Outside the station, taxis idled in the sodium light like cattle awaiting slaughter. She slid into the back of a gray Lada and said, "Kruglovka," praying her accent didn't give her away.

The driver studied her in his rearview. "Kruglovka?" he said. "What's in Kruglovka?"

She'd been ready for that. The village—a smudge on the

map halfway to Vitebsk—barely warranted a name. The only thing it had going for it was proximity to the border, which narrowed the reasons a stranger might ever want to go there.

"That's my business," she said evenly.

"You're making it my business," he said, voice hard.

"Is it a problem?" she asked, hand already moving to her purse.

"No one wants to go to Kruglovka."

"Will you take me all the way to Vitebsk?"

He shook his head. "Not across the line. You'll have to find another ride on the other side."

"Exactly," she said.

He looked out at the station. "Why not take the train?"

"Maybe I don't like trains."

"So, how did you get this far?"

She didn't answer. Instead, she pulled out a folded stack of rubles—more than necessary, but not so much to raise eyebrows—and held it out to him.

He counted the cash. "Going to need more than this."

"How much more?"

He hesitated. She gave him another thousand rubles before he could speak.

"Two thousand," he said flatly.

"Fifteen hundred."

He didn't blink, and she counted out two thousand rubles and handed them to him.

"And you're going to tell me what you're up to."

"That's not part—"

"Look, I'm not losing my license hauling some smuggler into a controlled zone."

"I'm not a smuggler."

"Sure."

"I'm a private detective, if you must know."

"A private detective?" he repeated skeptically.

"Yes."

"And what's that?"

She gave him a look.

"A private detective," he repeated. "Right. Out of my car."

"Calm down. It means I've been hired to find someone."

"Yeah? Who?"

"A client's daughter. She came through here from Moscow. I need to speak to the guards at the border and see if they saw her."

"She'd have taken the train."

"According to her ticket, she got off here."

He nodded slowly, then said, "What happens after you talk to the guards? You'll be stuck out there."

"That's not your problem."

"It could be."

"It won't be," she said, handing him another thousand rubles.

He studied her a moment longer, then grunted and turned the key. The engine coughed to life. "Buckle up."

They pulled out of the station, the Lada's headlights cutting the cold blackness like a searchlight sweeping a battlefield. Streetlight soon gave way to emptiness as the city fell away. The road was narrow, cracked and crumbling. There were no other cars. The driver kept both hands tight on the wheel.

Margot sat stiffly, her eyes flicking to the rearview every few minutes.

No tail.

They drove for nearly an hour, and when the driver broke the silence, it startled her. "Here or the border?"

She looked out at a smattering of farmhouses that gave

no light, no evidence of habitation, and hesitated. This was the last moment to turn back?

"Border," she said tensely.

They drove on, then slowed, pulling over a few hundred meters shy of the crossing. He looked back at her, and she got the distinct feeling he was already trying to erase her from his memory.

She tried to open her door but it jammed, frozen with ice.

The driver watched wordlessly.

What did he want? A tip? A confession?

She undid her seat belt and shoved the door with both hands. This time it cracked free with a sound like something breaking.

Then he said, "You're sure about this?"

She got out without answering.

The wind cut like a scalpel, slicing through her cheap coat. She clutched herself for warmth and turned toward the border post.

Low-slung, cinder-block, hemmed in by razor wire, it sat squat in a halo of floodlight that bleached everything to a harsh, surgical white. In the light, she made out four figures, still as statues in their arctic camouflage, rifles slung across their chests.

They watched mutely, and for a moment, she almost imagined they'd been waiting for her.

She trudged toward them, her breath billowing in the air. The folder felt suddenly flimsy—its lies thin, transparent. Each step, crunching the frozen ground beneath, felt like it would be her last.

Behind her, the Lada's engine revved, and she fought the urge to look back at it.

She focused on the guards. One of them moved to a

chain-link pen next to the post and unlatched a gate. Two dogs came out—lean and dark and muscular. They didn't bark, they just watched her, their eyes, even from the distance, reflecting the floodlight like coals.

She stopped walking. She hadn't meant to. She shouldn't have.

She was shivering, and it wasn't from the cold.

One of the dogs tilted its head as if it recognized her.

She took a step forward, and the silence deepened. Something shifted in the air, or maybe it was the pressure inside her own skull.

Then, one of the guards barked a command. "Yah!"

The two hounds lunged into motion like two wargs from a half-remembered nightmare.

Smooth and low, they came like greyhounds, all muscle and shadow and teeth. She fumbled for her gun.

The dogs didn't bark, they didn't growl, they only ran, snow pelting the air behind them as they closed the distance.

She took a step back, then another, her heart hammering in her chest like a train piston. The folder slipped from her hand, the papers spilling in the wind.

The guards watched, motionless.

She opened her mouth to scream. Nothing came.

68

Roman stood by Veronica's kitchen window, tilting forward, staring out at the darkness. Snow melted against the pane, smearing the streetlamp's glow into ghostly streaks that gave the room an unsettling, submerged quality—as though the world outside had slipped quietly beneath the surface of a shadowy, frozen sea.

Margot was in that sea—lost and alone—each passing second dragging her deeper into its abyss. He imagined her chained to an anchor, the pale glow of her skin vanishing fast in the inky deep.

He would have done anything to pull her back, but he only shut his eyes and swallowed hard against the emotion. It had a sickly taste—the bile of guilt. He was losing her. She was slipping away forever, and there wasn't a thing he could do to stop it.

A cat brushed his leg, jolting him from his thoughts. He was about to nudge it away when Veronica entered.

"Sorry about that," she said, tightening the belt of a sheer nightgown that shimmered in the half-light.

He glanced at her and felt something catch in his chest. Her silhouette—slender and vulnerable, unexpectedly intimate—unnerved him. It reminded him of something he'd long ago tried to smother. Desire. He looked away quickly, ashamed those thoughts could intrude even now.

"My fault," he murmured. "I shouldn't have just shown up."

"Nonsense," she said, her tone tinged with the same grief as his own. "You had to come."

He managed a thin, bitter smile, which she didn't return.

Instead—her voice cautious, tentative—she said, "Where's the girl?"

"The girl?" he said, still avoiding her eyes.

"Oksana. You brought her back with you?"

"I put her to bed."

"Don't say it like that," she said, accusation lingering beneath her words.

"Like what?"

"You dropped her at a hotel."

"Yes," he said flatly. "The Lafayette."

"Lucky girl."

"What's that supposed to mean?"

She didn't answer. The silence stretched out between them.

In the window, his reflection was warped by the water streaming down the glass.

She spoke, but only to say the words he'd been dreading.

"It's been too long, Roman."

He tensed, muscle tightening like a noose. She was right, of course—he knew she was right—but he couldn't bring himself to swallow that truth. Not yet. There was still a chance, he told himself—clinging to his hope like a drowning man grasping at driftwood. A chance she'd crossed the border. A chance she would yet call from Minsk, or Warsaw, or Berlin.

"Roman?" Veronica said.

"Not yet," he gasped. "For the love of God, not yet!"

She waited, then tried again, softer, gentler. "Roman."

"We threw her to the wolves," he said, his voice drenched in self-loathing.

"We did what we could."

He shook his head and her composure seemed to falter. He averted his gaze.

"I told her I'd be there," he said. "I told her, when the shit hit the fan, that I was the only one who'd be there. But when it came, I was already recruiting her replacement."

"Don't do that," Veronica said, her voice suddenly sharp as flint. "Don't sink into that. She deserves better than our self-pity. Both of them do. She and Irina."

He looked up, surprised by her change in tone, then nodded slowly.

"You did your job," she continued. "A nuclear meltdown hung in the balance. You did what had to be done. There was no room for anything but black and white."

"I was reeling in her replacement—while she was still out there, flailing in the water, gasping for breath, crying for our help."

"She never cried for anything."

"Oh, yes she did, Vee! I sat next to her in the car to the airport. She all but begged me. She wanted me to stop her, to forbid her from going, and I knew it."

"You knew nothing of the sort!"

"I knew it and I sat there, Vee—silent. Holding my tongue. Swigging Pepto-Bismol just to fill the silence." The words came out of him soaked in self-disgust—and hung there, rank and sour.

Veronica said nothing, the expression on her face breaking into something approaching despair as she watched him wrestle with himself. It was a fight he was losing.

"I signed her death warrant," he whispered.

She stepped toward him then, and he swallowed again, that same bitter taste, acrid and metallic, like blood or raw meat.

"I sent her to her death. And what's worse—I knew I was doing it." The words landed like a confession.

"Margot knew the risks she was running, Roman. She took them—like she did everything—headfirst."

"I wanted her to go, Vee. God help me, I practically pushed her out of the car." His voice was strangled and brittle. "I knew what it would cost her, and I pushed her anyway."

"Roman, it wasn't your decision—"

"From the moment I put her before the Council, her fate was sealed."

"She didn't go for them," Veronica interjected, still coming toward him, moving as cautiously as if approaching a wounded animal. "She went for Irina."

"Irina?"

"She owed it to her asset," Veronica said, tears tracing quiet lines down her face. "That's why she went."

The silence that followed was crushing, all-encompassing, broken only by the distant, mournful wail of a siren echoing in the night.

Veronica reached out, placing a hand on his shoulder, and he tensed, recoiling from her touch.

She withdrew her hand as if scalded by a stove and he immediately regretted it. It was too late, though. Like so much else.

He knew he should have touched her back. He should have reached out and held her. He should have said something, offered something, but he had no words. In his mouth was only dust. And in his chest, only a hollow chasm.

And so, they stood in silence, the two of them staring into the darkness, their two fractured reflections staring back like two ghosts.

Haunted by a name.

Margot.

69

Not *who*. Not *what*. Not even *why*.
Only *how*.
How did she get here?
How did it happen?
Had there been a stranger in the bed? A rat in the house? Or was it a plain, old-fashioned cock-up?

She is tied to a steel-framed chair, blood seeping through the fabric of her clothes from wounds so deep she knows she won't survive them. Her face is a pulp of blood and broken bone, unrecognizable even to herself. Her fingernails are gone. In their place—clots of blood, dark and dry as old bark.

She feels the pain now, pure and clean and sharp, like a razor being honed on bone. It moves through her body like cold water over a streambed. Like cold water in the lungs. Not a relief. Not a baptism.

Nothing is forgiven.

The interrogator stands before her, looking down like a god in judgment. He doesn't know what's true and what's false. He doesn't know the value of what she's given. Only that she might yet give more—if he can keep her alive.

The dogs are there too, each secured to opposite ends of a single chain, threaded through an iron hoop bolted to the wall. They lunge and snarl, and when one hesitates, even for an instant, the other surges forward on the chain, so close she can feel its stinking breath on her skin.

"Come now, Ms Pechvogel," the interrogator says. "Let's not draw this out any longer."

He knows it's not her real name, the tilt of his head suggests as much, but all the others he's heard—whispered or screamed, offered in trade or flung in rage—are no more reliable. Nothing she's given him is reliable. That's her intent.

She knows how torture works. She's been trained to understand the limits of the human body. The limits of the mind.

And she knows that the more pain she endures, the more pain she can force him to inflict, the less he'll be able to rely on anything she's said. Resistance is not futile.

They're both trapped, she and him, in the cruel, heartless logic of it. The interrogator must interrogate. He must put her to the question, as the inquisitors of old used to say, and not a single drop of what she spills—truth or falsehood—will be worth a damn. It'll all be buried under a mountain of shit.

That's the point of resistance.

"Let's return to Irina," he says, cradling an electric cattle prod like a constable holding a baton.

"I've already told you everything."

"Don't make me hurt you again."

She grimaces as he puts the end of the poker between her legs.

The Honeytrap

"Well?"

"Fuck you," she snarls. In that moment, she feels cleaner than she has in days. As if profanity were a kind of truth. The only one left.

He pushes the button.

Electricity jolts through her like heroin in an addict's veins. It lasts an instant. It lasts an eternity. She might have soiled herself—but there's so much blood she can no longer tell.

"Oh dear," he says, a sadist's smile twitching at the corners of his mouth. "That's not very nice, is it?"

To either side, his hounds yelp and snarl and growl, truly frenzied now at the sight of all that blood and piss.

"Did Irina go after Chichikov from the beginning?" he says, his voice like sugar. "Did she already work for you when they met?"

"I already told you," she spits, gasping for air, "the first time I met her was after the miscarriage."

"And I told you, it was an abortion."

"No it wasn't," she cries.

She knows he knows it wasn't an abortion. Chichikov's own doctors confirmed it. They tested Irina for every substance known to science and didn't find a thing.

But that's the logic of the questioner. Ask what you know, not what you don't. Cast doubt on certainty, not the other way around.

"Irina was a honeytrap from the beginning," he says, placing the prodder to her temple. "You sent her to infiltrate our leader."

Margot shakes her head. After so many hours of this psychological game, there's a part of her mind she can no longer trust. That's the part that wants to make him see now.

Wants to pry open his mind and force him to know the truth.

"No," she gasps.

"She was a spy when they met," he says. "She worked for Center 16. She knew how the game was played."

"She was loyal," Margot screams, her voice rising shrilly as the electricity begins its flow again. "To herself!"

The dogs yelp like little devils, and her vision fades.

Conscious or unconscious, she no longer knows. But she sees it—that first meeting with Irina. The bar. The glass and mirrors. The golden chandeliers clinking from the whoosh of the hand driers.

There's an absurdity to that place, the thousand-dollar caviar that tastes like nothing, the vodka-soused women who give up everything to be there, but want nothing so much as to forget it the morning after. It is a gilded cage. A house of horrors. Decadent and grotesque. Opulent and mean. Dazzling and hellish.

And even when she first set eyes on her, Margot knew Irina didn't belong. She was different from everyone else in the place—clean water in a diesel engine. Something pure where it shouldn't be.

"Half a woman," Irina said, passing Margot the paper towel. "That's what he calls me."

"He mustn't mean it," Margot said, though at that point, she didn't even know who they were talking about.

It was only later that she found out. Only later that they'd hatched their plan.

But that first night, looking at each other in the mirror, refreshing their lipstick, and adjusting the straps of their glittering dresses, they understood each other. They knew they were going to do something important. Something that

The Honeytrap 477

would make a difference. And they were going to do it together.

"You understand what this will cost us?" Margot said at one of their later meetings. By then, Irina was well and truly playing the honeytrap. And Chichikov's teeth were so far into her he would die of the poison. "You know what's going to happen."

Irina nodded. "It'll cost our lives."

And maybe Margot faltered in that moment. Because Irina said, "I think we're both half-women."

"Oh, really?" Margot said.

Irina nodded, and that was the moment it happened—the moment they passed some invisible electrical field, some portal from which they would never pass back.

"Not how Chichikov means it," Irina added. "Not my barren womb. But in the sense that we've both already put one foot in the grave."

And that was when Margot knew she'd go all the way. Quietly, carefully, like someone lighting a fuse, she said, "It'll be fucking worth it."

Back in the concrete tomb, Margot's eyes flicker open. The room is tilting. Her body is failing. She is gasping for breath she cannot catch, and she knows the end is near.

The interrogator is gone from view, but the dogs are still there—snarling and lunging, their fury mounting with the scent of her ruin.

Then she understands.

He's behind her.

His hands come down over her head, and she feels the wire—thin, cold, final—as it tightens around her throat. He begins to pull. Slow at first. Practiced. Cruel.

Her vision narrows to a pinhole. A scream coils in her chest but never escapes.

She doesn't struggle.

She doesn't beg.

Because none of it matters now.

It is as nothing.

A leaf in the wind.

And Irina is with her.

They were always in it together. From the gilded vanity of the Mercedes Bar to the raw concrete floor of this forgotten hellhole, they were in it together. They'd made a pact. A vow etched in blood.

And they both kept it.

That was enough.

That was everything.

They both kept fate.

Her last thought is Irina's voice—soft, unsparing.

"We've already put one foot in the grave."

And then, finally, the second foot follows.

AFTERWORD

First off, I want to thank you. Truly.

Thank you for reading *The Honeytrap*.

If you're seeing this page, it means you've made it all the way to the end, and that means more to a man like me than perhaps you realize.

There's a funny thing about writing. You do it alone. For months. For years. You live inside the minds of people who don't exist. You obsess over their choices, their fates. You chase the clearest descriptions, the perfect line of dialogue that gives away the soul of a character. And all the while, you wonder—more than you'd probably like to admit—if anyone will care.

And then someone like you comes along. Someone who gives the book their time, their focus, their imagination. Someone who turns the words into a real world.

That's magic. That's a gift.

So from the bottom of my heart, thank you.

And please hear me when I say: **you matter more than you know.**

Writers like me don't survive on awards or advertising.

We survive on word of mouth—on readers who tell friends, who post online, who leave honest reviews. Without that support, the stories vanish. Not metaphorically. Literally.

So if you connected with this book—if Margot or Roman or Oksana got under your skin, if the tension made your pulse quicken, if you found yourself thinking about the world differently even for a moment—please consider leaving a review.

It doesn't have to be long. Just a sentence or two. What you liked. What stuck with you. What made the story feel real.

Because those reviews? They matter. They push this book higher in the rankings. They convince a stranger to give it a shot. They tell the algorithms that someone out there cares.

Your review could make all the difference. Not just to this story, but to my ability to keep writing others like it. I truly depend on readers like you. So if you have a minute, I'd be deeply grateful.

And if you spotted something in the book that didn't sit right—politically, historically, factually—I'd love to hear from you. I try hard to keep my own opinions out of my fiction. When I write about governments and intelligence services, I do it to explore human behavior under extreme conditions, not to make a political argument.

I'm not here to preach. I'm here to tell a story.

If something felt unfair or off, or if you spotted a typo or an inaccuracy, please reach out. I've made corrections before based on smart, thoughtful feedback, and I always appreciate it.

saulherzog@authorcontact.com

Behind the Curtain

The story you've just read is fiction—but some of the threats, operations, and tactics described within it are rooted in chilling reality.

The Russian Federation (and before it, the Soviet Union) has a long, well-documented history of plotting—and sometimes executing—mass casualty operations beyond its borders, including on US soil.

Here are just a few real-world examples that shaped elements of *The Honeytrap*:

Operation Cedar (KGB)

This plot was revealed by Russian defector, Vasili Mitrokhin, and allegedly involved plans by the KGB to disrupt the US power supply during the Cold War. The program supposedly took place between 1959 and 1972 and targetted hydroelectric dams in New York, the Hungry Horse Dam in Montana, and numerous oil refineries and pipelines between the US and Canada. The operation was conceived in the Ottawa residency in 1959, and Mitrokhin claimed it involved immensely detailed reconnaissance of oil refineries and gas pipelines. Detailed photos and small-scale maps, similar to those used by Toko Sakhalinsky, identified vulnerabilities in the facilities, as well as the best getaway routes after the attacks were carried off.

Other Infrastructure Targeting (KGB)

During the Cold War, KGB agents in the US were caught on multiple occasions mapping utility grids, water reservoirs, transit chokepoints, and even schools. In one operation uncovered in 1984, a Soviet diplomat in New York was surveilled while compiling a detailed list of vulnerable targets in Manhattan—including hospitals and commuter tunnels.

❄

The world of espionage is filled with shadows, and often the darkest plans are the ones you never hear about—because they were never executed, or because they succeeded.

In writing *The Honeytrap*, I've drawn from Cold War archives, defectors' accounts, declassified CIA documents, and modern cybersecurity briefings. I've spoken with former intelligence professionals and read the memos that were once kept in locked safes. I've tried to shape a story that honors the real sacrifices made by agents in the field, while also acknowledging the psychological toll of a life lived in secret.

If you're interested in the real history behind this book, I highly recommend:

Red Horizons by Ion Mihai Pacepa

The Sword and the Shield by Christopher Andrew & Vasili Mitrokhin

The Dead Hand by David E Hoffman

Spymaster's Prism by Jack Devine

These books paint a haunting portrait of modern espionage and the long, often invisible war that still simmers beneath the surface of global affairs.

I'll end with this: the world is complicated. Human beings are messy. And the truth is rarely simple.

But stories can help us see more clearly. They can offer insight, catharsis, even hope.

If *The Honeytrap* did any of that for you, I'm glad. If it

Afterword

didn't, I hope the next book does. Either way, thank you for walking beside these characters. They lived and breathed because of you.

※

The next in the series, *The Dissonant* is already available to pre-order.

So grab your copy now. I promise, if you enjoyed this book, and built a relationship with the characters, you're going to love what comes next!

God bless and happy reading,

Saul Herzog

GRAB BOOK TWO
DON'T MISS WHAT HAPPENS NEXT!

Don't miss the stunning next book in the series. **The Dissonant** is an ultra-modern, hyper-realistic espionage thriller that follows Oksana, Roman, and Foxtrot on their next adventure.

Don't miss out!

THE LANCE SPECTOR SERIES

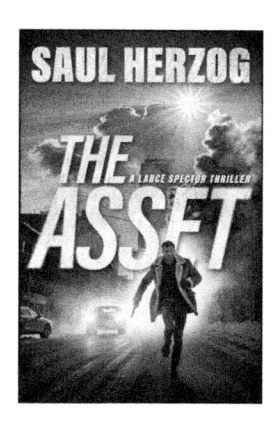

Don't miss the stunning nine-book series that made Saul Herzog a household name.

The Asset - Lance Spector Series Book 1

Montana, USA

When Lance Spector quit the CIA, he swore he was out for good. One more government lie and he would go off the deep end. They could find someone else to do their dirty work. As far as he was concerned, Washington, Langley, the Pentagon could all go to hell.

Yekaterinburg, Russia

A secret Russian expedition returns with a devastating new pathogen, harvested from the frozen corpses of mammoths. It's the biological super weapon they've been looking for, an apocalypse-level pathogen, a virus more deadly than anything ever to come out of a Russian lab. Something that will stop NATO and the Americans in their tracks.

A Biological Chernobyl.

Washington DC, USA

A mysterious vial, sealed in a titanium case, arrives at CIA headquarters. They have no idea who sent it, but it comes with a note.

"I will only speak to Lance Spector."

Printed in Dunstable, United Kingdom